THE IMMORTAL FORCE

STEPHEN PAUL SAYERS

Hydra
Publications

heart-stopping end." – Darcy Coates, USA Today bestselling author of THE CARROW HAUNT and CRAVEN MANOR

"A terrifying tale of demonic possession that is perfectly paced and will have you hooked. One you don't want to miss!" – Lee Mountford, bestselling author of THE DEMONIC and HORROR IN THE WOODS

"Everything you'd want in a riveting supernatural horror story. Crisp writing, engaging characters, and a brazenly refreshing plot pitting good against evil that will keep you turning pages late into the night." – Jeremy Bates, author of SUICIDE FOREST and MOUNTAIN OF THE DEAD

"A wildly engrossing novel that I literally could not stop reading." – The Haunted Reading Room

ISBN: 978-1-937979-73-7

Hydra Publications

Goshen, Kentucky 40026

www.hydrapublications.com

To Jeff Krug, who taught me that sometimes you just have to pick up the guitar and play.

Mother, you had me
But I never had you.
I wanted you.
But you didn't want me.
Mother — John Lennon

PROLOGUE

The weary house stood in the shadow of an overgrown maple, its dense leaf canopy burying it in perpetual darkness. Rot had formed in the window corners, and a scaly moss blanketed the roof's cracked shingles like a spreading disease. The dwelling remained partially visible from the main drag, but if you hiked along Barnard Street, past the broken-down service station and abandoned strip mall, you could see it resting at the edge of the crumbling parking lot.

The building emerged from the postwar housing boom when one-family residences had popped up like dandelions across America's landscape. Families had once lived there, celebrated Christmases, birthdays, job promotions, and graduations. Children had run through backyard sprinklers while parents kept an eye on them from plastic lawn chairs and sipped iced tea in the hazy New England heat.

Time passed. People moved away. But no one came back to visit Barnard Street.

No one stood at the edge of the parking lot and reminisced

about his childhood, wondering what the inside looked like now or who lived there. No one dug into the attic's moldy boxes to retrieve family photos depicting days on Barnard Street. In fact, most residents had abandoned the dwelling in haste, leaving belongings and haunted nightmares behind. For those who had passed through its hungry walls, the house held a legacy of misfortune, death, and misery. Barnard Street travelers could sense the house's deadly aura, gripping their children's hands tighter and quickening their pace as they passed, as if the living structure might come alive and snatch them.

The town of Chatham had tried to raze the structure after it had taken Marcus Bailey's young bride in the spring of '49, just days after the wedding. But when the city's excavator leveled its boom against the clapboard siding and pushed, the bucket somehow dislodged an electrical wire, sending it snaking into the cab and electrocuting the operator. After that, no one accepted the demolition contract, and the Barnard Street house remained.

The property stands vacant most of the time, but tonight a light burned in a smudged window.

A man stared through the dirt-caked, wavy glass into the world's bleak darkness, relieved he had finally found an out-of-the-way place to lay low. Why the house sat vacant, he didn't care. It had a roof. It provided a place to conduct his business, get back on his feet again. Propped against the wall, he tugged the boots from his aching feet and blew out a breath. As his eyelids slipped down over his burning eyes, he caught movement in the hallway. The walls shimmered as a thick, crimson fluid oozed from the drywall and clotted in pools along the floorboards' edges. A throbbing from beneath the man's feet pulsed like a heartbeat through his core, as if the musty house breathed with him, its stale air wafting over him with a metallic-iron blood odor. The man pressed his fists to his eyes, attempting to dispel the images as a shaft of glimmering light pierced the darkness from the back-bedroom keyhole. It grew like a beacon as the door swung open on its hinge.

The man stepped toward the glowing light, the soothing radiance beckoning him…inviting him in.

CHAPTER ONE

Thursday, March 17

RG

RG Granville dragged his knuckles across his eyes, wiping away the crumbled sleep. The streetlights lit the inky blackness and pierced the windshield from above like electric daggers as the car sped along Route 6. He jammed his bare foot against the accelerator, the Subaru shimmying as the speedometer ratcheted upward.

The dream had jolted RG Granville from a restless sleep, launching him from his bed, so disturbed and overwhelmed with the intrusive vision, he hadn't even awakened Kacey. Taking inventory, he glanced in the rearview mirror. Sweat clung to fevered skin, his disheveled appearance not much different than when he had rolled out of bed ten minutes ago.

He raked his fingers across a thick patch of wavy, brown

hair. Detective Stahl would assume he had finally cracked when he arrived, windbreaker slung over his bare chest, pajama bottoms cinched at the hips. Maybe he should have sunk back into the welcoming mattress and conformed to Kacey's beckoning shape, enveloped himself in her warmth, and forgotten about what he had witnessed. Chalked it up to the disjointed thoughts and images the mind weaves together in the night that disappear with the hint of morning. But the dream had been too real to ignore. Someone died tonight.

He had watched it happen. He should have nudged Kacey. She would have known what to do. She'd had dreams and visions like this before. Now he understood what it was like for his wife to have been born with the ability to see things no one else could, able to sense spirits outside the material plane. He had recently inherited the same power from his late father, Morrow, and could now witness what Kacey saw, malicious spirits from the afterlife—jumpers, who transitioned back and forth between worlds to prey on the living—and devoted caretakers, like his father, who battled them. He wasn't sure whether to thank the old man for his 'gift' or curse him, but in their short time as caretakers, RG and Kacey had faced some of the most powerful forces in the universe and lived to tell about it. Teaming up to protect the world from the spiritual realm's darkest evil would never have been his choice for a livelihood. Yet, here he was.

RG glanced at his wedding band, glowing with the forces his father had relinquished. His power was growing, and tonight he'd had a vision unlike anything he had ever experienced.

He had grown accustomed to Kacey's strange dreams revealing the future, events she could foresee but couldn't explain. He could sense her desperation upon waking, wrestling with her newfound knowledge and the burden of having to alter the future's outcome at times to protect loved ones. RG acknowledged the same emotions building inside him, but he couldn't do anything about what he had witnessed. Tonight, he hadn't glimpsed the future; his vision had occurred in real time.

But he had to be sure.

The headlights pierced the open road's dim shadows, the rhythmic thump of the highway asphalt lulling him into a trance. The dream flashed before his open eyes once again. Pictures and images replayed in high definition and color through the windshield, merging with the blacktop and painted road markings disappearing beneath the speeding car's front bumper.

The man's body had lain on the metal slab as the mortician secured lines into the incision points, whistling to himself as he worked. A cannula pierced an artery beneath the man's clavicle, and a drainage tube hung from a dime-sized hole in his chest wall. A line of glue sealed his eyelids and heavy twine snaked through the jaw and septum, tethering his mouth closed.

The mortician wiped his hands. "Now don't you go anywhere," he had chuckled to himself, spinning knobs on the gray-paneled machine beside the gurney as he exited the laboratory, his footsteps tapping along the tiled basement floor. The machine thumped and whirred as it sent the affixing chemicals into the dead man.

A shadow danced across the wall as the body on the slab shifted.

The cadaver tested his limbs, flexing his fingertips and rolling his ankles as cracks and pops erupted from the shriveled joint capsules. Lifting a hand off the metal embalming table, he pulled the cannula from the base of his neck and wrenched the drainage tube from his side. Pinching at his eyelids, the corpse ripped them open, the left lid splitting vertically as the glue maintained its oppressive hold. Removing the cotton folded beneath his eyelids, the dead man winced as brilliant white shards from the overhead surgical light burst through his lifeless corneas. He batted his hand forward, arcing the fixture into the wall beside him with a crash, glass shards raining onto the floor.

The commotion brought hurried footfalls clomping toward the room.

The corpse glanced at the row of instruments resting on the utility cart beside the table and wrapped stiff digits around the longest and sharpest one. Flexing the kinks from his fingers, he cradled the gleaming trocar until he could form a fist. As the mortician hurried into the room, the dead man rose from the gurney and pierced the mortician's throat with the sterling metal spear. The doctor's feet continued forward as his body went horizontal, head smacking the tile floor with a crunching thud.

The corpse snapped the string knots securing his jaw as the dying man writhed in his fluids, attempting to swallow and smack his lips, his hands folded gently around the trocar. Half the instrument protruded from the back of his neck and angled his head like a tent pole, his glazed, dying eyes aimed at the rear wall.

As the dream ended, a voice—her voice—had spoken into RG's head, its unforgettable intonation, pitch, and cadence burned onto his brain like a cattle brand since the moment of his birth. The last time her voice had breached the stillness, it barely rose above the beeps and pings of hospital machines keeping her alive. In the midnight silence, deep inside his head, Helen Granville once again whispered to her son.

"Be careful, RG," said his mother. *"There's something awful coming for you."*

* * *

Kacey

The German Shepherd's throaty growl rumbled like a mini earthquake through the bedroom's early morning calm. Kacey kicked her foot from under the down comforter to rub Baron's coat, but the furry mass she expected had vacated its usual spot at the foot of the bed.

"What now?" Kacey mumbled.

She tilted her head and glanced at the bedside clock. "Ugh." She rolled over, sandwiching her head between the pillows. *Way too early.* She hadn't had enough sleep, having stayed up late with RG trying to soothe his troubled mind. As a caretaker, her husband struggled under the burden of his powers, suffering with what the ring allowed him to envision. The evil existing between worlds and the danger humanity faced each day. He had devoted his life to those in need, working with Kacey to help the desperate, those who reached out to them for help through their cryptic online posts and classified ads. But they had to work in the dark, under the radar, tracking down lost loved ones and confronting powerful jumpers in the dark corners of the spiritual realm. For RG, his knowledge of the afterlife, parallel worlds, and the encroaching evil, left him wishing he could just come clean, stop keeping secrets and tell the world what he knew. Things they had a right to know.

Baron's growl roused her from drowsy recollection. She raised her head and spotted the mutt standing inches from the bedroom door, coiled like a live wire with hackles raised and teeth bared, eyes trained on the door handle.

"Easy, boy. What's the matter with you?" Kacey rolled over to nudge RG, but his side of the bed lay empty, the bedspread thrown back and sheets cold to her touch. She glanced toward the darkened bathroom. "RG, you in there?" She waited.

The canine forced another low snarl, something between a howl and bark, his agitation rising.

Kacey swung her legs over the side of the bed and snatched her cell, tapping RG's name from her favorites' list. His phone hummed as it danced across the end table on the other side of the bed.

"Dammit, where are you?" She blew out a breath. He had to be in the house somewhere—he never went anywhere without his cell. No doubt Baron sensed his padding around out there, explaining his unusual agitation level.

She scooped a sweatshirt from the floor and jumped into her slippers. Grabbing the dog's collar, she eased the door open and stepped out onto the landing, the Shepherd's muscled frame nearly pulling her off balance.

"Take it easy, boy." She reached and gave his taut shoulders a scratch, but the growl continued to rumble in his throat, his flews pulled back in a maniacal canine grin.

A distinctive creak sounded from the end of the hallway, Junior's bedroom door pressing against the squeaky hinges RG had yet to tighten. A flutter ignited in Kacey's chest.

She stepped along the hallway to Robert Jr.'s room and cracked the door. "RG, you in there?"

She leaned her head into the bedroom, letting her eyes adjust to the dark. A soft snore from the two-year-old boy in the race-car-shaped bed eased her thumping heart for a moment, the boy's hypnotic effect on her as calming as a combined love potion and sedative mixture delivered intravenously. She eased the door shut.

The full moon melted through the upstairs skylight and illuminated a path along the narrow hallway to the stairs. The first floor lay in shadows, barely visible from the top step. Baron growled at the darkness.

"RG, that you?" She half-shouted, half-whispered, her echoing voice more like a plea than a question. "Where the hell are you?" *Don't you know your wife is scared shitless right now?*

Kacey popped the baby gate open and descended the steps into the dark, fighting to control Baron pulling against his collar. His stocky eighty pounds bucked against her grip, straining her arms and shoulders as if she'd performed her circuit training regimen with just the one side of her body.

Flipping the switch at the bottom of the stairway, Kacey breathed a sigh of relief as the hallway filled with light. "Some caretaker you are, like a child afraid of the dark," she whispered to herself.

As she marched down the short hallway and passed the door leading to the garage, a draft of cool air rolled across her skin. The entryway door stirred as a breeze gusted through the carport, drumming it against the jamb. Through the door's sliver opening she could view the empty stall where RG's Subaru usually sat, the garage door wide open.

Gone? RG leaving without telling her, without at least giving her a kiss? And without his cellphone. What the hell's going on with him? Kacey considered the conversation that kept them up so late. Maybe his secrets had become such a burden that he couldn't wait until morning to shout them from the rooftops.

Another yawning squeak drifted from the upstairs hallway. Kacey stopped, pressed her hand against her chest and listened, using the other to reach for RG's Louisville Slugger nestled behind the hall tree.

Oh, and to hell with you for leaving me alone at a time like this!

Could Junior be stirring? At this hour? Even though they had worked so hard to train him not to get up before his

SpongeBob alarm clock went off, the boy would still try to get up and barge into their room. If it isn't RG, it has to be Junior. No other option, right?

Glancing toward the stairwell, Kacey squinted at the barefoot impressions pressed against each step. They hadn't been visible from the darkened hallway above. They appeared too small for RG or her to have made them, and the baby gate at the top of the stairs made it impossible that Junior could have—

Another creak from the landing.

She tiptoed to the base of the stairway and leaned against the bannister, craning her neck to survey Junior's bedroom at the end of the upstairs hallway.

The door stood wide open.

She froze.

She wasn't alone in the house.

She sensed secret hands gripping her insides and giving it a twist for good measure. She let go of Baron's collar. He bolted past her, sprinted up the steps, and smashed through the baby gate. Raising his hackles, the dog barked and growled as he reached Junior's room but hesitated at the doorframe. Poking his nose into the bedroom, Baron yelped and retreated, tail between his legs.

Kacey bounded the stairs two at a time and flew toward the end of the hallway, but something stopped her before she barreled into the room—a presence, a tickling sensation on the back of her neck, like a cold finger tracing her skin. Her instincts screamed at her to turn and run, but her protective motherly instinct pushed her forward, Slugger in hand. She stepped into the bedroom, only able to make out shadowed outlines in the darkened space.

"RG?" she whispered. "You need to come out here right now, this instant!"

She swiped her hand across her cell's touch screen and triggered the flashlight, aiming it toward the room's center. The cone of light captured the barefoot figure standing motionless beside Robert Jr.'s bed, hovering over him as it snaked a hand through his hair.

Kacey's jaw dropped and she struggled to pull a breath. She flailed for the doorjamb to steady herself.

She recognized the figure as that of a girl, her gaunt body appearing like a husk withered to nothing, as if someone had taken a straw and sucked the life from her. Trembling limbs barely held her weight, shriveled muscle cords stretching like elastic bands through sallow skin dotted with splotches and lesions. The girl appeared more dead than alive, the life all but drained from her meager frame.

She turned to face Kacey, her vacant gaze burning into her from behind dead eyes. The girl grinned and scooped Junior into her arms.

Get away from him! Kacey's mouth formed the words, but no sound emerged. She tried to advance, but her feet remained bolted to the floor.

Baron growled from the hallway and nosed his way into the bedroom. Kacey gave him a swipe on his haunches. "Get her, Baron!" The canine bolted into the room and leapt at the intruder, burying his teeth into Junior's collar and ripping him from the girl's grip as she vanished like a smoke wisp in a draft. Baron flew right through her and crashed into the dresser, pivoting his body to shield the boy from the impact. The crunching wood and dog's yelp woke the two-year old with a start.

Kacey raced into the bedroom and scooped up her sobbing boy, turning him back and forth to check for injuries. Clutching him to her chest, she soothed his whimpers.

As she squinted toward the floor, the faint barefoot impressions faded from the carpet.

* * *

RG

RG pulled onto Davis Street, blue light bouncing off house fronts and foliage as first responders' vehicles converged in front of the Bayless Funeral Home. Neighborhood residents in robes and pajamas viewed the scene from the safety of their front lawns and porches. Few ventured closer than the sidewalk, instinctively keeping their distance from a place where violent death had occurred. Police had cordoned off the block to secure the scene and deter the curious, making it impossible for RG to get closer to investigate. How the hell was he going to get in there?

RG pulled a U-turn and found a side street running behind the funeral home. Easing beside the curb, he killed the engine and gazed out the driver's side window. He couldn't see Mike Stahl's Crown Vic at the scene yet, but something told him he would be there soon. He would be RG's ticket in.

Stahl would understand. They had been through this type of thing before.

It had been less than a year ago that RG and Kacey had transported Mike Stahl through time to rescue his stepson from a volatile jumper abducting children from their world. And before that, the defeat of the burning man in Stahl's own living room had nearly killed him, leaving him with burns and bullets embedded in his hip and knee. Whether he liked it or not, Stahl was a conscript of this supernatural investigative team, and RG's case would have to take precedence.

If he couldn't find Stahl, he would have to sneak around back and find his own way in. As he pulled the key from the engine, the sounds of police activity through the driver's side window and the howling wind through the treetop leaves faded to nothing, replaced by an unnatural silence.

In the eerie calm, he gazed through the Legacy's windshield, the glass's clearness filling with shapes, colors, a story coming to life right before him. His mother lay in a hospital bed. But unlike the last time RG had seen Helen Granville alive, no tubes or wires protruded from her dying body. And, God, she looked so young, younger than he had ever seen her in any of the attic's mildewed photos. This time, she held a baby in her arms, her son, wrapped in a blanket.

She whispered to him as he cried. "Shhh, don't be afraid. Everything's okay. I'm right here."

RG scanned the hospital room, searching for Morrow, his father. But he couldn't find him. Why wouldn't he have been beside his wife comforting her at the birth of their only son? A nurse entered the room and stood beside Helen's bed.

"Please," Helen pleaded. "Don't." She gripped the baby tighter.

The woman placed a gentle hand on Helen's cheek before scooping the baby from her grasp. Helen's outstretched arms remained suspended as the nurse turned and left the room with the screaming child.

Where were they taking me?

RG stared through the windshield, the defining lines shredding into clear glass again, the moment from his past gone. RG pressed his palms against his temples, ignoring the street sounds rattling outside his window. First, his mother's warning. Then, a vision of her with her only child.

Had his mother been trying to communicate with him again? And what did his birth have to do with tonight's murder? He peered at the funeral home and stiffened in his seat, certain that hidden forces had led him there for a reason, wondering what he would find behind those doors. The answers had to be inside that funeral home. He would have to get inside, Stahl or not. But what if something happened? Chatham cops were not his biggest fans. They wouldn't be sympathetic to his plight and he could easily end up arrested at the crime scene or accused of murder…again.

Or shot.

Kacey would need to know where he was.

Just in case.

RG patted his pockets, then he leaned his forehead against the steering column. *Dammit! How could I have gone off without my phone?* He rocked his head back and forth against the padded steering wheel, scolding himself…unless… He jerked upright, threw his arm over the seat, scrounging for his professor bag. Thank God he'd left it in the car. With the weighty bag in his lap, he rummaged for the iPad pressed between crumpled research articles and lesson plans. *When all else fails…*

He cranked the ignition and scrolled through the Legacy's touch screen's settings until the WiFi icon activated. He pressed the home button to power up the device and tapped the 'Messages' icon.

Wake up - need to talk.

Not much chance Kacey was awake at 1:30, but she would be in a moment. She kept her phone and text volume so high it would wake the dead when his message pinged on her device.

Where r u? Had 2 chase off ghost in jrs room w/out u.

Wtf? u ok?

☺

Ghosts, visions and his mother's voice? They would need to talk to Morrow.

RG tapped the onscreen keyboard. *Dreamed I saw murder happen - at scene now.*

Tell me u r w/Mike.

He raised his head from the screen. Don't lie, RG. *Not here yet - but need 2 get inside now.*

Don't give them excuse to arrest u!!! Wait 4 him.

Forever the voice of reason. *Ok.*

Where r u? I'll come.

No, stay with jr.

R u ok?

Idk – but need 2 do this.

RG waited a long minute before Kacey's text jumped onto the screen. *Don't forget 2 come home.*

RG let out a breath. "I'll be home…I promise." The words tumbled from his mouth without conviction.

RG powered down the iPad and stared at the funeral home looming outside his window. He rubbed the gold band on his finger. Exiting the vehicle, he dashed across the grassy lot and jumped the fence onto the property.

* * *

Mike

Detective Mike Stahl jerked from a troubled sleep, his cellphone's shrill ring igniting a throbbing in his chest. Blinking his eyes open, he calmed himself with a few deep breaths and snatched the vibrating device rattling on the nightstand.

1:27 a.m.

Tempted to shut the sound off and roll back over, he groaned.

"Let me guess…" he flexed his opposite arm, the one positioned beneath his body as he slept. "You're calling to tell me I have the day off."

"How'd you know?" Chris Daniels mumbled as if he had emerged from a winter's hibernation. "Hope you were up."

"I wasn't."

"Well, you're gonna be for a while."

Stahl dragged a hand down his face. "I figured."

"We have a body over on Davis, the funeral home. It looks like Hal Bayless was at the wrong place at the wrong time."

Stahl couldn't help but recall his last visit with the man. His parents' deaths at the hands of a drunk driver on Route 6 had left a town in mourning, and a devoted son reeling. Bayless had done wonders with the bodies, considering what Stahl had witnessed when he ID'd them at the hospital. He had made them appear as if they might have been sleeping, as if they might wake up any moment. But they didn't.

"Ideal place for a body, don't you think?" Stahl quipped, attempting to dislodge the disturbing images in his head and quell the discomfort his recollections summoned.

"Not this body. And three others are missing from the freezers. Bring your forensics kit. As lead on the Sarnie investigation, I need a CIO. I'm sure you'd prefer getting a call from me at one-thirty in the morning instead of BCI."

As Criminal Investigations Officers with the Bureau of Criminal Investigations, Mike Stahl and partner, Chris Daniels, did double duty as Chatham detectives and forensic analysts, processing crime scenes across the Cape and Islands. It wasn't uncommon for them to team up on cases, with one serving as lead detective and the other as CIO.

Stahl switched the phone to his opposite ear, wishing he could figure a way to only work daytime murders. If criminals would just be more thoughtful. "So, what do three missing bodies have to do with the Sarnie case?"

"The Sarnies *are* the missing bodies."

Christ. "The wife and little girl, too?" Nearly everyone in New England had heard about the tragedy. A Chatham businessman, his beautiful wife, and five-year-old daughter drowned in a one-car accident near the Chatham-Harwich line, Sarnie's Lexus rolling off Route 28 and into Jackknife Cove. Alex Sarnie's company owned about every shipping contract into and out of the Cape, and with his hand in so many businesses, his death caused a palpable ripple across the region. The Cape's grocery store shelves, medical supplies, and construction materials dwindled to all but nothing in the days after his death.

"Listen, Mike, I'll be heading right past you, I'll pick you up."

"Give me five." Stahl disconnected.

Rolling his neck, he glanced at the queen mattress he shared with himself, a vast expanse of empty space beside him. Same as yesterday…and the day before, Claire's memory once again delivering a gut punch far too early in another of his endless days.

"Claire." His wife's name inadvertently tumbled from his lips, taking him by surprise, its sound an intrusion in the room's empty silence. Had it already been six months since she had walked out, taking his stepson with her? Even if she didn't go far, just across town, the scant distance didn't reflect the depth of the dwelling's hollow vacancy as well as the desolate hours did.

How often did Zach sneak into his mind each day? He'd stopped counting. But he couldn't shake the idyllic moments, the boy's goofy smile as he dashed out the front door and leaped off the porch to meet his car crunching across the shell driveway. Or when he absently grasped Stahl's hand as they strolled across the parking lot to school or hiked along the rocky shoreline of Aunt Lydia's Cove.

Stahl still shivered when he thought about how he had nearly lost him for good last summer, having to travel across time to rescue him from a dark corner of the past. Zach's return should have been enough to salvage things with Claire, unite the family. But it wasn't. She hadn't believed him when he told her of the constant war raging between the otherworldly forces of good and evil hovering beyond our senses, the truth about caretakers and jumpers. She couldn't accept the fact a jumper had abducted Zach and had taken him back in time. After he revealed the truth about RG and Kacey's caretaker powers, she had questioned whether he had been behind Zach's disappearance. She accepted the universe's reality now, but her earlier doubt and mistrust had been difficult to expunge from their history and move past. And she could no longer place Zach in the crosshairs of any more hidden battles, choosing to keep him far from Stahl and his time-traveling comrades.

He swung his legs over the edge of the bed and raked a hand through his pillow-sculpted nest of thick brown hair, glancing behind him at the space she once occupied. The sheets clean and taught, but cold as ice.

CHAPTER TWO

Thursday, March 17

Alex

Alex Sarnie had sensed the chemicals flush through his body as he lay on the metal slab, the embalming machine's electric hum pulsing in his ears. His body had expired, but death didn't faze him, not when he could jump into any human shell he desired. Living or dead.

But he had wanted his old body back.

He would show that no-good-sonofabitch that nothing could kill Alex Sarnie, not even his own murder. The scumbag's eyes would widen in terror as he recognized the man he had killed, sinking to the floor to beg a dead man for his life. A smile struggled against the restrictive twine still twisting through his jaw.

Killer beware—Sarnie was coming for him and would show no mercy…once he figured out who had killed him.

Sarnie rotated his dead hand back and forth. The raw strength he possessed brought a curl to his shriveled lips. He had never killed anyone before, but Dr. Bayless deserved his final judgment. A chuckle emptied from his parched throat as he eyed the mortician. Sarnie had done Cape Cod a favor—removing one more phony upstanding citizen from its shores. He had witnessed disturbing images in the man's head. Sarnie didn't question how he could tap into them like he could. He just accepted it.

Being dead clearly had its perks.

The man writhing on the floor had played the role of dour and caring funeral director for years, hands folded across his desk as he listened to grieving families recount their departed loved ones' final wishes. He would press his lips together as he feigned interest in the deceased's banal life, taking the bereaved family members' hands in his own as if he, too, had experienced their loss. Then, he would hand them a pen to sign the sizeable checks he would slip into his jacket pocket. Sometimes he would visit the widows in their homes as the lonely weeks passed by. He would bring food or flowers to comfort them and rub their shoulders with a compassionate gaze, encouraging them to live again, use him to escape their loneliness. If only for an afternoon.

Sarnie didn't care how he'd gained his newfound knowledge, but when he engaged the man's mind, he instantly witnessed everything Bayless had ever contemplated or experienced.

Even hidden things.

Like what he would do with young female accident victims lying prone and welcoming on cold examination tables. Sarnie closed his eyes to dispel the images.

Leaning over the table's edge, he locked gazes with the dying mortician grasping at the trocar impaling his throat. "You had it coming."

The mortician's final thoughts pinballed through Sarnie's mind, jolting his own recollection of the night the Lexus had careened out of control down the hill and flipped into the sea. It must have only been a few days since the accident, judging by his body's current state, but it seemed a lifetime ago. He had learned so much about the journey's next phase in the short time he had been to the other side, the dark powers he would own in the next world, and the things he would be able to do in time. But he wasn't ready yet. A simmering rage tugged at his soul, pulling him backward, earthly desires of vengeance and payback tipping the scales toward an unscheduled return.

The killer would pay for inflicting death upon him, but for now he would race home to his wife, Jessie, wrap his arms around her and convince her he was still alive, that there had been a terrible mistake. He would take the living room stairs two at a time to Marlie's room and tiptoe to her bedside to brush the hair from her eyes before kissing her forehead. He would leave the breakfast menu on her bedside table next to her butterfly alarm clock and await her footsteps across his bedroom floor the next morning. He would smile as she handed him the paper with the boxes checked in crayon— maybe cereal today, or toast with marmalade—a grin spreading across her lips as she wiped her sleepy eyes. Maybe they could make a life together again. His body could last another fifty years—

If embalmed properly.

Sarnie examined the dead funeral director on the tile, his wispy hair undulating in the crimson fluid pooling behind his head. He reached for the cannula, jamming it back into his neck and forcing the drainage tube through the hole in his side. He haphazardly spun knobs and flipped switches on the gray machine's panel beside the gurney, initiating a burst of pressure that rocketed the tubes from his body and ejected embalming fluid across the floor to mix with the spreading blood pool.

"Dammit!"

Hopping off the table, he collapsed onto the cold, tiled floor as his dead limbs failed under the weight. Massaging the rigor mortis from his stiff appendages, Sarnie took a deep breath, flinching at the stench rising from his core. With the embalming process halted, his body's own internal chemicals and enzymes were already at work breaking down its cells and tissues. As his body decayed, bacteria would proliferate and generate a rank odor that would only worsen the death stench wafting from his shell.

The dead man struggled to his feet, searching through cabinets for chemical jugs and embalming fluids, anything he could get his hands on to stave off decomposition. He lifted two different jugs off a shelf, unscrewed the tops, and guzzled the contents.

Stumbling from the preparation room on shaky legs, Sarnie grabbed a white lab coat hanging from the funeral director's coatrack to cover his naked body and waxy skin. He cocked his head, his gaze locking onto the Glade room freshener resting on a file cabinet. Pursing his lips, Sarnie snatched the canister and bathed himself in a cloud of apple-cinnamon vapors to quell the eye-watering aroma emanating from his core.

Pushing open the funeral home's doors, Sarnie drew a deep inhalation, but the brisk night air failed to reach his shriveled, inoperable lungs. Nothing worked. He pressed a hand to the left side of his chest, hoping for a telltale heartbeat, something to give him hope he could live in this world again. But he remained nothing more than a puppeteer operating a decaying marionette.

He strode along Main Street before taking a quiet side street toward his Chatham home. A shaft of moonlight bisected the clouds scattering faint light across the shadowed lawn. Sarnie quickened his pace along the driveway. Maybe he would wake them, shout from the bottom of the stairs. "I'm home now." *I'm really home.* Maybe Marlie would race down the staircase in her seahorse pajamas and jump into his arms from the third step like she did when he came home late from work. He imagined Jessie wrapping herself around him in her signature welcome-home hug, her body's contours perfectly tailored to his dimensions. Maybe her touch would kick-start his heart and get it beating again. But not a single light burned in the windows. As he approached the front door, he stumbled over a mountain of fading flowers, cards, and teddy bears piled on the front porch.

"What the…?"

Sarnie knelt and plucked a Hallmark from the pile, addressed to Marlie from her kindergarten class.

"We miss you, Marlie." Sarnie mumbled. Why do they miss her, hadn't she been to school? Did Jessie take her somewhere? It doesn't make sense. He glanced at the outpouring of affection scattered across the front porch. The card flitted from his fingers as the gears turned, roaring in his ears against the logic. *They only bring things like this to places when…*No! They're inside like they always are. It's just late. That's all. That's why the lights are off.

Sarnie pulled the spare key hidden beneath a space in the stone wall beneath the wraparound porch and let himself in. He raced through the foyer, shouting Jessie and Marlie's names. After racing up the carpeted stairway to the master bedroom, he paused and eased the door open. His face fell as he gazed at the bed, made neat as a pin. One of Jessie's outfits lay draped over a chair. Stepping across the room, he ran a palm along the material and pressed it to his face. He sucked the air with an exaggerated breath, hoping for a faint scent to trigger the sensors in his dead nostrils. He recalled wanting Jessie to wear the outfit, but she had chosen something else. The black dress, he thought. God, she had looked beautiful in it. He tried to remember the evening she wore it, recalling bits and pieces, but everything came across in a haze. Distant. What day had that been?

Laying the dress back across the chair, Sarnie stepped from the bedroom and approached Marlie's room across the hall. Triggering the light switch, Sarnie grinned at the assortment of toys and games scattered across the carpeting. On the desk, her jewelry box sat open. Sarnie leaned over and peered inside, searching for his favorite necklace, the one he had bought for her just weeks ago for her fifth birthday with the gold outline of Cape Cod dangling from the chain. He sifted a hand through her collection but couldn't find it anywhere. Where the hell could it be?

He dropped a silver bracelet back into the jewelry box, its curved edge catching a tincture of light. He picked it back up, stared at its shiny finish, just like the silver rim on his Lexus's steering wheel. The bracelet poured from his brittle fingers. He stumbled backward, pressed his heavy hands against his eyes, and released a scream to wake the dead. He fell to his knees. He didn't want to remember. That's not how it could have happened. Why was he seeing himself strapping Marlie to her booster seat, her Cape Cod necklace sparkling in the dome light's radiance? Why was Jessie sitting in the passenger seat, smiling at him as she threw a glance over her shoulder and straightened the hem of her black dress?

Sarnie lowered himself to a seated position on the carpet and rested his head in his hands. The memory had been his last, the night of his death.

His family had been in the car with him.

He struggled to his feet and retraced his route to the funeral home, mounting the steps in slow motion.

"Please, please, don't let them be here," he whispered. "Let me have remembered wrong."

Stepping into the preparation room, he sidestepped the gelling blood pool and entered the refrigeration unit. He pried the metal doors open, rolled out the metal slabs, and threw the sheets back until he found what he had come for. Hoisting the bodies across each shoulder, he slogged back to the house.

Sarnie kicked in the front door and stepped along the familiar route through the living room into the kitchen. No need to trigger the light switch. His useless eyes couldn't see anything anyway.

Propping Jessie and Marlie in the high-backed chairs around the granite-top island in the kitchen, Sarnie rummaged through the trash can and salvaged the breakfast list from his daughter's final day, crumpled and stained with syrup and coffee grinds.

He squinted at the list. "Eggs and pancakes?" He raised an eyebrow at Marlie. "Someone has quite an appetite."

Glancing toward Jessie, he expected the smile she returned days ago, but her skull's dead weight pulled it toward the countertop with a thunk. As he set to work whipping up a late-night breakfast, Marlie's body pitched sideways, hanging off the chair in a slow decent to the floor. Reaching across the island, he grabbed his cold daughter before she fell from her perch.

"It's okay, honey. I got you."

Positioning her securely in the chair, her jaw popped open as her head lolled backward, eyes staring unseeing toward the ceiling. He slid the plate in front of her and sent a gooey syrup waterfall cascading over the steaming, golden-brown pancake stack.

The sobs hitched his chest, but no tears escaped his dry, dead eyes.

* * *

Ellie

She lay motionless in the bed, one bare foot protruding from beneath the tidy sheets and blankets. The cool air on her skin gave her a slight chill, but she could do nothing about it. Ellie Daniels couldn't move, not so much as an eyelid. It had been that way for a while. Her body's wasted shell now resembled a balloon with a slow leak. Her skin had receded deep into her cheeks and the hospital johnny barely hid her protruding ribs. The nurses had positioned her hands around a folded towel to keep her tendons from shortening—as if it mattered, as if she'd ever use them again.

Her brother, Chris, visited her just about every weekend, making the long drive from the Cape to Boston's Mass General through weekend traffic. If only for an hour or two. She looked forward to his next visit in a few days. He would rest in the chair beside her withered form, a leg thrown over his opposite knee, looking over his case files and catching up on his detective work. Occasionally, he would glance above the manila folder at her ashen-faced shape sunk deep into the mattress, press his lips together and sigh. Ellie didn't entirely understand how she could discern him as clearly as she could, especially since she couldn't so much as open her eyes anymore. Still, she would view him there, plain as day, and glimpse the thoughts and pictures in his head as clear as if she had traded places with him.

She didn't understand how that could be, but it made her smile.

Her brother had a good ten years on her, despite being Ellie's closest-aged sibling. Growing up, he had been more like a father to her, especially after Brock Daniels' fishing boat took on the frigid February waters off Nantucket days before her fifth birthday. Her dad had been a strong man, that much she remembered, thick and mustachioed. He would reach down with his solid arm and hoist her onto his shoulders in one exhilarating movement, resembling the superheroes she would cheer for at the movies. But even Superman had his Kryptonite, and for Brock Daniels, it turned out to be the thirty-five-degree Atlantic in the dead of winter.

She used to wonder what went through his mind as his vessel took on water and the icy swells rose up to meet him, knowing he wouldn't have a chance. Could he spot the island's shores or make out the traffic and night sounds echoing across the encroaching waves?

Laying in her hospital bed one night, she finally discovered the answer.

She found herself with him—right there in his head—experiencing the frosty sea's biting cold as it climbed his pant legs and smothered his jacket, his muscles shivering and slowing until he couldn't move them fast enough to keep his head above water. She could sense his heart pounding in his ears and his clothing's anchoring weight as the layers of fabric swelled like sponges and pulled him below. She witnessed the peaceful grin stretching across his ice-blue lips as he relived a special memory: a brave princess with a spaghetti colander crown on her blonde head and an oversized wooden spoon chasing a thick, mustachioed dragon around the kitchen table.

She could also witness everything filtering through brother Chris's subconscious as he perched beside her, like a million twitter feeds playing simultaneously on her mind's homepage. She liked reliving his recollection of the girl she had been, the four-year-old covered in sand, resting on the beach blanket with her brother. The day he took her bucket and poured sea water into the sand beside the blanket, pressing the pasty granules with his hands until they took the shape of a heart, then handing it to her with a smile. She witnessed the freckled-faced, blonde teenager with the shimmering sea cascading from her pink and black wetsuit paddling out faster and farther than anyone else on Nauset Beach, surfing at dusk with the seals and sharks while the boys huddled on the beach. The chimes and dings from the life-prolonging machinery and oxygen whooshing through her air tube no longer registered in her ears, its company as familiar as the wall clock's tick or the fluorescent lights' buzz.

Where the hell was she? Did she still dwell inside that withered body somewhere?

When the accident happened—if one could call it that—Ellie had ended up here. The room teemed with activity day and night. Friends from school and her favorite surf spots, teachers and coaches, and family members from across New England poured in at all hours to sit with her, play her favorite music on their smartphones, read her poems they'd written, brush her hair and tell her all the latest gossip. They couldn't have imagined that from within her lifeless form she could see them, but she could. Sometimes they would cry, and she longed to reach out and hold their hands. And she would, only they didn't know it. Chris would wait his turn, viewing the room from the doorway until it slowly emptied. Then he would assume his position beside the bed, rubbing her hand as he settled in the chair next to her.

As time went by, Ellie didn't get as many visitors, but they still shuffled in from time to time. Somehow, she learned to pick up their thoughts, probing their minds for unrevealed secrets. Whatever new vision she now possessed allowed her to open her mind to everything, including the things they kept hidden. Her powers continued to grow as her body gradually withered away, as if fate had compensated for her physical loss. It wouldn't be long now before she would become…what? She didn't know yet.

She also dreamed of the unfamiliar woman and kept tabs on her from afar, a woman she sensed would help her and show her what to do.

Her brother never judged her the way other family members did, the older folks who couldn't fathom why such a beautiful girl with a bright future would ever get involved with that stuff. But on Cape Cod, more and more teens played this chemical form of Russian roulette and ended up meeting the round in the chamber. They blamed the Cape's isolation, its long winters and bored teens' curiosity. They blamed youth for acting irresponsibly. But Chris didn't blame the victims, he blamed the suppliers, the people manufacturing and distributing the stuff—the vultures cashing in on the spiraling tragedy around them. But when Ellie had smoked that junk after a night of drinking with friends—her first time ever—she didn't blame anyone but herself. The combination of depressants lowered her breathing rate and blood pressure until she simply fell asleep and never awoke. How stupid was that? Just for kicks on a Friday. It didn't matter that she had been at fault, Ellie could sense her brother's anger eating him alive, a vengeance percolating beneath the surface. He'd already taken his wrath out on one lowlife drug dealer, leaving him battered and bloody. She could sense he worried the department would suspend or fire him, and she feared he would have too much time on his hands. Too much time to think. And plan.

Before he had left her bedside last weekend, Chris's

prolonged stare had pressed against her sallow skin with a tangible heaviness. He did that a lot now. He struggled with the weight of the future, the time coming to accept the decision, honor the family's wishes. Soon, they would all gather to say their goodbyes, run their hands through her hair, and kiss her forehead for the last time.

Turn off the machines.

The doctors could still harvest her organs. She could still provide life to others. She liked that idea. But her brother's face had rested in a tortured grimace. She didn't like the dark images unleashed in his head, the ones he kept hidden, the ones she couldn't witness.

Things he had done. Things he still might do.

* * *

Alex

Alex Sarnie approached the dilapidated structure tucked behind the vacant strip mall and abandoned gas station on Barnard Street, paint peeling from the weathered exterior like sunburned skin. The once popular retail and service complex adjacent to the house had become a casualty to redevelopment, its fickle patrons leaving ages ago to frequent the newer, more colorful businesses along Route 28. Amidst life's daily bustle, the once vibrant edifices rusted and rotted through the heat and cold of passing seasons, dying in place as the town's residents traipsed past them year after year, pretending not to register their advancing decay, or how they mirrored their own mortal structures' decline.

Sarnie maneuvered past the rusted dumpster, scattering the broken glass and beer can pop tops littering the crumbling blacktop. Rotting food and garbage odors swirled about like a fetid cloud. The house rested beside a battered fence, untended grass, and overgrown weeds snaking their way up rotting wood slats. It would have to do. He couldn't stay at home with his dead wife and child as company. And with three bodies from the same family missing from the funeral home, the authorities would soon come calling. Not that they could stop him, but why draw attention? Better to find a place to hole up and plan his strategy in solitude.

Still, he wasn't certain he had gone unnoticed.

He had sensed a presence in the basement at the funeral home, a familiar aura, a power he perceived equal to his own. Whoever, or whatever, had witnessed his savagery even rummaged through his mind but had kept hidden. Well, he would take care of the watcher, as he would the people responsible for his wife and child's deaths. The payback would be excruciating and drawn out.

He would make sure of it.

Sarnie rapped his knuckles against Mick Sullivan's door and waited. Despite the late hour, a light burned through the grime-layered window.

"Who the fuck's out there? How many times do I have to tell you junkies not to come 'round here—" Sullivan's voice halted as he swung the door open, his eyes wide.

A stray dog's distant bark punctuated the silence.

"Surprised?" Sarnie snickered as he stepped into the run-down dwelling.

"Jesus Christ, Boss…You're supposed to be dead. The papers said—"

"You can't trust everything you read, you know," he interrupted.

"Well, it's good to see you. I—" His voice stopped abruptly as he took a sharp inhale, his face twisting into a grimace.

"Never mind the odor." Sarnie placed his glistening hands in his pockets, formaldehyde and interstitial fluid leeching from his pores. "I, um…had to avoid curious eyes so I jumped inside a dumpster in the parking lot. The uh…local feds don't want anyone to suspect I'm alive."

Sullivan scowled. "FBI? You in some kind of trouble, Boss?"

"Nothing like that." Sarnie perused the dwelling's interior as he stepped across a matted wall-to-wall carpet pressed against chipped floor moldings. A single light fixture hung limply from a worn wire bolted to the ceiling. "Someone tried to kill me, that's all. They got my family, but not me. They're investigating, but for now, we're all playing along like I'm dead."

Isn't that the truth?

The man gazed at his boss's face, inspecting his eyes. It occurred to Sarnie he had been staring at Sullivan through the split in his eyelid. He turned and ripped the dead skin from his eye socket with a slippery pop, flipping the membrane onto the carpet.

Sullivan swallowed as he eyed the curled leathery rind on the floor.

"That's the story we're going with, Sully. A ruse to fool my family's killers."

"Hey, I'm sorry about…your loss." Sullivan pressed his hand against Sarnie's shoulder, his fingers sinking into the toneless flesh. He flinched as he pulled it away.

"What the fuck happened to you?" Sarnie pointed to the cuts across the bridge of Sullivan's nose and discoloration under his eyes.

Sullivan pressed a tender finger against his face while leaning toward a stained mirror on the wall. "Some cop put the boot to me last week." His eyes darted back and forth between his own face and Sarnie's reflection behind him.

"What the hell for?" Sarnie asked.

"Don't know. This cop comes to the door…starts in on me about how I'm this scumbag drug dealer. Before I know it, I'm lying on the floor, covered up like a dog, walks over real calm like, and boots me in the stomach. Says, 'That's for Ellie.'"

"Who's Ellie?"

"How the fuck should I know? Figured it must have been a chick he knew. Maybe she got a hold of bad product."

"Was it…our stuff took the girl out?"

"Must have been. He came here, didn't he?"

Sarnie circled Sullivan like a shark. "Did he know about me, the organization?" He moved his finger back and forth between them. "Our connection?"

Sullivan's head swiveled back and forth, attempting to maintain eye contact. "I didn't tell him anything, I swear."

Sarnie stood behind Sullivan and placed a bony hand on the back of the man's neck. "Why didn't you inform me about this before now?"

"Well, I figured you were…dead. You know? I would have told you, Boss, but I didn't get a chance. Your…accident happened the next day."

Sarnie leaned forward and spoke into Sullivan's ear. "You didn't, uh…let my name slip or anything while he beat your ass, did ya?"

"Of course not. Why would I do that?" Sullivan covered his nose with the crook of his elbow as a pungent death odor wafted off the corpse behind him.

Sarnie tapped into Sullivan's brain, performing a gentle probe. He witnessed the conversation, the beating, the clean-cut cop with the brush-cut hauling off and flooring Sully with a quick jab square in the kisser followed by a shod foot to the midsection.

Sarnie grinned and spun Sullivan around, leaning forward to fix him with a stare. His dead eyes drew a look of terror from his henchman before the man averted his gaze. The man had been truthful, he hadn't betrayed him.

"I filed a complaint against that sonofabitch detective. He's gonna pay for what he did to—"

"You did what?"

"Bastard broke my nose." Sullivan raised his palms. "He had it coming."

"You should have taken the beating. If this comes out in a formal hearing, cops will be sniffing around the organization. And you gave them something to investigate."

"I didn't think about that. Geez, Boss, I'm really sorry, I—"

Sarnie raised his palm. "Listen, I need a place to stay for a while. I'm taking your room."

Sullivan swallowed. "Whatever you say, Boss."

"And you need to go out and get me some formaldehyde… and Axe body spray."

CHAPTER THREE

Thursday, March 17

Mike

Stahl reclined in the passenger seat of his partner's '68 Mercury Cougar Xr7. Most detectives welcomed the use of a government issued four-door sedan to wheel around in—no car payment, free gas—but Chris Daniels proved to be the exception. He'd told Stahl he wouldn't be caught dead in any vehicle he didn't consider a work of art, and no American automobile manufactured after 1971 qualified. Daniels recited his spiel every time they drove past a muscle car from the golden era. Stahl bragged to anyone who would listen how he had helped his partner restore his most recent classic. But in truth, his greatest skill as a mechanic rested in his ability to hand the correct tools to the guy fixing it.

Stahl's eyelids drooped as he melted into the cushioned

seats, the dashboard vents spewing out a stream of sleepy heat like an air-borne sedative, the rumbling engine sounds cloaking him in a blanket of comfort.

Daniels had curled a stick of gum into his mouth and balled up the silver wrapper, waking Stahl with a start as he flicked it against his temple. "Rise and shine, slacker. You're on the clock, you know."

Stahl massaged his eyes with his fingertips. "There's a clock? How come we never get to punch out?"

"Speak for yourself. I may be punching out for a good long time." Daniels body slumped in his seat, reminding Stahl about the hearing the following morning.

"You don't know that." Stahl reached across the console and dropped a hand on his friend's shoulder. "Just stay positive. I gave them my statement. The committee knows about Ellie. You might catch a break."

"Whatever's gonna happen, I got it coming to me." Daniels nibbled on his fingernails as he drove. "At any rate, it will all be over tomorrow. I'll either be sending out my résumé for the vacant security guard gig at the mall, or I'll have myself a nice, long, unpaid vacation."

"Jesus Christ, if that sonofabitch Matt Berrelli still has a job on the force, you don't have anything to worry about." The barrel-chested Chatham cop had the habit of using excessive force in his arrests, and an alarming proportion of the thug's annual salary went to fines, suspensions, and restitution.

Daniels smirked. "Well, we can ask him all about his experience since he's waiting for us over at the funeral home."

Stahl closed his eyes and leaned his head against the headrest. *Christ.*

Berrelli was the last person Stahl expected to run into. The last time he'd stood beside the explosive cop, a donnybrook had broken out in his backyard between Berrelli, RG

Granville, and nearly twenty of Cape Cod's finest until a well-timed swing from Kacey Granville's aluminum water bottle ended it, and transferred the pugilist's nose to the other side of his face.

Daniels rounded the corner onto Davis Street, the funeral home looming in his headlight's shadows. "Different day and age, Mike. They're cleaning up police forces across the country now."

"Don't get ahead of yourself. Let's see what tomorrow brings."

"Listen. After the hearing, I'm heading up to Boston for the weekend to visit Ellie…and the family. We have decisions to make about her. I need you to cover the Sarnie case for me while I'm away. Can you help me out?"

"Anything you need, brother. I wasn't doing anything this weekend anyway." *Wandering through the empty rooms of my house, maybe.*

"And if things don't go well tomorrow, you'll take over lead on the case." Daniels turned his head, the glow from the Cougar's dashboard painting his face in eerie, blue-green shadows. "You know most of the details, and you have copies of all the files. I already talked to Chief Defranco."

"Pump the breaks, kid. Let's cross that bridge when we come to it."

Daniels guided the Cougar in front of the mortuary, popping the column shifter into park as the engine idled to a low growl. "Just get up to speed as soon as you can."

A steady flicker of blue light bars pierced the dark calm of the sedan's interior. As Daniels and Stahl eased themselves from the vehicle, Officer Matt Berrelli waddled up beside Stahl. The image of a bulldog in uniform came to mind as the Chatham patrolman materialized from the darkness.

"How are you, Matt?" Daniels asked.

"Detective," he nodded. "And if it isn't Mike Stahl. Glad you could make it. Looks like we interrupted your beauty sleep, or is that how you always look?"

"How's the nose, Fuckwad." Stahl stepped closer to inspect.

"It's an improvement, actually." Berrelli moved into Stahl's personal space. "You'll have to thank your old girlfriend for me. Or maybe you could give me her number and I will…in my own special way."

Stahl closed the remaining distance between them.

"All right, enough you two." Daniels stepped between them, signaling to the second cop inspecting the scene from the funeral home's porch. "Hey, Officer…Stevens, right? Get your ass over here!"

The patrolman, who looked as if he would need an ID for an R-rated movie, hopped the steps and double-timed it to Daniels' side.

"Whatcha doing rook, guarding the crime tape?" Daniels shook his head. "Tell me what you got."

Stevens flinched as if Daniels had sprung a pop quiz. He squinted at his spiral-bound notebook. "Um, guy walking his dog about twenty-three hundred…a Ralph Boyer…sees the funeral home's door open. Doesn't think too much about it. Knows Dr. Bayless lives upstairs. Figures the guy's maybe out in his garage or something. But when he returns from the walk about a half hour later, he sees the same thing…door open, no sign of the doctor. Decides to take a peek inside." Stevens snapped the notebook closed and looked up. "That's when he gave us a call."

With crime scene tape angled in odd directions and draped along the grass beside the mortuary porch, Stahl could only imagine the state of the crime scene with these two in charge. "Guy live around here?"

Berrelli pointed into the dark. "House across the way. I told him he'd have to answer more questions tonight. He ain't going anywhere."

"Did he walk the dog in there, compromise the scene?" Stahl squeezed his eyes shut.

"I, uh…didn't think to ask," the rookie stammered.

"Did any of you get close to the body, touch it, check for vitals, before you put up the tape?" Daniels jammed his hands against his hips.

"No reason to. The doc was dead as a doornail. You'll see." A grim smile crept across Berrelli's face. "We took a peek from the entryway, that's all. Nobody's been inside."

"What do you say, Mike. Let's get to it." Daniels nodded toward the house and climbed the steps leading to the front door. He barked to Berrelli over his shoulder. "And get the dog guy back here as soon as you can, I'll have a few questions for him after we finish up inside."

As they entered the grand structure, Stahl surveyed the layout. A sitting area greeted the detectives to the left of the entryway, comfortable sofas and chairs assembled before a huge desk—the spot Bayless could show off to his potential customers. Stahl had been here before, and it hadn't changed much, an update of the hand-crafted furniture, a new painting or two adorning the somber walls. An expansive hallway flowed from the front door across a buffed wooden floor to a stairwell leading upstairs to what Stahl assumed to be Bayless's living quarters, and a second stairwell leading down to the laboratory.

I'm guessing he doesn't show off that room to the customers.

"Body's in the basement lab. Berrelli said we need to take the stairs…"

Daniels' words fizzled like a distant radio station as Stahl glanced across the hallway, the spacious viewing room looming to his right. He recalled the place well, hundreds of mourners dressed in black, filling every square foot of the room and spilling out into the entryway. The scene replayed in his mind as fresh today as it had been a decade ago. He had stood against the room's opposite wall, wearing his one and only black suit, the one his mother had helped him pick out years ago.

In case he ever had to attend a funeral.

Stahl closed his eyes and shook his head, attempting to dislodge the memory.

"Mike! You okay, man?"

Stahl rubbed his eyes and opened them. Finding his focus, he glanced between Daniels and the dark and vacant viewing room. "Yeah, Chris. I'm okay. Just give me a minute." He offered a shaky smile as he stepped across the hall and into the yawning space. He brushed his hand against the paneled wood and triggered the wall switch, the soft lighting bathing the room in a mourning tenor. He sucked in a burst of air pungent with pine-scented cleanser as he snapped off the lights, retreating to the hallway. He pressed his palms against the small table outside the viewing room entrance and leaned forward.

"Mike?" Daniels took a step across the rich walnut floor.

"Just a bit dizzy, that's all. Maybe from the car ride."

"The Cougar has that effect on people." He grinned and gave Stahl a chuck on the shoulder. "Let's get a head start on the scene before Russ gets here."

Russ Randle, the Barnstable County Coroner and Chief Medical Examiner, formed the third member of their investigative team and would rule whether Bayless had been a victim of homicide or a natural death. Based on Berrelli's description of the scene, it wouldn't be a tough call.

Stahl and Daniels hoofed toward the stairwell and followed

the angled steps to the basement. Here, the landscape changed, the walls and floors no longer embellished with expensive wood paneling, artwork, or hand-stitched furniture. Their footfalls echoed off the worn tiled floors, taking them closer to a stinging odor of embalming chemicals and formaldehyde. Another unmistakable aroma wafted from the laboratory—a copper-iron stench of blood.

They paused at the doorway, scanning the sprawling room, the storage facilities housed to the left. Two of the four-body refrigeration unit doors rested on open hinges, frosty air forming cool mist as it rolled into the warmer room temperature. To their right, an embalming machine sat humming beside a hydraulic table, and chemicals lined the shelves above the sinks and scrub stations. Resting on stainless steel utility carts, embalming instruments, drain tubes and trocars, suture needles and forceps reflected the glare from the bright surgical lights overhead.

Dr. Bayless lay in the room's center, clothes soaked with embalming fluid and his own body's chemicals. His half-lidden eyes remained open and head protruded backward, hands wrapped around the instrument protruding from his neck. His body settled amidst shattered glass from an overhead examination light, thick blood congealing around his head and wrapping his hair in a thick paste.

Stahl pictured the angel hair pasta swimming in a deep red sauce he'd eaten only a few hours earlier. His stomach squeezed, emitting a defensive gurgle.

"Okay, then." Daniels mumbled underneath a forceful exhale. "It's all yours. Tell me what you need me to do."

For the next hour, Stahl and Daniels processed the crime scene, taking measurements and snapping photographs. Stahl meticulously collected fibers, hair, and blood samples, and lifted prints from metallic surfaces, as well as a set of bare footprints tracking through the blood into the refrigeration room. According to Bayless's paperwork, he had stored three bodies in his refrigerators, but now they had gone missing. Daniels canvassed the neighborhood with Berrelli, knocking on doors and interviewing sleepy neighbors, including the dog-man who discovered the body. Afterward, Stahl and Daniels reconvened and mapped out potential scenarios, batting ideas and theories back and forth until the other would shoot holes in it, leaving them back at square one.

"Why the hell did the perp go barefoot when he took the bodies from the refrigerators?" Stahl snapped the latex gloves from his hands and tucked them into the biohazard bag beside his kit.

"I don't see any shoes anywhere."

"It's March, for Chrissake, who goes around barefoot?"

Russ Randle poked his head into the laboratory. "So, we're looking for a barefoot murderer who stole an entire family?"

"You eavesdropping again?" Stahl quipped.

"I couldn't help myself. You have no idea how much I enjoy listening to your half-baked theories. It's amazing you guys solve any crimes at all." He stepped into the laboratory with a dark-colored, zippered tarpaulin under one arm and an examination bag grasped in his opposite fist. He deposited them both on the nearest counter and pulled out a pair of latex gloves.

"Our theories get better over time," Daniels pointed out.

"Let's hope." Randle's well-manicured goatee expanded with his grin as he greeted his friends and set about examining the body. After establishing time and manner of death, he inventoried and organized the deceased's personal effects. Positioning the unzipped body bag next to Bayless, he recruited the detectives to help roll the body onto its side. Sliding the bag's open end beneath the body, he and the detectives gently rolled the corpse to its original position. Straightening the stiffening limbs, Randle positioned them inside the bag as he zipped it up in one well-practiced move.

"Chris, give me a hand with this, would you? If I ask this guy," Randle said, nodding toward Stahl, "he'll start rubbing his shoulder, making faces."

"Tell me about it." Daniels rolled his eyes. "Guy takes a couple of bullets and the rest of us have to do all the work."

Stahl winced and rubbed his shoulder on cue.

"Be right back," Daniels said, smirking.

After Randle and Daniels had carted the body bag from the laboratory, Stahl packed up the equipment and placed it in his kit. As he inspected the biological samples in the dry ice container, an argument erupted from the corridor.

Racing up the stairs, Stahl found RG Granville toe-to-toe with Matt Berrelli, the cop's night stick pressed against RG's jaw as he backed him against the wall. Chris Daniels and Russ Randle had a bear hug on each of the men, wrestling them away from each other. Bayless's body bag teetered half on and half off the cart, the scuffle dislodging it from its perch.

"I need to see Mike immediately." RG had grabbed the baton, but Berrelli still had the stick jammed against him. RG had arrived in his pajamas, bare chested beneath a light jacket, his hair sticking up and matted as if he'd just stumbled from Bayless's upstairs bedroom.

"You don't give orders at a crime scene, motherfucker." Berrelli reached his free arm over Daniel's shoulder and jerked the threat out of RG's hand.

Jesus Christ, what now? "RG, what the hell are you doing here?"

"Get this pit bull off me," he ordered. "I need to talk to you."

RG's expression conveyed a coded look. A knot twisted in

Stahl's stomach. He had only witnessed RG this agitated once before, when a jumper known as *the burning man* had abducted Kacey to the beyond. Stahl hoped he had misread RG's desperation; he wasn't certain he could take another brush with the supernatural right now. But why else would the man be in a funeral home in his nightclothes past midnight.

Fuck.

"All right, boys." He nodded to the team. "Let me have a minute with him."

"Fucker can wait out on the driveway 'til we're done here." Berrelli gave RG one last palm to the chest.

"Out, Berrelli. Now!" Stahl jabbed a finger toward the door.

"Sonofabitch comes barreling into a crime scene." Berrelli shrugged. "What the fuck am I supposed to do?"

"You do your job," Daniels said, then added. "You don't pick up where you left off last summer."

"Well, fuck the both of you." Berrelli turned and strode toward the door, hitching his belt and rubbing the back of his neck.

Stahl blew out a breath and turned to the team positioning Bayless's body back onto the cart. "Guys, I need a minute with Dr. Granville. I'll meet you outside in five."

"Got it, partner." Daniels positioned himself opposite Randle on the side of the cart and helped wheel the body from the funeral home.

"Jesus Christ, RG. What the hell happened? Kacey all right?"

"She's fine…I'm sorry. I didn't mean to cause a ruckus, but—"

"With Berrelli as the crime scene's guard dog," Stahl interrupted, "there's nothing you could have done to prevent it."

"Mike, we need to talk."

"Why?" Stahl crossed his arms. "You haven't gotten me into enough messes already?"

"He's dead, isn't he? Bayless?" RG pointed toward his throat. "Spear, right through here."

"How do you—?"

"Just show me where it happened."

* * *

RG

The men wound around the circular stairway to the basement, RG's voice picking up speed and volume as he explained what he had witnessed in his dream.

"I need to see the room, make sure what happened in my vision matches the scene."

As they entered the laboratory, tremors snaked along RG's legs, the location as familiar as his own living room, though he had never set foot here before. The shattered overhead light, the metal gurney against the wall beside the embalming machine, and the gleaming tools lined up on the cart beside the gurney—minus one—were all identical to what he had witnessed. He leaned his frame against the doctor's metal desk, closing his eyes and massaging the back of his neck.

"We may be in trouble. It all happened right here…"

His voice trailed off as he sensed the light receding through his eyelids, as if a curtain had dropped before him. He swooned as the blood drained from his head. When his eyes blinked open, Stahl no longer stood beside him. His earlier dream picked up where it had left off, but now he viewed it happening before him.

Dr. Bayless lay on the floor with the spear embedded in his neck. The doctor's angled neck positioned his eyes directly at him, beseeching him for help, his tongue swelling in his mouth as he attempted to swallow. Blood oozed from the tattered hole in his throat and dripped from his open mouth like lava from a dying volcano. The doctor's lips moved with a sick smacking sound, as if attempting to speak, but no sound escaped. RG stood to approach the corpse still seated upright on the metal gurney, but he couldn't press himself through the thick air, walled off as if viewing the scene through a plastic tarp. The dead man hopped off the embalming table and stumbled toward him. He had to pull his feet toward the desk to keep the naked corpse from tripping over him as it brushed past him. The moving images faded as the room darkened once again. But he had glimpsed the corpse's face, the man from the newspapers who had died a week ago, an identification he hadn't been able to make in the dream. The lights flickered again, the brilliant light once again flooding the laboratory, revealing Stahl resting against the entryway doorjamb.

"Hey, man." Stahl reached for RG's shoulder. "Are you sure you're all right?"

"Christ, now I'm seeing things." He steadied himself against the desk before bolting from the laboratory. "Come on, Mike," he shouted from the hallway. "I know who did this."

CHAPTER FOUR

Sunday, March 20

Kacey

The eyes bothered her most.

Something unearthly about them, blanched and cloudy, as if someone had blotted the color from their surface. They focused in no particular direction, but Kacey sensed their stare boring directly into her.

The girl stood motionless at the end of the restaurant's narrow hallway. She hadn't been there moments ago when Kacey traversed the corridor on her way back from the washroom. But something made her stop as she approached the end of the walkway—a presence, a tightening spreading across her scalp and through her shoulders. Kacey stopped and turned, her breath catching in her throat as the weight of the girl's vacant gaze fell upon her.

Kacey beheld a living corpse, but any reservations about her earthly status disappeared when knots in the wood-paneled wall appeared through her body's meager frame.

The girl spun and entered the restroom, gazing at Kacey as the door eased against its frame with a slow creak.

Kacey threw a glance over her shoulder toward the table where RG and his boyhood friends gathered. Matty Kelly had rented out the function room at the Flying Bridge restaurant overlooking the Falmouth Marina, celebrating the christening of his and Livy's daughter Chelsea. Church had ended less than ten minutes ago, but the empty bottles had already piled up on the tables, especially the one RG, Donnie, and Matty surrounded. Kacey attempted to get RG's attention, speak into his mind, but he proved oblivious to their shared special powers at the moment, distracted by one of Matty's epic tales.

Kacey swallowed and took cautious steps along the hallway until she had reached the bathroom door. "It's Sunday after church, middle of the day." She gazed at Father Ed, who had performed the ceremony, hoisting a Coors Light with an arm draped around Matty's shoulder. "Priest less than fifty feet away. You got this."

As a living caretaker, Kacey had gotten used to strange phenomena. She had already met the ghoul with the muddied eyes in Junior's upstairs bedroom. The time had come to confront her, find out why she had elected to stalk her family.

Kacey pressed her hand against the bathroom door and eased it open. Her shoes clicked along the buffed tile as she stepped into the chamber, their echo reverberating off the porcelain fixtures and flooring. The door closed behind her with a startling, soft thump.

A shuffling sound escaped from the first stall.

Kacey approached the line of wood partitions. Labored breath wheezed from behind the first door. As she pressed her palm against the cool frame, pictures exploded across her vision. Images spun so quickly past her she could only attend to one at a time: a teenage girl racing across a halogen-lit field, cheers erupting from the crowded sidelines as she twirled toward the goal, lacrosse stick spinning in her hands before firing a shot into the net's top corner; the same girl reclined on a cushioned wicker patio chair at her family's seaside home, her pink toenailed feet powdered with sand resting on the glass-top table, her gentle grin shared with her Goldendoodle as they bathed in the afternoon sun's hazy glow; three friends in a red convertible speeding along Route 6, the girl corralling her long blonde hair as her front seat companions laughed and sang along with the music blaring from the Harman-Karden speakers, surfboards protruding from the backseat like fins through water.

The vision halted as her hand recoiled from the stall door. She no longer sensed the girl's presence. Kacey stooped to a knee to peer under the wood divider.

Nothing.

It occurred to her she had been holding her breath, and she greedily sucked in a burst of air as she rose from the bathroom floor. Stumbling to the sink, she steadied herself against the countertop and splashed water on her face. The drips cascaded into the basin with a gentle plink as she reached for the paper towel dispenser. Burying her face against the gritty brown parchment, she swiped the towels from forehead to chin.

As she straightened, the emaciated figure's reflection appeared in the mirror behind her.

"Help me." A grizzled hand reached for Kacey's shoulder.

As the figure advanced, she backpedaled, crashing into the metal canister beneath the hand dryers. Scrambling to her feet, Kacey whipped the bathroom door open, crashing it against the tiled wall as she stumbled down the hallway.

In a frenzied rush, Kacey lurched toward the table, grabbing RG in a bear hug from behind. His arms flailed forward, sending a line of empty Coors Light bottles tumbling across the white tablecloth like scattered bowling pins, ricocheting off Father Ed's drink and sending a geyser of hops and barley across his cassock. Matty and Livy pushed back from the table and sprang from their chairs, hoisting their bottles upward to protect them from the spinning glass while assorted hands flung forward in a vain attempt to corral the frosty projectiles. Father Ed stood, holding his arms out to his side as foamy suds dripped from his fingertips.

RG gazed at Kacey kneeling beside him, her arms encircling his waist like a human belt. "Well, that did it," he whispered, eyeing a damp Father Ed. "Now we're definitely going to Hell."

"I guess Kacey can't get enough of you, RG." Livy punched Matty on the arm. "How come you don't hold me like that?"

Kacey rose to her feet, apologizing to Father Ed and her friends as she slunk from the table. Circling behind RG's chair, she grabbed his collar, nearly yanking him over the seat back.

"Get up," she whispered. "I need you…right now!"

Dragging him down the narrow hallway to the restrooms, she jammed the door open.

"Wow, Kacey." He unbuttoned his shirt, grinning like a teenager on prom night. "When you're in the mood, you find the craziest places to—"

"Easy, Romeo." Pulling him onto the tiled floor, she jerked her head back and forth. She paced the line of stalls, slamming the wooden doors open one by one.

RG searched her eyes for an explanation. "What the hell are you doing?"

"I'm looking for a dead girl."

* * *

Kacey had held it together throughout the christening celebration, but her encounter with the supernatural left her distant and distracted.

Not to mention, a bit embarrassed at the scene she had caused.

She raised her glass at every toast, made small talk with Matty's extended family—aunts and uncles, all tall and beefy like Matty himself—and caught up on the latest life events with best friend, Livy; but more than once, RG had to send a gentle elbow into her ribs to jolt her back to the present. Now, as they gathered in the parking lot, Kacey proved eager to get away. She needed to get into the car and talk with RG, try to make sense of what had happened.

She peered at RG's boyhood friends huddled at the edge of the marina. The gathering had been like old times, but an emptiness stirred in the pit of her stomach. Donnie Goudreau had one arm around his wife, Christine, as his two-year-old daughter, Kayleigh, did figure eights through his legs. Matty hunched beside the little girl, swiping a paw at her as she evaded his reach with delighted squeals. Glancing at RG, Kacey noted the melancholic smile pressed across his lips, one she chalked up to his difficulty re-engaging with his world, the one they had once inhabited.

Too many secrets now.

She proved no different, forever vigilant these days, unable to remain oblivious to the evil from accompanying worlds bleeding into their own. But she could compartmentalize, stepping up when external threats arose, then falling back into work, Red Sox, and Robert Jr. during the downtime. RG dwelled, letting the knowledge weigh him down and darken his daily life. And when it came to his old friends, he had pulled away, especially since Johnny D's death a few years earlier.

Kacey's psych 101 background convinced her denial fueled his self-imposed exile. He fooled himself into thinking Johnny D wasn't really gone…just away. RG would see him later, when the gang reunited again. But when they did, and Johnny wasn't there, reality set in and hung over him like a thunder cloud. She also understood his secrets set him apart from the others. And would forever.

As Matty rose to his feet, Donnie poked him in the ribs. "All right, you big sap, give us a kiss." He pursed his lips with a smacking sound.

In an instant, Donnie's head disappeared underneath Matty's rippling forearm, his face reddening as he sputtered to breathe.

"Hey, psycho, watch the hair." Donnie craned his neck to free his luxuriant, tinted locks from Matty's grasp.

"Ha! The pretty boy, Donnie Goudreau," Matty announced with a smirk, like a circus ring leader. "The Sun-Pig, champion ex-surfer masquerading as a respectable bank executive, still grasping at youth with long hair and perma-tan." He let Donnie go and turned to RG. "Still thinks he's prettier than we are."

"He is." RG shrugged.

"A lot prettier," Kacey and Livy replied in unison.

Matty scowled. "All right, off with the lot of ya. I gotta go back upstairs and settle up with the manager. I'll be putting in overtime 'til summer to pay this thing off."

Donnie pointed at the lone figure stumbling along the

marina walkway. "I'm guessing inviting Father Ed may have tripled your liquor costs."

Matty shook his head. "Yeah, he threw back a few, didn't he?"

"And he may have taken the rest with him," RG said, a suspicious clinking sound punctuating each of Father Ed's wavering steps.

"So, Donnie," Kacey said, "summer's coming. You ready to break out your boards?"

He grabbed Kayleigh in a bear hug as she pirouetted before him, hoisting her into the air. "Too many sharks out there now. Guy got killed out on Newcomb Hollow not too long ago." He gave his daughter a peck on the cheek as he lowered her to the ground. "I have too much to lose now."

"Not to mention that luxurious mane of yours." Matty grabbed him again and raked his knuckles across his dome.

Donnie slipped his grip and combed his fingers through the thick strands. "I'll get a few more years with it if you'll just keep your meat paws off it."

After giving final hugs and promises to get together soon, RG and Kacey strapped Robert Jr. into his car seat and cracked the windows. They took Route 28 from Falmouth to Chatham, slogging through each small town in a slow-moving traffic caravan stretching across the island. But it gave Junior extended nap time in the backseat and much needed car time for RG and Kacey to talk.

RG ground his knuckles against the steering wheel. "So, tell me what you think is going on. "You think your ghost was after Junior again?"

Kacey deliberated a moment. "I'm not sure yet. I had myself convinced when I caught her in Junior's room, but now…" She shook her head.

"Anything else unusual? I mean, besides running into a dead girl in a public restroom."

Kacey leaned against the headrest. "RG, I'm not so sure she was dead. As crazy as it sounds. She was…somewhere in the middle."

"Between life and death?"

"I think so. She sought me out, like she needed something from me. She said 'help me.'" Kacey wrapped her arms around herself as if bracing against a sudden chill. "I could have found out, too, if I hadn't panicked. She rattled me, for sure. Her corpselike appearance, so wispy…and her eyes." Kacey banged her hand against the dashboard. "Dammit, that pisses me off!"

"Don't beat yourself up." He reached across the passenger seat and kneaded the back of her neck. "It's been a while since we've made contact with the other world. Something like that would have frightened anyone. You're lucky you didn't get hurt."

"That's the thing, RG. Thinking back, I'm pretty sure I wasn't in any danger." Kacey blew out a breath. "God, what an ass I made of myself in front of Father Ed."

"And Matty and Livy…Donnie…" RG counted on his fingers. "…and let's not forget Matty's mom and dad, their cousin Ernie—"

"I get the picture," she said, cutting him off.

"I'm sure they all think you must really love me. You know, stumbling back from the bathroom and wrapping your arms around my waist like you did. The image will no doubt stick in Father Ed's mind for a long—"

"Enough already!" Kacey pressed her hands against the sides of her head. "Let's focus on the problem. This spirit, or half-spirit, whatever it is, had the power to find me, RG. She revealed herself in her grotesque dying form, but also she showed me pictures from her earlier life."

"Why would she do that?"

Kacey gathered her hair off her neck and shook it out. "I'm guessing she sensed my fear and wanted to show me she had once been just…a girl, with a life, and people who loved her."

A soft snore escaped the backseat as the Legacy slowed through Harwich, the comforting engine noise no longer exuding its pacifying effect on the boy.

Kacey reached across the backseat and rubbed Junior's feet. They drove the rest of the way immersed in their own thoughts, comfortable having some alone time but shared with another. As they pulled into the Chatham house's garage and killed the engine, RG leaned his forehead against the steering wheel.

"What's the matter?" Kacey asked. She reached across the seat and brushed an errant hair behind his ear.

"Does it burden you?"

"What?"

He tilted his head to face her. "The responsibility."

"You mean, the things we know? The afterlife? Jumpers and caretakers? You know it does, RG."

He shifted in his seat. "You handle it much better than I do."

"One more thing to add to the list." A grin swept across her face.

"I'm serious, Kace. I've never been good at keeping secrets." He stared through the windshield. "When I first learned about Morrow, I had to keep it from you, and it just about ate me alive. Now I have a hundred times more knowledge building up inside me. It's like I'm going to burst. It's too big to carry around."

"What's the solution?"

"I don't know." RG threw up his hands. "Tell the people what's out there. What they can expect when they die."

"And you'll do this…how?"

RG pressed a palm against his forehead and rubbed both temples.

"I can picture the headlines now. 'Fugitive Professor' says he can visit the afterlife, talk to the dead." Kacey shook her head. "They'd crucify you…again."

"There must be a way to leak things, get people to investigate these happenings."

"I figured there might be deeper scrutiny when we returned the children from Plymouth last year, but it didn't happen."

RG scratched his head. "I know. That's so weird. It's as if no one wanted to know how children missing for decades could show up again."

"The region buried its head. That's what happened." She chewed the corner of her lip. "It just shows you the truth might be too much for people."

"I'm not so sure. I think the human race tends to rally in the face of the darkest truths."

"So, here's a question. Would sharing our secrets help others? Or just you?" She read RG's grin as a subtle acknowledgment of her insight.

"This time it isn't about me. I understand everything appears worse after seeing the gang. I can't talk to them. I can't share what I know. Possessing these heavy secrets cuts me off from them, and I have trouble with that. But shouldn't people understand what's out there? Don't we have a responsibility to wake them up?"

Junior startled, rousing from his long nap. His fussy cries rose in intensity inside the silent vehicle.

"We're responsible for the people reaching out to us for help." Kacey glanced into the backseat. "And to our little guy back there. That's all."

"Maybe." RG slipped from his seat and opened the back door, hoisting Junior into his arms. The boy drifted back to sleep with his cheek pressed against his father's shoulder. Mounting the stairs, RG carried his son to his room. He eased Junior onto the mattress and perched on the edge of the bed, draping the down comforter across the boy's warm body.

Placing his hand against the side of Junior's face, RG grinned as his son snuggled against it. Kacey had a front row seat from the doorway as RG gazed at the boy, studying his china doll features, possibly the delicate curve of his nose, the small mole just beneath his right ear. The boy's mouth twitched and morphed into a secret sleepy smile, and Kacey could only imagine what dreams flitted through his mind. After the boy's breathing had settled into a steady rhythm, RG ran a quick hand through Junior's hair and crept from the bedroom. He closed the door just enough to let a patch of light in from the hallway, the way Junior liked.

RG shuffled down the hallway with an arm draped around Kacey's shoulder before dropping beside her onto the pillow-top mattress. "So, what do we do now?"

"Well, we could use an expert opinion about what's going on around here?"

"Morrow?"

"Tell him to meet us…the usual place."

RG reached for her hand and squeezed. "And what do we do about the ghost stalking our son."

"We wait. She'll be back."

"How do you know?"

"Because she needs something from me." Kacey paused a beat. "I'm just not sure what."

CHAPTER FIVE

Monday, March 21

Kacey

The sweet smell of griddle-fried potatoes, sizzling bacon, and fresh-brewed coffee lulled Kacey into a contented trance as she reclined against the worn cushion of the Pancake Man's high-backed booth. She fingered the corner of the matching red duct tape square slapped over a small tear in the seat fabric and freed a sliver of pale, spongy foam from the crevice, adding it to a collection building beside the sugar packets. The din of spirited conversation combined with clinking silverware and plates dropping into plastic bins grew like a living presence within the diner, greeting her like an old friend. She squeezed RG's hand as she gazed about the room. It appeared to be a diner, but it wasn't. Not really. Kacey had brought RG, Mike Stahl, and

Robert Jr. to a portal leading into the next world, an exact replica of the South Yarmouth eatery she had created in her mind from childhood memories of Sunday breakfasts with her parents. She could spot a younger version of herself, in French braids and a favorite dress, sharing silver dollar pancakes with her mother and father while sipping a strawberry milkshake, giggling at her father's dumb jokes. Foam cushion tufts accumulated in a matching pile beside the little girl's plate.

She released RG's hand and swiped a napkin across the Formica tabletop to dry the waitress's haphazard cleanup job. She picked at the hard syrup nodules protruding like frozen raindrops and rubbed the ancient food stains discoloring the speckled laminate pattern, her lunchroom monitor instincts getting the best of her.

"I'm not sure why you bother wasting your time with that thing, RG. She flicked the menu, causing him to flinch. You're just going to order the usual…Lumberjack, double bacon, large OJ, coffee, maybe finish up with some pie."

"True, but I like the pictures, and they put me in 'pre-game' mode, kind of like when Mookie Betts has 'em play "I Love My City' for his walk-up music. Gotta get motivated if you're gonna be in top form."

"I've never met someone who takes food as seriously as you do. Thank God you're working out again."

He flexed a bicep with a grin. "What are you having, Mike?"

"I'm not so hungry."

"Really?" Austerity didn't square with Kacey's recollection of the man. "Since when?"

"I'm about to find out if the murder suspect in my one case and the victim in my other are the same person." Stahl pressed the middle of his forehead with two fingers as if trying to accept the logic. "My stomach is in knots. You sure he's coming?"

"He's on his way," RG reassured him, eyeing the menu. "But you gotta eat. And you won't get a better breakfast anywhere in the universe."

Kacey raised her eyebrows. "He means that literally."

Stahl reached for a menu resting in the wire holder and skimmed the columns. "So, what's in the Lumberjack?"

RG counted off on his fingers. "Stack of pancakes, three eggs, toast, fried potatoes, ham, sausage, and bacon."

Stahl glanced up over his menu. "And you double the bacon?"

RG tilted his head. "You say that like it's a problem."

"Well, it's nearly an entire pig," Kacey pointed out.

"Calories don't count over here." RG licked his lips. "No saturated fat or cholesterol, either."

Stahl threw a glance toward Kacey. "Wait a minute. The last time I ate here I gained about five pounds."

"Maybe that's some kind of cosmic payback for how you eat back in our world." Kacey smirked.

He tossed the menu onto the table. "I guess it's the fruit plate for me."

The next world's burgeoning color flooded the entryway as the diner door swung on its hinges. Morrow glided through the waiting crowd of patrons craning their necks and gawking for an open table or booth. He palmed his forties-era gumshoe fedora and slipped out of his black linen jacket, depositing them on the coatrack with a practiced hand. He jostled through the patrons clogging the aisle and sank into the booth beside Stahl as the waitress appeared beside the table.

He nodded at his awaiting party. "Miss, we'll have three Lumberjacks, one with double bacon and a slice of pie, and…" he pointed at Kacey… "silver dollar pancakes with a strawberry milkshake."

Kacey smirked at Stahl. "So much for your fruit plate?"

He shrugged. "I suppose life is too short to pass up triple pig meat on the same platter."

Morrow grinned as he reached across the table to tousle Robert Jr.'s hair, loosening the tie hanging from his crisp, pearl-white button down. Pivoting to face Stahl, he rested a hand on his shoulder and gave his neck a squeeze "Michael, a pleasure. You're becoming quite the regular on this side."

"Not sure if that's a good thing or not, but it's nice to see you, too."

"I came as quickly as I could. So, someone fill me in, tell me what's happened."

RG waved his hand in a mock greeting. "Uh…good to see you, too, Dad."

Morrow peeked at Kacey over the top of his glasses.

"He needs constant affirmation," she said, grabbing RG's chin.

RG scowled and fished into his front pocket, pulling out a crushed Kit Kat. He pressed it back into shape and tossed it onto the table in front of Morrow. "Sorry I don't have any more. We left on short notice."

Morrow quickly stripped off the orange wrapper, snapped off a section of the chocolate candy, and popped it into his mouth. His eyes closed as he leaned his head back. "Don't worry. I forgive you."

Morrow devoured another chocolate section.

Stahl scratched his cheek, eyeing the caretaker. He leaned across the table. "It's like he's never had chocolate before."

"It's not available over here," Kacey said.

"Really?" Stahl pulled his lower lip, as if considering the possibilities of such an afterlife.

"Check this out, Mike. We can make him do tricks." RG grabbed a section of candy and waved it in front of his father. "Roll over! Heel!"

RG's hand flew open as Kacey aimed an elbow into his ribs, the Kit Kat dropping onto the table.

"Ow!" RG grabbed his side.

Kacey glared at him as she slid the candy across the table to Morrow. "Serves you right."

"Can someone tell me what's going on, please?" Morrow asked.

Kacey leaned across the table. "We suspect something might be brewing, something from another realm, and we need to understand what we're up against."

"Tell me what you know?"

RG pressed his palms against the table's edge. "I'm not sure where to start. I'm either hallucinating or I'm losing my mind."

Kacey reached over and cupped RG's drumming fingers. "Just tell him what you saw."

With a half-hearted smile, RG folded her hand into his. "Okay, I had a dream more real than anything I've ever experienced before. Too vivid." He put the fork down and clasped his hands down on the placemat, curling and tightening his fingers. "And in the dream, I witnessed a murder."

"You suspect something more than a dream?" Morrow asked.

RG leaned forward on his elbows, talking with his hands. "It had all the hallmarks of Kacey's visions, the tangible ones she describes where she can picture what's going to happen."

"So, you're witnessing the future now?" Morrow asked.

RG waved his hand. "This one wasn't something about to happen, but something that already had, or something happening in real time. I couldn't tell. Once I got to the murder scene…I experienced it again, from start to finish, and this time I could identify the killer."

Morrow rubbed his chin. "So, when you arrived you had a vision, but different than what happened in the dream?"

"Not different, but from a different angle. I stood by the door and could view the killer's face. During the dream, I couldn't make it out."

Morrow wiped his glasses with his pocket handkerchief. "The ring gives you powers I never passed on to you. I've had visions, but I've never experienced memory residues attached to a particular place before."

RG reached over and twisted the gold halo from his finger. "I wish I could understand this damn hunk of tin!" As he glanced down, the once-severed finger shriveled and sprouted the scars and fissures from his run-in with a previous jumper and subsequent finger reattachment surgery.

"Hunk of…? Watch yourself, buster." Kacey wagged her finger.

"I didn't mean it like that." He raised a hand and positioned the ring back in place. Immediately, the finger grew to its original length, appearing as healthy as its equal on his opposite hand. "This thing can heal me, yet it keeps coming up with different ways to complicate my life."

"Gifting my power into an object representing the union of souls has augmented its capacity more than I could have ever imagined."

"So, does that mean love makes it stronger?" Kacey asked, squeezing RG's hand.

Morrow grinned. "The most powerful force in the universe."

"Listen, Mr. Morrow, I have to chime in here." Stahl gave his water glass a quarter turn. "RG's vision has to be false. He says he witnessed what happened, but he ID'd a man killed in a car accident about a week earlier, a guy named Sarnie. I'm investigating his death. I've seen the accident photos. The guy couldn't have been any...deader. He had been partially embalmed for Chrissake."

RG shook his head. "I know what I saw. He's come back. It's the only explanation." He folded his arms and leaned against the booth's backrest.

"Mr. Morrow," Stahl began, "I have to move forward in this case with a plausible explanation until I can accept the implausible could happen."

RG gave Morrow a tentative glance. "Well? What do you think?"

"What, the dead coming back to life?" Morrow mumbled.

"How about a jumper who comes back for his own body?" RG asked. "Can they do that?"

Morrow shrugged. "I'm not aware of its happening before. A jumper invades the body of the living and controls them from the inside. If the body isn't alive—"

"He would have no way to control it," Stahl interrupted. "You see, none of this makes sense, RG. There has to be a rational explanation. That's all."

"Rational explanation?" RG leaned against the backrest. "You, of all people...after all you've been through, and *you* need a rational explanation? A guy who has traveled through time?" The more excited RG got, the more his hands took over the conversation. "If you need reminding of how irrational things are, look around you. We're sitting in a portal between worlds, waiting to devour noncaloric food, and at least one of us at the table is already dead. Can anything I say, at this point, sound less rational than that?"

Morrow inspected his arms and hands. "I'm very much alive, if I do say so myself."

Kacey glanced around the table. "You are to me." She smiled and grabbed Morrow's hand.

"I'm just trying to make sense of it," Stahl said. "I witnessed the bodies at the house, all arranged around the table."

"And Sarnie's body wasn't with them," RG said. "He must have pulled the bodies from Bayless's cooler and carried them home. Who else would have done something like that?"

"You'd be surprised, RG." Stahl swirled his water glass. "I've witnessed a few strange things in my world."

"I have, too, Mike."

The table fell silent as a team of waitstaff delivered steaming plates and dishes in multiple shifts, struggling under the weight of their trays. A moment of strained anticipation followed as the group eyed each other, RG breaking the stalemate by stabbing a dripping slab of ham with his fork.

Morrow followed, clutching a bacon slice and chewing the crispy end in deliberate bites. "I wouldn't be so quick to dismiss RG's vision, Michael. It's not outside the realm of possibility that a jumper's living presence inside a dead body could manipulate the dead tissue to get the limbs to work, the mouth to speak."

"But the burning question remains why?" RG garbled a response through a barrier of meat. "Why would he need his old body when he could simply commandeer a new one?"

"Maybe he simply liked his old body," Kacey offered.

Morrow turned to Stahl. "You mentioned something about bodies around a table. Tell me more."

"When my partner and I arrived at the Sarnie residence, we found the family propped up at the kitchen island, pancakes and syrup on plates sitting in front of them."

Morrow dropped his bacon and wiped his fingertips with a napkin. "Very symbolic. Showed a need to have his old life back. Clearly this…Sarnie wanted his body back and wanted his family around him." Morrow sighed. "That's why he took them home. He wanted things the way they used to be, if only for a moment, until he could process things."

"If Sarnie's behind this, he's running on borrowed time," Mike said. "His body will decompose."

Morrow pointed at RG. "Didn't you say the doctor embalmed him?"

"Before the murder, Sarnie lay on a gurney with tubes sticking from his body. He ripped them from his body before he impaled the funeral director with one of his metal instruments." RG chewed the corner of his lip. "I'm guessing the doctor didn't complete the job before Sarnie finished him off."

"He has a desire to either relive his life on earth, or he has unfinished business to attend to." Morrow dipped the edge of his bacon in the syrup pooling on his plate. "If he's come back from the dead, he's done it for a reason."

"In the funeral home, Sarnie passed close by me. I shared his thoughts. He wants someone to pay for what happened. He doesn't know who it is yet, but he's going after the person who wronged him, took his family and his life from him."

"Revenge?" Stahl asked.

"Not a surprise. Often the simplest emotions remain in the transition to a new life." Morrow wiped his hands on a napkin and threw it on his plate. "But if he can't stop his body from decaying around him, he won't have long to solve his own murder. He may try to buy some time, bring his body back to life. And God help us if he figures that out."

"Isn't there a theory about a jumper who can live forever?" Kacey asked.

RG turned to his wife, dropping his fork. "Where did you hear that?"

"I've been reading a few books Morrow recommended."

Morrow beamed at her like a professor with his star student. "Those in the next world and beyond believe a jumper could someday solve the problem of mortality and open the door for other dark souls to join him."

"Join him where?" Stahl asked.

"In whatever realm he originated from. You see, the body cannot die a second time in one realm. It's impossible. A jumper housed in a body that cannot die would become… unstoppable. An immortal force."

RG's fork tumbled from his grasp, rattling his plate. "God, this can't be good."

"Immortal force…" Kacey's voice trailed off. "But how would he revive a dead body to become immortal?"

"That's the mystery." Morrow folded his hands. "No one knows. I imagine that's why it has never happened before. The immortal force remains a theory. But Sarnie has come back for a reason, and no jumper I'm aware of has ever reclaimed its own body like yours has. The longer he stays in his previous body, the more likely he learns how to keep it alive."

"And if he finds the answer to death?" RG rubbed the back of his neck.

Morrow picked at his plate. "It would be catastrophic. Such power wasn't meant for your world. And if other dark forces joined him, it would throw the cosmos into turmoil. A caretaker could do nothing against such a force. And for the people of that jumper's realm, they would be at his mercy."

"Why can't we go back in time like we did before," Stahl asked. "Stop the accident that killed him, or something? Then all this wouldn't be a problem."

"He's right," RG said, glancing at Morrow. "We both have the power to travel through time."

"You travelled back in time because someone constructed a portal leading directly to Plymouth in 1946. There are thousands of portals leading back in time, all of which you can access. But none that lead back a week ago. And it takes years, decades to construct a portal."

"But you built one right in front of me," Kacey interjected. "You opened one when Malachi's portal closed."

"I only reconstructed the remnants, like putting together a jigsaw puzzle. If we had waited much longer, I wouldn't have been able to put the pieces back together, and you'd still be back in Plymouth."

"So, time travel not an option here."

Morrow shook his head.

"So, what do we do?" RG asked.

"We need to find this Sarnie fellow." Morrow pointed at Stahl. "You're involved in the investigation, correct?"

Stahl nodded.

"So, you'll be talking to people who know him, people who may have wanted him dead. You need to find out who killed him, and you need to find out before Sarnie does. That way we can head him off before he tries to exact his revenge. Right now, his focus appears to be on retribution, but that could change." Morrow shifted in his seat. "Dark forces guide the wayward. He's already inhabiting his former body. The step to becoming an immortal force appears to be closer than ever. Evil forces may reach out to influence him, direct him toward realizing his destiny. We need to take him out before he gets an inkling about immortality."

"Then he may not be alone in this?" Kacey asked.

"We don't know. But it's up to you and RG to stay alert. You two are the only true threat coming from this realm. Others may seek to eliminate that threat." Morrow turned his gaze to Stahl. "Mike, keep the team posted on what you find out in your investigation, so we can find this Sarnie fellow. We need to stop him before he discovers the depth of his power."

"And if Mike can't find him?" RG asked.

Morrow peered over the top of his glasses. "I wouldn't worry, the way you describe your connection with him, eventually he'll find you."

* * *

RG

RG leaned back on the porch swing of Morrow's ranch-style house, sharing a beer with the old man as a chorus of cicadas, or their otherworldly equivalent, buzzed in the afternoon heat. The alcohol on Morrow's side contained unfamiliar and sometimes foul-tasting grains and sugars, but RG had come to savor every bitter sip. Their father-son ritual was something he never took for granted, something he had only imagined doing years earlier, before he learned his father wasn't as dead as he had come to believe.

Morrow's home rested beside a clear-running stream at the edge of an endless field somewhere in the next world, the tall wheat grass bending in successive waves with the breezy gusts rippling across the meadow. RG took in his surroundings like he would a work of art, the boundless hues and contrasts exploding through the visual field like a psychedelic IED, as if someone had administered an IV hallucinogen at the maximal tolerable dose.

"I just remembered something." RG reached into his pocket and extracted a second mangled Kit Kat square and placed it on the end table beside the swing.

Morrow grinned and took a sip from his bottle. "You've been holding out on me."

"Not sure how well this will go with our suds." RG swirled the bottle's contents. "But it's all yours."

"I think I'll enjoy it later. Savor it a bit."

"Wow, Dad. Showing some restraint."

Morrow chuckled as he leaned against his wraparound porch railing, his back to the scenery. "You didn't tell me everything back at the Pancake Man, did you?"

RG hauled himself to his feet. "Not everything."

"Why not?"

"I wasn't sure how you'd react. You see, in the dream, a voice spoke to me." His eyes bore a hole through the porch floor before glancing up at Morrow. "Mom's voice."

"Helen…" Morrow's eyes drifted. "She spoke to you?"

"Clear as a bell."

He removed his glasses and wiped them with his shirt. "I'm sure it wasn't—"

"It was." RG placed a steadying hand on his dad's shoulder. "She warned me specifically about the vision I had. She told me to be careful…that there's something…awful, that's how she put it…something awful coming for me. Somehow, she knew about Sarnie."

"I agree. In all likelihood, her warning is not a coincidence. But, as you know, she has no special powers. If she's contacting you through your dreams, then she might not even be aware she's doing it. It has to be the ring." Morrow snatched the Kit Kat from the end table and held it for a moment before turning it in his hand. "Somehow, the ring is drawing Helen to you."

"I also saw something I can't explain. A vision of her holding me in the hospital when I was born."

Morrow smiled. "I remember the day well. Tell me what you saw."

RG leaned against the porch rail and stared across the field. "She held me in her arms, but she seemed so sad. I witnessed a woman come and take me out of her arms." He glanced up at his father. "Was I sick or something?"

"No one took you away, Son. She didn't give you up to anyone."

"And where were you? I didn't see you there."

"I'm not sure what you witnessed in the vision, but I never left Helen's side." Morrow dropped a hand on RG's shoulder. "Or yours."

RG threw his hands up. "Then I don't know what I saw. Maybe I should pay her a visit and find out what's going on. She could be the key to this whole crazy mystery." Deliberating a moment, he turned to Morrow. "Why don't you come with me?"

His father clenched his teeth, working his jaw. "I worry it might be too much for her, both of us together. She wouldn't recognize us, of course, but the emotion might be too overwhelming."

"But if she doesn't know who we are——"

"Doesn't mean she wouldn't sense us," Morrow interrupted. "We don't completely shed the things we've learned and experienced in previous worlds. But they remain dormant." As he spoke, his fingers stripped the orange wrapper from the candy and slid a section into his mouth.

RG raised an eyebrow.

"Don't say a word," Morrow said, pointing at him. He threw another square into his mouth.

"You mean, about restraint?"

Morrow waved him away. "You go visit your mother…and take Kacey with you. If Helen has spoken to you once, she will have more to tell you."

"But how will we communicate? She won't recognize me, and I can't just blurt out, 'Hey, Mom, I'm home.'"

"Don't worry. The ring will help tell you what to do."

RG choked down a gulp from his bottle and dropped onto the porch swing.

"Something's still troubling you, isn't it?"

"You probing my mind?"

Morrow lowered himself onto the seat beside RG and squeezed his arm. "A father doesn't have to when it comes to his son. He can sense it."

"Dad, I've been thinking. Isn't it time we stop this whole charade and let people know the truth?"

"About what? You mean caretakers and jumpers, the next world? What makes you ask such a thing?"

"Because I'm tired of keeping this secret." RG rested the beer bottle on the end table and leaned his head back. "It's too big to hide. Throughout history, the worst things have happened when people hide the truth. People deserve to know. We're wrong to suppress it."

"But it's something they weren't *meant* to know." Morrow leaned forward, resting his elbows on his knees. "It's not like something waiting to be discovered, a cure for cancer or the answer to a mathematical proof. This knowledge is not discoverable. You only discovered it because I broke the rules and told you."

"You're wrong." RG shook his head. "Kacey discovered her powers long before you came around. Maybe there are others. Maybe this point in time represents part of our evolution."

"I never anticipated how difficult this might be for someone still connected to the physical world as you are. But knowledge of the afterlife would change…everything in your world."

"Ninety-five percent of the world are believers anyway," RG argued. "This would only confirm what they already know, flesh it out a bit, bring hope to the other five percent."

"Or terror," Morrow added. "Imagine telling the world the

dead might be stalking them, but they can't do anything about it. Why would you want to tell them?"

"Because it's never been more important than right now. If the immortal force proves real, the world may soon be in peril." RG rose from the swing and paced the porch. "Every time our world faces tragedy, we unite. We accomplished great things. Wars, natural disasters, terrorism, diseases. Our world would rise together to face an apocalyptic threat like this. Maybe this would be the event that would knock down walls and unite the world. Change history."

"You have admirable faith in your people. I'm not sure I do." Morrow rested a palm on his chin. "If people remained rational, devoid of emotion, then yes, there could be value in it. But a panicked populace can only bring about chaos." Morrow lowered his gaze. "I've burdened you with this secret, and for that I'm sorry. But I can't imagine the world is ready yet."

"Maybe not." RG exhaled and took the last swig from his bottle.

"But if Sarnie's for real, and what we suspect is indeed happening…your world will know soon enough."

CHAPTER SIX

Tuesday, March 22

Mike

Mike Stahl aimed the lumbering Crown Vic through the chain-link fence surrounding Sarnie Trucking and came to a stop at the glassed-in security booth. Stahl had been pacing the department halls all morning, finally bursting through the double doors and fleeing the confining walls. If he couldn't do anything to influence Daniels' long-awaited hearing, at least he could cross one more task from the to-do list on the Sarnie case.

But he'd had to make a quick detour to pick up his new partner.

Stahl chuckled at the man in the passenger seat, adorned in one of Stahl's oversized sport coats and a fake badge hanging over his belt. RG Granville looked like a fish out of water, tugging at his sleeve and flapping his wing like a bird, unaccustomed to a thirty-eight-caliber hunk of iron nestled in his armpit.

"Don't get me wrong, Mike. I appreciate you dressing me up like a cop, but it feels like I'm trying to sneak a refrigerator out of a department store." He pulled at his armpit beneath his jacket.

"You have to look like a detective. You only have to wear the holster for a few minutes, and you can leave it in the glove box when we're done. The only weapon I really care about is that ring on your finger."

RG flapped his arm again. "I don't even know what I'm doing."

"Just relax and follow my lead. I'll do the talking. Keep your mouth shut and try not to draw too much attention to yourself."

Stahl's mind weighed heavily with thoughts of jumpers and immortal forces and having to track down an otherworldly killer bent on human revenge. If he could crack Sarnie's case in time, figure out who killed him, the team might be able to stop him before he discovered immortality's secret. But unlike RG and Kacey, Stahl entered this clash without gifts or powers, no magical weapon with which to battle the next world's dark evil. When the shit hit the fan, he would be the first to fall. So, he had insisted on a little supernatural back up if they expected his help.

And fuck you all very much for putting me on the front lines!

Death hadn't mattered to him as much when he'd been fighting for Zach's life last summer. He had resigned himself to it, the odds remote they would ever emerge from that dark corner of the past. But now with his boy back, life had taken on greater meaning. He wasn't just going to take one for the team here. He had a marriage to salvage and a family to reunite. He had Zach, and he hadn't yet taught him how to shave, how to drive a manual transmission, or tie a perfect Windsor knot.

On top of that, he had two murders to solve. He had already learned who killed Hal Bayless, but that murder would always remain unsolved. If he put out a BOLO on a perp who had died a week before the victim he allegedly murdered, that would pretty much be the end of Stahl's career.

As would being caught dressing up RG Granville as a detective and taking him on an interview.

Stahl accepted the risk to his livelihood and even the investigation's integrity, but he didn't expect any information they gathered to see the light of day in a court of law. The adjudication of this case would occur elsewhere.

Rolling down his window, he gave a friendly nod to the portly, older man encased in the glass booth. The guard raised a finger and struggled to shimmy from the tight quarters out the side door, the structure a near seamless fit to the man's current dimensions. Before long, the company would either have to build the man a new booth or hire a smaller man to grow into it.

"Detective Mike Stahl." He flipped his badge and rested it on the open window. "And Detective…" Stahl drew a blank, not having gotten that far in the planning. He threw a glance at RG. "um…Detective Hutch."

Hutch? RG mouthed.

"We're here to speak with Wilson Sarnie. He's expecting us."

The guard lumbered over to Stahl's open window. "Let me check the list." Flipping through his clipboard's curled pages, he squinted through his horn-rimmed glasses, an ancient coffee stain visible on his breast pocket. The man continued to check his lists, his scowl affirming no one had informed him of

Stahl's arrival—a security guard cut out of the loop when it came to security.

"How 'bout I just sign in somewhere?" Stahl gave the man a wide smile, hoping to move things along.

The man continued to squint and stare, stretching Stahl's patience.

"Let me call up to the office, detective. It'll just be a minute."

Maybe. The man shuffled back to his booth.

"Hutch?" RG said. "That's the best you could do?"

"I had about ten cop shows spinning through my head."

"I've always been more of a David Soul fan."

The guard returned to the Crown Vic and rested his forearm on the roof. "Main building." He pointed across the gravel parking lot. "Mr. Sarnie should be in the business office up the stairs to your right."

"Thank you. Stay safe, now."

Stahl pulled ahead, checking his rearview as the guard shuffled back to his booth.

"Ready for your first day of school?"

* * *

RG

Stahl swung the Vic into the last open space at the lot's far end. RG eased the door open, careful not to ding the vehicle beside him. He hesitated a moment to appreciate the fully restored '70 Dodge Challenger poised beside the Crown Vic like a big cat ready to pounce.

RG whistled. "Damn! This one might even be nicer than the one in Daniels' barn."

"Don't tell him that. You couldn't afford the donuts it would take to win him over again."

The pair trudged the length of the building and entered through the main doors. An abandoned workstation lay to their left, what looked to be contracts and invoices assembled in haphazard piles across the desktop. A cigarette burned in a ceramic ashtray beside a stylish new computer as emails pinged and phone lines buzzed in the empty reception area. Stahl peered into the warehouse directly in front of him. Forklifts sped across the cement floors, zigzagging through the natural corridors the stacked boxes and skids created from floor to ceiling throughout the sprawling space.

"Detective Stahl?"

Stahl glanced toward the landing above the stairway to his right, a man's head appearing around the corner, John Lennon glasses stretching across a boyish face framed by long stringy hair. "Mr. Sarnie?"

"Sorry, Deb must be on another break." He gave a quick wave. "Come on up."

RG and Stahl joined the man in the first office at the top of the stairs, the name Alex Sarnie still stenciled across the door's glass window.

"Please, have a seat." The man drew a hand across the scraggly beard.

"Thank you, Mr. Sarnie."

"Call me Wilson." A framed photo of the muscle car out front hung behind the desk.

Stahl gestured toward RG. "This is Detective…Starsky."

"You're shitting me."

RG shrugged.

"Clearly destined for this line of work, I guess."

Stahl sank into the plush leather seat opposite Alex Sarnie's old desk while RG leaned against a file cabinet, making a show of scanning the room. Stahl coughed and nodded toward the chair.

RG dropped onto the cushion and flipped open a tattered, leather-bound notebook, clicking the plunger on his borrowed pen for emphasis. He examined the man seated before him, searching for the DNA string tethering the man with his brother, Alex, the man from the newspaper photos. Maybe the eyes, but not the face or build. The jawline…close. Gray threads bleeding into his dark mane separated the brothers by several years. The man had already arranged the desk with his own personal items, framed photos, planners, and nameplates, his late brother's paraphernalia resting in boxes outside the office door.

Stahl pointed to the photo. "So, I take it you own the old classic in the lot?"

Sarnie grinned. "You like?"

Stahl nodded as he pulled out his own notepad and pen from his jacket pocket. "I have a colleague who restores them. If he'd come with me, we would probably still be in the parking lot admiring it."

Sarnie shifted in his chair, squinting at RG across his desk. "You look kind of familiar, detective."

Fuck me. "Curse of having an average face, I guess."

Sarnie rubbed his chin. "Swear I've seen you before. Maybe in the papers, a big arrest or something?"

RG pulled at the refrigerator beneath his armpit. "Nothing yet. I'm still pretty new at this."

"Yeah, very new." Stahl cleared his throat. "So, we should probably get down to business. First, let me express my sympathy for your loss. There's nothing to prepare you for these kinds of things, and the last thing anyone wants to do during times like this is to talk to the cops."

"I appreciate that, detective." His eyes didn't leave his laptop's screen as he pecked at the keyboard.

"We're hoping you might be able to shed light on anyone

who may have wanted to possibly…how do I say this?…humiliate the family after the unfortunate accident."

Wilson Sarnie leaned back in his chair and locked his fingers behind his head. "Horrifying…the whole thing…and coming right after the shock of their deaths."

"Did your brother have enemies?"

Sarnie blew out a breath. "When you're in the shipping business, never fails someone ends up pissed off. Contracts cancelled, expanding into other's territory, undercutting the competition, you can understand. To get where Alex got, he pissed a few people off?"

"Enough to steal his body?"

"God!" Sarnie rubbed his eyes and pulled his palms down his face. "I can't imagine someone who would do that."

"Anyone ever threaten him?" Stahl folded his arms.

Sarnie clasped his hands and tapped his index fingers against his chin. "I remember a guy named Billy Massey. He got it in his head Alex had undercut him and cost him his company."

"Did he?" RG asked, glancing at Stahl and folding his arms, too.

"Maybe." Sarnie shrugged. "Hard to say. If someone gives you an opportunity to take their business, Alex would do it. The guy called the office and told Alex he would kill him."

"How long ago?" Stahl asked.

"Eight, nine years…still operating out of Boston at the time."

"Did this…Massey ever come by?" RG leaned forward in his chair, making a show of checking his blank notebook. His eyes darted to Stahl.

"We upped security for a while, but he never did."

"Guy ever show up unannounced, sit in a car outside the

gates?" RG slowed his cadence, clicking the plunger on his pen up and down. "Send threatening letters or emails?"

"Never heard from him again."

"Sometimes the confrontation itself gets the point across." Stahl glared at RG. "So, Mr. Sarnie, what do you do here at the company?"

"Cyber security, programming, that kind of thing." Sarnie continued tapping at the keyboard.

RG could picture it now, an aging computer hacker. Maybe a gamer in his youth. "Computer expert?"

"Every company needs one. We have hundreds of companies' personal and business information stored in our servers. They have to be confident it's protected from hackers."

"Takes one to thwart one, I imagine."

Sarnie nodded. "And it's not only the professional hackers, it's the thirty-year-old living with his mother with nothing to do but fuck around in someone's system, plant a virus, and cause headaches for everyone."

"Mostly your head, though, right?" Stahl cracked a smile.

"Don't you know it?"

The tidy, well-appointed office gave all indications of a business doing well. But RG couldn't imagine the company had so many security threats to warrant a cyber security officer. I mean, this wasn't Google or Amazon.

"So, would accounts received and billing be part of your job responsibilities, too?" Stahl had done his homework.

Sarnie's face fell as if the detective had punched him in the gut. "Well, we all chip in to help however we can. I work with Deb on that."

"How long you been with the company?"

Sarnie pulled his glasses and wiped them on his shirt. "From the beginning. Started with Alex up in Boston before the move."

"You must know everything about the business if you've been here as long as you have."

"That's why I'm up here right now trying to keep it afloat. He would have wanted me here."

"I'm sure he would have." Stahl's eyes shifted to the boxes of personal effects piled in the hallway.

As if anticipating Stahl's question, Wilson Sarnie said, "Can't keep the office like it's a museum exhibit." He shrugged. "Not good for company morale."

A framed photo of a woman and little girl perched on the shelf behind Sarnie's desk brought a squeeze to RG's chest. Must be the wife and daughter. Their images remained the only evidence Alex Sarnie had once occupied the space.

Stahl turned his head toward the door, pointing toward the line of doors along the corridor. "Which office are you moving from?"

"Downstairs." He shot Stahl a forced grin.

"On the floor? I didn't spot any offices but Deb's work-station."

Sarnie folded his arms. "The basement actually. Only place in the building with the square footage for the servers and computer equipment."

RG stood and leaned against the file cabinet, clicking his pen. *Time for a little good-cop, bad-cop.* "A bit out of the way..." RG let his statement hang, giving Sarnie the chance to fill the awkward lull with more information.

Sarnie pulled off his glasses and fixed him with a stare. "Like I said, the basement had the most functional space for the work I did." He scanned his new office. "But now I'll have to be more hands-on if I'm going to be running things."

RG unwrapped a stick of gum and folded it in his mouth. "Pretty big jump from billing to company president."

"What the hell, Starsky!" Wilson gripped the chair's

armrests, the cords standing out on his neck. "Did you come here to ask questions about me or about Alex?"

"Just routine." Stahl held up his hands. "If we had run into Deb at the front desk, we would have asked her about her office and how long she'd worked here, too." Stahl redirected the conversation to the inner workings of the business, other employees, anyone who might have had a beef with Alex Sarnie. But Sarnie's employees remained many of his lifelong friends, closer than family, and faithfully devoted to him.

"You mentioned the floor manager, a guy named…" He checked his notebook. "Griggs. He available to talk?"

Sarnie let go a heavy sigh. "I had to let him go this week, too many things slipping through the cracks lately. Almost sunk us."

Stahl raised an eyebrow. "Do you have a forwarding address or contact information?"

"I can have Deb get in touch with you."

Shifting his weight as he rose from the chair, Stahl reached into his sport coat pocket. "Have her contact me at this number."

As he stood, Sarnie grabbed the card from Stahl. "Are we done here?"

"We don't have anything else. But if you think of anything, would you give me a call or text? The smallest recollection could still be helpful in a case like this."

Sarnie nodded as he tossed the card onto the desk.

"I appreciate your candor today, Mr. Sarnie. Thanks for taking the time to meet with us."

"No problem, detectives. I'll show you out." He gestured toward the door. They exited the office and headed down the steps to the first floor.

Stahl gazed toward the warehouse floor. "So, who officially owns Sarnie Trucking now?"

"Well, Alex left everything to Jessie. If she died, then to Marlie." Sarnie blew out a breath. "With everyone gone, the company goes to our mother."

"Your mother?" Stahl gave a slight head shake. "Not you?"

"Well, for all intents and purposes, it goes to me. My mother has no intention of running a trucking company, and when she dies, I'll inherit it. I'm her sole living heir." Wilson shrugged and shifted his weight to his opposite leg. "Typical Alex. Just a little sibling rivalry to fuck over his older brother."

"Family dynamics are tricky, aren't they?"

Wilson smirked his agreement. "As much as I had hoped, we never had a close relationship. We worked together but didn't talk much outside the business."

"Again, I'm sorry for your loss. And thanks again for your time."

"You bet." Sarnie grasped Stahl's outstretched hand. He nodded to RG and turned toward the stairwell.

Stahl pushed against the front door but hesitated. RG nearly ran into him from behind. "Can I bother you with one more question, Mr. Sarnie?"

Halfway up the stairs, Sarnie pivoted and checked his watch. "Shoot."

Stahl stepped back into the reception area. "It's a bit sensitive, so forgive me. I remember reading the papers a few years ago, a couple investigative reports about the company."

Sarnie chuckled. "The drug rumors? Stories about how we made our money shipping heroin up and down the New England coast?"

"Didn't paint the company in the best light."

Sarnie shook his head, descending the stairs. "Lots of local reporters started sniffing around, but their stories were nothing but wild conjecture. In truth, we had an employee, one of our drivers, with a serious problem. Made a few mistakes. Instead of firing the man, Alex made sure he got the help he needed. He cleaned up and he's still working for the company. So, Alex helps a friend, and we get a reputation."

"Can I ask his name?"

"Guy named Michael Sullivan." He glanced over the top of his glasses. "I'm sure you Chatham cops know all about him."

RG tilted his head. "Never heard of—"

"Mick Sullivan," Stahl interrupted. He pressed his lips together and stared at his shoes. "Yeah, we do."

Wilson stared at RG.

"Just back from vacation." RG shrugged and flapped his arm. "Missed the morning briefing."

"Well, one of your guys decided to use him as a punching bag?"

"An unfortunate incident, I'm afraid."

"Might be time for the Chatham PD to clean house over there."

RG glanced at the boxes accumulating on the landing as Sarnie climbed the stairs.

Talk about cleaning house.

* * *

Mike

Mike Stahl paced the hallway at Chatham Elementary School, perusing the sponge-painted masterpieces pinned to the chipped corkboard outside the art room. Every fourth or fifth piece revealed a spark, an inkling of artistic talent the same way PE class exposed Darwin's theory of favorable genetics in motion. Through the glass, Zach Simpson huddled with his classmates around paint-spattered tables with lumps of clay pressed to parchment paper, hands and faces tinged with chocolate mud. Tongues danced along lips as they fashioned mugs and pinch pots, soon to be glazed and fired into fixtures on their family's kitchen mantels. Underneath each, crude initials and date would mark the moment and bring tears to parents' eyes when they would one day peek into boxes marked fifth-grade memories and puzzle over how time had flown by so fast.

Judging from what he'd observed through the art room window, Stahl had a hunch Zach's talents wouldn't rest on the potter's wheel. The boy proved a whiz with computers, but Stahl couldn't tell what Zach's other gifts would be yet. Someone had placed courage and bravery inside the boy's heart, though. Last summer, Zach had faced a continuing, haunting nightmare, one he couldn't share with anyone, not his friends or school counselors. Not with anyone but Stahl, who had been there with him, who had rescued him from a cage in a hollow pit beneath a graveyard seventy years in the past. Despite Zach's stepping up as the hero, saving Stahl and every other child from that living hell, the boy's fear persisted. His stepson needed him more than anything right now. He needed a father to help him feel safe and protected. Yet, just seeing him at drop-off or pickup, maybe a few hours on the weekend or an overnight, wasn't enough, at least not for Stahl. The boy appeared so far away now, as if still interred in that fetid cave. And Stahl could do nothing but stand there, unable to reach him.

He continued to stare through the glass, his own reflection merging their shapes until they fit seamlessly within each other. His heart dropped in his chest as a second reflection appeared beside his shoulder.

Claire Simpson gazed past him into the classroom. "Aren't I picking up today?"

Beautiful as always. Stahl shifted his weight from one foot to the other. "You are. I'm just grabbing a quick peek." He nodded over his shoulder. "I have a meeting with Kacey."

Her eyes narrowed. "Oh? Something going on with Zach?"

"No, he's fine, it's…something else."

"Just a friendly visit then?" She crossed her arms.

"Claire, it's nothing like that. RG will be there, too. I need to talk with them about something."

She drew a deep sigh. "Still playing supernatural sleuth?"

Here we go again. "Something's going on, and I need advice, that's all. I'm not—"

"And you question why I keep Zach as far away from you as possible," she interrupted. "You don't seem to understand I need to protect him if you won't."

"Protect him?" He struggled to keep his voice from carrying. "Are you forgetting who traveled through time to protect him? Who brought him back to you?"

And who took him away from me. He didn't say it.

"With the way you hang around strange people, who's to say you didn't lead that evil directly to him? Who's to say it won't happen again?"

"How could you say that?" The tenor of his raised voice startled him. He glanced at the other parents huddled in the hallway, their eyes quickly darting away. "After everything you and I have been through, to say I'm the cause of what happened. How could you think such a thing?"

"Look, I don't want to argue with you. Haven't we had enough of that?"

"Apparently not," he muttered, glancing at Zach through the glass. The boy's gaze locked onto his and his face illuminated in a grin, a misshaped pinch pot raised in a stained hand.

Stahl replied with a wink and a hearty thumbs up.

"Listen, you might as well know I've been offered a job as lab director with Boston Scientific in Cambridge." Her words spun Stahl from the window. "They want an answer by the end of next week. If I accept, I plan to take Zach with me—"

"You don't get to make that decision," he interrupted, digging his fingers into his palms as his blood flow picked up, whooshing in his ears. "We're still married, you know. This separation didn't come with rules, but you decided where and when I could spend time with Zach, and for how long. I went along with it. But you don't get to take him away. You'll have to divorce me first, and then there *will* be rules you have to follow."

"Do you know why I left you?"

"Claire, we've been over this…why do you want to—"

She ignored him. "I left you because I couldn't let what happened to Zach…ever happen again. I needed to keep him safe."

Stahl jammed his hands on his hips and gazed at his shoes. "You don't get it." He raised his eyes to meet hers. "There's no safe place. If one of these…things…wants you, it doesn't matter whether you're Zach or me or Tom Brady. He's gonna get you. Maybe it's best if we stay close to the people who can help."

"Like your ex-lover…?"

Stahl threw up his hands. "Christ! Is this about Zach or about you now?"

Claire shook her head. "I'm just tired. I'm tired of the dreams, waking up in the middle of the night and racing down the hall to check on Zach, hoping he's still there. I'm tired of waiting for the other shoe to drop."

"I worry, too. Every day. You don't have to go through all this alone." He filled his cheeks and blew out. "Come home. Bring Zach home where he belongs."

She stepped back and folded her arms in front of her. "This can't only be about Zach. I need to be in there somewhere."

"You are. You've always been."

Claire reached a palm to his cheek. Stahl recoiled, and she dropped her hand. "Do you know the other reason I left you? Why I left the only man I've ever loved?" She sighed. "It may be the most important reason of all."

Stahl lowered his gaze.

"Because you can't forgive me."

Stahl continued to stare at his shoes and said nothing. He couldn't argue with the truth. He had never been good at forgiveness, not for himself, and not for Claire either. He had never forgiven himself for a moment of weakness in his youth, throwing then-girlfriend Kacey to the floor when he'd been fighting the bottle. And he hadn't been able to forgive Claire for the things she accused him of after Zach's disappearance.

"I studied your eyes…the night you returned from that… place you and Zach had been. You figured bringing my son home would be enough to make things all right, like before. Before all those things I said."

"It's been hard to get over, that's all."

"Good God! My son had disappeared, I'd just been inter-rogated by the cops." She raised her hands. "Your colleagues, people I knew, asking me what I'd done to my son. I was beside myself. And you start in with the incomprehensible, ranting about caretakers and jumpers, the existence of worlds within our own. My mind short-circuited. I lashed out at you. How did you expect me to react?"

"It doesn't matter anymore what—"

"Of course, it does! It's the reason we're in the place we are right now."

Stahl rubbed his temples. "I just hoped you knew me

better than to assume I might have caused harm to Zach."

She explored his eyes with such a heavy gaze it made him turn away. "I search for it every time I run into you. That… spark behind your eyes. But they haven't changed at all. I keep waiting, wondering when you'll be back. But there's nothing there anymore, nothing for me."

"Claire—"

"You can't get past it." She didn't let him finish. "And I can't spend the rest of my life hoping for forgiveness, for that light to come back in your eyes when you see me."

"I haven't stopped loving you. It's just—"

"It doesn't matter what words you say. Your eyes tell me otherwise."

"Zach needs a full-time father now. And we can get back to where we were. It may just take time."

"We've had nothing but time since you've been back, and I'm not settling for ninety-eight percent of you. I need the whole thing, the man who fell in love with me." She straightened her jacket and fixed the leather bag over her shoulder. "So, if I can't be with you, I want to be as far away from you as possible. Zach will be safer, and I'll be able to move on." She stared upward and blotted the corner of her eye with a knuckle. "But this…" she gestured back and forth between them, "…I can't do anymore."

As she shook her head and strode across the corridor, Zach burst through the classroom door aiming for his stepfather. He appeared ready to leap into his arms, but hesitated, caught between the worlds of childhood and preadolescence and its new set of rules. But as Zach glanced at his mother seated in the line of chairs by the main office with the other parents, head buried in her hands, his full emotions swelled across his face.

"What did you do to her?"

CHAPTER SEVEN

Tuesday, March 22

Alex

Alex Sarnie slipped through the gap in the chain-link fence behind the garage on the southeast perimeter of Sarnie Trucking. A sliver moon provided the only illumination to the meandering pathway from the parking area to the main building.

Light…dark…it didn't matter anymore to Sarnie.

A few days before his accident, he'd stumbled upon the breach in the enclosure after chasing off a homeless couple who had been drinking, drugging, and god-knows-what-else in one of the eighteen wheelers' cabs parked at the fence line. He chuckled. Served him right. In all likelihood, they were strung out on the stuff Mick Sullivan had brought in from his northern distributers.

Perched beside the fleet of new trucks, Sarnie gazed across

the compound at the recently remodeled main building housing the business office. The company had been on the verge of bankruptcy less than a decade ago before a chance meeting with a die-hard Red Sox fan changed the company's fortunes. After downing more than a few overpriced beers in Fenway Park's packed right-field bleachers one sweltering July night, Sarnie had struck up a conversation with a guy beside him named Billy Massey. Turns out he had had a small business in Dorchester and was looking to contract auto part shipments to the South Shore. After Big Papi had curled a ninth inning, Andy Pettitte breaking ball around Pesky pole—and more late-night celebratory beers along Lansdown Street—the deal was done. After a summer working together and attending regular pre-game business meetings at their favorite watering holes in Back Bay, Sarnie had learned his new business partner had more than just auto parts he wanted to ship. The relationship had been lucrative, but Sarnie considered Massey nothing more than a stepping stone. He had eventually cut out the middleman and went directly to the source, Jimmy 'Big Mac' McKinnon, the south Boston crime boss, and started shipping his product exclusively. Expanding distribution throughout Massachusetts and New England, Sarnie took a fortune from Massey's pocket and cost the man his livelihood.

But such is the price of doing business.

Sarnie paced across the asphalt parking lot, staring at his glowing office window on the top floor of the main building. He could make out a silhouetted figure getting comfortable behind his old desk. Reaching his hand to his neck, Sarnie rewound the bandage that had snagged on the chain-link fence. He resembled a monster from a 1940's B-movie, wrapped from chin to ankles in medical wraps, but he had to keep the decomposition in check. His gait had become mummy-like, but at least he had staved off the oily death odor leeching from his pores.

He had Sullivan to thank for that. His new roommate had stepped up, procuring a variety of embalming fluids and helping cinch up Sarnie's body in a gauze jumpsuit. Sarnie couldn't figure out why the man hadn't deduced the obvious—that his old boss was deader than roadkill—but it could be the acceptance of the unimaginable took longer in a simple mind. The man didn't so much as utter a word as he wrapped Sarnie, the pressure from the medical tape squirting gobs of maggots from the fissures in Sarnie's body. Eventually the man would figure it out, come to his senses. Maybe Sarnie being dead or alive didn't matter to Sullivan. As long as the boss gave the orders, Mick Sullivan would follow them. But the moment the unfathomable dawned on the man, Sarnie would have to act.

Tie up loose ends and all.

Sarnie tried the main entrance and found it unlocked. He slipped inside the doorway and climbed the carpeted steps to his office, rapping the glass with his knuckles before sliding through the open door. "You're looking pretty comfortable in my chair, big brother."

Wilson Sarnie's eyes widened. The egg roll balancing between his fingers dropped onto the cluttered desk with a greasy splat. "Holy shit! Alex…" He sprung from his chair. "I thought you were—"

"That's the story we're going with right now," he cut him off. "I'm the only one who made it out of the car."

Wilson shuffled around the desk, his nose twitching as he inhaled the powerful odor fighting its makeshift restraints. "What is that smell…? Where the hell have you been?"

"You wouldn't believe me if I told you."

"Why didn't you tell us you were alive?"

"What do you think I'm doing here? Feds are keeping my survival a secret right now, trying to protect me while they find my would-be killer." He hesitated, gauging whether his deception would fly. "But I'm doing an investigation of my own."

"Killer? What are you talking about? It wasn't an accident?"

He shook his head. "Someone made it look like an accident."

Wilson pressed his lips together. "What happened?"

"Someone tampered with my car. I'm driving one minute, the next minute the car has a life of its own. The doors lock, the gas pedal is pinned to the floor, and the thing steers itself through the guardrail and into the drink."

Wilson Sarnie circled his desk. "Some kind of electrical failure?"

"I don't think so. Felt deliberate somehow."

"Jesus, Alex. Is that possible?"

"You're the tech guy. You tell me. Can someone hijack a car if they're not in it?"

Wilson Sarnie shrugged and scratched his head. "How did you get out?"

I didn't. Alex Sarnie fixed him with a stare.

"Never mind." Wilson gazed at the bandages masking his brother's neck and hands. "Were you injured? You should be in a hospital." He turned and reached for the desk phone.

Alex slammed his hand against Wilson's, pinning it to the table. "Don't. That's the first place they'll look."

Wilson rubbed his bruised knuckles. "Who?"

"Whoever killed Jessie and…" He pressed his palms against the desk, his head bowed, unable to mutter his daughter's name. *My pumpkin pie.*

"Their funerals were supposed to be in a couple days. I took care of the arrangements myself over at Bayless, but…"

"He's dead, the sick bastard." His lips curled into a grin. "He's gonna need his own undertaker right now."

Wilson picked up the previous day's *Cape Cod Times* folded on the desk. "They're reporting someone stole the bodies, including yours."

"Well, mine's right here, and I'm gonna find the person responsible."

Wilson leaned over the desk. "I just had a visit this morning from a couple detectives." He maneuvered the business card between his index and middle fingers. "The guys asked a bunch of questions but didn't say anything about a murder. They have no clue you're alive."

Alex Sarnie snatched the cheap cardboard ID from his brother's hand. "Detective Michael Stahl." He eyed his older brother. "Local cops don't know about me. We're keeping them out of it. Why are they poking around here, asking you questions?"

"Gotta question family, I guess. I am still your brother. Wanted to know if you had any enemies."

"What did you tell them?"

"I gave them Billy Massey. He's the only one I can remember who ever threatened you."

"There are others, and I'm gonna find them." He turned to leave.

"So, what do I do now?"

"The older brother, never failing to need direction." Alex's gaze darted about his former office. "You can start by getting your ass back to the basement and worrying about networks and cyber security, and whatever else you do down there."

"Geez, Alex. I'm trying to keep the company going. What do you suppose I'm doing here all hours of the night?"

Alex glanced about the office. "Looks like you're upgrading."

Wilson threw his arms up. "How the hell could I have known you were still alive? Someone had to step up and keep things running."

"What happened to Griggs? He's been manager for as long as the company's been in business. No one knows more about operations than he does."

Wilson scratched his head. "You're not gonna want to hear this, but, well…I had to let that sonofabitch go."

Alex Sarnie couldn't stifle his chuckle. "Christ. Did you wait till my body was even cold before you parked your ass behind my desk and designed a new organizational chart?"

"The last week has been crazy 'round here, nobody thinking straight, things slipping through the cracks. Shipments not going out. Routes not assigned to drivers. And no one paying attention to the details that kill companies overnight. I couldn't sit back and watch what you'd built come crashing down just days after you left us. I stepped up to salvage things." Wilson crossed his arms. "You could at least show me a little gratitude right now."

Alex reached out and rubbed his sibling's shoulder. "You always did need lots of encouragement, didn't you?"

Wilson jerked away. Alex couldn't tell whether big brother's response grew from anger at his comment or revulsion at his lifeless touch.

"I guess I didn't praise you enough for the company's grunt work."

Wilson turned and waved him away. "I knew you appreciated what I did here."

"Well, enough of this mutual admiration society bullshit. So, here's how it's gonna be. I want you out of my office. I don't care where you go, but you're moving out of here. And before you do, you're gonna put my stuff back on the desk." Sarnie nodded toward the nameplate and photographs packed in hallway boxes. "I won't be back for a while…too dangerous right now…my assassins can't suspect I'm still alive…no one can. Run the show from up here during the day, for all I care, but don't forget whose office this is." Alex's eyes darted back and forth amongst his brother's personal effects decorating the desk and shelves. "And take your shit back downstairs." Sarnie stepped behind the desk and dropped into his chair.

"Of course, of course." Wilson salvaged Alex's items from the hallway boxes and wiped them off as he arranged them back on the desktop.

Company man. Seeing his older brother lounge behind his old desk nearly made him laugh. Wilson Sarnie had been a good foot soldier for the company, buried in accounts payable, brilliant enough to design company software and develop security systems to thwart hackers, but dumb enough to be pushing paperclips and chasing Deb around her desk. Jack-of-all-trades, master of none. Expendable were it not for his last name.

Thinks he can run a company all of a sudden.

Alex glared at his brother. "I need you to go through the shipping logs and contracts. Find someone who I might have…how should I say this?"

"Screwed over?"

Alex grinned. "Exactly."

Wilson shook his head. "I'm not gonna be able to find much in the logs. So much gets moved around off the books, most of the time I'm not entirely sure what's being shipped, or where."

Plausible deniability. Sounds like a politician. "But you do know who I've pissed off."

"You mean, besides Massey? Maybe."

"Put him on the top of list and go from there. I'll check back with you soon." Alex turned toward the door.

"Maybe you should just let the feds handle this. They'll figure out who did it, and then whoever it is will answer for the crime."

"No, they won't."

"Why not?"

Alex slipped through the office door into the hallway. "Because they'll have to answer to me first."

* * *

Ellie

The first time Ellie left her body, her brother had just exited the room and hiked along the buffed, white corridor floors to the elevator. She had been curious about what lay beyond the door, the hallway tile pattern, the wall color outside her door, and what artwork hung upon it. So, she jumped inside him. She wasn't sure whether she could accomplish the task until she tried, but she found she could burrow inside him and take in all the world offered from inside his head. At first, she could sense nothing but his love for her seeping from every corner of his soul. But, a darkness emerged, revealing things laying hidden below the surface. Things he kept secret. Things she couldn't detect.

The moment she entered him, he had stopped for a moment in the hallway and rubbed his chest, thinking maybe he had eaten something that disagreed with him or had suffered a bout of heartburn. But he continued along the corridor. She discovered she had control over his movements. She tested her skills by having him scratch his ear and run a hand through his hair. She had him stop and stare out the third-floor window, toward the hospital's blue neon sign by the parking lot and to the stream of halogen lights piercing the night. She imagined people heading out to dinner or meeting friends for ice cream.

She missed those things most.

As she took in the colorful hallway hues tastefully appointed with African sculptures and artwork, she sensed she had a job to do. Just as her brother had been her protector, she understood her role would be to return the favor when the time came.

She hoped the woman would explain everything to her, so she knew what to do.

Ellie had sensed her kindness and compassion. She had made such an awkward attempt to contact the woman, she feared she had frightened her off. If she just hadn't come across like a creature from a horror flick, maybe she would have had more success. And she shouldn't have picked up the child in the woman's house. That had been a mistake. But she sensed an overwhelming sense of love wash over her when she encountered the little boy. Maybe because she would never have a child of her own, and God or the cosmos, or whatever turned out to be navigating her strange journey, gave her one fleeting moment to experience what such love would be like. To be a mother. To take care of someone who couldn't take care of himself.

She would have to reach out to the woman again, maybe come to her as she had once been, not what she was now. In the restaurant washroom, she had embedded images of her into the woman's mind, pictures from her youth when she wasn't dying. Maybe the woman wouldn't be as scared the next time she showed up. She had also considered reaching out to the kind man. She sensed him, too.

What proved compelling about the pair wasn't so much their power, but their hearts. They shined as if goodness and love originated inside them, pure radiance bursting from their souls. In the new place she found herself, such brilliant energy had not surfaced within the other wandering souls she had encountered. She could only hope she ended up like the man and woman, not the others—the ones who gave off a dark, vengeful aura.

Ellie would reach out to the woman one more time. She felt empowered, but vulnerable, like a hatchling crocodile that would one day rule the Nile, but that now served as nothing more than prey for egrets and heron. And the sooner she could shed her withered, human shell, the better.

She was ready for what would come.

* * *

Wednesday, March 23
Alex
Blood.

The voice whispered to him inside his head, the word playing over and over, bouncing through his skull like a mantra.

Sarnie woke in Mick Sullivan's back bedroom. Well, woke wasn't completely correct. His body didn't need sleep anymore since it no longer lived and breathed, but his mind needed rest, time to reset, take a break from the bitter musings it housed.

Blood.

He glanced at the space between the medical wraps securing his body, an oozing line of exudate dripping from his ribcage, carrying with it a pungent stench. He cinched the bands tighter and wiped the excess fluid from his fingertips onto the bedsheets.

He couldn't say for sure whether he had been dreaming, but someone had spoken to him in the night. Whispered to him again and again.

Blood.

When he closed his eyes, the images had come. Rivers of blood flowing out of severed arteries and limbs, droplets of red rain tumbling from the heavens and staining his slick skin a deep crimson.

Blood. The whispering voice repeated.

Sarnie turned over, wrapping the pillow around his head to quell the sound, dislodge the images racing through his head. Just his 'sticky brain,' as Jessie would have called it. When something lodged in his head and couldn't shake it. Like images of her.

Those he could never shake.

Back when his body surged with life, just the idea of her sent a shudder through his chest. Now, a dull ache resided where his shriveled heart remained.

Jessie. He had met her in one of Jimmy McKinnon's clubs in Saugus. The Charlestown boss controlled a small piece of Boston's organized crime interests, with the Russian and Italian syndicates staking their claim on the rest. The FBI had infiltrated the other crime families, but they had never been able to breach the tight-knit Southie faction and bring Big Mac's organization down. The times they had tried, they had found their agents floating in the Mystic River with their tongues torn from their throats.

Big Mac epitomized Boston Irish, Beantown born and bred. He ran several legitimate businesses in Charlestown and along the north shore, from limousine services to recycling and sanitation. But his gentlemen's clubs provided the cover for his more lucrative escort services. Sarnie had cultivated a relationship with Big Mac when he undercut Billy Massey and took over Big Mac's liquor and food distribution contracts, and the more lucrative, off-the-books contracts. Sarnie would regularly visit *The Reveal* in Saugus to pick up his envelope, share a

Jameson with Big Mac, and strike up conversations with the dancers. But the new girl from the Jersey shore had caught his attention.

Jessie Bolduc had been dancing at the time, swaying with the horns from that Al Green song and creating a visual snapshot vivid enough to live forever beside the song's auditory imprint. Something had pulled him toward the stage, as if her soft green eyes had him hooked on a retractable leash. She told him she hailed from Avalon, her smile spinning the words into an erotic whisper as it rolled off her tongue. Compared to the places Sarnie had spent his youth, towns like Ludlow, Chicopee, and Holyoke, he imagined Avalon as Jersey's version of the Emerald City. She was so beautiful, so *not*-Boston, and every Friday evening when he pulled into the parking lot for his envelope, his heart would flam like a jazz drummer on a smoky, bourbon-soaked riff.

Sarnie worked out a deal with Big Mac for a regular appointment time with his new star employee. But their sessions weren't enough for either of them, and their trysts spilled over into next days and following weekends in out-of-the-way places where Big Mac's paid eyes and ears remained none the wiser. Despite his friendship with Big Mac, the thug protected his stable of thoroughbreds and would not let Jessie out of her commitments. Sarnie suspected Jessie had advanced to a level higher than just business to Big Mac, but never questioned her about her past...or present. Finally, Jessie convinced the crime boss to let her go, but Sarnie came to understand that Jimmy McKinnon would have a hold over Jessie long after their friendship fizzled, and the shipping contracts ended.

He would glimpse one of Jimmy's limos parked at the far end of the couple's Back Bay neighborhood or idling on the curb outside the North End restaurants the pair would frequent, windows blackened and hiding an even darker heart.

But when Sarnie moved Jessie and his business to the Cape, Jimmy's surveillance faded, as if the boss's world effectively ended at the boundaries of Southie's Fort Point and Telegraph Hill.

But Sarnie had no illusions he would leave them alone. He learned soon enough that, contract or no contract, Jessie still had obligations to fulfill.

She would disappear for an afternoon or evening, saying she had been visiting friends, but when he snooped, her smartphone's GPS would place her back in Southie. And she still had a wild side Sarnie had never tamed. He had stumbled upon the others, the men at her gym and yoga classes, the cops, bartenders, and lifeguards. But he overlooked those things because she never failed to come home to him. In the end, he had faith she loved him as much as he loved her, and nothing else mattered.

And someone had killed her…along with Marlie. His pumpkin pie. The sound of his daughter's nickname brought a grin, then a dull ache from somewhere down deep. A moan escaped his lips, surprising himself as he rolled onto his side. He wanted his heart to flutter again when he pictured his girls. He wanted to experience something inside the decomposing shell he wore like a cheap, dime-store suit. He wanted blood to course through his veins again. Blood was life. Blood was the magic elixir, the gas powering the engine. Living or dead.

Blood.

He bolted upright in the bed. He closed his eyes, imagining his body as an immortal engine and the fuel that would give him life in this world. A picture formed in his mind, the dark figure of a man. Not a memory or someone he had envisioned, but a living being who had visited him in his mind. A palpable presence filled Sarnie's space, and the man's voice echoed through his brain.

"Open the door to the forces of darkness."

He sensed a tiny blip in his chest, his heart struggling to beat like a recently hatched bird, head back and mouth open, snapping at the air and awaiting that first worm forced into its gullet.

Another blip, a faint beat. His own heart.

He would have to feed it…with blood.

* * *

RG

RG stared out the passenger side window as he rumbled along the silent Chatham streets in Mike Stahl's Crown Vic. The detective had shown up unannounced before dawn, rousing him from his bed as Kacey stifled a yawn from the hallway.

The one day I don't have class and can sleep late.

Whether he liked it or not, as Stahl's honorary partner, he was now on the job full-time. But so far this assignment wasn't shaping up to be as much fun as the previous one. Stahl had told him he wouldn't need a gold shield on his belt or the thirty-eight-caliber stopper stored in the glove box. The detective had even confiscated his notebook and pen.

Just when I was getting the hang of this detective thing.

"So, are you punishing me for the good-cop, bad-cop routine the other day?"

Stahl deliberated a moment, squeezing the steering wheel. "As far as bad cops go, you set the bar pretty high."

RG scrunched his face. "Thank you." *I think.*

"Let's see how you do at a crime scene. Maybe this assignment will better suit your strengths."

Stahl had informed him that they were on their way to Sarnie's residence. But unlike their last visit, RG wouldn't have to sit in the car as the Chatham cops swarmed the place and removed Jessie and Marlie's chilled bodies from the kitchen. He and Stahl would have the place to themselves, on a search for clues the first round of detectives might have overlooked. Any nugget that could shed light on the jumper's whereabouts.

As long as they didn't find him in the house, RG would be okay with that.

Despite the calendar welcoming spring, a crisp morning frost gripped the tree branches and finely manicured lawns like icing on a pastry. The image directed his hand into the Dunkin' Donuts waxed paper bag beside him on the passenger seat to extract a frosted vanilla glazed from the Munchkin cluster.

Stahl snagged RG's wrist, halting his fingers inches from their target. "Hey, those are mine. You already finished yours."

RG eyed the empty paper bag between his legs. "I thought cop partners shared everything."

"You watch too much TV." Stahl released his grip, palmed a powdered jelly and popped it in his mouth.

What is it with cops and donuts?

Stahl cracked the windows and elevated the heat, the combination neutralizing the other's benefit. Still, it seemed to satisfy the man's odd duality, his need to balance yin with yang. He aimed the boxy sedan along Main, veering onto Route 137 toward the mid-Cape highway.

"Where we going? I thought Sarnie lived by the water."

"He does. I gotta pay a quick visit to my maybe-soon-to-be ex-partner, Daniels. Poor bastard."

RG had heard about the incident. "I take it the hearing didn't go well."

"A disaster." Stahl scarfed another Munchkin. "The community members on the panel and suits from internal affairs are done with Berrelli-type cops, even though that ain't

Daniels. They threw the book at him. Placed him on indefinite leave, took a hefty chunk of his salary. But the panel showed mercy for his family circumstances and didn't demote him."

"So, you looking for a new partner?" RG raised his eyebrows.

"Don't get your hopes up."

Chris Daniels' modest dwelling rested on a plot of scrub brush, set back several hundred feet from the high-traffic thruway between Chatham and Route 6. A wall of knotty pines shielded the house from the road noise's relentless rumble and offered a modicum of privacy. Pulling onto the property, Stahl looped behind the pastel shingled one-story ranch. The gravel driveway gave way to deep muddy grooves circling the house beside what once might have been a well-tended yard, but which had evolved into a temporary grave-yard for a half dozen project cars settled amongst the weeds. Stahl eased his ride to a stop in front of the renovated barn behind the residence, the crisp wooden exterior and recent upgrades contrasting the main house's general malaise.

Killing the engine, Stahl threw the Vic into park and opened the door. With one foot on the gravel driveway, Stahl peered across the passenger seat. "You coming?"

"Maybe I should wait in the car."

"What for?"

RG rubbed his chin. "I don't get the feeling your partner likes me too much."

"Because you started a brawl on my lawn with half the Chatham police force last summer?"

"Well, there's that."

"Or is it because he thinks you had something to do with his old boss's death?"

RG blew out a breath. "Maybe that, too."

"Well, he thinks I had something to do with it, too, if that's any consolation. I think I might have a solution. Maybe an olive branch." Stahl slid the remaining Munchkins bag across the front seat as he threw open the car door. "This will go a long way toward healing old wounds."

RG peeked into the bag. "Really?"

"The tried and true currency of the law enforcement world."

Cops and donuts. Who knew?

* * *

Mike

Stahl used the car door for leverage as he unfolded himself from the front seat. His hip groaned as he transitioned to his feet and paced across the hard-packed dirt, a smattering of pebbles scattering underfoot. As RG gathered the pastry bag from the front seat, Stahl resisted the urge to sneak another Munchkin handful. With Claire and Zac gone, he had reverted back to his old ways, Dunkin' for breakfast, fast food for lunch, and over to Carmine's at the end of the day for a couple of monster pizza slices. If he only had access to Kacey's diner and the calorie-free Lumberjack, maybe he could ease the mounting assault on his uniform's strained seams.

The pair approached the sliding door, cracked open far enough to catch Cool 102's classic rock filtering from the state-of-the-art sound system mounted into the barn's far wall. Stahl poked his head through the door and scanned the high-tech workshop. With a multi-post car lift, engine hoists, air compressors, transmission jacks, and a full metal fabrication bay, it didn't take a genius to figure out where Daniels invested his paycheck each month. He eyed a pair of gleaming muscle cars in mid-restoration with tarps covering two more near the rear wall. If Daniels never made it back to the force, he wouldn't have to worry about how to put food on the table.

In the far corner Stahl spotted Daniels hunched over a countertop, sifting through a pile of papers stuffed into an old cigar box. As he edged closer, he could make out the tattered photographs, postcards, and letters spilling over the edge. The crimp in Daniels' posture hinted at the weight pressing against his sagging shoulders.

"What's doing, partner," Stahl half-shouted, snatching the remote from the nearby workbench and calming the radio's volume.

At the sound of Stahl's voice, Daniels swiped the back of his hand across his eyes and stuffed the mementos into the cigar box, snapped the top shut, and jammed it into the desk drawer like a teenager caught with a dirty magazine. A pair of photographs fluttered from the drawer like falling leaves and landed on the floor between them.

"Shit, you surprised me." Daniels' voice wavered as he dropped to a knee. Stahl leaned over to help gather the fallen Polaroids, but Daniels hand shot forward. "It's okay. I got 'em." He turned them over and stuffed them into his back pockets. "So, what're you doing here?"

Daniels' forced grin couldn't fully mask the torment his puffy, bloodshot eyes betrayed.

Must be Ellie. Stahl wouldn't ask about her today. "Just passing by on my way to the Sarnie residence. Thought you might need a little something."

RG pulled out the Munchkin bag, minus one or two chocolate glazed.

"Thanks, Dr. Granville." Daniels face lit up as he reached for the bag. "Haven't had any breakfast yet."

"Not sure I would call this breakfast. It's more like fried balls of fat with sugar attached."

"That's breakfast in my book." Daniels reached into the paper bag, the fresh pastry aroma wafting into the room, inciting Stahl's mouth to water like one of Pavlov's mutts.

Scanning the barn, Stahl's gaze rested on a late sixties Mustang 428 Cobra Jet on the lift and a seventy-something Dodge Challenger resting in the second bay with its hood stripped from the body.

RG stood marveling at the vehicles. "Beautiful restorations. You do them all yourself?"

"Little hobby of mine. You a car guy?"

"He drives a Subaru Legacy, so…" Stahl interjected.

"Hey! I watch *Velocity* channel! Love the Xr7 out front. Sixty-seven, is it?"

"Sixty-eight." Daniels grinned and turned to Stahl. "Your friend's got taste."

"Well played," Stahl whispered to RG as he strode toward the pair of muscle cars. "See you're keeping busy on your vacation."

"Got hooked up with a wealthy Boston client." He nodded toward the Challenger. "Saw the car at the Great Woods auto swap back in May. The guy has the money…now I have the time."

Stahl glanced at the tangle of wires cascading from the Dodge's dashboard. "Rewiring?" he grinned. "Maybe I could help."

Daniels chuckled, in all likelihood recalling Stahl's wiring fiasco with the Cougar. He had followed Daniels' directions, crimping the wires and making the terminal connections, but when Daniels finally got the car on the road, the horn blared every time he stepped on the brake.

"I know you're a quick study, but this may be beyond even you."

He scrunched his eyebrows together as he stared at the wire nest. "What the hell is all this?"

"CAN bus system. Part of the onboard diagnostic system that allows different microcontrollers in the vehicle to talk to each other."

"Microcontrollers, huh?" The thing looked more like a computer motherboard than a car part. "Whatever happened to plugs and points?"

"Way more complicated now." Daniels talked through a glazed Munchkin. "There's a shitload of electronic control units in modern cars, things that govern the transmission, air bags, mirrors, power windows, cruise control, power steering, anti-brake systems, you name it—even in that hunk of shit you drive."

Stahl splayed a hand across his chest as if hurt.

"But they need to communicate with each other somehow. This thing," Daniels held up the motherboard, "is like the master computer coordinating these systems. Just program the software and you're good to go."

Stahl shot a glance at RG. "Pretty soon regular guys like us won't be able to change their own oil."

"That's why you regular guys will need people like me," Daniels said with a grin.

"So why the hell are you installing it in a forty-five-year-old muscle car?" RG asked.

Daniels rolled his eyes. "The new millennium car enthusiast. They want all the modern conveniences and safety features housed in a classic body. It's like buying a historic property and putting a Jacuzzi in the living room. Drives me fucking crazy."

"But if the price is right...?" Stahl asked.

Daniels hesitated. "Well, it drives me less fucking crazy."

Didn't quite seem fair to Stahl that Daniels could make

more money while on suspension than Stahl could make on the job. He clapped his partner on the shoulder. "Well, I'll let you get back to things here. Just wanted to make sure you got fed, since that's been part of my job responsibilities from the moment I brought you to Chatham PD. I also have a couple of cases to solve."

"You got my notes on Sarnie."

"I do, but I gotta start over. I'm gonna walk the residence and see what I can find." Stahl nodded to RG and turned toward the door.

"Jimmy McKinnon."

Stahl glanced over his shoulder. "Huh?"

Daniels shoved his hands into his front pockets and rocked on his heels. "Talk to Jimmy McKinnon."

"The crime boss, Jimmy McKinnon?" RG whispered to Stahl.

"Christ! I'd rather dine with Michael Corleone in an Italian restaurant."

"He had a history with Sarnie…and his wife, Jessie," Daniels said. "Find out his whereabouts that night."

Stahl tilted his head. "Didn't spot McKinnon's name in your notes."

Daniels' gaze drifted to the floor as he shifted his weight from one foot to the other. "Just look into it. And Mike…keep me in the loop. I'm off the case, but I'd like to know the sonofabitch responsible for killing the family." The cords tightened in his neck as he swallowed.

"So far, the evidence points to a car accident."

"A body's missing, and someone propped up the others around their kitchen table. That ain't no accident."

"I agree with you there. I'll keep you posted, brother." Stahl gave Daniels a nod as he gathered RG and slipped through the barn door.

Stahl stepped across the driveway to his car. He stood for a moment with his hand on the door handle as RG dropped into the passenger seat and secured his seat belt. How the hell did Daniels know Sarnie had been mixed up with Big Mac? He backtracked, poking his head through the barn door, but hesitated before slipping inside.

Daniels leaned over the counter with his back to him, his fingers rummaging through the old cigar box again.

CHAPTER EIGHT

Wednesday, March 23

Alex

Sarnie shuffled from the back bedroom into Mick Sullivan's dimly lit living room. The day's radiance failed to penetrate the tattered curtains pulled across the grime-spattered windows, leaving the room bathed in a palpable gloom.

The teenage girl curled up under an unwashed sheet on the pullout couch beside Sullivan. The perks of being a low-life drug dealer, Sarnie guessed. But the girl's youthful glow had receded to a dull weariness and neglect. Her skin didn't shine like it should have at her age, and her veins' ropy thickness and scarring revealed a history that belied her years.

"Sully," he called.

As if attempting to wipe away the previous evening's recollections, Mick Sullivan rose onto an elbow and rubbed a palm against his forehead. "Whatta ya need, Boss?"

"Who is that?"

"Just one of my regulars who needed a fix last night. Didn't have no money, so…"

"I see. Well, I need something from her."

Sullivan grinned. "She's all yours, Boss."

Sarnie scowled, disgusted at Sullivan's insinuation that he would stoop to degrading this woman for a base human need. "I need you to fix an IV. I need…blood."

Sullivan swallowed as he glanced at the slumbering waif beneath the covers. "For what?"

"Since my accident, I've developed this…condition." Sarnie rubbed his chin. "It requires blood. You worked as an EMT once. You've had medical training."

"Sure thing, Boss. I have my kit around here somewhere." Sullivan rummaged through drawers and closets until he had recovered a worn, black pouch filled with syringes, needles, and plastic bags and lines. "What if she doesn't want to give you her blood?"

"Oh, she will."

The girl on the filthy mattress woke with a start, as if locked onto a vague threat. Her eyes darted back and forth between the two men as she reached for her clothes to cover herself.

"Sully, give me a moment with her." He waited until the man had shuffled into the kitchen before dropping onto the mattress beside her. "What's your name, young lady?"

She flinched and pulled her tee shirt in front of her nose.

The damn smell again.

"Destiny." A muffled response.

Well, isn't that appropriate. "You are a beautiful young lady, Destiny. Do you know what I want from you?"

She sighed, uncovering her nose. "I think I can guess." She let her clothing fall, revealing the colorful history tattooed across her exposed skin. "You can have it," she whispered, "if you can get me one more fix from Sully."

"Oh, no, you misunderstand." Sarnie reached for her shirt and gently maneuvered her head through the stained collar, using his opposite hand to sweep her long hair free as if delivering a glissando across a harp's strings. One at a time, he helped her arms through the sleeves. She flashed a grin, and Sarnie could imagine her as a child, a mother and father pulling a soft cotton shirt over her silky head after a warm bath. Sarnie gave her mind a quick probe, lowering his eyes as he found no such memories.

"You don't want to mess with that stuff anymore, Destiny. It brings back all the sadness, the things you try to forget." Sarnie gave her mind a gentle push, nudging the painful memories from behind its bolted door.

Destiny's eyes glazed over as the images burst from their slumber: the beatings from her crack-addicted mother and the punishment she would exact with cigarettes against bare skin; the twisted body of her cat, Pickles, its sandpaper tongue protruding from the side of its mouth after her stepfather wrung its neck and left it on her bed; the crooked smile of first crush, Bobby McGavin, who handed her to three men behind an abandoned gas station in Hingham in exchange for a nickel bag of marijuana.

"You can have peace, if you want it." Sarnie stroked her hair, imposing his will with another gentle push.

"That would be nice." She lay back on the pillow and closed her eyes, a child-like smile brightening her weary face.

"And you could give life to others. Wouldn't it be nice to trade in all the pain for something better?"

"Mmm." She rubbed her eyes. "Maybe start over somewhere else. It's been hard here, you know."

"Indeed, it has. There isn't much here for you anymore. Why don't you rest a while? We'll take care of things for you."

Sarnie signaled for Sullivan to prepare the transfusion. A bead of sweat migrated from Mick Sullivan's temple as he wrapped a worn rubber tourniquet around Destiny's bicep to engorge her veins with blood. "The easiest way to do this would be a direct vein-to-vein transfusion. We'll need to have her stand up, let gravity assist the blood flow from her vein—"

"No, that won't do," Sarnie interrupted as he stroked Destiny's hair. She smiled, but kept her eyes closed. "She's resting, and I want her to stay that way."

"Okay," Sullivan raked a hand across his stubble. "That makes things a bit more difficult. I could tap an artery and use her heart's pumping action to fill your veins. I've never done that before. It's a bit riskier."

"It won't matter at this point."

"What do you mean?" Sullivan rested his hands against his hips.

Sarnie ignored him. "How long will this procedure take?"

"Depends on how much blood do you need?"

Sarnie stood. "All of it."

Sullivan's jaw dropped as he stepped backward in an instinctive retreat.

Sarnie reached out, squeezing Sullivan's ratty shirt collar in his fist. "Don't you go anywhere. You have work to do."

"But Boss, if you remove all her blood…" his voice fluttered. "I'm not going to kill—"

Sarnie squeezed his eyes shut and pushed himself into Sullivan's mind, imposing his will, removing the doubt from the man and setting a clear path for him to follow. Sarnie understood he could have simply jumped into Sullivan's body, hijacked its muscles and limbs and made it do whatever he wanted it to. That's what his kind did. But he sensed the critical juncture he had approached in the preservation of his body, and he didn't dare abandon it. Plus, the notion of dirtying himself in Sully's foul frame made the bile rise in his throat.

Sullivan swallowed, his face assuming a somber calm. "To drain her body of blood, we'll have to try another approach. I have four, five…" he swept his hand through his medical bag, "…maybe six 20-cc syringes we'll use to draw from her veins and inject into yours." He scratched his head. "We'll have to do a shit load of blood draws."

He set out six syringes on the mattress and rested a half-filled bottle of contact lens saline against Destiny's outstretched leg, one he had found behind the bathroom mirror. "We'll have to clean the syringes to keep the blood from clotting."

"How long will this take?"

"We're gonna pull about four liters of blood from her, so it's gonna take most of the day. She'll be in some pain." He nodded toward the sleeping girl on the bed.

He touched her forehead. "She won't feel a thing."

Sullivan fixed a tourniquet around Destiny's upper arm and inserted the first syringe into the vein in the crook of the elbow, pulling back on the plunger and filling the clear plastic tube. He turned to Sarnie, tapping his finger against his sticky forearm to locate a vein. He grimaced and glanced up at Sarnie with questioning eyes. "What happened to your veins?" He rubbed his thumb against his fingers in a circular motion, as if to wipe off whatever sticky film remained. "I can't find any. And your skin is…lifeless, it's like——"

Sarnie spoke deep into his mind, a gentle push against his deductions. "I'm dead, Sully. You've known for a while, but your simple brain hasn't allowed you to accept it yet. It's time to come to terms with it and move on. Just find a vein and fill the syringes with her life-giving blood."

Sullivan's mind clouded over as he set about performing his job, saying nothing as he transferred blood from Destiny's arm into Sarnie's. As the girl's veins collapsed one after another, he struggled to pinpoint deeper ones in the wrist, the feet, under the tongue, anywhere he could stick a needle. The work proved slow and arduous, the hours passing with little progress. Sometimes he would hit Sarnie's vein and release blood through his circuitry; sometimes he would miss and inject blood into his muscles and interstitial spaces. Every ten minutes or so, he dismantled the syringes and cleaned them with saline, slowing the process.

As Sarnie lay prone on the mattress beside Destiny, Sullivan plunged a deep red plasma bolus into his arm. Warmth grew in a meandering pathway toward his shoulder and into his chest. A faint palpitation fluttered against his chest, then another.

"Quick, inject me again!"

Sullivan pulled another twenty cc's from Destiny's arm and transferred it into Sarnie's. The warmth grew, and he sensed his heart pound out a series of tentative beats before quitting.

"Son of a bitch!" Sarnie rose from the mattress. "We have to speed up the process, Sully."

"There's no way, Boss. I told you it would take—"

"What if you had all the blood right beside you?" Sarnie cut him off, rising from the bed. "You could fill your syringes one after another and inject me, correct? I could inject myself, too."

"Well…if I had a bucket of blood beside me, and someone to help, yeah." He chuckled. "It would cut the time in half, I'd say."

A bucket of blood. Sarnie rubbed his chin and peered about the apartment. "Where do you keep your cleaning supplies?" As if he ever cleaned this shithole.

"Hallway closet beside the bathroom. Why?"

Sarnie ignored him as he dashed across the living room and pulled a bucket from the closet, a dried-out mop head stuck to the bottom. He shook out the dirt coating its bottom and placed it beside the mattress. Positioning Destiny's head partially off the pullout couch's mattress, he pulled a gleaming blade from his pocket. The girl's external jugular vein pulsed blue against her pale skin. She stirred from her slumber, reaching her hands to her throat as if sensing a threat.

"My arms hurt," she mumbled, reaching down and rubbing the venipuncture sites in small circles. She attempted to raise her head but couldn't, Sarnie's imposed comfortable fatigue thwarting her efforts.

Sarnie closed his eyes and pushed her again, granting her mind peace. She would be in no more pain. He placed her arms by her side. "It's nearly over, Destiny. Close your eyes and you'll be home soon."

A small grin played on her dried lips. "Thank you."

Sarnie positioned her head off the end of the mattress and jammed the knife into her neck, aiming for the blue jugular, but sending the knife much deeper. The high-pressure carotid artery he had severed sent a blood geyser jetting across the mattress and onto the floor as if sprayed from a firehose, costing them much of Destiny's precious life force.

"Grab the bucket!" Sarnie shouted.

Sullivan corralled the bucket and held it against Destiny's neck, shielding them from the blood shower.

As Destiny's heart slowed, the blood ebbed from the wound, slowing to a gentle trickle. Sullivan placed the bucket beside the mattress where it caught the runoff from her neck.

"Fill the syringes and hand them to me."

Sullivan pulled back on the plungers two at a time, slurping the viscous arterial blood into the syringes. He handed one to Sarnie and injected the boss's vein with the other, falling into a steady rhythm of filling and injecting, filling and injecting. After an hour, they had emptied two thirds of the bucket. Sarnie's heart now tapped out a steady rhythm, his limbs and torso exuding a warmth palpable to the touch.

Sarnie glanced at Destiny's withered body, almost forgetting she was there, her skin whiter than the bedsheet underneath her still frame. Her life force remained strong, and she held on valiantly to her fading existence. He entered her mind and found himself at the edge of a grassy field, the summer sun shining with exuberance as the heat bugs buzzed around him. Destiny traipsed through the waist-high grass, one hand cradling Pickles to her chest, the other popping cattails and releasing their billowing fairy dust. She leaned her head back as the fluffy seed heads danced in the air, her face exuding a peaceful radiance rivaling the anticipation in her soul.

He spoke into her mind. *"Thank you, Destiny. You can let go now."*

And she did.

* * *

RG

Weaving the Crown Vic through the narrow streets along lower Chatham's beachfront properties, Stahl pulled into the driveway of the late—or maybe not so late—Alex Sarnie. The home looked like something from a movie set, a three-story mansion with multi-level rooftop decks perched on the edge of a windswept bluff, the heaving Atlantic shimmering behind it.

"Holy shit!" RG gaped from the passenger side window as Stahl threw the vehicle into park. "I didn't think people actually lived like this."

"A bit grander in the daylight, huh?"

"I'll say. I guess Sarnie did pretty well for himself."

"Self-made millionaire. I read up on the guy. Came from nothing, some blue-collar town outside of Springfield. Put himself through community college driving trucks for Brockway Transport. Struck out on his own and built Sarnie Trucking from the ground up."

"The American dream. So, who would have killed him?"

"Million-dollar question." Stahl deliberated as he stared through the glass. "We answer that, and we'll find…the spirit, the jumper, whatever the hell Sarnie's turned into. He's looking for his killer, too."

"So, that's why we're here, to find his killer?"

"Anything pointing in that direction." Stahl popped the door handle and exited the vehicle.

"I don't get it," RG said across the car roof. "This isn't where Sarnie died. It's not like we're gonna find any of the killer's DNA in here."

Stahl leaned his forearms above the doorframe. "It's not all CSI stuff, partner. If we're gonna find Sarnie, we need to learn about his past, his friends and family, and his enemies. The people who wanted him dead. Those answers could very well be within these walls." Stahl tapped the roof and turned toward the walkway. "We just have to find them."

Mounting the steps to the porch, Stahl patted his pockets for the key to unlock the front door. RG cupped his hands and peered through the front door glass.

"Remember, in the places where life happens, secrets tend to leech into the bedding, the carpets, behind dressers and between the couch cushions. The answers all remained hidden somewhere."

"You told me Daniels had been through the residence from top to bottom. What the hell could I possibly find that he hasn't?"

"You're a fresh set of eyes." Stahl located the key and pulled it his jacket pocket. "And I need to witness up close what photographs and notes in a case file can't provide. I need to wander the empty rooms and make connections between what I observe and some note scribbled on a margin, or a word circled in red pen a hundred pages into the report. I need to let those things come to life…give birth to a theory, a hunch, or a direction to take the investigation."

"I'm just not sure how much I can help. I can't do what you do."

"Not yet, but you're a researcher, and your mind finds patterns and makes connections among variables. That's kinda what we do."

"That can't be the only reason I'm here."

"Well…" Stahl hesitated.

"What?"

"I can only witness what's here. You can sense what…isn't. Your…other abilities…well, they could be useful, too."

"Counting on me having another vision?"

"I'm counting on you to protect me from Sarnie, first and foremost. Anything else that happens is icing on the cake."

Icing. RG smacked his lips as visions of Dunkin' Munchkins flashed across his vision.

Stahl pushed the front door open and the pair entered the foyer, stepping onto a marble floor slab extending from the entryway to the French doors at the back deck. A monstrous stairwell loomed to their left, the polished banister curving upward to a plush, carpeted landing. A modest office nestled below the stairwell, across from a formal dining room. RG craned his neck upward to take in the entirety of the dwelling. Ornate crown moldings framed the walls and ceiling, and a dazzling chandelier dangled beneath a skylight like a flaming glass fountain, sending blue and yellow sparks of reflected sunlight spinning across the floor like a disco ball.

"So, here's the plan. We'll split up and go room by room."

RG scratched his head. "So, what am I looking for again?"

"Something. Nothing. Try not to think of it as searching for anything in particular. In fact, the less you actively search for, the more you'll find."

"What are you, the Zen detective?" RG jammed his hands against his hips. "Should I listen for sound of one hand clapping?"

Stahl waved him off. "Just use your observation skills. If something odd whispers to you, or something feels out of place, come get me. We'll take a closer look."

Whispers to me? What the…? RG shuffled up the steps to the second floor with a homework assignment that made no sense. *God, I hope I'm not that vague with my students.*

He wandered through the rooms, content to take the mansion tour. Stahl might be waiting for the house to whisper sweet nothings to him, but so far RG heard nothing but silence. He pressed a hand to his forehead and padded along the hallway until he came to the master bedroom. Sunlight poured through the generous windows, leaving rectangular patches at his feet like gold stepping stones across the wood flooring. RG's footsteps echoed too loudly in the empty house as he proceeded across the room, pausing to peek into closets, pull out drawers, and sift through the treasure-filled jewelry boxes and baskets atop dressers and nightstands. Was he supposed to be searching through this stuff? Or not searching?

To hell with Stahl, he didn't plan to just sit in the middle of the floor and chant 'Om.'

Graduating toward the master bathroom, he flipped the wall switch to reveal a tiled fortress with a glass-encased, walk-in shower that could easily fit five positioned directly in front of a full-length wall mirror. He couldn't hide his discomfort at the notion of showering in a display case for the world to see or catching his reflection as he dragged a soapy washcloth across his undercarriage. There weren't many features of Sarnie's house RG *didn't* envy, but he would take the modesty of his house's old Re-Bath tub and shower curtain any day.

As he stepped through the bathroom and into the walk-in closet, he ran his hand along a line of designer dresses and outfits hanging on Jessie's side. Not a speck of dust on any of the fabric. She must have worn them all. He rummaged through shoe boxes and storage bins but found nothing out of the ordinary.

Returning from the closet's far end, Stahl ran a hand along Alex Sarnie's silk suits and sport jackets on the opposite side. As he reached the end of the line, his palm smacked something embedded within one of the garments. Backtracking, he squeezed each dangling jacket until he uncovered a stone-age flip phone in one of the sport coat's breast pockets.

"Well, I'll be damned. A millionaire with a ten-dollar pre-pay TracFone?" RG mumbled, turning the device over in his hands. Had to be a burner. The guy had secrets he kept from someone.

RG tossed the phone in the air and snatched it with his opposite hand.

"Om."

* * *

Mike

Stahl wandered along the lower floor, waiting for even the smallest clue to speak to him. Except for the Chatham PD's active crime scene sticker posted on the front door, the home appeared as it had before the accident, as if the residents would be back any minute to pick up where they had left off. Ascending the stairway to the second floor, a heaviness pressed against his chest as he stepped into the little girl's bedroom. A bunk bed with mini wooden stairs leading to the upper level settled against the far wall. A bedspread hanging from the upper mattress sheltered the lower bunk, creating a secret hideout. Stahl pulled back the cover to reveal colorful crayon drawings taped to the wall and a family of dolls arranged on the bed for a tea party.

Marlie's hidden world, the place she had played and dreamed.

A sharp inhale surprised him, and he steadied himself against the bunk bed's frame. Another crime scene revealing life's cruel tendency to end in mid-sentence, when least expected. He had seen it before. A toothpaste tube with the cap off, an appointment card clipped to a fridge calendar, eyeglasses folded on a nightstand beside a tented book, or a set of car keys tossed on a kitchen counter—life's final moments frozen in time. No one gets to tidy up, pack everything away, and call it a day. Always left for someone else.

And nobody knows when it's coming.

As he toed the child's carpeted floor, Stahl's eyesight darkened as if a thunder cloud had passed above. The room glowed and flickered out like an old lightbulb, then sprang to life. As the light rose, he glanced about the space, now transformed into something different than Marlie's bedroom. He inspected the dark mahogany walls and buffed hardwood floors surrounding him, the soft light glowing from wall-mounted fixtures triggering a dazed panic.

What the fuck….?

Stahl closed his eyes and exhaled, hoping to calm the thumping heart rate pounding in his ears. A dampness spread beneath his arms. Stahl recognized the place. He had been here recently—and long ago in one of his darkest moments—but couldn't comprehend the physics of the events leading him here. He envisioned the handcrafted furniture and soothing artwork hanging from the walls of the sitting room behind him, even before pivoting to face his dark remembrances of the place. He could almost picture the funeral director, Hal Bayless, behind the huge desk, expressing his condolences as he slipped the check into his jacket's breast pocket.

Before his churning mind could fathom an explanation, throngs of mourners dressed in black flitted past him, hands reaching out to rub his shoulder and squeeze his hand as they made their way across the hallway of the funeral home and into the viewing room. He peered through the double doors, the scene's shocking familiarity playing out in his memory like a television re-run. Stepping forward, he squinted at the chamber's occupants through the sepia haze, some seated, some hovering about the room's perimeter, some kneeling before his parents' matching caskets at the front of the room, adorned with flower arrangements and dripping velvet bows. He swayed as he spied a younger version of himself against the opposite wall accepting the gentle pats on the shoulder and hugs from friends and acquaintances with a forced smile plastered to his lips. Hushed voices had created a somber murmur confined within the maple walls as he stood like a sentry beside his mother and father, as if protecting them, making up for what he couldn't do days earlier on Route 6. His eyes darted amongst the mourners, anticipating the exact moment they would sit or rise from their chairs, approach and press his palm, or drop to their knees before his parents' casket.

Stahl attempted to shake the images. He pressed his palms against his eyes and paused a moment before opening them, steadying himself against the doorframe.

When you open your eyes, it will be over, Mike. This isn't real.

Opening his eyes, Stahl's gaze tracked to his shoes still planted on the funeral home's hardwood flooring. Stahl either remained interred deep inside his own twisted memory or served as the guest of honor at Sarnie's elaborate alt-world funhouse. The mourners had vanished, seemingly into the woodwork, leaving Stahl alone in the pine-scented hallway outside the darkened viewing room.

Piercing the silence, a voice floated from the stairwell.

"Michael, we're down here. Please help us."

Oh my God. He bent at the waist and pressed his hands into his knees, sucking at the air. "It can't be."

All rational thought stalled as he dashed along the hardwood. Reaching the stairwell, he hobbled down the steps two at a time until he reached the basement landing.

The voice…her plea…

He hurried along the basement corridor and into the preparation room, the soles of his shoes screeching as he skidded to a stop. He rubbed his eyes again and shook his head in disbelief. His mind had to be playing tricks on him.

This can't be real. She's been dead for ten years.

But there she was…his mother, staring at him from a shiny autopsy table with her husband beside her.

* * *

RG

"Mike!" RG shouted as he quickened the pace along the

Sarnie mansion's hardwood floors. He held the burner eye high, hell bent on showing Stahl that all his Zen bullshit couldn't unearth a clue like the one he had in his hand. Maybe he did have a future as a cop after all.

Approaching the bedroom at the hallway's far end, RG yelled to his partner once again. Flickering light spilled from the room, sending a strobe light pattern flashing across the floor.

RG entered the child's room and toggled the light switch, squinting inside the dimming chamber. The little girl's pastel-colored walls remained visible in the dark, but with each burst of light, rich wood paneling emerged from the decorated drywall.

"Mike, where are you?"

He pressed his eyes shut and placed his hand over the ring, hoping it might show him something. Anything. It didn't take long before the inside of Bayless Funeral Home grew before his eyes, morphing into a three-dimensional shape against Marlie's bedroom wall. No. Wait. The wall panels extended *through* the little girl's room, the two structures appearing to balance at the crux of different worlds. He sensed a lurch in his stomach, a hidden force pulling him into the unknown. He reached for the doorjamb and braced his legs to maintain one foot in each realm as the room swayed. He sensed he had a choice as to whether he should stay put or flip into the vision, if that's what it was, and end up back in Bayless's house of bodies. His odds of success would plummet without Kacey or Morrow with him, but his friend had stumbled into something beyond his capabilities and would never find his way out without him.

Dammit! And this was my day to sleep late.

RG waited for the light flicker to expose the funeral home's chestnut walls before reaching over to twist his ring. Marlie's room appeared to bend and fold before him, leaning at an impossible angle, as if the home had separated from its foundation and dangled from the bluff. RG grasped at the bedpost for purchase, but the pivoting room poured him from the carpeting onto the buffed floors of the funeral home's sitting room. He tumbled forward, wrapping his arms around his head for protection as he skidded along the polished floors and impacted the near wall with a crunch. Jumping to his feet, he reached to his woozy head to confirm the wall hadn't knocked it from its perch before stumbling toward the laboratory basement. Picking up speed along the corridor, he sprinted down the curved stairwell until he reached the preparation room and peeked his head through the doorway. Hal Bayless gripped the overhead hose's nozzle and hosed off Stahl's naked, dead parents. Blood leaked from the gashes in their faces and necks and slurped into the floor drain below them.

A stunned Mike Stahl stood gaping at the bodies.

"Dr. Granville, so glad you could join us," the doctor said, waving him inside. "Your friend only had a chance to view his beloved mother and father after I finished with them. But now he can take a good look and see what I had to work with."

RG stepped into the room as Stahl gazed across his parents' broken figures frozen in death's paralyzing mold. His father's head resembled a melon left too long in the sun, soft and mushy at the point he had vaulted through the windshield and impacted the oncoming vehicle. Even from a distance, RG could view the scrambled brain matter beneath the shattered skull pieces, and the man's neck bent at a near impossible angle. His mother's face revealed a roadmap of lacerations and slashes from flying glass, and her sternum remained crushed from the impact, maybe the steering column. She resembled one of those Saturday morning cartoon characters after an anvil had dropped from above.

Stahl approached the bodies. "Oh, God."

"Don't worry, Mr. Stahl. I'll stuff lots of filler into her. You won't even notice the indentation." Bayless turned off the hose. "And I'll rebuild your father's skull. It'll be like trying to reassemble a cracked egg, but I'll make it so you can't even tell."

Stahl reached for a white laboratory coat hanging from the rack to cover his mother's naked body, but it fell from his grip when her eyes fluttered open and she snapped her head to the side. One of her eyes lay crushed and oozing from the socket.

"You sonofabitch!" She sat up.

Stahl backpedaled, crashing into the metal cart behind him, autopsy tools, chisels and scalpels, flying from their perch and clanging onto the tile floor.

"Too busy to drive us home that night, were you? Sure you were. Now look at us!" She reached over and palmed her husband's head, pressing her fingers against the swollen skull until she punctured another section with a soft pop.

Stahl's Adam's apple bobbed up and down in his throat as he tried to swallow. "Mom, I—"

"We called you over and over. Figured you were probably drunk again. Isn't that what we thought, Ralph?" She poked her mangled husband. "Well, he's no help."

Stahl's eyes darted back and forth between his parents, his mouth frozen in a contorted gasp.

"All this is your fault." She reached into her eye socket and scooped out the gelatinous paste with a finger, flinging it onto the floor with a splat. "Just look at this mess."

As she glared at him with contempt in her one good eye, a smacking sound rose in RG's ears, pulling his gaze toward the source. Bayless stood in a pool of blood behind Stahl, a gleaming trocar jutting from his neck. His swollen tongue protruded from his mouth as he struggled to swallow.

RG glanced toward the metal examination tables, but the bodies of Stahl's parents had disappeared, or had never been there; he couldn't be sure. Sensing a presence building like a wall behind him, RG pivoted to face the threat. Tendrils from a decay- and formaldehyde-rich odor snaked into his nostrils.

Where are you, you sonofabitch?

The room grew silent, his ears muffled as if wrapped in a wet towel. The voice grew from the middle of his brain, swirling like a gale and bouncing off his skull as it rose in a hellish crescendo. "Get out of my house!"

RG and Stahl locked gazes, the detective's wide eyes an obvious tell that he had heard the voice, too. "We gotta get out of here, Mike! Follow me!"

Exiting the preparation room, RG and Stahl hit the stairs and double-timed it to the sitting room. "Grab my arm. This may be a bumpy ride."

As Stahl hooked a claw around his bicep, RG twisted the ring. His vision flickered as the room shifted beneath his feet. His legs dropped from underneath him as the room pitched and yawed, Bayless's sitting room wall opening into Marlie's bedroom. The pair flipped into the mutual dimension, shooting across Marlie's floor, their limbs ending up tangled in a heap beside the bedroom door.

"What the hell just happened?" Stahl dragged himself from the floor and rose to a knee.

"Sarnie having a little fun." RG stood on shaky legs. "Let's get out of here before he loses his sense of humor."

They legged along the hallway and down the sweeping staircase, Stahl's bad hip slowing their progress. Stumbling across the marble floor, RG threw open the heavy door and the pair scrambled off the porch. Collapsing into the front seat, Stahl keyed the engine and jammed his foot on the gas, leaving twin tire impressions in the seashell driveway. As they put more distance between the Vic and Sarnie's home, the detective let out a sigh and cranked the AC, resting his hands on the wheel and raising his elbows to let the icy breeze dry his armpits.

"Sarnie showed me…terrible things."

"I know. I saw them, too, Mike. It wasn't real. None of it." But RG sensed that what they both saw today was an accurate rendering of what may have been.

"I'm thinking it's time to go back to being a detective, leave the supernatural encounters to the experts."

"What you saw would have shaken anybody up, trust me. But we still need you, if that's any consolation. Thinking we could sneak up on Sarnie was a mistake." RG reached into his pocket and pulled out the cell. "I almost forgot. I have something for you."

Stahl reached across the passenger seat and grabbed the phone. "What is this?"

"Oh, just a little something from the house."

"Where'd you find it?" Stahl turned the device over in his hand.

"I sat in the lotus position in the master bedroom chanting, and it just dropped into my lap."

"Fuck you." Stahl pressed the 'on' button but couldn't revive the dead device. He pulled the vehicle to the curb and reached behind his seat, pulling out a manila envelope. He pulled off the paper strip and dropped the device inside. "We already recovered an iPhone from Sarnie's body after the accident, so this one has to be a burner."

"So, today wasn't a complete failure. You learned about Sarnie's connection with Big Mac, and I found you some evidence."

"And I witnessed part of my parents' autopsies…" Stahl blew out a breath and dragged the back of his hand across his eyes. After composing himself, he tossed RG the evidence envelope. "Hold onto this. We'll bring it to the tech guys at the station, have them charge it up and analyze the SIM card. See what's inside."

"Looks like Sarnie had secrets."

"Where secrets lay buried, lies grow." Stahl tapped the steering wheel as he stared through the glass. "But beneath the lies, you find the truth."

They drove in silence before Stahl pointed to the envelope and mumbled under his breath. "Too bad you're the 'Fugitive Professor,' or you might have made a good cop."

RG settled into his seat with a grin. *My thoughts exactly.*

CHAPTER NINE

Thursday, March 24

RG

The sunlight glinted off the rich aqua-blue seawater and pierced his retinas like July Fourth sparklers, forcing his eyes closed and leaving diamond-star imprints across the back of his eyelids. RG inhaled the salt air as he leaned against Kacey. The humid, seawater taste leached down his throat as he swallowed and revived memories of a lifetime by the ocean.

But RG had never seen this ocean before.

This one didn't have a name RG knew of. It swelled and rolled along the surface of a parallel world, one only described in his father's pained recollection. The rich sky and ocean blues took the visual spectrum into overdrive.

The tidy, weather-beaten inn stood like a sentry across the street from the sea, listing imperceptibly forward, as if bracing itself against half a century of battering winds and storm surges. Vivid, colored flowers, nestled inside hanging planters, swayed in the breeze as the woman reclined on a swing suspended from the knotty pine beams spaced along the underside of the wraparound porch's overhang. The guests had finished brunch along the patio, and she had settled the tabs and cleared the dishes. Now, a cool drink sweated on the table beside her as she pressed a palm against her forehead.

The innkeeper took a sip from her beverage and gazed toward the ocean. RG recognized the stoop in his mother's overworked frame, the effort lines carved into her hands and face as if they'd followed her here, staking their claim on her from across a distant plane. Her haggard appearance reminded him how hard his mother struggled to make ends meet after his father's death. How she would return home and collapse on the couch in the tidy Revere beach house's sunroom, a palm pressed to her forehead, the window slats cracked no more than a few inches, but enough to allow the salt air to perform its healing ritual. A moment's rest before she had to do it all over again. And amidst the struggle and fatigue, the eternal mourning for his father. RG squinted through the glare at the face he hadn't beheld in over a decade, trying to hone in on the truth between the composite his memory had constructed and the living image before him.

He perched on a bench against the seawall extending along the waterfront. Casual eateries, bed and breakfasts, and gift shops dotted the boardwalk, just like on every other water-front in every universe—at least the ones he had visited. Swiping a line of sweat from his forehead, he shed a clothing layer as he glanced toward the inn, spring in his world not matching the season in which he found himself in this one. Wherever *this* was.

RG reached for Kacey's hand as he gazed at his mother's

form, like viewing a distant recollection in real time, and his mind quickly sifted through a bittersweet memory burst: rolling along Beach Street in Revere with the windows down as they warbled off-key to forgettable songs from the eighties she loved so much; Monopoly and Scrabble on the living room's threadbare carpet, a fevered July breeze shimmying the curtains as an ensemble of heat bugs played a spiraling buzz-saw finale; staring at the heavens with his mother's head nestled on his pillow, hundreds of glow-in-the-dark star stickers pressed into the ceiling creating the illusion he could gaze straight through the roof and into the sky, a hidden universe existing just for them. RG fought the biting urge to mount the inn's creaky steps, throw his arms around her, and bury his face into her neck. Then sit beside her like he used to, revel in her distinctive laugh. His throat hitched as reality reasserted its presence.

She wouldn't even know who he was.

She would have no sense of displaced longing, no loss for a son she never had, no overpowering need to be near him or to run a hand through his hair. Still, the ring had told him to come, had directed him here for a reason. Its potential had blossomed in ways he could never have imagined when he first accepted it from Morrow. He figured he would be able to communicate with her in some way, he just didn't know how yet.

He absently twisted it around his finger. Kacey gave his forearm a squeeze, as if she could sense his anxiety.

"So, what's the plan?" she asked, parting the blowing curtain of hair from her face as the wind picked up off the ocean.

He rubbed a hand across his stubbled chin. "I think we wait."

"You think?"

"I don't know yet."

"Maybe we should just go up and talk to her. See if—"

"Out of the question," he interrupted. "The ring will let me know what to do. It brought us here, didn't it?"

She nodded. "So, we're winging it again?"

"I think our seat-of-the-pants approach has served us pretty well till now."

"Well, we haven't died yet. Should have on more than one occasion…wait a minute, you actually did once."

"That doesn't count."

"Getting blown out of a house doesn't count?" Kacey turned toward the inn, her jaw dropping. "Um, don't look now, but your mother's heading straight toward us."

RG bolted to his feet as Helen scampered across the street and descended the steps to the boardwalk leading past their bench.

Kacey yanked his arm and dropped him onto his seat, his teeth clicking together from the abrupt impact. "Real smooth. You trying to draw attention to yourself?"

"Shit, I didn't expect her to come *this* way. What do we do?"

"Why don't you ask the ring?"

RG rolled his eyes.

"Just relax. If she makes eye contact, say 'hello.' That's all. Tell her what a beautiful day it is."

"Beautiful day…" he mumbled.

"Or you could say, 'Hi, I'm your son from another world. Oh, I'm sorry, let me get you some smelling salts.'" She squeezed his hand. "How about I handle this."

Helen Granville stepped onto the boardwalk and ambled toward RG and Kacey.

"Any word from the ring?" Kacey mumbled from the corner of her mouth.

Helen nodded to them with a smile as she strolled past, then stopped and glanced across the street at the inn. "You two choose the wrong bench?" She spoke to them in a language they understood implicitly, the language of every living creature, the language of all realms.

"Pardon?" Kacey smiled at the woman, sending a gentle elbow into RG's ribs. But he remained parked with his mouth open, his eyes glued to his mother.

"You're missing the scenery. This one gives you a beautiful view of the ocean." She pointed to the bench opposite them. "Yours only lets you stare at that dilapidated old inn."

"We think it's a beautiful inn, don't we, honey?" She jabbed RG in the ribs again, but he remained frozen like a statue. A brief grunt tumbled from his lips. "Do you work there?"

Helen lowered herself onto the opposing bench, its parched wood creaking under her weight and years of exposure to the salt air and elements. "I own that old hunk of lumber and drywall." She threw a thumb over her shoulder. "Bought it many years ago…"

RG strained to listen, but her voice trailed off, winding down until it disappeared in a silent vortex, like water circling a drain. Kacey continued to engage her, their lips moving but no sound escaped their throats. The two women mimed an imagined conversation. His hair whipped in the ocean breeze, but he no long perceived the wind's howl thundering across the sand. The world's rhythms had died to a disorienting nothingness, a complete absence of sound. He shook his head, trying to dislodge the wedge inside his brain separating him from the surrounding world. He glanced at his ring, the band glowing with phosphorescent radiance.

"*Hello, RG,*" the voice whispered in the silence. "*My baby boy…coming to visit me after all these years.*"

A mist filled his eyes as the voice's unbearable familiarity reached his ears, or another part of his brain, maybe. He couldn't be sure as none of the cognitive circuitry appeared to be operating properly. He snapped his head around, searching for the source, fixing on the soundless conversation between his mother and Kacey, like a silent film flickering around him. His mouth gulped at the air like a fish out of water, attempting to feed his oxygen-starved brain but he couldn't sift out enough of the precious gas to assemble coherent thoughts. When he gazed at his mother across the boardwalk, she hadn't so much as glanced at him. She had leaned forward to engage Kacey, showing her a book she had pulled from her shoulder bag, her mouth moving as they spoke.

"She doesn't recognize you, but I do," the voice sounded. *"Your presence floods her with good feelings. That's why she's jabbering away with a complete stranger."*

RG closed his eyes. *"Who…who are you, then?"* His lips didn't move, his voice resonating from his mind and into another's. But he already knew the answer to his question.

"Well…I'm her, I guess." She chuckled.

"How can that be? I'm imagining this," RG reasoned. *"I've waited so long to find you. I must be imagining your voice."*

"You're not," the voice assured him. *"I'm here, but I'm from a place she doesn't know exists. A place deep inside where we keep all our memories, our past, the pieces of the lives we've lived, the worlds we've been."*

Kacey rubbed RG's arm and turned to him. He tried to read the question communicated in her eyes as she engaged Helen, tried to read her lips, but he couldn't decipher her intentions. In the numbing silence, he simply nodded his head.

"Don't worry, you answered her. I imagine Kacey expected you to engage more, but she doesn't understand how distracted you are right now."

So, Kacey couldn't hear the voice. How could she not? She

had keener powers than he did, more practiced and refined. Her powers could probe the mind, perform split-second scans of the brain's living history and relive life's accumulated thoughts and images through long-forgotten memory residues. And she couldn't pick up his mother's words pounding in his brain? Somehow, they remained walled off from hers as they spilled into his. Something had happened here deeper than anything Kacey had ever tapped into, and greater than he had ever experienced in his short time with caretaker powers. He grasped his ring, its glowing edge warm to the touch.

"I sensed your father once." She reflected a moment. *"Benton came to me, but he didn't stay long. I suspect he recognized an uneasiness, a longing inside me. He thought he had caused me pain, but he had set me free, unleashing feelings I hadn't confronted for many years. I wish he had stayed longer. I wish he had returned."* Helen continued to engage Kacey on the boardwalk, but her eyes fluttered closed for a moment, as if flooded with a bitter memory.

"Being near you proved too hard for him," RG said. *"Not being able to reach out to you."*

"How do you know?"

"He told me all about it."

"You…see him?"

"From time to time. He has a unique power." The women had risen from their benches, still immersed in conversation. Helen pointed toward the horizon across a sparkling sea. RG could only imagine where their conversation took them. Taking his cue, he rose to his feet and joined them but still remained entombed in a glass-walled, sound-proof chamber, his only focus, the still communication between him and a long-buried part of his mother.

"I sensed that about him. I also recognize something surging inside you. Something even bigger. In Kacey, too."

"We both have dad's gift."

"Is that how you're able to find me across the boundary of life and death?"

"You're the one who found me. You're the one who spoke to me in my dream."

"I sense darkness, something getting closer to you. It has you in its sights."

RG couldn't be sure whether she glimpsed the future, or the recent past. *"How do you know?"*

"You're my son, and a mother senses things about her child. When you were a boy, I could read everything about you in your face…your joy, your sadness, every little thing hidden within your smile. I couldn't explain it then. Just like I can't explain the darkness hovering around you now."

RG hesitated. *"You said…something awful is coming for me. What do you foresee?"*

"I can't say for sure, RG. I don't share your gifts. But I sense danger."

"I've been in danger before. How come you've never spoken to me before? Why now?"

"I've never had a feeling like this before. It's as if you possess a spiritual light that glows inside me. It speaks to me. Not in words, but in light and darkness."

"I don't understand." RG lifted his gaze to Helen, the Helen who didn't recognize him. Her features hardened as she swept her hair back against the wind. Her voice resumed.

"A horrifying darkness has invaded me. It's powerful and it's competing for your presence, blotting out your light. I fear it's…stronger than you. That's why you're in danger. Kacey, too."

"Tell me more."

"I don't have anything else for you. Just be careful."

His mother checked her watch and secured her bag over her shoulder. He didn't have long.

"Can I come back to see you again sometime?"

"I'd like that."

"I want to hug you, but I'm guessing I shouldn't."

Her soft chuckle sent a burst of warmth through him. *"That might startle her. If she ever spotted you coming again, she might walk the other way."*

"She? You mean…you."

"She…me, they're the same. Best to just remain close. Come to the inn for a meal sometime. Bring Kacey. They'll talk…and I'll come find you again."

The sounds of the world rose in RG's ears like a crescendo of wind and pounding surf, the women saying their goodbyes.

"What a nice treat chatting with you." Helen gave her son a polite nod. "Maybe we'll run into each other again."

"I'm sure we will. We love the beach. And this spot…" Kacey surveyed the landscape. "… could be something right out of heaven."

"You come by the inn sometime and say hello." Helen squeezed Kacey's arm.

After Helen had put distance between them, Kacey collapsed onto the bench, throwing her hands up in the air.

"We travel across worlds to see your mother, and you don't say anything?"

* * *

Monday, March 28
Alex

In the days following Destiny's sacrifice, physical changes surged through Alex Sarnie. He had a physical connection to his body he hadn't experienced since before the accident. Instead of manually controlling his body like a crane operator, dormant nerve fibers awakened to transfer the commands from his brain to his muscles. The jelly-like pus seeping through his skin had cleared, and he could sense the heated blood bathing his muscles and tendons underneath the dermis. The maggots disappeared, along with the formaldehyde odor, allowing him to shed the medical wraps constricting his midsection. He experienced thirst…and hunger, savoring the variety of food and drink he only thought he had appreciated during his short stay on earth. He could detect light and dark bursting, his vision sharpening with each passing day. But while his heart continued to squeeze the healing elixir through his core and extremities, the pump would flutter and halt after a day or so, sputtering like a car engine sipping the final drops of gasoline from a dusty fuel tank. Somehow the serum's life force didn't sustain the positive effects. Maybe the dirty, drug-infected serum in Destiny's veins corrupted his recovery. He didn't know. But he would need to search until he found the right donor.

It fell on Mick Sullivan to become a different type of supplier for Sarnie, to harvest the life-building blood from his regular customers, and anyone else he could find, by luring them to the Barnard Street house. Sarnie had made it clear he wanted the purest blood he could find, the blood of the young and healthy. But if any more blonde runners in sports bras and Spandex disappeared in Chatham, it would raise red flags, and he agreed Sullivan's contacts proved safer and quicker to gather. Sullivan had them coming in and out all hours of the day for his product, and no one appeared to notice when one of the forgotten souls never returned from the run-down structure behind the abandoned service station.

Sarnie's right-hand-man had transformed the kitchen into an efficient transfusion center, like something you would find in a licensed medical facility. He had arranged the room with an array of different gauge needles, plastic blood bags and lines, antiseptic wipes, cotton balls and medical tape resting on a small table beside a gurney and IV stand. They had emptied the refrigerator of spoiled meats and cheeses and scrubbed out the mold, allowing Sullivan to do the initial work on his donors and store the blood until Sarnie required his transfusion. It also fell on Sullivan to dispose of the victims once he had drained their blood. Along the moldy bathroom floor tile, now stained red, Sullivan had assembled a variety of hacksaws, blades, and chisels to solve the most stubborn bones, tendons, and connective tissue. A chest freezer had been set up beside the tub, and various-sized cuts of meat wrapped in butcher paper and packed together like jig-saw puzzle pieces filled the confined space. Sarnie had reminded Sullivan he would need to come up with a disposal plan, either heave the meat chunks down the steep highway embankments he travelled at night or brave the Atlantic swells to feed the marauding great white sharks circling off Nauset Beach. His choice, but he would need to make a decision soon.

The house had gotten a bit crowded.

Ellie

Ellie lay upon the freshly washed bed sheets at Mass General, her limp body clean and odor free from the sponge bath she had received that morning. The nurses had positioned her hands at a wider angle around the towel, and her knees' knobby protrusions pressed against each other beneath the sheets. Despite her body proving nothing more than an imposition to her, Ellie appreciated the attention the hospital staff showed it. She sympathized with the staffer who drew the short straw and had to wipe down her living corpse.

But, her fading shell did provide a place to rest, a weigh station between this world and the next. She could regroup and recharge her batteries before she ventured out and explored.

As she rested, a tug jerked at her body—or her mind, she couldn't tell—drawing her from her resting place. She plunged into a pitch-black, soundless chasm, the weightlessness registering as a lurch in the pit of her stomach, like the sensation of being on her board and taking a drop along the face of a wave.

This is it. I must be dying.

As she tumbled along the soothing passageway, fragrances and sounds swelled in her senses, rising in intensity as if growing around her. The darkness parted as light appeared, the outline of a familiar structure looming in her cloudy vision. She stepped forward and cracked open the front door, glancing at the lettering stenciled across the door's frosted glass.

The Pancake Man.

"Where in the hell…?" Ellie scanned the bustling diner as she stepped inside, winding her way through the crowd jostling for open tables. Wandering the aisles, she took in the red-cushioned booths and rotating counter stools, the checkerboard black and white tiled floor, and the gleaming corrugated tin adorning the walls behind the counter. A colorful Wurlitzer in the diner's back corner spun out a familiar tune she couldn't name.

She glanced through the server's window and grinned at the sounds of spatulas scraping home fries from the greasy grill and wire whisks swishing eggs in tin bowls. An imposing figure emerged from the kitchen and filled nearly the entire doorframe. He wore an intimidating scowl, grease stains pasted across his apron like buckshot. But Ellie had seen that expression before, his 'don't order another breakfast burrito' face.

"Sal!" Ellie held her arms out and raced into the man's

bear-like embrace. "Are you trying to scare away the customers again?"

"Makes for an easier workday, doesn't it?" Sal lifted her off the ground and whirled her around. "Ellie, my friend. I've missed you so much." He held her at arm's length as if inspecting her for the first time, a wide grin spreading across his weathered face. "You must be hungry. You sit at the counter, and I'll make you my special French toast."

"With powdered sugar?"

Sal grinned. "The way you like it."

Ellie positioned herself on an empty stool and leaned her elbows on the counter. "Sal, what are you doing here? Are you…" She didn't want to ask.

He chuckled. "I'm alive and well, as are you. And you've never looked as beautiful."

Ellie glanced down at herself. She lifted each arm and inspected them. She stood and peeked at the mirror behind the counter. She wasn't the gaunt, emaciated figure from the hospital anymore; somehow, she had gotten her body back. Maybe the trip through the darkness had restored her, but she also considered that she might have chosen her old form before venturing out.

"Here." Sal hoisted a slice of apple pie from beneath the glass-covered plate and placed it in front of her. "While you wait for your French toast."

Ellie grasped her fork and dug in, the crispy wafer crust and sloppy apple filling tumbling into her mouth with a euphoric flavor burst. When had she last eaten?

Sal leaned over and pinched off a piece. "So, what brings you back here, Ellie? Itching to put an apron back on again?" He raised an eyebrow. "We got a full house and could use you on the floor."

She had waitressed here since the summer she turned

sixteen but couldn't bear the thought of jumping into the fray at the moment. "I'd love to." Her voice fell as she placed the fork on her plate. "But I think I'm here for another reason."

The words had barely escaped her lips when the diner's back door swung open. Ellie glanced at the familiar woman peering about the room and rose from her stool. "Hold on a minute, Sal," she said, raising her index finger. "I suspect my reason just walked through the door."

Ellie stepped to the middle of the aisle as the woman scanned the restaurant. They locked gazes. Ellie sensed the invasion, the gentle probing of her mind. At the same time, the woman's imaginings came alive in Ellie's head, and she witnessed her life in an instant, a high-definition burst of joy and pain, encounters with the worst the universe had to offer —a man on fire and a troll-like child. She did not resist Ellie's invasive probe, but let her view it all, everything inside her. The woman possessed a boundless energy revving within her frame like a race car's engine perched at the starting line, ready to protect those who needed it, bolstered by a deep, flowing love for those around her and the world she inhabited. She had come here to find Ellie.

The woman navigated the crowd until she stood toe to toe with Ellie. She reached for her arm. "What do you say we find a table?"

"How 'bout we sit at the counter? Sal's whipping up some French toast for me, and I don't want to miss it. I'm starving."

"I'm guessing it's been a while since you ate."

They lowered themselves onto the counter stools. Ellie offered Kacey a fork and pushed the pie toward her. "What's your name?"

"Kacey Granville."

Ellie told Kacey her name, reaching her hand out in an

awkward teenage introduction. "I've been looking for you. I think we're supposed to meet."

Kacey took a bite of pie. Her gaze darted from Ellie's eyes to the pastry and back again. "Thanks. I guess I'm starving, too."

"Good, isn't it? Sal's a master with dessert."

Kacey's eyes fluttered closed as she took another bite.

"How did you find me?"

"I sensed you, Ellie. The same way you've been tracking me. I'm just not sure how you ended up here. This place only exists in my mind. It's not real."

Ellie glanced about the diner. "It has to be real, doesn't it?"

"I guess so, but I suspect it's more complicated than that. I figured only I could find this place, but somehow you have, too."

"Maybe you brought me here. I'm glad you did because it's like coming home. I used to waitress here." Ellie glanced about the diner. "But it looks different from the Pancake Man I know."

Kacey glanced about the space. "It's constructed from my childhood memories. It's how I remember it."

"Well, that explains things. And I guess you haven't met Sal yet, either."

Kacey rested her chin against her fist. "I don't think he worked here when I used to come here as a child."

"God, I figured Sal has always been here." Ellie pressed a finger into the apple pie filling pooling on the plate and licked it clean.

"I heard that." Sal's booming voice thundered from the kitchen.

Kacey and Ellie stifled a laugh as they finished off the pie.

"Somehow you've added your own memories to my vision,

made it your own." Kacey rested her fork beside the plate. "Ellie, this is a special place."

"I know."

"Not just because we like the food or because our friends are here." Kacey chose her words with care. "It's a door, Ellie…to the next world."

"What? Like…heaven?"

"Not exactly." Kacey dabbed the corners of her mouth with a napkin. "But it's *this* world's last stop."

Ellie rubbed the goosebumps spreading across her arms. "So, it's *my* last stop?"

Kacey dropped her hand on Ellie's forearm. "You must have had an idea, lying in that hospital bed."

"I guess so. But hearing it from your mouth…" She lowered her head.

Sal appeared behind the counter with two steaming plates of French toast, confectioner's sugar sifted across their surfaces like a light snowfall. "After watching you guys with the pie, I figured two servings might be best."

"Thanks, Sal," Ellie said. "You read my mind."

Sal nodded at Kacey as he retreated into the kitchen.

Kacey poured a dollop of syrup onto her stack and dug in. "You have great things in store for you, you know. You have powers."

"Like yours?"

"Just like mine. You're a protector, a caretaker. And these powers will blossom as soon as you move into the next world."

"But you're not…dead." Ellie leaned closer and tested Kacey's arm with a gentle poke. "How do you know about the next world?"

"For some reason, I acquired these powers in life. When you…move on, you'll be responsible for a human soul, to protect him and guide him into the next world when it's his or her time."

Ellie pictured her brother Chris. "I suspect I've already gotten my assignment."

"Already?" Kacey smirked. "Funny how we just understand these things, isn't it?"

"I've also been drawn to you, Kacey. And I'm sorry about startling you at the restaurant…and in your home. I shouldn't have picked up your boy. But he was so beautiful. I couldn't help myself."

"It's okay. I just got scared. That's all."

"The way I looked must have been frightening. So…horrendous."

Kacey lifted Ellie's chin. "But look at you now."

Ellie forced a grin as she caught her reflection in the mirror behind the counter.

"I'm glad you found me. It's my job to show you what you need to do in the next world, teach you about your powers."

"When do we start?"

"How 'bout now. Well, after we eat." Kacey stuffed another syrup-drenched forkful into her mouth.

Ellie glanced about the diner. "Would it be all right if I stayed here for a while? Before I…" She glanced at the front door. "Well…you know."

"Of course. The longer you stay, the more I can teach you."

"I'd like that. I'm not sure I'm ready to go through that door yet."

"The last step remains the hardest. But you'll be ready." The two sat in silence as they finished their French toast. "And I'm not going to let you leave until I've shown you everything you need to know."

Sal's hulking frame emerged from the kitchen with an

apron dangling from his hand. "Couldn't help overhearing your conversation. If you stay, you gotta earn your keep." He tossed Ellie the apron as he surveyed the bustling restaurant. "We could use the help."

Ellie fashioned the cloth around her waist and dug into the pockets, pulling out her order pad. She blew out a breath as she gazed at the sea of hungry bodies. "Wish me luck."

"You'll be fine." Kacey rubbed Ellie's arm. "Everyone here, they're all good people."

"Can we start our training after the rush?"

"I'm not going anywhere." Kacey checked her watch and handed Sal her empty plate.

"Well in that case," Sal said, grabbing a plate from the server's window. "How about an order of silver dollar pancakes?"

CHAPTER TEN

Monday, March 28

Alex

Sarnie rested on the wooden bench across from the inn. The ocean exploding against the shore behind him triggered memories of Jessie and Marlie at the National Seashore, silhouettes skipping through the frigid surf against a sparkling blue horizon. He shook his head to deflect the recollection. Closing his eyes, he welcomed the brilliant noonday sun pressing its heat against his skin. But the scorching rays didn't satisfy him the way they used to, when he had a fully functioning body. Something was off, despite his body's tingle after recently feeding his veins with a robust infusion and warmed blood circulating through his limbs; despite his heart tapping out a steady rhythm in his chest and a sturdy pulse throbbing beneath his skin. It would get better, he promised himself. If he could consume enough blood, it would ignite the life force inside his body once again. But he would have to keep trying until he found the right donor.

He glanced to his left at the shops and restaurants along the boardwalk, tourists and beachgoers parading about under a cloudless sky. After having a bit of fun with the detective prowling around his home, Sarnie had rested his eyes a moment as he reclined on Mick Sullivan's couch. When he opened them, he had found himself here. He wasn't sure where he was, but the vivid colors and contrasts told him he had traveled far from his former world. He also sensed he wasn't dreaming, and someone—or something—had brought him here for a reason.

His own powers both surprised and confused him. Some things he could control, like when he entered people's minds and scanned their memories in an instant, or when he controlled their thoughts and actions with a gentle push. He had controlled, and even fabricated, the detective's remembrances in ways he had never imagined. But other things controlled him, leaving him questioning whether he had charge of his powers or the other way around. Like today. Sarnie had no idea how he ended up in a seaside town in a world he didn't recognize.

As he contemplated his odd circumstances, he glanced at the inn across the street, catching sight of a woman on the porch. She rubbed a forearm across a weary brow, stringy hair wisps escaping her clip and tumbling into her eyes. She navigated a table maze in the outdoor café, clearing plates and dishes into plastic bins, repositioning tabletop centerpieces, and pushing in chairs.

Setting a heavy bin on a table, she paused to rest, glancing across the street toward the beach. As she scanned the scenic waterfront, she met Sarnie's gaze. She tilted her head as if she recognized him, or maybe she just imagined she did. Sarnie almost expected her to wave, and he threw a quick glance over his shoulder to check if someone else may have been the intended recipient of her focused stare. When he returned his gaze to the inn, the woman had resumed her work, disappearing from the porch with her bin of dirty dishes.

Blood. A voice whispered in his ear.

He snapped his head to the left and right to pinpoint its source. A chuckle echoed deep inside his brain. "Who's there?" Sarnie shouted and sprung to his feet, drawing cautious glances from the nearby boardwalk travelers. "What do you want?"

"It's not what *I* want," the voice responded. "It's what *you* want."

Sarnie pounded the sides of his head with both fists, as if he could dislodge the voice's transmitter embedded inside his skull.

"Blood, Mr. Sarnie." The voice changed, pulling from deep within and now coming at him in stereo head on, as if it had swung through his head on a pendulum. A man materialized before him, blocking his view of the inn. "You need more blood."

Sarnie sensed the sunlight dim and the warm breeze fall to a chilly wind as the man's shadow crossed his path. Sarnie jumped to his feet and gazed upward but could no longer find the sun. Everything had vanished, including the clouds and sky. The world's vivid colors faded into a chalky haze, and the sound had diminished to nothing. The boardwalk winding along the beach had emptied, replaced by an ancient stone pathway proceeding in either direction into darkness. Sarnie didn't need to turn around to recognize the ocean waves had disappeared. Somehow, beauty no longer existed in this place. He immediately lamented the loss of their thundering payload and predictable cadence. Their comforting presence.

"How did you…?" Sarnie sputtered. "Who the hell are you?"

"Thought we could talk better if you could see me…I'm the voice in your head," the man spoke, a subtle lisp slipping across his teeth. "You can call me Luther."

"Did you do all this?" Sarnie raised his hands. "Make the world go away?"

Luther tilted his head in question. "This *is* the world. My world." He gestured toward a stone slab beside the walkway. "Please. Sit."

Luther slipped from his long black overcoat in a graceful, practiced sequence and seated himself alongside Sarnie, placing the folded garment beside him and smoothing it out with his hand.

"You mean, you didn't take me there. The boardwalk across from the inn?"

Luther raised an eyebrow. "I brought you to no such place. The Barnard Street house brought you here, nowhere else."

"Sullivan's house?" Sarnie gazed at his surroundings, stone pillars climbing hundreds of feet high within the dark, rocky cave. "I guess it sent me on a short detour before I got here."

The man peeked inside Sarnie's mind, sneaking through his memories and conjuring the image of the boardwalk and the old woman on the inn's porch.

"Who is the woman?" Luther asked.

"How should I know? I closed my eyes, and there she was."

He scrunched his face and gave a quick head shake. "No matter. I must say I'm quite pleased to meet you."

"You've been contacting me, haven't you?"

Luther nodded. "We've been waiting for you a long time."

Sarnie dropped onto the bench. "Who's we?"

"All of us." Luther placed a leg over his opposite knee. He folded his hands in his lap.

Sarnie inspected the wiry man in the thick wool trousers and spotless white linen shirt, a gold pocket watch chain dangling from his vest. He resembled a historical photo, but without the nicks and blemishes, his clothing possessing a flair absent from an era when function trumped style. His tailored garments hugged his slender body with creases that traced an impeccable line along his lithe limbs. He had hailed from the leisure class, no doubt, his dialect carrying the lilt of east coast Ivy League education and old money.

"Who's us?"

"You must appreciate by now, you aren't the typical dead." Leaning an elbow against a protrusion on the stone slab, Luther rested his head against his fist and fingered the curled end of his handle bar mustache with his pinky. "It can be confusing at first. You have gifts and powers, and there are dark forces at work making decisions about who will get them and who won't."

"And you make these decisions?"

Luther pursed his lips and shook his head. "That's above my pay grade."

"But I made the cut?" Sarnie folded his arms.

"That you did." He pressed his hands together as if in prayer, tapping his fingers against his lips. He glared at Sarnie with reverence. "Do you realize no jumper has ever accomplished what you have?"

"And what's that?"

"You have successfully taken over your own body and somehow kept it alive, placing you one step closer to immortality." Luther leaned forward. "That makes you a very important man to those in my world."

"Why would immortality matter to you? I don't have any connection to you or anyone else of your kind."

"We are all connected, linked by the darkness inside." He pointed to his heart. "And we have awaited your coming." Luther stood, pacing along the stone pathway. His movements had the grace of a ballet dancer, but a savagery remained in his eyes that offset his delicate pageantry. "We have awaited the one who returns to life. He will have the power to open the doors of his world to all of us and give us eternal life."

Sarnie pressed his palm to his chest. "You're talking about me?"

Luther dropped onto the slab beside Sarnie. "You would give us a place to call home."

"What's wrong with the one you've got?"

"Observe this place where I dwell." He gestured with his hands, glancing about his domain. "I don't get a boardwalk by the sea, surrounded by light and color. I get a cold, dark, empty place, hidden away, shifted askew from everyone else's reality." He inspected his well-manicured nails as he spoke. "I deserve more than to live in shadows, relegated to the darkness. We all do."

"Listen, I appreciate your problem, but I have things I need to accomplish right now. My wife and daughter—"

"Murdered, no?" he interrupted. "Hmm…and let me guess…you're planning to take revenge on the perpetrator responsible for your death and your wife and child's." Luther's eyes changed and Sarnie could glimpse something deep inside him, as if he had peeked through a window into a dark corner of his soul where something bad had happened. So far, Luther had covered that outward layer with a colorful costume, a façade he wore to deflect from the truth and shield the unbridled fury simmering beneath the surface, as if masquerading at his own ball. A monster from hell lay coiled beneath the surface of Luther's androgynous shell, ready to rip through the lining of his skin, but when Sarnie meandered through the man's thoughts, the images disappeared in a flash.

Luther grinned. "Like what you see?"

"I could ask you the same question."

"I've seen enough inside your head to recognize you are just like us. Predators."

"Maybe I am." Sarnie leaned forward.

Luther folded his hands together. "I must say, most show a hint of fear when they witness my...hidden friend. The other side of me."

"I don't scare so easily."

Sarnie sensed a breach inside his head, Luther treading carefully through his thoughts, searching for scraps.

"You're wondering, Mr. Sarnie, how I came to be here."

"If you're gonna sift through my mind, why bother talking?"

"I prefer conversation. It's a bit more genteel and refined."

Sarnie shifted his weight. "Have it your way."

Luther stood and paced along the rocky ground. "Your world proved cruel to men like me, men who were...different. You can't imagine life years ago for a man with my...sensitivities." He brushed a piece of lint from his vest. "I longed to live as a great winged bird who could fly away from the torment, the judgment. After those men did what they did..." his eyes drifted upward, as if lost in a memory. "As I lay dying, I vowed I would return to your world and exact my revenge, like you, destroy my tormentors in unspeakable ways." His lips peeled back to reveal incisors like those of a horrific beast, something hidden inside but anxious to be let off its leash. "I imagine most of us had unfinished business in our worlds that darkened our souls and put us here."

"So, I'm heading for a place…like this?" His gaze darted about the desolate space.

"When your mission ends, you will end up like us. Somewhere between worlds. In darkness."

"In…Hell? Is that where we are?"

Luther barked out a thin, strident laugh. "My hell, perhaps." He waved his hand. "You will end up in a hell of your own choosing."

The weight of Luther's statement hung between them, leaving them in silence.

"But you can end our hell, Mr. Sarnie. Help us while you help yourself. You can lead us from the darkness."

Sarnie considered his eternal choices, hidden away, existing somewhere between worlds, or living forever in his current world. A no-brainer. "So, what's the answer?"

"Blood. That's what I've been telling you…whispering in your head."

Blood. The word hammered in his brain. "Blood will give me everlasting life?"

Luther nodded "And us."

"I'm not so sure. The blood isn't working. I've been filling my veins just about every day, and I'm still decomposing."

"Think of it as building up a tolerance. You're getting ready for the blood that will give you eternal life."

"A tolerance…to blood?"

"The life-giving blood you seek is so pure and powerful, it would kill you if you didn't build up to it slowly." Luther grinned and lowered himself onto the stone slab beside Sarnie. "It would be like injecting pure, uncut heroin into your vein. An old junkie does it and he's fine. A suburban housewife graduating from Oxycontin tries it, and she's dead."

"So, when will I be ready?"

"Soon."

"How will I know when I find it? It could be anywhere."

"You don't need to worry, it's closer than you think." Luther grinned. "And I know where it is."

* * *

Tuesday, March 29

Mike

Mike Stahl crept past the battered dumpster and approached the aged, ramshackle dwelling on Barnard Street tucked away behind the abandoned strip mall and service station off Chatham's main drag. After his adventure at Sarnie's mansion the previous week, he had vowed he wouldn't be going solo in this investigation anymore. But when he got to RG's that morning, hoping to rouse his new partner before his foggy brain could come up with an excuse, Kacey told him her husband had already left for an early class. He thought about recruiting Kacey, but with Robert Jr. in her arms and car keys jingling in hand, it was obvious she had her own day unfolding before her. He convinced himself he wouldn't need either of them for this gig. Just a quick talk with one of Sarnie's truck drivers.

No big deal.

His feet scattered paper and debris across crumbled asphalt as he crossed onto the dirt-patched lawn and stepped to the front door.

His pounding fist rattled the doorframe. "Chatham PD. Open up."

Stahl could sense a presence on the other side of the door, hesitating, waiting him out.

"Mr. Sullivan, I gotta ask you a couple of questions." The silence stretched between them. "C'mon Mick, open up."

"Fuck you! Last time you guys came around I ended up with a broken nose. I'd be a fool to let that happen again."

Stahl had no answer. The man had a point. "I understand, Mick, but nothing's gonna happen to you. We need your help." His words sounded flat and untrue as they left his mouth. Wilson Sarnie had provided Stahl with his only local lead to track down his brother. "We're trying to find Alex Sarnie's body. Someone stole it from a funeral home, and we don't have a damn clue where to start." He paused to gauge whether Sullivan bought his pitch. "We're talking to everyone who knows him. I'm aware he helped you a while back, and I'm hoping maybe you can help me."

After a long minute, the door swung open. A shirtless Sullivan gave him a nod. "Come on in."

"Thanks, Mr. Sullivan." He handed him his card. "Detective Mike Stahl."

As he stepped across the stoop, a coppery hint of blood and formaldehyde rushed past him, the same odor he had encountered during his unplanned return to the Bayless Funeral Home with RG. It swept past him like a humid wind through a subway tunnel, as if eager to escape the structure's gloomy confines. The room reeked of death and the afterlife, two things Stahl had become too familiar with lately. He glanced about the dim premises, blood stains stippling the grimy carpet and walls, the back-bedroom door closed.

Turn around. Get out.

The door clicked shut behind him, extinguishing the only natural light in the darkened hovel. Sullivan receded into the living room, a network of tattoos zigzagging across his back. Stahl's plan had been to get Sullivan talking about Sarnie, maybe extract a clue as to his whereabouts. Then he would alert the cavalry, let RG and Kacey ride in on their supernatural horses and do the rest. But his plan changed.

The weight in the pit of his stomach told him he had already found Sarnie.

He sensed the jumper's presence, coming from somewhere behind the bedroom door. Waiting. Stahl was no caretaker, but repeated trips to different worlds and encounters with their spirits must have opened up a sixth sense within him or had taken the existing five and ratcheted them up a notch. If only it had done something for his common sense. He should have waited for RG. He was foolish to think he might outsmart Sarnie again, so soon after the bizarre incident in his mansion, and his plan failed to factor in a contingency.

The jumper's unmistakable aura kick-started Stahl's adrenaline, the way a lion might initiate its prey's muscular twitches in anticipation of the coming chase. The residue from brutal atrocities performed in this place burned in his nostrils. He withdrew his HK45 but lowered his extended arm. The useless hunk of iron, even with a full magazine, would not deter what dwelled here. He listened to the fight-or-flight response choosing to wait for reinforcements. He ignored Mick Sullivan's half grin, daring him to open the door. The confident man stood like a skinny kid on the playground with a big older brother behind him, assured his protector behind the closed door would come to his rescue.

"You appear a bit antsy, everything okay?" Mick Sullivan leaned against the doorjamb separating the living room from the kitchen, enjoying his newfound advantage. Stahl could read in the man's eyes a confidence the cop would never set foot in daylight again.

"Just fine, Mick." Stahl glanced at the back bedroom, the door now cracked open. Beads of sweat slid down his temples and stung his eyes. *Keep it together.*

Sullivan chuckled. "Are you?"

Stahl considered a mad dash for the front door, but his legs weighed him down like two pillars of concrete embedded in stone. Nothing he could do at this point. He couldn't outrun a jumper. If Sarnie wanted him, he would catch him. His eyes drifted again toward the back bedroom.

Why doesn't he just come out and get it over with?

The wall clock's minute hand ticked like a hammer in Stahl's brain, marking each painful second in the still house like a countdown of his remaining breaths or heartbeats. He gazed at the bare walls, the ancient, chipped paint lighter in spots, in the shape of framed photos or art that had once warmed the room. People had lived here once, and laughed here, before the baseboard moldings bore the stains of spattered blood and matter. His eyes glazed over as he pictured his world outside this horror and death slaughterhouse, Claire and Zach leaning against him on the creaky porch swing as the ocean sounds rumbled in predictable waves through the summer's humid breeze.

Stahl waited, anticipating Sarnie's entrance. He holstered his sidearm and lowered himself onto the couch, resigned to his fate.

Might as well get comfortable.

Stahl gazed at Sullivan, leaning against the kitchen doorjamb, arms folded. "So, what do you want to talk about?"

Alex

Sarnie cracked the door of the back bedroom. He sensed the detective the moment he shuffled around the corner past the old service station and crossed the crumbling parking area to the house. His mind's assemblages streamed from his head, sailed across the open space, and slammed into Sarnie's mind like the moan of a ship's foghorn carrying across water. Sarnie glanced downward, staring at his hands' waxy skin. His body craved replenishment, and the detective's blood could serve him well.

But Sarnie hesitated.

The detective's proximity brought strange vibes emanating from the man, different than he had encountered in anyone since his recent resurrection. Sure, he had played with Stahl earlier from a distance, sending his thoughts and memories into overdrive and showing him horrific images that once had been. But the man had something about him, something special. He could sense Stahl's mortality, but he now recognized the man had been places most humans hadn't. He had no special powers, but he wore the residue of different worlds and reeked of encounters with Sarnie's kind.

He needed to understand more about the man before he killed him.

He shuffled through the man's indistinguishable and forgettable memories, but others burst forward, vivid and alive. Sarnie focused on the mind pictures approaching him, joining the detective in his own head. He paced the rickety porch behind the hanging swing as the detective rested a cheek against the woman's dark hair and sipped an iced tea, eavesdropping on their intimate conversation, hushed in the presence of their child. He swam behind him through the frigid underground pipes of downtown Plymouth, through the pitch black, silent fluid. He sensed Stahl's heart twisting and thumping against his chest, the oxygen stalled within his burning lungs. In the pipe, Sarnie reached for the detective's leg, hoping to slow him down and disrupt his remembrance, possibly bring about a different outcome and drown him in his own memory. He hesitated a moment to consider whether he could even do that, and Stahl slipped away from his grasp.

As Sarnie continued probing his mind, the detective

conversed with Sullivan, relaxed and casual, even though he sensed Sarnie's presence in the back room. The detective waited for him to show himself, get things over with, not from fear but acceptance of whatever fate awaited him. The man's bravery or indifference must have come from his experiences in the next world. His knowledge that something else awaited after this world's dress rehearsal may have helped alleviate death's universal dread.

Sarnie continued his probe, flipping through the detective's memories. He witnessed his trips through different portals and back and forth in time, his earlier confrontations with the fiery spirit in his house before the explosion, and the half-human, half-jumper he shot in the strange diner between worlds. In each recollection, another man and his wife appeared with him, along with an older man. The special three had defeated the fiery one in the detective's home and the grotesque child jumper from the past. Together, their powers proved formidable.

He stopped the sequence when he could view Granville's face.

The familiar features froze before him as he paused to examine them more closely. Granville's broad grin revealed a single tooth turned a fraction inward and reckless hair tumbled across his forehead into coffee-colored eyes. Sarnie leaned closer, squinting, as if looking at an old friend. Where did he recognize him from? He had twice sensed the man in the basement of the funeral home, once as a witness to the good doctor's murder and again when he and the detective trespassed through his house.

Looks like we're destined to meet, my friend.

Sarnie sighed. Stahl continued to engage Sullivan in the living room, as indifferent to his fate as he would be chatting with a friend. He searched the detective's mind once more to gauge what he knew so far. Thoughts and pictures swirled before his eyes, directions the case had taken him, how it had brought him here, but it remained a jumble of names, Billy Massey and Big Mac, along with wild theories and odd connections not adding up to much, yet. Nothing Sarnie hadn't gathered already.

He pressed a hand to his cold chest, feeling no heartbeat, nothing but deadness within. Sarnie had hoped his reclaimed body would have resurrected his physical senses by now, but until he could fill his veins with the immortal blood Luther had described, he would be stuck with a half living, half dead shell he wore around on his back like a turtle. Before long he would combine his otherworldly powers inside a healthy, living body and have the best of both worlds.

He should just go ahead and kill the detective, take his blood for a temporary fix.

But Sarnie also detected a meticulous and thorough nature to the man's thinking, the way the disparate images and concepts weaved together and refined his early deductions. The man could serve as a useful resource. Sarnie could tap him for his blood, but if he let him go, he could follow him and learn what he knew about his family's death. The detective would surely find out who had killed them. Sarnie could keep tabs on him as he led him directly to his killer. He could also let Stahl lead him to Granville and his team of supernatural interlopers.

Above all, Granville remained a key piece to the puzzle, inexorably linked to Sarnie's quest for immortality.

He would have to stop him.

Sarnie glimpsed Mick Sullivan through the bedroom door crack, now resting his ass on the dingy brown armchair, his rapt attention turned to Stahl. Sullivan's thoughts jabbed at Sarnie like a bee sting now. He had holed up together with the man in this shit shack out of necessity, but it had finally reached a tipping point. Sullivan stood in the living room salivating over the detective, nearly quivering in anticipation of another forced transfusion. The man had been reluctant at first with Destiny but had quickly warmed to the procedure. Sarnie occasionally caught him whistling at times while dismembering the bodies. God, the man irked him, and his patience with him had worn thin.

The man had led his pursuers to him, and Sarnie would have to tie up loose ends sooner than anticipated.

A frown curled across Sarnie's lips as he opened the bedroom door and advanced into the living room.

* * *

Mike

At some point in their conversation, a calm descended over Mike Stahl, a sense Sarnie had opted to let him go and the danger had passed. He had been in the presence of volatile jumpers before and witnessed their rage, their eagerness for destruction. But Sarnie's ire had passed like a cloud's shadow skimming across a patch of lawn. At the same time, an increased agitation had overtaken Mick Sullivan, his face resembling a child on the verge of a tantrum denied his favorite toy. Stahl could read the disappointment in his body language, the awareness Sarnie had spared the cop, for whatever reason, and whatever Sullivan had expected to happen here today wasn't going down.

Stahl leaned forward to engage with Sullivan. "Sarnie's in the back, isn't he?"

"Not sure what you're talking about?" Sullivan's eyes shifted between Stahl and the back bedroom.

Stahl shrugged. "Any reason to keep it from me at this point?"

Sullivan deliberated a moment. "I guess not."

"Why hasn't he come out?"

"Can't say for sure." Sullivan's mouth twisted as he scratched his head. "I figured you'd be dead by now."

Stahl gestured about the room. "How did you guys end up as roomies?"

"I…owe him."

"Because he helped you out a few years back, when you fell on hard times?"

"He gave me my life back. He——"

"You know he's dead, don't you?" Stahl interrupted.

Sullivan's face changed, as if he waged an internal battle between what his subconscious mind told him and what he witnessed with his own eyes. "He's just sick or something." He rose from the edge of the chair and circled the room. "I'm helping him get back on his feet." Sullivan glanced toward the kitchen.

Stahl followed Sullivan's gaze, craning his neck to peer into the room, now transformed into a low-tech medical center. A gurney and IV stand rested where a kitchen table once did, and needles and plastic blood bags lined the counters.

"The blood makes him feel better."

That's what keeps his body alive. "And you're helping him?"

Sullivan nodded. "Like I said, I owe him."

"Where do you get the blood?"

Sullivan grinned. "Where do you think?"

Stahl lowered his gaze. "How many so far?"

"Just a handful of junkies, don't matter none. Ain't no one gonna miss 'em."

"A couple young girls who run through the area have been reported missing. Know anything about them?"

"We take what we can get."

Jesus Christ. "What do you suppose happens when Sarnie's done with you? Who do you imagine ends up strapped to your gurney?"

The door to the back room opened with a slow creak, and Sarnie strode into the living room. He moved with the ratchet-like cadence of a marionette, as if someone guided his body from above instead of from within.

"Our arrangement doesn't concern you, detective," he said in a raspy voice, as if his vocal cords vibrated inside a dusty box.

Stahl stood and met Sarnie's gaze, but something about the eyes weren't right. They appeared flat and glassy like dolls' eyes, sightless and resting in their sockets. Dead skin dangled from a torn eyelid.

"I figured you might be here." Stahl viewed the living corpse before him, a body in a state of obvious decay, the skin waxy and moist. Thick gauze protruded from his open collar and wrists, cinching his body tightly to stanch the odor permeating the stuffy enclosure. The jumper's inner force guided nothing more than an inanimate shell, afforded moments of sputtering life with the infusion of living blood. But the nourishment hadn't done much for him. He would rot before long.

"My presence doesn't appear to bother you much."

Stahl shrugged. "This ain't my first rodeo."

"I gather." Sarnie chuckled. "My apologies for having a little fun with you last week. But you were trespassing in my house. I figured that gave me license to trespass in your head."

"Fair enough." Stahl wrinkled his nose. "The blood isn't working. You're rotting."

Sarnie's gaze drifted toward the kitchen. "I'm working on it."

"You could have jumped into any body you wanted. Why did you choose—?"

"Because it's my body, goddammit!" Sarnie interrupted, revealing the simmering tempest beneath the human cloak. "And the ones who did this to me will pay!"

"The ones who did what?" Stahl asked.

"The ones who killed me."

RG had been right. "And who do you suppose did that?"

"You're the detective. You tell me."

"I haven't figured that out yet." He caught his breath. "You thought about killing me today, didn't you?"

"Long and hard."

"But you changed your mind. Why?"

Sarnie stepped closer. Stahl gagged as the corpse's odor rolled over him in waves.

"There's a man I'm destined to meet. A powerful man… named Granville. I've sensed him on several occasions now. He pulled you from your vision last week. A friend of yours, I assume?"

"He and his wife, yes. But you may not want to meet them. They have a knack for sending jumpers like you into oblivion." *Maybe I shouldn't have warned the guy.*

Sarnie nodded. "As I have seen from your memories. Oblivion may be a better choice than where I'm heading. You must tell Granville I am looking forward to meeting him. It appears we share a certain destiny."

"Tell you what, give me an hour, and I'll bring him by. His wife, too. I'm sure they'd both like to meet you." *And send you back to hell.*

Sarnie grinned and shook his head. "Two against one isn't fair. Or three against one, for that matter. Who's the old man?"

"Another nightmare for you."

"Well, you bring them all by if you'd like. But I won't be here. Our meeting remains destined for another time."

Sullivan appeared jolted from a daydream. "What? Are we leaving?" Sullivan asked.

"Can't stay here now." He pointed at Stahl. "We've been compromised."

"But we can still kill him, feed you his blood? I can throw his body to the sharks, like the others. No one will ever know."

"No, Sully." Sarnie draped a waxy arm around Sullivan's shoulders. "I like the way you think, but it's time to move on."

"What happens to me?" Sullivan gave a quick peek toward the kitchen.

Stahl sensed the man's mind racing, his usefulness now in question.

"Don't you worry." Sarnie tapped Sullivan's cheek with his palm. "I have other important jobs for you."

"Thank you, Mr. Sarnie." He blew out the breath he'd been holding.

Sarnie stepped toward the front door and opened it, the sunlight and fresh air reviving Stahl's dulled senses. "You tell Granville I eagerly await our meeting. And when I'm done with him and his lovely wife, you and I will continue where we left off." He pointed toward the kitchen. "I gather you know what we do here."

"I have a pretty clear picture."

Sarnie leaned and whispered in his ear. "We're getting really good at it."

Stahl swallowed.

"Now, get out of my house…again. Before I change my mind."

Stahl stepped past the jumper, squinting his eyes to adjust to the brilliant daylight. As he strode across the lawn, his legs cycled faster and faster, his survival instinct finally whisking him away from the danger. When he reached the crumbling parking lot, he glanced back to catch Mick Sullivan peering out the front door like a child forced to stay home while his friends went off to play. Sullivan opened his mouth as if to speak, but the door slammed shut before he could say anything.

CHAPTER ELEVEN

Tuesday, March 29

RG

RG had advanced to his final PowerPoint slide when the auditorium door flew open, diverting the class's attention. "So, it's not simply caloric intake versus expenditure that leads to weight gain," RG continued over the growing murmur, "but a multitude of genetic and metabolic issues that enter into the equation."

Squinting through the overhead projector's glare, RG spotted Mike Stahl's silhouette pacing the aisle behind the last row of seats. "Okay, let's wrap it up early, gang. Don't forget, I put quiz four up on Canvas until 5:00 pm Friday."

He peered at Stahl, hobbling down the aisle toward him. He approached the dais as the room swelled with sound, the clunk of tablet arms dropping beside seats, the rustle of backpacks slung across shoulders, and the growing surge of competing conversations.

"What the hell are you doing here?" RG drew his eyebrows together as he gathered papers strewn across the table and stuffed handfuls into his professor bag. "Just had to witness one of my stunning lectures on energy expenditure?"

"I found him." He dragged a forearm across his brow, dripping sweat as if he'd run the entire way from Chatham.

RG hesitated, lifting his gaze in slow motion. "Sarnie?"

Stahl nodded. "Who else?" He told him about his trip to question Mick Sullivan and surprise encounter with Sarnie. "He's alive, and he knows all about you and Kacey." Stahl glanced away. "He got inside my head."

"Don't blame yourself. It's not your fault. I suspect he knows about me from more than your memories. The same way I know about him." RG slung his bag over his shoulder and dimmed the ceiling-mounted projector. "There's a connection, somehow. He's sensing it, too."

RG led Stahl from the auditorium. The men advanced along the corridor in fits and starts against a sea of oncoming students and faculty.

"Sarnie told me you have a shared destiny."

RG repositioned his bag from one shoulder to the other to maneuver through the oncoming bottleneck. "Not sure if that's good or bad."

"Sounds fucking bad to me."

"Appreciate you not holding back." RG clapped him on the shoulder. "I guess it could be worse."

"Well," Stahl hesitated. "It might already be."

RG stopped. "What the hell does that mean?"

Stahl jammed his hands against his hips and stared at his shoes. "I may have taunted him a bit."

"Taunted, how?"

"You know, played up your powers a bit." Stahl swiped a paw through his mane. "Maybe pissed him off a little."

"Shit." RG shook his head. "The *one* jumper in the universe on the verge of everlasting life, and you decide to push his buttons?" He caught himself before he said something he couldn't take back. "Not helping the odds much for us mortals."

"He's not immortal yet, but he's working on it. He's using blood to keep his body alive."

"What? He's a fucking vampire now?" RG asked, drawing head turns from a cluster of students behind them.

Stahl lowered his voice. "He's not drinking it. He's filling his veins with it."

Jesus Christ. RG directed Stahl to the hallway's side exit and leaned against the metal push bar, freeing them from the cacophony and allowing them to speak freely. They paced along a deserted walkway winding behind the building until they arrived at the edge of the east parking lot where Stahl had ditched the Crown Vic.

"You're saying blood's the answer to immortality."

"I'm not sure. He's turned Mick Sullivan's house into a slaughterhouse to get blood, but he's still rotting. I suspect he's running out of time."

"When did you find all this out?"

"Earlier today. I tried your cell, Kacey's too, but neither of you picked up. I decided to hightail it over here."

RG flipped on the cell's ringer. "Sorry, teaching all day." He tried Kacey's cell, but the call went to voicemail. "She must be in a meeting." He holstered the cell in his back pocket. "By the way, how the hell did you get out of there?"

"He let me go."

RG patted him on the back. "Something wrong with your blood? Well, lucky you."

Stahl shrugged. "He needed a messenger. Wanted you to know he's looking forward to meeting you."

"So how about we pay him a visit?"

Stahl stopped and turned to RG. "Listen, we're not gonna find him. He knows I'm bringing the cavalry."

"Where do you think he's heading?"

"No clue, but his sidekick, Sullivan, sticks pretty close to him. We find Sullivan, we find Sarnie."

RG scratched his head. "Does this guy...*know* about Sarnie?"

"Kind of. I told him Sarnie was dead, but it only half registered. I suspect Sarnie has him under some type of spell. He's conscious and communicating, but I'm not sure he understands what's going on completely." Stahl stepped over the curb to the Crown Vic. "And you were right about Sarnie. Somebody killed him and his family. He's hell bent on finding the people responsible."

"We still have to find him," RG said. "We can't let him find a way back to life."

"Guess it's back to the drawing board for me."

RG leaned against the Crown Vic. "You found him once. You'll find him again."

"Yeah, but the next time I find him, I'm not sure he'll be as generous. He's already used me as a messenger boy. I doubt he'll find another reason to keep me around."

"So, what do you suggest we do?"

"I need you and Kacey to come with me to Barnard Street. I'm putting out an APB on Mick Sullivan for the death of god-knows-how-many people in that house. But I'm not going to let my boys wander into a bloodbath...*if* he's still there. If he's gone, he's gone. But if he isn't, I need you and Kacey to be Chatham PD's first line of defense."

RG sensed the ring pulsing on his finger. He reached down

and felt its glow warming his hand. A burst of heat rose up his arm and into his body like a fiery injection traveling through his bloodstream.

He opened his mouth to speak, but his vocal cords and tongue had somehow forgotten how to work together. Images of an abandoned structure perched beside a weather-beaten fence and deserted parking lot formed in his mind. He found himself outside the structure, standing on the dirt-patch lawn. His vision penetrated the solid walls and locked onto the blood-stained carpeting, human matter spattered on the base-boards, saws and chisels strewn across the moldy bathroom floor, and body parts draining in the tub. Behind him a vicious wind arose, a vortex swirling around him, pulling him toward the house as if it hungered for more flesh and needed a quick snack. The updraft picked him up for a moment, his shoes tickling the grass as his body spun airborne. He stretched his arm to reach for Stahl, hoping that his body still stood in the hidden plane beside him, and that detective could help pull him back. He turned his head, but only spotted the crumbling asphalt behind the decrepit service station.

"Mike! Grab my hand!" He slapped at the air, hoping he flailed in the right direction and Stahl could somehow sense him. His hand impacted a solid form. Two meaty arms firmly gripped him around his chest. RG's feet remained elevated at eye level as the wind swirled and increased its intensity. A tug pulled at him as Stahl yanked him through a fissure running through the vision. RG flew through the air and landed on top of Stahl beside the Crown Vic.

"Jesus." Stahl rose to his knees. "You damn near flew away!"

"I saw the house." He pressed a hand to his forehead, his palm moist with perspiration. He whipped his head back and forth to check whether anyone had witnessed his new levitation trick. "I think it wanted me. It tried to pull me into it. Sarnie must still be in there."

"Then what do we do?"

"We need to get over there quick."

"You sure you want to do that?"

He deliberated, gazing at the ring on his finger. "Absolutely not, but I don't have a choice."

"Then get in the car, partner. We'll grab Kacey on the way."

* * *

After RG and Stahl had exploded through the doors of Chatham Elementary and hauled Kacey out of her morning meeting, the three sped along Route 28 toward Mick Sullivan's shack behind the vacant service station's rusting metallic remains. Stahl told her about his encounter with Sarnie, and RG recounted his earlier vision, how Stahl had grabbed him and prevented a swirling vortex from sucking him into... where, he didn't know.

"What the hell happened?" Kacey asked.

"Damned if I know. That was a first."

Stahl glanced over his shoulder into the backseat as he steered the unmarked with his left hand. "I ended up playing tug-of-war with his body. Something had hold of the other end. I'm sure of it."

"This Sarnie," Kacey began, "he's been playing with you in your dreams and visions, but what the hell's gonna happen when you actually get to the house?"

"Just help me keep my feet on the ground, and I should be fine."

Stahl rolled the car across the parking lot's crumbling asphalt. A tangle of branches draped Sullivan's house in shadow, moss collecting on the cracked and broken roof shingles. It appeared to be a well-chosen plot, several side streets removed from the beaten path and hidden from the curious eye, where the Cape's beauty gave way to the creeping neglect most residents ignored or pretended didn't exist. Secluded. Forgotten.

As they exited the car, a chill descended from the warm breeze. RG grabbed Kacey's hand with a shiver. "Did it just get cold?"

Kacey glanced up at the cloud cover settling before the sun. "Like instant nightfall."

As RG stepped across the thinning lawn, he gazed at the structure, sensing its life force. He could all but smell the walls and floors decaying like the human remains festering inside. The house betrayed a subtle swell like that of a bloated body, its siding appearing to bow outward as death's putrid gases pushed against the frame. "Feels like I was just here."

She squeezed his hand twice, reassuring him.

"You okay, RG?" Stahl asked, arms held to his sides like a linebacker, ready to bear hug him in case the winds picked up.

RG nodded and gave him a reluctant thumbs-up. "Not much time for putting together a plan, though."

"Planning's overrated." Kacey grinned. "But I have been thinking. We've gotta find a way to separate that bastard from his body."

"Oh, that's all?" RG raised his eyebrows.

"Just listen. If one of us can get inside him and expel him, the other could hack his carcass into pieces, cut off its head, burn it, anything to prevent him from getting back inside."

"He would lose his one chance at immortality," Stahl said.

"Not a bad idea, but easier said than done. He won't give up his body that easily." RG recalled his earlier vision, the body parts filling the tub, an array of ghastly tools to perform the separations soaking in the porcelain sink. To defeat Sarnie, they would have to stoop to his level, slash him to pieces, and replicate what he had overseen inside the slaughterhouse.

The door rested open a crack, as if beckoning them to enter.

"Well," Stahl stepped forward. "What do you say?"

They entered the house one by one, RG bringing up the rear.

"Oh, my god." Kacey threw a hand over her mouth and took a step backward, bumping into RG.

It took a moment for RG's eyes to adjust to the dim light, to process the scene before him. But before his eyes took in the savage details, his nose had already taken the brunt of the heinous stench wafting from the shape suspended from the rafters. Extension cords tethered the feet to a pipe running across the ceiling from the far wall. The body hung upside down, viscera protruding from the jagged tear in the belly as if someone had scooped them out by hand. A neat incision had punctured the carotid artery in the neck, inviting the occasional blood droplet to plink into the bucket resting on floor beneath the corpse's head.

"It's Mick Sullivan." Stahl swiped a hand across his chin and stepped through the living room, checking the other rooms in the house.

Kacey slowly dragged her hand away from her mouth. "Jesus. Why did he hang him—?"

"Sarnie's feeding off the blood." Stahl shouted from the house's far end.

"Looks like he did a bit more than that. Did he consume him?"

"He's draining the blood and injecting it." Stahl returned to the living room. "Anything else he did was extra."

Kacey winced as she turned from the corpse. "So, blood's the answer. It's giving his body life."

"Whatever he did, I don't think it works." Stahl pointed to the bathroom. "There are a bunch of body parts in there, enough blood to have provided an ample supply, but he's not getting better. At least he wasn't earlier today."

"So, he hasn't figured it all out yet," Kacey said. "There must be something else he needs for immortality."

"Looks like it." Stahl pulled out his cell. "Hal, Mike. We got bodies. I'm gonna need you to send everybody." He gave the address and disconnected, glancing up from the cell. "He must have just left, RG. I can still smell the formaldehyde."

Where are you? RG concentrated on the space around him, the place Sarnie had been, imagining him traversing the worn carpeting, his energy and aura filling the space between the walls. With closed eyes, he rubbed his hands together. The warmth of the ring penetrated the skin as heat burst through his bloodstream. The lights flickered, sending shadows across his eyelids.

"You guys ought to make yourself scarce. Chatham PD's on its way, and your presence at a murder scene will raise questions. Why don't you head up to the Java Hut on Main, and I'll pick you up when I'm done…"

Stahl's voice faded as the air shifted in the confined space, pressing against RG like a weight. He blinked at a dusky cloud raining around him. He searched for Kacey and Stahl, but they had disappeared.

Everything had disappeared.

RG waited for the world to resume and for the ring to speak to him. Sarnie appeared beside him through a shimmering veil, circling Mick Sullivan as he shivered in terror. Rushing forward to reach the man hanging from the ceiling, RG's body smacked into an invisible barrier. He pounded his fists against the impenetrable facade, but he couldn't breach the force holding him at bay. He stepped back, sensing that the ring had revived this earlier event and showed him its residue, the way an odor might linger long after the source had disappeared. But somehow Sarnie had helped queue it up just for him. He could do nothing now but watch as the scene unfolded.

"But I helped you, Mr. Sarnie," Sullivan cried from inside the hallucination. "You said you would take me with you."

"No, Mick," Sarnie said, raising a finger. "I said I had other important jobs for you." He placed a finger along Sullivan's neck searching for a pulse. "This *is* an important job."

"Why? Why me?" Tear stains streaked across his eyebrows and forehead, gravity sending them slaloming along a new trajectory.

"I've found the blood that will give me everlasting life. I'm close now."

"Mine? My blood will give you—?"

"God, no, you horse's ass! You're just a snack between meals, like all the others. You'll hold me over for a couple days, that's all. But I've been educated, you might say. I need to find her, and I'll be whole again."

"Her? Tell me who, and I'll help you. Let me live. Please." Sullivan struggled against his restraints. "I'll help you harvest her blood."

"I have the procedure down now. You've become obsolete."

"I'll help you track down your family's killer."

"Why? You want to find out what I'm going to do to them?"

"I'll even help you do it. Just let me down! Mr. Sarnie, please!"

Sarnie knelt and met Sullivan at eye level. "Ah, the magic

word. How about I show you what I'm gonna do to them." Sarnie stepped from the living room and rummaged through the closet beside the bathroom, returning with a cleaning bucket he propped below Sullivan's head.

"Oh, God! No, Mr. Sarnie!"

"I'm gonna start like this." Sarnie placed a gentle hand along Sullivan's stomach and splayed his fingers like a rake, embedding them through the man's skin and through his abdominal wall.

Mick Sullivan's final scream pummeled RG's eardrums.

He pounded on the veil separating his world from the vision but couldn't break through to intervene. Sarnie turned toward RG and grinned as he ripped Mick Sullivan in half.

RG dropped to the floor as the scene in his mind ended. The light rose in his eyes as Kacey and Mike's faces materialized before him. "Oh, Christ."

"What happened?" Kacey knelt beside him.

RG gazed at the corpse turning slowly in an arc. "Sarnie just gave me a front row seat to Mick Sullivan's execution."

* * *

Kacey

After Stahl dropped RG and Kacey at Chatham Elementary, the couple drove back to Hyannis to pick up RG's car from the college. Kacey pulled into the faculty parking lot and eased into the space beside the Subaru perched farthest from the main building. He had to be getting his steps in every day if he chose to park this far from his office. Not that he needed them anymore. She gave him a quick once-over, her heart experiencing an unexpected quickening in pace as a lock of hair spiraled across his forehead.

Focus, Kacey.

But she couldn't help herself. Her desire for him often came at the most inopportune times. Maybe not like his desire for her, showing up in restaurant bathrooms after church when she had a ghost to catch, but how different was this, really? She took a deep breath as she threw the car in park, fanning herself with both hands.

RG loosened his seat belt but remained in his seat, staring out the windshield. Kacey pulled the key and waited, the cooling engine's tick peppering the silence.

"He's taunting me now." RG shifted in his seat. "You should have seen the way he smiled at me while he ripped out the man's innards. The way he smiled and stared straight at me…he wanted me to see it."

"He's a jumper. That's what they do. They kill. In horrific ways. We've seen it before."

"The thing is, he didn't have to." He pressed his palms to his temples. "He only needed the blood."

Kacey touched his shoulder. "Maybe something personal happened we don't know about. Maybe Sullivan had something to do with his murder, or his family's murder. That's the main reason he's come back, right?"

"He would have said something to him. If he's come back to this world for revenge, he would have at least mentioned it."

"What did he say to him?"

RG focused on something beyond the windshield. "He said he'd found the blood that will make him immortal."

"Sullivan's blood?"

RG shook his head. "That only charged his battery until he gets to his primary target. I'm sure he's on his way there now, and we have no idea who it is. He's won this game, and we haven't so much as lifted our asses off the bench yet."

"You don't know who or what is standing in his way. This isn't over yet. You gotta have faith."

RG pulled his car keys from his pocket and swung the car door open, still not exiting the car. "Listen, I'm going back to the house."

"Then, I'll follow you home."

"Not that house." He turned his head to face her. "I'm going back to the Barnard Street house."

"You know it's a crime scene, right? Cops will be all over that place."

"I'll wait until dark when cops and forensics guys have cleared out. I can slip through the crime tape, no big deal."

"Why? You expecting another vision?"

"I'm not sure." He took a deep breath. "But I got the strangest sensation back there. Bad things have happened in that house."

"Yeah, I saw it hanging from the ceiling."

"Sarnie killed people in that house, for sure. But I sensed a darker history there. The house exudes evil. It seeps from the walls. Things that happened decades ago."

"I didn't experience anything like that." Kacey stroked her forehead with her fingers. "Could I be losing my edge or what? Maybe the ring helps you sense things I can't."

RG shrugged. "The feeling overpowered me, like entering a portal. I need to go back."

"Well, I'm going with you. We'll drop Junior at Morrow's—"

"I don't think that's a good idea," he interrupted. "I suspect the house acts as a passageway, and it goes some-where…bad."

"We've seen bad."

"Not like this."

Kacey raised her eyebrows. "Plymouth wasn't bad?"

"Someone wicked lived there, true, but the destination

wasn't evil. Barnard Street is the doorway to something we've never experienced. I don't want you to go."

Kacey grabbed a package of breath mints resting in the cup holder and started bouncing them off RG's head one by one, picking up speed as she went.

"Ow!" he yelped, holding up his hand as a shield.

"Stop doing that to me!"

"Doing what?"

"Your typical 'I'm the big, strong caretaker with the powerful ring and I'm gonna protect the little lady' bullshit. Doesn't work that way, goddammit!" Kacey popped the final breath mint into her mouth. "We're a team. We don't hide things, and we don't try to go it alone. Haven't we learned that already? We're stronger together than we are apart, so I'm coming with you."

"I know, it's just…." RG rubbed his temple at the impact site and stared at his hand. "This ring may give me supernatural powers, but it doesn't change my *human* side, my primary instinct to protect you. Whatever I may become, I'll never stop being that guy."

Moments like this reminded Kacey that her husband's foibles had been borne of his strengths, his deep devotion to her and Robert Jr., his friends, not to mention frightened children held in cages in a remote corner of the past he had never met before. He would always be a protector, despite how it made her feel sometimes. Could she ever really stay mad at him?

"Just close the damn door so we can get out of here," she said.

"Not yet." RG climbed out and dashed around the vehicle, pulling Kacey from the front seat. "Come on," he said, taking her hand, "we have research to do."

CHAPTER TWELVE

Tuesday, March 29

Mike

Mike Stahl pecked away at the battered laptop perched on his desk at the Chatham Police Department, pausing every few minutes to scarf a bite from the egg sandwich resting on the crumpled fast food bag. After dropping RG and Kacey back in Hyannis, he had spent most of the morning at the Barnard Street house, assisting detectives from several jurisdictions assigned to the 'House of Horrors' case, as the local media had dubbed it. He already had two murders on his plate, so he had no problem handing this one off. The detectives would no doubt find Mick Sullivan responsible for the murders of the dismembered men and women in the bathroom, but Sullivan's murder would be unsolvable. Like the murder at the Bayless Funeral Home, no one could reasonably conclude Alex Sarnie could be responsible. Stahl sighed. At least he wouldn't be the only one with an unsolved murder hanging over his head. But two? That wouldn't fly. He had to solve Sarnie's murder, or else find himself on weekend traffic detail during the tourist season. He downed a gulp of medium warm Java, but paused mid sip, gritting his teeth as the wheel of death appeared on his screen, spinning in defiance as his computer buffered.

"Sonofabitch!"

"You ought to let us upgrade that thing." Malcolm Meyer's voice chimed in from behind him, a tangle of USB cords and chargers dangling from his hands as he scurried from cubicle to cubicle. "You'd get—"

"Yeah, yeah," Stahl interrupted. "I'd get twice the work done in half the time." According to that calculation, he would end up doing four times as much work each day. *Not much of an incentive.* Truth was, Stahl had finally gotten comfortable with the old Windows operating system. He could navigate the programs and webpages, knew the shortcuts, where his bookmarks were, and how to manage his files and folders. Why reinvent the wheel? Most upgrades had no true purpose, designed to make computers appear fresh and new while keeping tech guys like Meyer employed. The detective languished at least three versions behind the rest of the department, which, according to Meyer, doubled *his* work when it came to problem-solving software glitches and digging around for obsolete codes and patches. In the end, Stahl figured Meyer's working twice as hard beat his potential four-fold increase. He would fight any upgrade tooth and nail.

"Stahl!" Jack Defranco's voice rattled the office. "We're ready for you in 'A.'" The Police Chief still referred to the station's conference room by its number stenciled on the glass window, placed there when plans existed for a 'B' that never materialized.

"On my way, Chief." Stahl scooped his sandwich and coffee, balancing them on the laptop wedged against the crook of his elbow. He chuckled. Every other meeting in the department happened at a desk or water cooler, but with Boston PD's Digital Forensics and Cyber Crimes guy on the premises, Defranco had pulled out all the stops. He had stored the microwave and fridge in Daniels' empty office and stashed the department's softball gear in the electrical closet. Today, 'A' bore little resemblance to the storage room it had become.

Stahl entered and dropped the laptop onto the table, his Styrofoam cup tumbling off the keyboard and sending a coffee river flowing across the table top.

"Shit," Stahl mumbled, grabbing a handful of napkins from his sandwich bag. He mopped at the stain and nodded at the Boston detective, his seat pushed back and feet raised as a java-colored waterfall poured off the table and pooled beneath his chair.

"Um, sorry about that."

Defranco sighed. "Detective Stahl, Frank Doyle from the Digital Forensics team in Boston. Detective Doyle, Mike Stahl."

"Nice to finally meet you after all the phone calls." Doyle extended his hand as he stood, the other clutching a dripping sheaf of papers. He appeared younger than the man Stahl had imagined over the phone, with a smooth face and smattering of freckles across his fair Celtic skin. As a detective, he would have undergone rigorous law enforcement training, but his soft physique suggested his strengths didn't rest with a gun, but a mouse.

The men shook hands. "Hope you had a nice drive down."

"Listen, guys. I…um, just learned about the bodies they're pulling from that house downtown."

"Barnard Street," Stahl added.

"Just what this town needs." Defranco pulled his wallet and badge from his pocket and tossed it on the table. "The local media has already dubbed it the 'House of Horrors.'"

"I know it's in your jurisdiction, Chief. If you need to concentrate on other things," Doyle said, tossing a thumb over his shoulder, "I could come back when things settle down—"

"Appreciate it, but I've already been down there. Nothing more I can do but let forensics do their work. Either way, we gotta keep moving on our other cases, too. Including the Sarnie case." Defranco raised his cell and displayed the messages pinging on its screen. "Besides, I'm getting constant updates."

"All right then, let's get down to business."

Stahl dropped into his chair, pulling his egg sandwich from the takeout sack. "What have you got, Doyle?"

Defranco scowled as Stahl scarfed a chunk of sandwich, an egg string dangling from the corner of his mouth. "We could come back when you're finished."

"Come on, Chief, you know I hate to eat alone." He swallowed another bite and washed it down with the remnants of his spilled coffee. "Surprised you're here so soon, Doyle. Figured it would take longer getting a warrant for the phone records."

"Turns out you didn't need one."

"Court order?" Defranco tilted his head.

"Neither."

Stahl raked a hand through his mop. "Didn't the Supreme Court ban police access to cellphone data without a warrant?"

"They did, but the rules get a bit murkier when someone's dead. Especially if the phone could hold critical clues, like this one." Doyle flipped it over in his palm.

"Those the phone records?" He glanced at the stained papers laid out on the chair beside Doyle.

Doyle sighed, holding up the papers drip drying in his grip. "Not exactly. With burners, prepaid phone records aren't much different than what you find on the smartphone call log." Doyle leaned back in his chair. "The unit itself gives you text messages, incoming and outgoing calls, time, date, duration of the call, and detailed location data." Doyle shook off the stapled list and slipped it across the table. "We made things easier for you by matching numbers to names."

"That'll help." Stahl leafed through the sodden pages.

"How did you get the thing open?" Defranco asked, pointing at the cell.

"Had to charge it up and break the guy's passcode."

"Easier said than done, from what I hear." Defranco folded his arms.

"Helps to have a staff of code breakers. Just took all the family names, birthdates, anniversaries, all the data Stahl sent." Doyle acknowledged him across the table with a nod. "We put them all together and had the computer prioritize from about a million different options. We had our team working 'round the clock until we cracked it. Damn lucky, really."

Stahl turned the phone in his hand and powered it on. He located the call log and scrolled through the lists of numbers, glancing at Doyle's identification index. The dates and times on the screen went back to the previous year, the first calls belonging to Sarnie's brother. Numerous calls all hours of the day and night, week after week. Hadn't Wilson told him he and his younger brother rarely talked? Stahl shook his head. *Why does everyone lie to the cops?*

Stahl scrolled through the call log, numbers blurring as they flew across the screen beneath his thumb. As he advanced to the most recent calls, he identified Jimmy McKinnon's number from Doyle's list, another flurry of calls in the weeks before Sarnie's death. Chris Daniels had been right about their connection. Just business most likely, but now he would have to make a trip to Southie. *Sonofabitch!*

As he scrolled through the list, Stahl's mouth dropped. The phone number all but jumped off the screen, the string of digits fuzzing the longer he stared at it. Stahl could barely make out anything against the background distractions, Defranco and Doyle's muffled conversation sounding as if it came from somewhere down the hall or maybe from a different room… "For a guy who runs a business, his cellphone security had been pretty lax"…"Maybe because he used it as a burner"…Stahl continued scrolling, the number bleeding into a solid wall across the touch screen from top to bottom…"You ever run into that 'Fugitive Professor' guy? Doesn't he live down here?"

Turning pages from Doyle's handout, Stahl searched for the name associated with the number. He blinked a few times, certain he misread the device's blaring screen. *Isn't that…what the hell?* He grabbed his cell from a back pocket, convinced he was wrong. He pulled up the number from his 'Recents' list, a contact that lit up his cellphone just about every day. He held it beside the burner. *Damn! That's impossible.* With fingers flying, he flipped the report to the final page. The last name matched his cell number. *Well, fuck me…*

Doyle rose from the table and handed Defranco a clump of damp pages. "Here's a copy of the list I gave Stahl. Feel free to——"

"I'll take those off your hands, Boss." Stahl reached out and intercepted the packet before Defranco's hand closed around it. "You have enough to do 'round here with the 'House of Horrors' case revving up."

"Mike Stahl taking work *off* someone else's plate?"

Defranco spoke in a deliberate cadence, raising an eyebrow as he pushed his chair back. "Alert the press."

"Got this one, Chief," he slid the papers onto his laptop keyboard before closing it. "Nothing I can't handle, just a bunch of names and phone numbers."

Defranco held up his hands. "Your call." The police chief narrowed his eyes. "Jesus Christ, Stahl. You look like you just got out of a sauna. You okay?"

Stahl dabbed at the layer of sweat on his forehead. "Just a bit hot in here, that's all. I guess I need a breath of fresh air."

"As long as you're not having a heart attack on me. I don't need the extra paperwork."

"Appreciate your concern, Chief."

"I'm joining Doyle for a late lunch before checking back at Barnard Street." Defranco gathered his belongings on the table, depositing them in different pockets. "Why don't you grab a bite, get that fresh air."

"Whatta ya say, Stahl." Doyle checked his watch.

"Too much on my desk right now." He raised his egg sandwich. "This'll have to hold me over until dinner." He stretched a hand to Doyle. "Great meeting you. Can't thank you and your team enough for your hard work on this."

"You let me know if there's anything else you need." He nodded. "Ready, Chief?"

As the two men hastened to the glass doors, Stahl collapsed in his chair and checked the name on the list one more time. He needed help with this one. He would have to call Chris Daniels. He remained the only person who could help him figure this out.

But his first question would be the hardest.

Stahl would have to ask his partner why his phone number popped up all over Alex Sarnie's burner.

* * *

RG

Kacey and RG huddled together inside a carrel on the mezzanine in the college library, staring at a glowing seventeen-inch computer monitor. Kacey pulled the Milk Duds box she grabbed from the lobby vending machine, glancing at the 'no food or drink' sign as she poured the contraband into her hand.

RG's blank stare registered his disbelief.

"What?" She garbled through a thick chocolate paste. "It's a contradiction to sell food in a place you can't eat it. It's like going to the beach but not being allowed to swim. Should be a crime."

"The point is, I don't want to be the professor that gets thrown out of his own college library because his wife can't follow the rules."

She narrowed her eyes and poured another handful of chocolates before closing the box and stuffing it in her pocket. "Fine. Okay, where do we start?"

RG glanced to the left and to the right. "You can start by giving me my share." RG cupped his hand.

Kacey grumbled as she relinquished the contraband. "Fine."

RG's jaws quickly worked the candy. "I can't remember the address. Let's try a Chatham property search under Mick Sullivan, maybe we can find some history on it." With a few keystrokes, RG had pulled up the house's previous MLS listing along with the sales history, square footage, current owner, and real estate office managing the property.

"We're not looking to rent it."

"Okay, let's try this." RG entered the house address into Google, followed by the words, 'murder,' 'accident,' 'death,' and 'crime,' but none of the hits included the key words he entered.

Kacey grabbed the mouse. "You're too literal. Let's see if there's any legend surrounding the place." Kacey commandeered the keyboard and typed in 'haunted' and 'Cape Cod.' Thousands of hits filled the screen. "Now we're talking."

But after twenty minutes of scrolling through commercial Cape Cod ghost tours and haunted hotspots designed to wring money from the out-of-state tourists, she could locate nothing specifically describing the Barnard Street property.

"Let me take a look." RG grabbed the keyboard, scrolling down the list until she came across a blog called 'Haunted Chatham.' He clicked on the link and arrived at a low-tech website with lists of B&B's and hotels on the Cape and South Shore with a history of ghost sightings, hauntings, and paranormal events.

"Hey look, Plymouth. The John Carver Inn." Kacey grinned. "Why do you suppose they included that place?"

RG rolled his eyes and kept scrolling. "Can't imagine."

At the bottom of the page, a number of books by Cape Cod authors popped up on the screen, self-published judging by the cheap cover art.

"Hang on, RG."

She grabbed the mouse and scrolled through them. Most appeared as lighthearted short fiction and historical accounts, but one caught her attention.

"*Cape Cod Death Houses*," she mumbled. "By Raymond Knoll."

RG squinted at the screen. "This one comes across a bit darker than the others." He clicked on the title, and an Amazon webpage popped up.

God, Amazon will publish anything. He tapped on the 'Look Inside' feature and scrolled the Table of Contents. This book didn't have the same tongue-in-cheek approach to ghosts and hauntings the other books and websites displayed, or list adventures for tourists and families heading to the Cape for daytrips. This one had a grim cover, a grainy black and white crime scene photo of an old cemetery with a partially clad bodies lying in a heap amongst tall grass. He advanced to the first chapter. "The Whiteside Inn?"

Kacey leaned in to read from the screen. "You know, the place in in P-town? Don't you remember the story?"

He shook his head.

"Back in the seventies, a cook butchered his wife and two children with a meat cleaver in an upstairs apartment, then leapt from an open window, impaling himself on the wrought iron fence. They say he lived for over an hour, confessing to the crimes as he lay skewered on the fence."

RG scrolled down the pages to find more black and white crime scene photos painting a visual picture from Kacey's recollection. "Oh my god." RG turned away at the grisly photos, blackened blood pools seeping into the wood floors, a child's half lidded eyes devoid of life's spark, empty, and a body hanging over a fence with two iron rods protruding from its back.

They scrolled further through the chapter headings.

"Hey, wait," Kacey whispered. "The Pine Grove Cemetery killings. I remember hearing stories about this as a kid. This drifter dismembered four women in the crypt and left their bodies beside gravestones with teeth marks all over them. The women had their hearts removed. They caught the guy, but they suspected he may have done the same to seven or eight women all together."

RG fixed her with a prolonged stare. "Geez, how long do you have to be married to someone before you learn they're obsessed with serial killers and murderers?"

"Imagine what you'll discover in the next ten years."

"This book…" RG scrolled through the cemetery photos "…like a goddamn snuff film, a 'true crime' novel on steroids. Truly dark stuff, Kace. The author included a chapter on 'The Lady of the Dunes,' too."

"'The Lady of the Dunes,' huh? Not a drunken July Fourth weekend you're recalling, is it?"

"Ah, did we find a Cape Cod murder you aren't aware of?" RG returned to the Table of Contents, scrolling through the chapters until he came to 'Chatham's Hidden Horror.' Beside the page number a coarse photo of a sturdy house from the fifties or sixties appeared on screen. RG pressed the control key and twirled the mouse's wheel to zoom in. The small hairs on his arms lifted.

"That's the Barnard Street house."

"Quick, go to the chapter." Kacey clasped her hand over RG's and advanced the pages. "Dammit, the free preview ends before the chapter."

"You have your Kindle with you?"

"It's in my school bag in the car." She fished into her back pocket and pulled out her cell. "Here, order it on my account, it'll be there by the time we get to the parking lot."

RG pulled up her Amazon page and located the eBook. RG hesitated, his finger poised over the 'Buy' button.

"What's the matter?"

"There's no way I should have to pay $8.99 for an eBook. Who does this guy think he is, Stephen King?"

"Jesus, RG."

"It's the principle of the thing."

Kacey rolled her eyes. "Just buy the damn thing, you cheapskate."

Friggin' eBooks. Unlike Kacey, who had hundreds of titles stashed in her Kindle, RG shunned the technology, cherishing a physical book's braille-like cover, the smell of print on the smooth paper, and the weight of it resting in his hands. The combination of sensations never failed to trigger the magic of his childhood dalliances with the written word, something digital could never replicate. But he also acknowledged envy when Kacey finish one book long after the bookstores closed, press a button, and download another without having to adjust the bedroom pillows.

Taking the library steps two at a time, RG and Kacey reached the Quad's grass carpet, sprinting across the campus to the far end of the east parking lot. When they had settled in Kacey's car, she powered up the Kindle to find the purchase waiting in her library.

"Here it is." She handed him the Kindle. "Pretty amazing technology, I'd say." She gave him a quick elbow to the ribs.

RG frowned as he found the chapter in the Table of Contents and hit the 'Go To' button. He tilted the Kindle to allow Kacey to read along from the driver's seat. She fished a pair of readers from her bag and leaned over the console, draping an arm around his shoulder.

The chapter displayed pictures of the Barnard Street house throughout the years, the sturdy dwelling featured in forties and fifties era black and white photos and graduating into the gaudy colors of sixties and seventies instant camera film. They scrolled through dozens of images, many with young couples or growing families standing before the structure. But no smiles graced their faces. No child stifled a grin or shared a joke with a sibling as the camera's shutter snapped. No proud husband beamed as he stood in front of his castle, arm slung around his wife's shoulder and pressing her close. The photographs appeared to represent a requirement to fulfill, an obligation to the house. Evidence that everything appeared fine. Normal. And while the home appeared crisp and clear in each photo, shaded with impeccable lighting and contrast, the people huddled before it often remained blurred or in shadow.

RG continued to scroll but could find no recent photographs. "Nothing past the early nineties. I wonder why?"

"Could be when the house fell into neglect and disarray. It definitely coincided with the urban decay in the area, the abandoned strip mall and gas station. Maybe the house didn't want to be seen like that."

"Kacey, look." An iciness descended his spine. "The angles."

She adjusted her readers and leaned in. "Jesus Christ. They're identical. Every one. How can that be?"

Looking closer, RG inspected the images again, noticing a peculiar similarity. The photographers snapping these pictures spanning over sixty years had all stood in the exact same spot. *Impossible.*

"Hold on. Let me check something. He pulled out his cell and pulled up the website featuring Chatham properties. He scrolled through the MLS information until he came to the photograph at the bottom of the listing, a recent image judging by the time stamp. Unlike the earlier pictures, this one revealed the state of the house's disrepair, the moss-covered roof, rotted windows, and chipped clapboard. A canopy of tree branches hung low, as if trying to hide the decay, but the image angle remained identical to the ones in the book.

"Look, RG. Exact same spot."

"It's as if the house can only be pictured from this spot, as if another angle might reveal something it doesn't want anyone to see."

RG and Kacey read in silence for the next few minutes, processing a litany of tragedy, accidents, murders, and disappearances happening in and around the house: a two-year old child drowned after falling into an emptying bathtub, her ringlets pulling her into the drain; a family of four vacationing from Hartford killed in their sleep after carbon monoxide seeped from a furnace exhaust pipe; an eight-year-old boy's arm wrenched from his body after getting it caught in washing machine; a new bride electrocuted in the kitchen while changing an overhead lightbulb.

"All those lives." Kacey leaned her head against the headrest. "They should have torn the house down decades ago."

"You think it would have let them? I want to talk to this guy…" RG checked the author's name, "…Raymond Knoll, find out what he knows about the Barnard Street property. He's done his research, and we need to understand what we're walking into." He tapped the Kindle and found the author page. "Guy's a local. Cape resident his whole life, it says."

"Shouldn't be too hard to track down." Kacey pulled out her cell and Googled the author's name, tapping the 'whitepages.com' entry her search returned. She turned her cell to RG.

He inspected the Eastham address. "Half-hour drive."

"Pft! For you maybe." Kacey cranked the engine and jammed the car in reverse.

* * *

Mike

Stahl juggled his cellphone with one hand and the steering wheel with the other as he sped across Chatham with a controlled recklessness. He had tried numerous times to reach Daniels, but he wasn't picking up. *Where the hell are you, goddammit?* He powered along Route 137 toward Daniels' residence, leaving a blackened skid on the pavement as he spun the wheel and maneuvered into the driveway. Rolling across the dirt and gravel pathway up to the house, he blew out an audible exhale. He killed the ignition and leaned his head against the headrest.

He hadn't planned in advance what to say, how he would probe Daniels about his connection with Sarnie. He kept going over it in his head, but his emotions swung like a wrecking ball between confusion and anger, knocking down everything in between. He wanted to reach out to Daniels as a friend, and, in the same breath, reach out to him with a closed fist.

Why did you lie to me, you sonofabitch!

Stahl pried his hands loose from the steering wheel, unaware his hands had gone numb. He shook them until the stinging dissipated and the blood flow returned. Maybe he could ask Daniels why the little voice in the back of his head whispered to him, telling him his partner must have been involved with something, sending his imagination running wild.

Fuck.

As he sat there, the little voice abandoned its whisper, using its outside voice to remind him Mick Sullivan and Alex Sarnie had been working together. If Daniels assaulted a drug dealer bringing in the stuff on Sarnie's trucks, how much of a jump would it be to go to the guy running the company? Would he have done such a thing for Ellie? Now the little voice spoke up again, advancing to the podium and tapping the microphone, pointing out that Daniels fought for lead investigator on the Sarnie case but had never mentioned any relationship with the man. He had been keeping secrets, compromising the investigation. If he had been involved and gotten himself in too deep, he could control a lot of the information by taking the lead.

Don't go there, Mike…not yet.

Stahl eased himself from the front seat, pausing a moment to accommodate the standing weight on his bad hip. He limped to Daniels' front porch and struggled up the steps, the splintered wood groaning beneath his hobbling mass. Stahl rattled the screen door with his fist, cupping his hands and peering through the kitchen window.

Stahl couldn't pick up any music coming from Daniels' workshop, but the open barn door gave him pause. He shuffled across the driveway and slipped into the dim warehouse, triggering the wall switch.

"Chris," he called out. A fresh air smell and cool afternoon chill permeated the space, blanketing the familiar gasoline and machinery odor. As he turned to leave, Stahl's gaze shifted to Daniels' workstation in the far corner. A cigar box rested on the table, its contents scattered about.

Ellie's keepsakes. He recalled the last time he had surprised an emotional Daniels in the workshop.

Stahl stepped to the desk, glancing at the collection. He had met Ellie at one of the Daniels' family Memorial Day beach cookouts. He recalled the teenager surrounded by friends, scarfing down Daniels' meaty burgers, and dancing to Justin Timberlake as the thirty-somethings rolled their eyes and lamented the dearth of quality music these days. She pulled people toward her as if she were the sun and they were planets and had no choice but to revolve around her. Later, when he'd visited her at Cape Cod Hospital, before her transfer to the long-term care facility in Boston, her transformation had stunned him. It wasn't only that her body had changed, but the glow surrounding her had disappeared, as if the room's ventilation system had sucked out her essence. He recalled his initial reaction as he advanced into the room, and Daniels' curious glance, as if his friend could read the ruminations streaming from his mind.

She's gone, Chris. It's not her anymore.

Stahl reached for one of the photographs, hoping it would trigger a smile and a few positive recollections to take through the day.

He brought the photo closer. He squinted, attempting to reconcile the conflict between the image he expected and the one he viewed.

It wasn't Ellie.

Stahl couldn't identify the woman in the snapshot right away. He perused the handwritten notes and letters and checked the signature at the bottom. Then it hit him as if the Mustang in the second bay had barreled into him and knocked him across the room.

The woman had been beautiful when alive. Stahl had only seen her face after they had hauled her from the bottom of Jackknife Cove. He hadn't recognized her beauty at the time, her final struggle to breathe and fight to stay alive had contorted her gentle features into a death mask. But in the pictures, she remained flawless.

Jessie Sarnie.

He picked up a handwritten letter from the cigar box, mumbling the words as he scanned its heartfelt prose. Now everything came together, like the reels of a spinning slot machine clicking into place and hitting jackpot. Stahl couldn't feel his feet beneath him, and he reached for the table to steady himself.

Chris Daniels had been Jessie's lover. And judging from the depth of emotion revealed in the letters, she had been in love with him.

No wonder Doyle couldn't find any cell records for Alex Sarnie, the phone didn't belong to him. It belonged to Jessie. Stahl hadn't so much as considered that possibility. But with Daniels' number all over it, along with the discovery of photographs and love letters, the truth couldn't be more obvious. No doubt Sarnie had discovered his wife's burner after becoming suspicious and had hidden it in a jacket pocket to explore later.

But later never came.

Why didn't you tell me, Chris? Confide in me?

Stahl figured Daniels' despondency over the past weeks had been due to Ellie's deteriorating condition and the decision the family would have to make to take her off life support. But his friend had been mourning more than his sister. The little voice in Stahl's head had been joined by a choir all chanting the same chorus. Killing the man who had supplied Mick Sullivan with his product would be sweet retribution for Ellie. But what if Daniels had wanted Sarnie out of the way to have Jessie to himself? Sarnie's Lexus plunged into the cove without a single shred of physical evidence anything had been wrong with it. Operator error. An accident. He'd read the reports; he'd talked with the mechanics who had inspected the vehicle's hardware.

Daniels understood a lot about cars…

Could he have made it look like an accident? *Stop it, Mike…* Stahl had no evidence vaulting Sarnie's death from an accident to murder, but now he had a pair of deadly motives: love and revenge. Maybe Daniels' plan had backfired, and he hadn't expected the family to be with him that night. Could he be responsible for three deaths?

Stahl kicked himself for entertaining such notions. How he could imagine his friend could be involved in something like this?

The little voice again. *Because he kept things from you.*

Stahl shook the thoughts from his head. Daniels had pressed Stahl about his progress in the case, but had he done so to find out who killed Jessie or to keep tabs on how much

Stahl had uncovered? He banged his fists against the workstation and leaned his palms on the desk top.

Raking his hands through his hair, Stahl slogged to the barn door, his gait struggling against the two-ton weight added onto his shoulders. As he approached the exit, he came face to face with Chris Daniels, blocking the entryway.

"Whatcha doing in here, Mike?"

CHAPTER THIRTEEN

Tuesday, March 29

RG

Kacey zoomed along Route 6 past the Orleans/Eastham rotary, winding along the small connector roads until they reached Cable Road, heading straight toward the ocean. They took a left onto Nauset Light Road, pulling past the iconic red and white cast-iron lighthouse overlooking the National Seashore, searching for the address. A half-mile down the road, they turned into a sand driveway, sideling the Outback beside a wood-framed, saltbox house nestled in the beach grass less than one hundred yards from the sea.

They knocked on the door. A gaunt shape loomed behind a porch window, darting away with the curtain's sway. Feet shuffled inside before the bolt snapped and a gnarled and leathery figure appeared through the sun-faded door. The man bore a faint resemblance to the weather-beaten home he lived in, but unlike the rugged structure surrounding him, his stooped posture and thin frame wouldn't have stopped a stiff wind sweeping in off the ocean.

"What can I do for you?"

"Are you Raymond Knoll?"

"Who wants to know?" the man answered, revealing a salty lifelong New Englander suckled on piss and vinegar.

"I'm Robert Granville. My wife, Kacey."

She extended her hand. "It's nice to meet you, sir."

The man nodded, grasping her hand with his left, like a politician. "Ma'am." He remained behind the door's safety, tilting his head as he inspected RG's face. "Robert Granville. The name sounds familiar."

"I'm sorry, have we met? I teach over at Cape Cod Community if that helps."

"You're a professor?" he asked.

"Yes, sir."

"The 'Fugitive Professor,' perhaps?"

Here we go. RG closed his eyes. "Some have called me that."

Knoll's face lit up as he threw open the door, the breeze sending a ripple through his clothing and revealing the man's haggard, tent pole frame. "Well, I'll be gobsmacked! Come in, I'd hoped to run into you one day, and here you are, right on my front stoop."

RG glanced at Kacey before stepping through the door. *"Now what have we gotten ourselves into,"* he said, speaking into her mind.

"Must be nice to be famous."

RG's eyes adjusted to the dim surroundings, the dwindling afternoon light fighting the gloom. Books lined the man's shelves from floor to ceiling, several aligned vertically while others had been stacked to fill free space. The overflow found its way onto the hardwood flooring, tomes piled eye high, carving snaking pathways through the house. A writer's warren if he ever imagined one. A small, open kitchen joined the main room almost as an afterthought, as if the builder remembered those living here would have to eat at some point. Knoll shuffled over to an ancient rolltop writing desk and rummaged through a sheaf of papers, ignoring the grand view of the Atlantic through the bay window. RG's eyes drifted to the sleeve pinned above his right shoulder.

RG's eyes darted to Kacey's. *"Now I understand why he shook hands with you the way he did."*

Peeking into the crowded bedroom off the main room, RG discovered a roomful of odds and ends and collectibles, television consoles from the sixties, a hand-crank Victrola with brass gramophone horn, and a pearl-colored Ludwig drum kit nestled beside a twin mattress. He signaled Kacey with a head nod.

Kacey squinted as she peered behind RG into the bedroom. *"A one-armed drummer?"*

"Could be a Def Leppard fan."

"Please sit." Knoll pointed to the flower-print sofa beside the fireplace. "I'm a writer, if you haven't figure it out by now." He gestured toward the bedroom. "Or a hoarder. Take your pick. I'm writing a book about strange happenings on Cape Cod, and your case intrigues me." He gathered his notebook computer and tucked it under his arm. "I have so many questions."

"Sir," Kacey began, "we're hoping to ask you a few questions, too. About your book."

"Ah, which one?" The man snaked a self-conscious hand through his hearty gray locks, as if revisiting a time when his appearance had mattered. The man had an Einstein quality to him, all hair, untended and flowing. Even the tufts sprouting from his ears blended in with the surrounding mane. "I have several published under my imprint, Cape and Islands Press. Have you heard of it?"

"I haven't," RG confessed. "But we just bought *Cape Cod Death Houses*. Priced a bit steep for an eBook if you ask me—"

"We had a few questions about it, Mr. Knoll," Kacey interrupted, pinching RG's side and twisting for good measure. "If you'd be willing to talk with us."

His face hardened. "Depends. What did you want to know?"

"We need information on the Barnard Street house. The one in Chatham. A number of accidents have happened—"

"I know the house," Knoll said, raising a hand. Stepping to his recliner, he rested his computer on the end table before sinking into the cushion.

"Mr. Knoll," Kacey leaned forward. "I'm sorry if this sound insensitive, but how did you lose your arm?"

"A childhood accident." He turned to RG. "Why the interest in the Barnard Street house?"

"Things have happened at the house recently. Dead bodies have turned up there. It's all over the news." RG searched for a television but didn't spot one.

"Oh, Christ." He rubbed his temple with his thumb and index finger. "Will it ever stop?"

RG reached for Kacey's hand. "Will *what* ever stop?"

He raised his head and blinked, blood-red vessels etched across pearly sclerae. "The evil."

"What do you know about the house? Besides the stories in your book."

"I lived there. I know more than anyone. More than I've ever shared in my books." His gaze drifted toward the fireplace. "If I wrote about things I've witnessed, people would say I'm crazy. But then again, I imagine if you told people everything *you* know, they'd say you're crazy too, right?"

RG deliberated for a moment. "I'm not sure what you mean."

"I read about an eight-year-old boy at the Barnard Street house who lost his arm in a washing machine," Kacey said.

His gaze drifted toward the sleeve pinned above his shoulder. "Yours truly."

RG leaned against the sofa back. "We have a lot to ask you."

"Well, I've got questions, too."

RG crossed his legs. "Go ahead."

"I'm writing a chapter about a mysterious death in Chatham. A Falmouth police chief, killed in your friend's house, if I'm not mistaken. An explosion, wasn't it? One that nearly killed you."

"Just a gas leak. Could have happened to any—"

"If you're gonna lie," Knoll interrupted, "you and your lovely wife are welcome to get the hell out of here. You want to know about Barnard Street, you'll have to do better than that. I want to know what happened on Old Harbor Road two years ago."

RG debated how much to tell the man. He wanted to spill his guts, tell him tales of caretakers and jumpers, secrets of an afterlife different than Knoll could possibly imagine. But when he glanced at Kacey, he sensed her reticence. He recalled Morrow's warning. But RG would have to give the man something or they wouldn't get far with him.

"We had a visitor the night Detective Stahl's house exploded. A man of fire. Not sure entirely where he came from, but he wanted to take us back with him. He's gone now."

"Is he?" Knoll asked. "By your hand?"

RG curled his fingers around Kacey's. "Many hands."

"I had a visitor at the Barnard Street house. But he kept coming back. A man named Luther Greer." Knoll's blank stare drifted toward the ceiling. "You see, I used to live in the back bedroom of the house. One night I woke to find a strange man sitting on my bed. He told me he had died at the house years before, on the front lawn."

"Luther Greer? I don't recall the name in *Death Houses*?"

"He holds the distinction of being the first victim of Barnard Street. But I didn't write about him. He wouldn't have…agreed to that."

"What happened to him?" Kacey asked.

"Luther was a flamboyant fella, especially for his time, if you know what I mean." Knoll closed the notebook and placed it on the end table beside his chair. "Impeccably dressed, but a bit ostentatious for many of the hardworking folks in Chatham. He lived on a large estate overlooking the sea but loved to be around the bustle of downtown. Right after the war, lots of soldiers had returned stateside. One day, Luther passed several flyboys on the street and made a… suggestion the other man didn't take kindly to. The man gathered a few of his friends and chased him down Main Street and through back streets until they caught him on Barnard. They beat him to within an inch of his life and finished it off by throwing a rope across a tree branch and garroting him in front of the house."

"Oh, my god," Kacey cried.

"Luther chose to visit me at night. I'm sure it sounds crazy, but he found a way inside me, or inside my head, I couldn't tell. But wherever he was, he was real. One night, he tells me the house has a magic room. I'm staring at the back-bedroom wall through the darkness and it doesn't make sense because now there's a staircase leading right through it. Never seen it before. Luther just wanted to show it to me."

"Weren't you scared?" Kacey asked.

"What did I know? I was eight years old. I'm sure I chalked it up to a dream. At any rate, I made the decision to step through the wall and check it out." Knoll edged up in his chair, sitting on the edge, eyes alight. Kacey sensed his eagerness to finally tell someone what he saw. "When I reached the bottom step, Greer stood in the center of a cold, dank cave. Stone walkways crisscrossed the floor, and solid rock towers rose hundreds of feet into the air. It resembled Hell, the one an artist might depict in religious paintings or our Sunday school Bible for children."

Kacey closed her eyes and nodded, as if remembering a similar hell.

"People milled about, but they didn't appear to belong there. They wore different style clothes and haircuts, as if I gazed back in time decade by decade. I recognized one of them, Missy French, a classmate from my school. She had disappeared on Barnard Street not long before Luther began visiting me. She always had a big smile plastered across her face. But when I glimpsed her in the cave, she didn't quite resemble herself anymore. Everything human or childlike about her had long disappeared."

Knoll folded his lips, as if recalling the horror of what he saw.

"Go on," RG prodded.

Knoll shook his head silently. "I'm not sure you'll want to hear the rest."

"Please. We need to know what's there."

"The worst part had to be the bodies. Luther had hung them on these wood hangman poles, some upside down. Many gutted. I just stood there on the step, staring at this world existing under my house. I had this churning in my gut that if I set foot on the cave floor, if I moved from that final step, the door above me would shut and I'd never get out of there. I'd turn into a shell of myself, like Missy French, or wind up hanging from a wooden post. So, I turned and raced back upstairs as fast as I could. I escaped just as the open wall sealed shut behind me. After that, I slept in the bath."

"Did you ever run into Luther again?" RG asked.

"No, but he let me know he wasn't pleased with me. Wasn't long after, I'm helping my mother with the laundry. She's outside hanging clothes on the line while I'm loading up the new washing machine my father had hooked up the day before. I get this creepy sensation Luther's in the room with me. I guess I should have been frightened, but on a beautiful spring day with a sweet pollen scent blowing through the window screens, it just didn't register. And my mother was standing at the clothesline a stone's throw away, singing to herself. Why should I be scared, right?"

Kacey smiled and shook her head.

"But then the washing machine lid slams down on my arm and the lights and dials start flashing and turning. The thing begins bouncing along the floor and grunting like some living, breathing animal." The cords in Knoll's forearms tighten as he pulled on the sleeve where his arm should have been. "The lid presses down harder and harder, and I'm losing feeling. The barrel inside is spinning like a turbine, and I can feel the whoosh of air passing above and below my arm, nearly giving it lift. I think to myself, if I move my arm an inch, the machine's swirling spokes and edges will pulverize it. But then the lid bites down on me."

"Bites?" RG leaned forward.

"I'm aware how crazy it sounds, but the thing had come alive, and its teeth sunk deep into my skin, snapping the bone.

Luther had been inside it, controlling it, and he took my arm. They never found any of it either, just an explosion of splattered blood on the inside of a new Whirlpool."

Knoll strolled across the room and cracked the window. The steady ocean swell pounding the sand stretched through the room's prominent silence.

Dropping into his chair, Knoll scratched his stubbled chin. "I'm convinced if there's a hell on earth, it's located beneath the Barnard Street home."

"You might be right, but we need to get back there." RG signaled to Kacey, and they rose from their seats. "You've given us a sense of what we'll be facing."

"Don't go back there." Knoll didn't move from his chair. "If you do, you'll never come back."

"We know what we're doing."

Knoll lifted his gaze in a slow arc. "You can't possibly know what you're doing…or what awaits you."

Knoll rose from his chair and escorted the pair to the door, hesitating before unsnapping the bolt. "Another story caught my attention. Causing quite a buzz on social media. Children around here returning home, some after many decades."

RG and Kacey locked gazes.

Knoll pivoted with his back toward the door, blocking their exit.

"And yet, they come back unchanged, the same age as when they left." The floorboards creaked under Knoll's shifting weight. "I keep stumbling across your friend's name in social media posts, Mike Stahl. How grateful people are for what he has done. And what would that be?"

"He works with social services helping find foster homes for children. He's been doing it for years," Kacey said.

"Foster homes, huh?" Knoll rubbed his chin. "You see, I suspect the detective had something to do with these children returning home. And since he's your friend, I'm convinced you had something to do with their return, too. Tell me I'm wrong."

RG's gaze drifted to the floor. "I don't know what you mean."

"Second time you've said that." Knoll leaned forward to inspect RG's expression. "And, I'll tell you, keeping secrets only burdens the soul. It does not protect those we think we're protecting."

RG opened his mouth, but Kacey interrupted. "Mr. Knoll, thank you for your time today, but we have to be going." She extended her hand.

"Well, I guess that's it then." Knoll grasped their hands with his good one and stepped aside. As RG and Kacey strode from the house, RG glanced back at Knoll, the man's jaw clenching as his gaze fixated on the couple.

"I hope you're better at fighting the dead than you are at lying," he huffed, "or you won't be coming back from Barnard Street." He disappeared behind the door.

* * *

Mike

Stahl froze like a home intruder caught on video, his brain scrambling for a convincing excuse to explain his presence in Daniels' workshop. He wanted to come clean, talk to his friend, but the little voice told him to play his cards close to the chest. He had discovered too much in too short a time, and he needed time to process the information, figure out how to proceed.

He gaped at Daniels, the man he had worked beside for the past two years, the dedicated cop he had trained to be a top-notch detective and forensics expert, the man who had come to be his friend. He wasn't sure he recognized him anymore, the weight of Stahl's newfound knowledge adding a distorted layer to the man, obscuring his view.

"Hey. I've been looking for you. Figured you might be out here." He tossed a thumb toward the second bay. "Looks like the Cobra Jet's coming along."

Daniels entered the barn and brushed past Stahl. "You been here long." His eyes darted toward the cigar box and back to Stahl.

"Just long enough to admire your handiwork. I tried the house."

"Had to run out for a couple of parts." He raised the plastic Auto Zone bag and stepped toward his workstation. Dropping the bag on the counter, he scanned the photographs and letters scattered across the table as if attempting to discern whether anything appeared out of place. He lifted the hand-written letter Stahl had perused and placed it back inside the cigar box.

He knows I know.

Daniels rubbed his hand along the Formica countertop. "So, what brings you out here?"

Stahl froze, his mind a blank. "Can't I stop by and pretend I'm on vacation, too?"

"Usually when I spot fresh skid marks near my driveway, I suspect the person making them had a more pressing reason."

"Daydreaming behind the wheel, that's all. I almost missed the turn."

Daniels crossed his arms. He wasn't buying it. Stahl would have to give him something.

"Ah, fuck it!" Stahl pressed his hands against his hips and scuffed at the floor with his shoe. "I have to talk to you about the Sarnie case. Things aren't adding up, and I have questions."

"Questions about the case," he asked, glancing at the cigar box, "or about me?"

Stahl scratched his head. "I'm not sure yet."

"Well, what the hell does that mean?"

"It means you haven't been straight with me."

Daniels didn't answer.

"Why did you ask me to talk to Jimmy McKinnon?"

Daniels packed the contents of the cigar box and placed it inside a drawer. "Because he's involved."

"How do you know?"

Daniels shifted his weight from one foot to the other. "I can't tell you. I just know."

"Well, I did find a connection to Jimmy McKinnon." Stahl paced toward the far end of the barn before turning to face Daniels. "Nothing in your reports, of course. Suddenly it's right there in front of me. I didn't find it until today, but a week ago you're telling me to investigate Jimmy McKinnon." Stahl filled his cheeks before blowing out a breath. "It's like you knew something and weren't gonna bother telling me. Or maybe you *forgot* to put it in the report." He air-quoted the word with his fingers.

"What connection?" Daniels' body deflated like it had a slow leak, as if he anticipated the answer to his own question.

"Just something in the weeks before the accident." Stahl wasn't about to reveal what he knew, that McKinnon had been calling the woman Daniels loved before her death, or that he had also found his partner's number in Jessie's burner.

"Something between McKinnon and Sarnie…or with Jessie?" He called her by name.

Stahl didn't have a clue how McKinnon had known Jessie Sarnie, but judging from Daniels' response, the reason had to be the oldest one in the book. "I can't tell you."

Daniels jammed his hands against his hips. "I guess we're both keeping secrets now."

"You have the balls to say that to me?" Stahl said, squeezing his fingers against his palms. "You're a hidden fountain of knowledge about this case. Anything else you can tell me now to save me time? You know, before I find it myself."

Daniels jaw clenched. "That stings."

"Does it?" Stahl turned and limped toward the door. "You fought for lead on this one. You've been controlling the direction of this case from day one."

"You're out of line." Daniels eyes blazed with a heat that warmed the air between them.

"All you have to do is talk to me. I have questions, and I'm gonna find answers one way or another, with you or without you."

"All right, then." Daniels held his hands up. "Go ahead, ask me anything."

Stahl leaned against the doorjamb. He wasn't ready to reveal everything he had discovered, the detective in him overriding their friendship at the moment. "I'm heading to Boston to talk to McKinnon tomorrow, but you've got to tell me everything you know about him."

"Okay." Daniels leaned his elbow on the counter. "Alex Sarnie used to work for Big Mac."

"When?"

"I'm not sure, seven, eight years ago."

"Jesus, Chris, that's ancient history." Stahl threw his hands out to his sides. "How's that relevant now?"

"The guy ran Sarnie out of town. He wanted him dead."

"How do you know?"

"Just talk to him," Daniels said. "Oh, and bring some backup."

Stahl rolled his eyes. *Thanks for that.* "Anything else you want to tell me before I head up to Southie?"

"Like what?"

"Like…am I wasting my time?"

Chris Daniels stared at the floor, hands on his hips as if faced with a complicated riddle. After a moment he raised his head. "What the hell does that mean?"

"I'm giving you a chance to talk to me."

"That's what you say when we're playing good-cop-bad-cop and sweating someone out under the lights."

Stahl remained silent, eyes fixed on Daniels.

"Is that what this has turned into? An interrogation?" Daniels dropped onto the stool beside his workstation. He buried his head into his hands for a moment before raising his eyes to Stahl. "You're forgetting something. I'm your partner. Not to mention, your friend. I learned about the 'House of Horrors' on my way over here. Mick Sullivan's place. You gonna arrest me for that, too?"

"Not my case." Stahl turned and headed toward the door. "I'll be back when I'm done with McKinnon. He's gonna answer my questions, and when I get back, and so are you."

CHAPTER FOURTEEN

Wednesday, March 30

Mike

Stahl's fingers drummed the Crown Vic's moist steering wheel as he pushed the beast along 93 North toward South Boston, the highway swollen with late-morning traffic inching along from the Braintree split to Quincy. Stahl blotted his palms on his shirt and took a deep breath. He had arranged a meeting with Jimmy McKinnon at The Kells on Broadway, one of the crime boss's favorite haunts. Despite his suspicions, Stahl owed it to Daniels to give Big Mac a once-over, his partner adamant the crime boss had orchestrated the Sarnie family's deaths. No evidence linked the thug to the accident so far, least of all a bunch of calls on Jessie's cell, but nothing ruled him out, either. He would have to be sure.

The ride north had given Stahl ample time to find ways

to eliminate Daniels from suspicion, but he couldn't ignore the little voice in his head. Sure, Big Mac may have had a history with Sarnie, but two scenarios closer to home pointed to the dead man, and Daniels remained the common denominator in both: a brother exacting revenge for a dying sister and a jealous lover in way over his head. In Stahl's experience, passion proved a deadly wildcard, leaving many good men caged in a six-by-eight cell, puzzling over how something that had once swelled their heart had eventually darkened it. And after what he'd read in the letters from Jessie Sarnie, Daniels had been caught in the snare. Stahl needed answers.

He took the Columbia Road exit toward Dorchester/South Boston. Despite an effort at gentrification—upscale restaurants and a Starbucks' catty-corner from each trendy new clothing boutique or smoothie bar—the place couldn't shake the gritty, working-class underbelly from which it sought to distance itself.

"Still a fucking shithole," he mumbled.

He had shaded the truth with Big Mac, telling him he needed to understand more about Alex and Jessie Sarnie, and why someone might have stolen their bodies. The tricky part for Stahl would be gauging Big Mac's level of involvement without giving away his intentions. He had told him the meeting would be informal, just a few questions off the record. But tapping an unpredictable and ruthless killer's mind on his home turf wasn't something to take lightly, informal or not.

Stories of Big Mac's violent temper remained legend around Beantown, including his alleged beheading of a local informant in a crowded Southie pub during the St. Patrick's Day parade a few years back. Stahl's carrying a shield from a small town on the Cape wouldn't afford him any special privileges if things went south. And Stahl would be outnumbered.

Big Mac never traveled alone; he would have plenty of help to get rid of a body if his temper got the best of him.

Chief Defranco had insisted on backup for Stahl's endeavor, assigning Matt Berrelli as his security detail. Despite wanting to go it alone, Stahl agreed the former Southie tough might be the ideal cop for this gig. If the shit went down, Berrelli wouldn't hesitate to come in with guns blazing. Not so much to protect Stahl, but to make sure he got a chance to shoot someone. He had insisted Berrelli follow in an unmarked and park down the street outside the meeting place and wait for his cell signal if needed. Separate vehicles would ensure Stahl's presence would appear less threatening to Big Mac, but also guarantee he didn't have to spend a single minute in a car with the volatile cop.

As he pulled the car in front of The Kells, a shiver tickled the back of his neck. "It'll be fine," he muttered, glancing at his nervous reflection in the rearview. *What's the worst that could happen?*

He had never met Big Mac; he had been introduced to him through a grainy image on surveillance photos in dusty case files. But Stahl didn't need any visual aids to pick out the man wedged in the deserted café's corner table. He possessed a brazen aura, a palpable energy surrounding him like an electrical field. He rolled a pencil along his index, pointer, and ring fingers like a baton, then back again, his eyes darting between his two men securing the entrance and the other leaning against an old Wurlitzer along the back wall. Stahl's blood pressure kicked up when he scanned the eatery, not expecting it to be uninhabited so close to the lunch hour rush.

Big Mac's physical appearance didn't jibe with Stahl's expectations of an underworld crime boss—he wore no designer suit or Italian shoes, and his body wasn't soft around the middle from an indulgent life. Instead, Big Mac looked as if he spent as much time in the gym as he did running South Boston. Baggy jeans cinched a narrow waist, and a short sleeve polo shirt cut to mid-biceps hugged his upper body. A shock of Irish red hair and wide eyes completed the picture, conferring a youthful innocence to a murderer's face. His muscle dressed with a more casual flair, Celtics tee shirts over waffle knit thermals or hoodies and sweats. Stahl wasn't naïve enough to imagine they chose their mufti for any other reason than to hide a deadly arsenal beneath the bulk.

Stahl gazed about the dim café, catching his uneasy reflection in the mirror running the length of the rear wall. Thick overhead beams and wood flooring muted the ambient light peeking from the wall fixtures spaced like sconces along the rich wood paneling, resembling a medieval Irish castle with Big Mac perched on its throne.

As he advanced into the café, a heavy hand descended onto his shoulder from behind, bending his knee and stopping him in his tracks.

"Slow down," Big Mac's lieutenant said. A scar snaked from the man's eye to his chin, and his teeth appeared as if someone had extracted them with pliers and returned them to the wrong sockets.

"What?"

"You'll get Mr. McKinnon nervous." Scar kept his hand planted on Stahl's shoulder and eased him from the door to Big Mac's table. The thug's heavy boots, no doubt another weapon in his arsenal, punctuated each deliberate step.

"Detective Stahl?" Big Mac waved a hand at the chair opposite him. "You look about as comfortable as a nun at an orgy, but Southie does that to some people. Especially cops. Have a seat."

As Stahl lowered himself into his seat, his line of sight fell below the wall mirror in front of him. He wouldn't be able to monitor Scar and his companion while seated, leaving his flank exposed.

Dammit!

Rule number one: never sit with your back to the door. At least the tough beside the Wurlitzer remained in his direct line of sight and he could keep an eye on him.

Stahl winced as he adjusted his position on the hardwood chair.

"Still nursing those bullet wounds, I see. Hip and shoulder if I remember correctly. I read about you a few years ago. You were all over the news." The pencil rolled across his knuckles and between his fingers. "What did the press call his fucking pal?" he shouted to his cronies.

"The 'Fugitive Professor,'" Wurlitzer offered.

"This man," Big Mac spoke up, pointing at Stahl, "solved a case from a hospital bed. Freed a man wrongfully accused of murder. That, my friends, is dedication."

"I read he takes care of little children, too," Scar added from the entryway. "Finds homes for them and everything." McKinnon's men chortled.

Big Mac pressed his eyes shut and gave a dismissive head shake. He gestured toward the man behind the bar. "You want something from the kitchen? Sean, over there, can whip up just about any dish you can imagine and still add a bit of Irish to it."

"I appreciate the offer, but if you don't mind, I'd like to get down to business. This nun has to get back to the monastery."

Big Mac snorted a chuckle and folded his thick arms. "Okay. So, here are the ground rules." His face dropped into a more somber veneer. "You called an informal meeting, and we're off the record. The way I see it, we're like two old friends getting together for a talk."

Where's he going with this?

"And when friends come to visit, they have to relinquish their firearms."

"Mr. McKinnon, I'm a police officer."

"Not today, you're not. You're a guest in my house, and in my house, you follow my rules."

Stahl held up his hands. "I'm no threat to you—"

"Everybody's a threat to me," Big Mac interrupted, "and I don't know you from Adam. You give up your piece or you get back on 93 South."

Under normal circumstances, Mike wouldn't accept such terms, but the fate of the world hung on his finding Alex Sarnie, and to do that, he had to find out who killed him. He also had a burning desire to find out whether his partner played a role.

Stahl assessed his situation. A stranger alone in a deserted Southie eatery with the most ruthless crime boss in Boston history, three hired guns tracking his every move. He needed information, and only Big Mac could give it to him. And he had no way to defend himself. But on the plus side, he had Berrelli outside if things went south. It didn't exactly equal out, but he reached under his jacket and unholstered his HK45, pulling it out butt first and laying it on the table.

"Helluva stopper, detective. I'd bet you could solve the Cape's shark problem with this thing." Another chuckle arose from his men, a bit too loud. From the front door, Scar clomped toward the table and confiscated the piece, jamming it into his waistband.

"So, what do you want to talk about?" Big Mac folded his fingers around his pencil and leaned back.

"The Alex Sarnie investigation."

"Not sure I can help but I'm happy to try. You must be pretty desperate if you're coming to me."

Stahl shrugged. "Hate to say it, but we are. I hoped

someone acquainted with him might be able to give me a little direction on the case."

"Shame about what happened to him." He shook his head, scratching a thumbnail along the pencil eraser. "Tough way to go out. What do you suppose happened to his body?"

"If I had any clue, I wouldn't have spent my morning stuck on 93 North. We're going on the theory that whoever stole the bodies may also have been responsible for the family's deaths, but we have no evidence that what happened was anything but an accident." Stahl leaned forward. "Tell me about your relationship with Alex Sarnie."

The crime boss snaked a cigarette from the pack resting on the table, positioned it in his mouth, and reached for a matchbook. "Alex and I go back a ways," he said, the unlit butt bobbing up and down like a conductor's baton as he spoke. "He used to stock all my clubs and restaurants with food and booze before he moved to the Cape."

Big Mac ignited the tobacco. He slid the pack across the table, but Stahl shook his head.

"How long has it been since you've been in contact with him?"

"Hadn't talked to him in years." Big Mac took a deep drag.

Yeah, but you talked to his wife, didn't you? "At one time he worked as one of your main distributors, correct?"

"My only distributor."

"And your business relationship ended because…why? He moved to the Cape?"

McKinnon tapped his cigarette ash into a dented soda can. "What does my business relationship have to do with his missing body?"

"Nothing at all," he assured him. "Just trying to get the full picture."

Big Mac narrowed his eyes. "Go on."

"So, would you say you had a falling out?"

"A difference of *opinion*. We thought it best to cut ties."

"Anyone you can think of at that time who had a beef with him? Who might either want him dead or humiliate him after death?"

Big Mac balanced the butt in his mouth as he twirled the pencil across his fingers. "If you think these are the types of people I would know, you must not think very highly of me."

Stahl grinned. "No offense intended."

McKinnon pressed his fingers against his cig and sucked in a nicotine-rich breath. "Alex had been a regular in my clubs. Got to know all the boys." He gestured to his thugs securing the café. "Never caused any trouble."

"As you know, his wife, Jessie, also died in the accident." Stahl hesitated a moment to gauge Big Mac's reaction. A twitch pulled at the corner of the crime boss's eye. "Did you know her at all?"

Big Mac relaxed. A wisp of smoke trailed from his cigarette, spiraling toward the ceiling. "Jessie Bolduc came to me from New Jersey, looking to be a star. She ended up as a dancer in one of my clubs."

"Do you recall if any particular customers took a special liking to her?"

"They all did." Big Mac's demeanor softened, his guard dropping for a moment. "She had…something…the other girls didn't." Big Mac gently rubbed the pencil between his thumb and index finger.

"Off the record, was she…just a dancer?"

"Detective Stahl," he said, pressing a hand to his chest. "Are you insinuating the activity in my clubs might be illegal?" His men's forced laughter rung across the café.

"Off the record."

"You might say she did a little of everything."

"Anyone ever get violent around her, threaten her in any way?"

Big Mac stared at Stahl, his hand gripping the pencil in a fist. "If they did, they'd have never left my club."

"Have you been in touch with Jessie since she moved to the Cape?"

A vein in Big Mac's neck throbbed as his voice rose. "What the fuck kind of question is that?" Big Mac's body grew before his eyes, mirroring the man's agitation level. "You got someone out there who stole three bodies from a funeral home and arranged 'em around a kitchen table. You got a third one missing…and you're asking me if I've been in touch with Jessie?"

"Mr. McKinnon," Stahl backpedaled, "someone with a beef against you could have taken it out on them. We just don't know. I'm trying to gather information to explore every angle and rule out any possibilities."

Big Mac leaned his elbows in the table. "I'm gonna be frank with you, detective. I agreed to help out of respect for the dead. I'd like to help you with your case. You believe that, don't you?"

Stahl raised his palms off the table. "You wouldn't have agreed to meet if you didn't."

He blew smoke from the corner of his mouth. "Jessie and I continued to see each other off and on, despite her being married. She wasn't what you call a one-man woman. But we were discreet."

"When's the last time you saw her?"

"It's been a few years." The way he said it with his eyes staring off for a moment, Stahl glimpsed the man's vulnerability. "Four maybe?" He stopped rubbing the pencil.

"I don't mean to pry, but did your falling out with Alex Sarnie stem from Jessie?"

"I had finished with her when Alex and I parted ways." Big Mac waved a hand, his hardened exterior returning. "I gave her to him. He just happened to fall in love with her."

"What about Alex? You been in touch lately?"

"Not since he left Southie."

Stahl shifted in his chair. He had the distinct impression that if Big Mac couldn't have Jessie, no one would.

Big Mac's cell chirped in his back pocket. He held up his finger as he placed it to his ear, listening for a moment. "Who is this?" Big Mac gazed at the table as the time stretched, his eyes tracking upward until they locked onto Stahl's. The muscles in his jaw rippled as he clenched his teeth. "I appreciate your telling me." Big Mac disconnected, never taking his eyes from Stahl. He signaled to Sean behind the bar.

"Now I have a question for you, detective." Big Mac rose from his chair, standing like a monolith before him and blocking the light filtering from the frosted windows. "What are you *really* doing here?"

Sean wandered toward the front entrance.

Shit. "I'm just gathering—"

"You building a case against me?" Big Mac interrupted, pulling his chair around and straddling it.

"Like I said, I need all the help I can get on this one."

"Something you probably don't know about me. I got friends everywhere. They let me know when something ain't right." His knuckles blushed white as he choked the pencil, snapping it in two. "You may have solved a murder from your hospital bed, but you can't solve one from the morgue."

Calm him down. "Mr. McKinnon, I'm not sure what's gotten you so upset. You're misinterpreting my—"

"You want to know my whereabouts the night they died? That your next question?" he asked, a grin spreading across his face. "I'll answer it for you. It doesn't matter, because I have at least four men in this room that will vouch for me."

Big Mac's eyes migrated upward, coming to rest on what Stahl assumed to be the vein pulsing in his temple, as if estimating his racing heart. "You come here alone?"

Breathe, Mike. This had turned too quickly.

Big Mac leaned forward. "Big mistake," he whispered.

He needed to signal Berrelli. Stahl pulled out his cell. "You need to understand something. I press this button, and I'll have more cops swarming this place than you can—"

"Stay away from the poker tables, Stahl," Big Mac interrupted, eyes blazing. "You can't bluff for shit. Go ahead. Press your buttons. Call the cavalry." He rubbed a hand across his chin. "I know most of those Boston boys personally. A lot of them grew up right here in Southie. A couple of them stood right beside me when I put Billy Crowder down right over there." He pointed to a spot beside the bar. "Like a dog. Forty-five magnum to the back of the head. You ever see what a firearm like that can do to the human brain? Let me give them a call, get 'em down here. They can watch what I'm about to do. And they'll tell you what you should have already known."

Stahl swallowed. "What's that?"

"The first rule of being a cop…always make it home at the end of your shift." He nodded at Sean.

The front door bolt clicked.

"I imagine the worst thing about being a cop is you never know when that day's gonna come. One minute you're out doing your job, the next…"

Think, Mike. Think!

Big Mac grinned. "At least now you know." He rested his elbows on the table and leaned forward. "Don't worry, your pension will take care of Claire and Zach. I just hate to see them left all alone. But that's the problem with cops…sometimes they die."

His family's name rolling off Big Mac's tongue struck him like a blow to the head, shaking off the fear and waking him from his stupor. Stahl stood and pointed at McKinnon. "What the fuck did you just say to me?"

Two sets of footsteps scraped the wood floor, Big Mac's muscle advancing from the front entrance.

Big Mac rose from his chair and glanced at Wurlitzer. "Guys got some big balls for someone about to be scattered around a Southie landfill."

With Big Mac's gaze diverted, Stahl peeked into the wall mirror above the jukebox, catching sight of McKinnon's two henchmen moving toward him, Scar holding Stahl's HK45 at arm's length. He anticipated it would be a head shot, up close. Too risky to shoot from anywhere else with Big Mac directly behind Stahl. They may have had overwhelming firepower, but they had no training and advanced toward him single file. The second man had deferred to Scar for the hit, his gun still resting in his waistband, but if forced to shoot, he would have to fire through his compadre to hit Stahl. That meant one gun to worry about from the rear.

Stahl directed his gaze from the mirror back to Big Mac, not wanting to reveal his intentions. He would have to time his move with expert precision. But Scar had given himself away. Twice. Stahl had counted the thug's twelve clomping footfalls, first when he had led him to Big Mac's table and again when he confiscated his weapon. He could sense the advancing killer only steps away, gun clutched in an extended arm, approximately twenty-four inches from shoulder to fist for the average sized man, Stahl calculated…about the length of a full step at his size. Stahl would feel the cold steel against his head somewhere around step eleven. The footfalls crept closer…six, seven, eight…

Stahl closed his eyes. Waiting.

Slinging his left hand over his right shoulder, Stahl grasped the semi-automatic handgun at the barrel just inches behind his head. He yanked it forward, jolting Scar off balance, jamming the henchman's finger against the trigger. The bullet exploded inches past Big Mac's head, shattering the wall mirror and sending the crime boss scrambling beneath his chair. As Scar stumbled forward, Stahl's elbow flew back, crunching his face and loosening a few of his snaggled teeth as he dropped him to the floor. Scar's limp hand dropped the HK45, but Stahl caught it midair and pressed it between Big Mac's eyes.

"You want to know who dies? Two-bit crime bosses like you." Blue cables stood out on Stahl's neck as he repositioned the stopper. In an instant, Stahl stared down the muzzle of Wurlitzer's Tech nine, and sensed the weight of another automatic pressed against the back of his head. The metallic clink of cocked hammers filled Stahl's ears.

Heat surged through his twitching muscles, and he stared at Big Mac with a controlled fury. "If I go…you go, too. You ever seen what an HK45 can do to the human brain?"

Big Mac swallowed. A single bead of sweat trickled from his temple to the corner of his eye.

"Tell them to drop their pieces and kick them over to the bar."

Big Mac nodded to his men. The firearms thunked one-by-one onto the floor and skittered across the hardwood surface.

Turning his attention to Big Mac, Stahl pressed the gun's muzzle harder into Big Mac's forehead. "You don't get to mention my family. Understand? Make no mistake, if I catch you anywhere near them, I'll shoot you and feed you to the sharks, dead or alive. You pussy out and send any of these sonsofbitches to do your dirty work, they'll get the same. Then I'll come back for you. Do whatever the fuck you want here, rule your shit kingdom for all I care, but I'd think twice about heading south."

"You got balls on you, Stahl. I'll give you that."

He pulled the stopper from Big Mac's forehead, leaving a barrel-size ring burning against the man's skin. "All of you. Stand over there where I can see you." Stahl waved the HK45, corralling the boss's underlings behind Big Mac. Sean dragged the unconscious Scar across the floor, his boot heels leaving skid marks in the hardwood.

Returning to the table, Stahl pressed his palms against the surface and leaned forward, his face inches from Big Mac's. "I'm done with my questions."

He stepped toward the front door, pausing to scan the café. His heart had eased its assault against his ribcage as he took in the sight of the biggest crime boss in Boston and his killers huddled behind a table in the corner.

Big Mac rose from his chair and stepped around the table, locking gazes with Stahl. "Don't come back to Southie."

"Don't worry." Stahl holstered his stopper. "The place is a fucking shithole."

CHAPTER FIFTEEN

Wednesday, March 30

Kacey

As the sun settled below the horizon, Kacey nosed into the parking lot behind the withered service station, deep cracks running like fault lines across the crumbling tar. Angled sunlight bathed the Barnard Street house's back porch, its broken balusters stretching jagged shadows toward the police vehicle idling in the parking lot, as if straining to pierce the officers through the glass barrier. Crime scene tape circled the clapboard house like ribbon around a Christmas present. Stahl had informed Kacey and RG the cops and forensic teams had finished their work, and he would meet them there when he returned from Boston. The two had waited more than an hour, but Stahl hadn't shown up. They had tried his cell over and over, and he hadn't picked up or returned their call.

Chatham PD had assigned at least one detail to monitor the 'House of Horrors' and dissuade the curious, now assembling along Barnard Street. But Kacey and RG wouldn't get close to it without Stahl.

"How the hell are we going to get into the house now?"

"Time to take matters into our hands."

"We can't just march past everyone and go through the front door."

Kacey pinched RG's cheeks, forcing his lips open. "Um… yeah, we can."

She turned the car around and disappeared behind the service station and out of sight from the patrolmen. A metallic shudder gripped the Outback as Kacey cut the engine and pulled the key. She extracted the small locket from around her neck.

"What are you doing?" RG asked.

"We have to find a way past the crowd." Kacey turned the locket over in her hand. She had received the ornate piece of jewelry from a caretaker who hadn't made it back from his mission in Plymouth the previous summer. If his gift could free up a mere thirty seconds, they could make it past the cops and explore the Barnard Street house's secrets without detection.

"You sure you want to do that? If I recall, the experience isn't so pleasant. It's like a workout at the gym, but without the air conditioning."

"If you have another idea how to get into the house, I'm all ears." Kacey exited the car and blew out a breath. "You ready?"

RG shrugged. "Can I stretch first?"

"You're stalling."

Kacey closed her eyes. Grasping the locket, she extended her arm from body and twisted her hand into a fist. The air thickened as the world's sounds muffled. Time ground to a halt before them with a metallic screech, like an old set of wheels on a neglected junker spinning to a stop. Kacey could imagine the world slowing on its axis, fighting the physical laws fixed on keeping it in motion.

"Let's go, we don't have much time." She pictured her friend Wilder's garish dress and long flowing locks, her smile tempered by the irony that he had gifted her the power to stop time but hadn't been able to prevent the stoppage of his own.

"I'm trying." RG's voice came from a distance, like a bad phone connection. Each air molecule's atoms no longer vibrated in their orbitals but hung suspended in the frozen atmosphere and formed a barrier to the sound, as if the words traveled through water.

They trudged through the molasses-thick air in slow motion, their bodies laboring to make it to the house before time resumed its natural progression. Kacey gazed at the interrupted world as she slogged through it, men and women's tongues twisted in mid conversation, a fly hanging motionless in the air as if encased in resin. She glanced at the officer in the squad car as they passed, a sugar blizzard from his powdered cruller frozen in a motionless cascade toward his lap.

The house appeared detached from the world's disruption, alive and breathing, daring them forward. As RG approached the front door and dipped below the crime scene tape, Kacey faltered, her hand releasing its grip on the locket. The world gave a lurch forward, hurling them against the door.

"I can't hold it any longer," she cried, her body drenched in sweat.

RG pushed the door open and the two stumbled inside just as Kacey released the locket. The world shuddered and emitted a violent shriek as physical and mathematical laws of motion and gravity asserted themselves.

"Well, that wasn't so bad." Kacey rose and slammed the door, draping the chain around her neck and positioning the locket underneath her shirt.

RG pressed the bruise forming on the inside of his elbow. "Could be worse. No doubt will be soon."

"The eternal optimist." Kacey shook her head as she crept to the front window, gazing through the frayed curtain at the murmuring crowd on the sidewalk and police officer gutting his pastry. "We're good. They don't have a clue." She glanced at RG. "Now what?"

RG peered through the darkness to the back bedroom. "There's only one place that matters in this house. Let's get this done."

RG reached for Kacey's hand and stepped through the living room, past the kitchen and bathroom, and through the hazy hallway. He hesitated at the bedroom door and gave her a brief smile. Grasping the handle, he eased the door open and let a long breath escape.

"Still smells like Sarnie in here." He wrinkled his nose, the hint of formaldehyde still embedded in the room's fabric.

As RG stepped deeper into the room, the door slammed shut behind him and the rickety house shuddered, throwing Kacey backward into the hallway. She rose from the pitching floorboards and limped toward the door, dragging her hand against the wall to steady herself as a thundering howl shook the bedroom. She gripped the handle and twisted, but the door wouldn't budge.

"RG! What's happening?" She slammed her palm against the wood. "Talk to me!"

The house gave another lurch and fell silent, throwing Kacey to the floor a second time. The bedroom door swung open with a creak. She crawled toward the room, pulling herself up on the jamb.

She peered into the room, but RG had vanished.

* * *

Mike

Mike Stahl wound the Crown Vic along Route 28, returning from the Lobster Claw in Orleans after dinner with Claire and Zach. It had been like old times, Claire's giggle evoking a familiar tug in Stahl's chest. The weight of recent news in Chatham and Stahl's near-death experience in Southie earlier in the day gave way to the pure joy of being with the people he loved most. As they sped along the two-lane road, Zach played on Claire's phone in the backseat, the device's glow illuminating the vehicle's darkened interior.

Stahl snatched his cell and scrolled through his contacts, searching for RG's number. He was running late and should have met them at the Barnard Street house by now. He would call and tell them he would be there shortly.

"I need to let them know this week, Mike."

Stahl chewed his lip and disconnected, dropping his cell into the cup holder. He had avoided conversations with Claire about packing up and moving to Cambridge, hoping the crisis would just disappear. When he pictured a permanently empty house, the visual added a level of gloom that pressed against his shoulders like a yoke. He had convinced himself he only lived with a partial emptiness, a fleeting inconvenience brushed away the moment he ran into the two at pickup or drop-off, or when he had Zach for his visits. The upcoming emptiness would be permanent, the silence deeper. Louder. He has already missed so much of Zach's life during the separation, filling their cereal bowls over the comics at the breakfast table, walks on Aunt Lydia's Cove, and Zach's sneak attacks mounted from the couch back that would leave them wrestling on the ground amidst Claire's giggles. Stahl had never appreciated the in-between moments the way he did now, the moments you didn't plan, when life truly happened. Now, they would be gone forever.

"So, what's it going to be, Mike?"

Forgive her. Let it go.

Why couldn't he? Every time he gazed in her eyes, he relived her contempt, the mistrust. She had once believed he had harmed Zach, had been part of his abduction the previous summer. The scars of that betrayal ran deep, and he hadn't been able to let her off the hook.

"I guess you need to do what you have to do." The single headlight beam growing in the rearview blinded him as he glanced at Zach in the backseat, the approaching vehicle's engine rumble swelling in his ears. Stahl slowed to allow the car to pass, but it downshifted with a winding growl and settled just a few yards off the Crown Vic's back bumper.

Couple of teens showing off, that's all.

"Is that what you want then?"

Stahl nodded toward the backseat. "Let's talk about it later."

"We don't have later."

"Claire—" The wheel jerked in his hand, pulling the Crown Vic toward the center lane. "Jesus Christ!"

"What's the matter?" Claire craned her neck toward the backseat where Zach had glanced up from the phone.

"I dunno," he mumbled. "The wheel must have—"

The dome light flashed on and off as the radio kicked on, The Rolling Stones' "Paint It Black" pounding to full volume. The trailing vehicle's single headlight pierced the darkened interior. Stahl's car burst forward as the accelerator pinned to the floorboard without Mike's help. *Who's controlling the fucking Vic?* Yanking against the wheel, he attempted to straighten the lurching vehicle. The picket fence posts along the roadway rocketed past the vehicle, picking up speed.

Zach dropped Claire's phone and pressed his hands against his ears. "Dad! Make it stop!"

"I'm trying…I'm trying…it's out of my control!"

Claire banged her hand against the stereo's power switch, hoping to quell the ear-splitting noise, but the volume continued to spiral upward.

The vehicle thundered forward. Stahl jammed his foot against the brake, but it simply flopped against the floorboard. Claire wrestled with the gear shift and struggled to pop it into neutral while Stahl wedged his foot under the accelerator like a lever. He attempted to pry it off the floor, but it hugged the carpet as if someone had nailed it to the floorboards.

Stahl glanced into the rearview mirror. The pursuer's headlights closed the gap between their bumpers. Claire gripped Mike's forearm and, with her free hand, corralled Zach's tee shirt in a death grip.

No way could he race around the upcoming bend in the road without flipping the Vic.

The whining engine roared against Zach's screams from the backseat. The surrounding chaos decelerated, time slowing to a crawl, but the Vic continued speeding toward the inevitable. He turned his head toward Claire. Her mouth moved, shouting words he couldn't hear. Small flecks of spittle flew forward then back. Stahl gauged the danger with split-second analysis, begging for a saving solution. The fence at the bend threatened to rocket the Vic airborne and send it careening into Jackknife Cove's inky black waters. He almost chuckled at the irony…the exact spot Sarnie's vehicle had met tragedy.

The insubstantial picket posts loomed in his headlights. He eased his hands from the wheel. What could he do? The car steered itself. He turned his head to meet Zach's eyes, pressing his lips together in an apologetic gesture, resigned to their fate.

In an instant, time came alive again at breakneck speed along with the radio's increasing volume and his passengers' screams. "Everybody, hold on!" he shouted as the Vic exploded through the wooden guardrail and flew through the salty night air.

* * *

Alex

Alex Sarnie stood in the doorway of The Reveal's upstairs office, the setting sun pulling long shadows across Jimmy MacKinnon's worn carpet. Big Mac squinted at the door from his desk. "Jesus Christ!" His hand swung as he jumped in his seat, knocking a Coke can across the desktop, spraying caramel foam through the air.

"Nice to see you, too, Jimmy."

"What the fuck…? You're supposed to be dead. I read about your accident in the *Globe*."

"The reports of my death have been greatly…well, you know the quote."

"Had a cop asking about you today. Ironic you'd show up."

"It's coincidence. Not irony."

"Fuck you, too." He peered around Sarnie at the open door. "How did you get in here?"

"Your security isn't what it used to be. If someone was, let's say…trying to kill you, it wouldn't be difficult."

"Whaddaya want?" The crime boss made the obvious reach for a button on the underside of his desk, a move Sarnie interpreted as a signal for his muscle to get their asses upstairs. Along with the office's faux wood paneling and shag carpeting, Big Mac's security team needed an upgrade.

"No need to bother with the panic button. I gave Davie and Mikey the night off. In fact, I gave them the rest of their lives off."

Big Mac's stoic features disclosed no fear as he stepped to the wet bar and poured himself a shot of Irish whiskey. "Can I get you one?" Big Mac raised the Jameson bottle. "Like the old days."

"This isn't a social call. I have questions that need answering."

Big Mac downed the shot and poured another, inspecting the man in front of him. "When did you become all tough and scary?"

"It's a recent thing."

"I'm sure I should be shaking in my boots, but you don't appear well. A bit peaked." Big Mac crinkled his nose. "Shower broken, too?"

The smell of decay escaped the Axe-spray barrier he'd applied. "Did you have her killed?" He needed to hear him say it.

Big Mac cocked his head. "I suppose you're talking about Jessie. Why would I do that?"

"Because you were in love with her."

"Hardly." He dismissed Sarnie with a wave. "She was the gift that kept on giving. That I'll admit." Big Mac's glance darted to Sarnie, as if waiting for a reaction. "And don't forget, I had her long before you did."

"And after."

"Can I help it if Jessie kept coming back to me? What did you expect me to do with a beautiful woman like that?" Big Mac asked with a grin. "She let men treat her body like a playground...but you already knew that. I bet I'm not the only guy you've wondered about."

Sarnie pictured the cellphone he had found in her bedside table. "That doesn't matter to me now."

Big Mac smirked. "It always matters." He stepped from the wet bar and extended a glass to Sarnie. "Why don't you go downstairs and pick out another one of my dancers to fall in love with? Call it even."

"I would, but I'm visiting old friends today. Tying up loose ends." Sarnie took the drink and threw it back, unable to sense the burn in his throat's dead tissue.

"Feeling a bit nostalgic today?"

"Just got back from Billy Massey's. You remember him, don't ya?"

Big Mac swirled the Jameson before throwing it back. "You sure fucked him over, didn't you?"

"Takes two, Jimmy."

"How is old Billy?"

"He found God. I didn't have the heart to tell him."

Big Mac stepped behind his desk and sank into the plush leather chair. "Tell him what?"

"Never mind." *You'll find out soon enough.*

"I need something from you." Sarnie sensed the maggots flitting underneath his skin, burrowing toward the surface. "A quick fix before I become immortal."

"Immortal, huh? My, you've developed an ego. But fixes are what I handle," he said, spreading his arms. "Didn't know you partook, but we can work something out. Tell me what you need."

"I need to know if you killed her." He would admit it, dammit.

Big Mac clenched a pencil in his strained fist. "I moved on from her years ago. Why would I waste my time?"

Because you loved her.

Sarnie entered Big Mac's mind, bent on discovering the truth. Images of Jessie and Big Mac playing out before him, the things he did to her and made her do. So many things. He fast-forwarded through them, stopping on a more satisfying set of images of Big Mac: sitting alone in the backseat of his limo, breath hitching in his chest as he stalked Jessie and Sarnie through the dark glass; pacing the moon-drenched living room carpet in his Southie fortress with a hand cupping the phone receiver, begging Jessie in a whisper to meet him again, just one more time, pleading he couldn't live without her; excusing himself from the table at his son's fifth birthday party and stumbling down the hall to the bathroom, turning on the faucets and bracing himself against the sink before bursting into tears. Sarnie advanced through Big Mac's life, focusing on the recent past. He hadn't been anywhere near them on the night of their deaths. He searched for deception in his thoughts, something he might have hidden, but he found nothing. No meetings with his thugs to arrange the accident, no phone calls checking whether the hit had proceeded. Off the hook, at least for their murder.

Sarnie pulled the rubber tubing and syringes from his jacket pocket, laying them on Big Mac's desk.

"Pretty elaborate set up there." Big Mac chuckled. "You must be desperate for a fix. But I've got just the thing." He reached into the desk's top right drawer.

Sarnie eyed Big Mac's pulsing carotid, imagined the coming bloodbath. He had gotten better at swiftly severing the artery but could never prevent the inevitable geyser. He searched the room for a garbage pail, anything to preserve as much precious blood as he could. He located Big Mac's trash bin beside the desk, hoisting it to the cluttered surface and resting it on the blotter. When Sarnie returned his gaze to Big Mac, he found him standing behind his desk with a gun pointed at his chest.

"Expect to just walk out of here?" His laugh rattled through the room. "I'm about to show you how mortal you really are."

He emptied the chamber into Sarnie's chest, abdomen, and neck, nine-millimeter automatic shells raining onto the shag carpet.

Sarnie felt nothing but the projectiles' thump against his body's casing and a tumbling pressure as they transected his core and embedded themselves in the walls behind him. "You're out of bullets."

The blood drained from Big Mac's face. "Holy Christ," he muttered. The gun dropped from his grip.

Sarnie could sense the man's mind churning, attempting to process something beyond his capability. "Have a seat. You'll feel better."

Big Mac took a seat, unable to tear his gaze from Sarnie as he mumbled to himself.

"Here." Sarnie placed the garbage pail in his lap. "Hold this."

"Huh?"

Sarnie placed his arm around Big Mac's shoulders and tilted his chin upward with the other until their eyes rested inches apart.

"I'm doing my damnedest to preserve this body and you go put holes in me? Shame on you."

Sarnie grabbed Big Mac by the neck, squeezing until his face flushed a deep crimson shade.

"And another thing…she never loved you." Sarnie thrust his hand upward through the soft palate and into Big Mac's brain while pressing him into his seat with the other. His knuckles scraped the inside of his cranium as Big Mac's head detached with a ratcheting crack, like a vanquished Rock 'Em Sock 'Em Robot. Ripping the thin skein of ligamentous cord attached to McKinnon's neck, Sarnie freed his skull from the body. His head rolled across the carpet, nestling against the corner of the wet bar. His lips smacked and puckered as if they had just sucked on a lemon. Easing Big Mac's body forward, Sarnie directed the spurting blood into the trash bin resting on the dead man's lap, preserving the liquid gold and minimizing the mess.

Glancing at the syringes, Sarnie set about getting to work. The maggots had advanced through the bullet holes.

CHAPTER SIXTEEN

Wednesday, March 30

RG

When the house shimmied under his feet, RG stumbled to his knees in the back bedroom, the floorboards beneath him jumping like piano keys at a ragtime revival. A glowing light filtered upward through the cracks and into the dusky room like a series of translucent walls constructed from orange luminescence and dust particles.

His eyes drifted to the crumbling back wall in the room's corner and the stone stairway leading into the glowing earth, a hungry throat about to engulf the human morsel resting on its hardwood tongue. He leapt for the door, locking his hands onto the wobbly handle as the wind picked up and pitched him horizontal to the floor. This time, he had no Mike Stahl to ground him. The room shook again, ripping his hands from his earthly tether and sucking him into the portal like a vacuum cleaner over a breadcrumb. He tumbled down the steps and slammed against the cold stone ground.

He raised his bruised head and surveyed his surroundings with a woozy gaze, pressing his fingers to his scalp to check for gashes. The subterranean cavern loomed before him just as Raymond Kroll recalled it over fifty years ago, only his depiction of hell had been an understatement.

Human bodies hung suspended from crude gibbets dotting the cavern, faces frozen in eternal terror and forever preserved in a netherworld no nightmare could mimic. These were lost souls, the targeted and the missing, those who had the misfortune to have passed Barnard Street when the house had been hungry, or when Luther Greer had grown bored and needed entertainment. He gazed at the corpses dressed in the fashions and style of past decades who never made it home from whatever errand or curious detour had led them past Barnard Street. Several hung upside down, disemboweled in the same manner as Mick Sullivan, and displayed like trophies for the jumper who patrolled these grounds.

RG sensed Luther Greer behind him before he registered his voice.

"So, you're the one they all talk about?" Luther's heels resonated across the dense rock corridor as he stepped over RG's battered form and seated himself on one of the stone slabs lining the walkway. Pressing his palm against the makeshift bench, Luther leaned to the side and threw one leg over the other. He plucked a microscopic tangle of lint from his pants, rubbing it between his thumb and pointer finger before flicking it to the ground. "You make quite a graceful entrance."

"You should see me on a dance floor." RG rose to his knees and gazed at the angular man dressed as if might be attending a formal dinner at the statehouse. His form-fitting wool suit and felt pork pie hat paid the perfect complement to his handlebar mustache. His graceful movements contradicted his human form, as if some nimble beast resided below the surface. RG attempted to latch onto Luther's mind and view its images, but they remained locked behind a heavily fortified barrier. He sensed Luther boring into his own mind and penetrating his flimsy defenses, extracting each imagining and memory assemblage like a dentist pulling teeth.

Luther gawked at RG with a knowing grin, like that of a late-night friend with whom you've overshared. "Who is she, by the way?"

"Who?"

"The woman at the inn?"

The blood froze in RG's veins. "What do you care? Just stay away from her."

"Oh, I'm not about to get in your business. It's just…I've seen her before, that's all. Have no fear. I wouldn't want to anger a man such as yourself. You've assembled an impressive résumé, Mr. Granville…Victor Garrett, Malachi. But you certainly appear lost down here."

RG surveyed his surroundings. "No, I'm in the right place, just expecting someone else."

"And who would that be?" Luther twirled the end of his mustache.

"Oh, just this dead guy I keep seeing all the time." RG rose to his feet and stood before the jumper. "Friend of yours, I think."

"You must be referring to Mr. Sarnie, but he doesn't live here. You must have known whose home you stumbled into after talking to the little Knoll boy."

"He's not so little anymore."

Luther smoothed an eyebrow. "I'll have to make a point to visit him again, tell him how disappointed I am."

"He won't be surprised again by any major appliances."

"I'm forgetting my manners." He extended a hand, sharp, polished nails pointing like daggers toward RG. "I'm Luther."

Grabbing Luther's hand and cupping it with his left, RG's ring brushed against the jumper's skin and ignited a barrage of flowing memories from his dark mind. The flurry of thoughts and pictures jolted RG, his fingers locking onto Luther's hand with a reflexive muscular burst as everything went dark.

When the world resumed in his vision, he found himself on the Barnard Street house's lawn beside Luther, the young man's body battered and bloody. The painful blows and kicks to the man's face, ribs, and groin in his final moments of life nothing more than a dull fluttering against his form, the signals traveling to and from the brain mercifully short-circuited by the protracted beating. RG sensed the unbridled hatred not only from the three men surrounding Luther on the front lawn, but from the crowd gathering to gawk at the spectacle from the sidewalk's safety. They had run into the man before, maybe downtown or at a restaurant or the theater, his gaudy dress and effete manner raising their hackles. The gallery stood far enough away to remain detached, uninvolved but still close enough to cheer when the bastard got what he had coming to him.

The man closest to Luther, tall and heavily muscled, gazed at him through an alcohol fog as he fondled the knotted cord he had ripped from the clothesline beside the house. He handed the rope to a man with rat-like eyes spaced too closely together, who secured it around the semi-conscious man's neck and tossed the end over a sturdy tree branch. Fueled by the mob's energy, the third man yanked on the cord and hoisted

Luther's body upward, his face bulging and sputtering like a squawking bagpipe. Luther's arms swung like pendulums as his shoe tips dragged against the trampled grass, a pummeled ballet dancer en pointe. His eyes remained bloodied and swollen shut. The light faded through his eyelids' opaque filter as his breath ceased.

Luther's memories sped forward, his three killers older now, fear etched across their features as judgment arrived in a chill, stone cave. Luther had waited patiently. When he found the men and entered them, they had understood their penance would be harsh, the man they had tortured having the power to right wrongs. Their minds had hurtled back to that hazy, dreamlike day in Chatham, convinced it must have been a drunken hallucination. But Luther had reminded them it wasn't. RG witnessed the savagery, the men suspended upside down from makeshift crucifixes as Luther transformed into a clawed creature, running a talon from stomach to throat.

RG entered another memory flurry, bursting toward him like a snow squall. Luther and Sarnie rested along the stone pathway, at nearly the exact spot RG now stood. He listened while Luther fulfilled his role as Sarnie's dark mentor, explaining Sarnie's task, his destiny. Morrow had predicted wayward forces would reach out and guide Sarnie, attempting to push him toward immortality. Could it be coincidence Sarnie had set up shop on Barnard Street, in a house with a portal into Luther's territory? Luther had brought him there. He had brought Mick Sullivan there, and the fate of humanity rested on the words Luther imparted to his protégé. They talked about the blood that would make him immortal.

"How will I know when I find it?" Sarnie had asked. "It could be anywhere."

"You don't need to worry. It's closer than you think." Luther grinned. "And I know where it is. The blood you're putting inside you is just a temporary fix," Luther had said. "It's priming the heart and blood vessels, keeping your body going until you find the right blood."

"The right blood?" Sarnie drew his eyebrows together.

"The purest form of blood, from the blessed giver of life." Luther placed a gentle hand behind Sarnie's neck. "She was a beautiful woman."

"Who?" Sarnie's chest rose and fell with labored breath.

Luther twirled his mustache with a finger. "I think you know."

"Mother?"

"Your mission isn't complete yet, and you're so close. She will give birth to your new form."

Sarnie turned his head to meet Luther's gaze. "You want me to drain blood from my mother's body?"

"Shhh…there, there now." Luther leaned and whispered in Sarnie's ear. "It's the only way."

Sarnie stumbled to his feet and backed away, steadying himself against a stone pillar behind him. "She's my mother, for Chrissake!"

"On the contrary, she's your salvation." Luther stood and donned his overcoat, laughing to himself as he turned to leave.

"Wait a minute!"

Luther glanced over his shoulder.

Sarnie jammed his palms against his head and paced along the stone walkway. "How can you ask me to do that? I can't kill my mother!"

"Then I'll have to make room for you down here. You can't live anywhere but the dark places between worlds." Luther gestured with his hand. "Take a good look at your new home."

"I won't do it." Sarnie locked his fingers behind his head.

"You have no choice. You're running out of time."

"What are you talking about?"

Something bulged behind Luther's eyes, the beast within rising to the surface and pulsing against his body's seams, like the unseen energy beneath a wave. Luther lunged at Sarnie, slashing his shirt from collar to belt with nails that had sprouted into talons. "Look at yourself. You're body's dying."

Sarnie glanced down at his tattered shirt. A maggot squirmed beneath his skin preparing to gnaw a hole through his stomach.

"And if you die, we can't live. Lucky for you, I have a solution."

Luther leaned forward and placed his hand on Sarnie's head, locking onto his thoughts, clawing at the images and pictures embedded in his consciousness and unwinding the emotional connections between Sarnie and his mother as if untying a knot strand by strand, memory by memory. Sarnie appeared to fight against the invasion, grasping to hold her but losing his grip, unable to counter Luther's strength. In his head, Luther left Sarnie with nothing but random visions of a woman he might pass on the street without a moment's consideration, Luther stripping each image from its meaning as if husking corn and throwing away the ears. A serenity descended over Sarnie as he pressed his eyes shut, the jumper leaving him with nothing but rage, a burning desire to slaughter the useless woman.

"Thank you, Luther," Sarnie mumbled.

"It's been a pleasure. Sometimes a jumper needs help when he first gets here. But don't forget. You have a job to do…and I'll be watching."

"Are you sure it will work?"

"She gave you life once. She will do it again. Use your powers…push her. She will agree to it. What mother would not want to provide her son everlasting life?"

"And if she…resists?" Sarnie asked.

Luther bared his teeth, and for a moment RG pictured what this man's tormentors witnessed in their final moments.

Placing a hand around Sarnie's shoulder, Luther purred, "Then you'll have to be more persuasive."

The torrent of memories scattered across RG's vision as Luther rocketed to his feet and yanked his hand from his grip, cradling it as if he had burned it. "What the hell just happened?" Luther's eyes dropped to the glowing band on RG's hand. "Where did you get that?"

"Jared's, Chestnut Hill mall?"

Something rose from behind Luther's eyes, like a living shadow in the shape of some hellish beast escaping the man's shell, a great winged bird but with a hellhound's maw. It lashed out with a clawed hand. RG reared back, doing the limbo to avoid having his chest ripped. The arcing blow caught the edge of RG's shirt, tearing a gash across the front and sending him tumbling to the stone floor. Glancing upward, RG twisted the ring on his left hand, igniting a golden barrier around him. Luther grinned and straightened his vest as the twisted fowl charged again with talons raised, attempting to breach RG's defenses. As it made contact with the glowing force field, the beast let out an agonized bellow, fizzling like a moth against a bug zapper.

Luther crumpled to the ground, a hand pressed to his chest. He raised his head. "Looks like I've underestimated you?" Crinkling his nose, he fanned the acrid burnt feather smell.

"Sorry about your budgie." Struggling to his feet, RG inspected the gash across his shirt, marveling that his viscera hadn't found a new home on the cave floor.

"Don't worry, I have others." Luther straightened his vest. "I apologize for my…outburst. I don't like being spied on."

"Neither do I."

Luther stroked his chin as he circled RG. "You have a power I haven't encountered before in the human species."

RG twisted his head from shoulder to shoulder, following him with his eyes. "How about from your understudy?"

"Ah, yes, Mr. Sarnie."

"And why isn't he enjoying your home's wonderful ambience today?"

"He's out in your world somewhere, tying up loose ends."

"Loose ends?" RG crossed his arms. "Like running off to kill his mother? Fill up with a blast of that high-octane blood?"

Luther grinned. "You've learned a lot from me, haven't you?"

RG extended his hand, fanning his fingers to display the ring.

"But don't forget, I've seen inside of you, too." Luther folded his arms behind his back. "I may have to make a stop at Jared's."

"Ninety days same as cash."

Luther waved him away like a gnat. "Mr. Sarnie gets a bit emotional, I admit. He needs to right a few wrongs. But he'll be back soon. He will fulfill his destiny and free us from the darkness."

RG picked up the subtle movement around him. Shapes emerged from the shadows, from behind stone towers and within the dusty caves and earthen pits dotting Luther's underworld. RG could barely make them out in the dark, but he didn't have to see them to recognize he had stumbled into a jumper's lair. Hundreds of them congregated in this holding pen like holiday travelers in a busy airport anxious to get to their final destination, advancing toward him like an army of assassins.

"They've come from every plane of existence, Mr.

Granville, every time period, past and future." Luther gestured with his hand. "They've been called. They understand something great awaits them. Once Alex has carried out his true mission, his blood will transform us, let us become just like him. Then we will live forever. We'll march together through that little house and out of the darkness, live in the light of your world."

"And who says you're welcome there?"

"It doesn't matter if we're welcome. We will claim it as our foothold in the universe. Your kind will have no chance. Your scribes' prophesizing the apocalypse will be proven correct after all."

"What will you do with the people?"

Luther chuckled, glancing at the wooden crosses dotting the landscape. "You need to ask? Your world is a failed experiment, and it's time to suspend the protocol."

They'll kill everyone. "You're nothing but a bunch of butchers."

"You think we're bad?" He glanced at the jumpers approaching him from all sides. "The powerful in your world never fail to exploit the vulnerable and decide who lives and who dies. Execution, ethnic cleansing, abortion, war, the holocaust, master races, infanticide. Should I go on? Time you had a taste of your own medicine."

"Even if everyone got a drop of Sarnie's blood," RG shouted, gesturing across the sea of jumpers, "he'd be bled dry. He doesn't have enough to satisfy this horde."

"Not at first he won't. A living body manufactures blood slowly, but over time there will be enough."

"So, you'll have to prioritize? Who gets what...and when?"

Luther rubbed his chin. "At first."

"Oh, I get it now." RG nodded. "Someone like yourself,

maybe, will decide who's worthy to be immortal and who's not?"

Luther glanced over his shoulder at the approaching forms. "Someone will have to be in charge, to make the decisions," he whispered. "Even jumpers need someone to lead them or else existence would be chaos."

"So, some will be in power. Some will be vulnerable. You intend to perpetuate the same structure you despise in my world. You're no better than we are."

"I'm infinitely better, and I will rule your world. And the first to go will be phony caretakers like you…and your wife, Kacey."

RG's mouth went dry. "So, you've already made the decision to be the ruler of my world? You don't suppose you need to discuss that with Sarnie?"

"He doesn't need to discuss anything with me." Sarnie stepped from the shadows. "I'm the immortal force, and no one else decides who gets my goddamn blood." He cast a dismissive glance at Luther. "Including you."

* * *

Mike

The airborne Crown Vic flew through the fence beside Jackknife Cove, Stahl's rear end coming off the seat as the car dropped from under him, his body weightless for a microsecond as the car arced forward and pitched gradually to the right. He reached for Claire and pulled her toward the center console, away from the impact zone, but she slipped from his grip as the car impacted the water with a thundering crack.

Claire's body glanced off the airbag, the vehicle's angle of decent forcing her against the side window. Her crumpled body came to a rest against the doorframe as the Crown Vic rolled onto its side and bobbed for a moment before settling upside down in the pitch-black sea. Slipping beneath the surface, the Vic's roof crunched against the rocky sand as the vehicle came to rest at the bottom of the bay. The twin beam headlights reflected off the murky water and illuminated the car's interior with a greenish hue as water rushed in through cracks in the Vic's body.

"Claire! Oh Christ!" Stahl unsnapped her shoulder harness, her limp body tumbling onto the ceiling. Her scalp left a blood smear along the head curtain.

"Dad, I'm stuck!" Zach tugged at his seatbelt as he hung inverted in his seat, his other arm pressed against the ceiling. The rising water crept over the boy's hand, up his wrist and to his elbow.

This was happening too fast!

The boy jammed his hand against the belt release button, but he couldn't disengage the belt. The rising water swamped Zach's eyes and nose.

"Dad!" he screamed, moments before his head disappeared beneath the water.

"Zach!" Stahl flailed behind him with a free hand but couldn't reach Zach's belt without releasing Claire and letting her slip below the water. No time to think or he would lose both of them. He let Claire go and leaped across the backseat, hands extended. The rising water had reached Zach's waist, and Stahl could no longer visualize the release button. He groped madly beneath the surface as Zach's muffled screams roiled the surface. Grasping the lap belt, Stahl shimmied his hand toward the spot where it met the shoulder harness, somehow triggered the belt release, sending Zach tumbling into the water. The boy gasped and sputtered as Stahl hoisted him to the surface, seawater spilling from his lungs.

Pushing himself back to the front seat, Stahl reached for Claire, pulling her from under the water.

"Mom!" Zach's scream felt closer, louder in the rapidly shrinking space, the water now pooling just below Zach's neck.

Stahl's mind spun. He'd been trained in underwater vehicle escape. Some retreat in Boston a few summers ago. But in the heat of battle, he couldn't remember. The speed at which the car had filled with water told him they only had another thirty seconds or so before the Crown Vic became their watery tomb. They were running out of time.

Stahl grabbed the Vic's window crank handle and pulled as hard as he could. The lever snapped off in his hand, the water pressure forcing the glass against the frame too powerful to overcome. He kicked at the glass with his boot heel, hoping to smash it and let the water come barreling in. But it was like kicking a wall. He hurled his shoulder against the door like a battering ram, but it wouldn't budge.

"We have to let the car fill up, equalize the pressure, then we can swim out, okay?"

Zach nodded, but his eyes betrayed his spiraling terror.

Stahl dragged Claire into the backseat, cradled her in his arms and holding her bloody head above the rising water. They pressed their heads against the floor carpet, necks craned as the gasped the last gulps of air.

"Ready?"

Zach delivered an unsure nod.

"All right, brother. Deep breaths. And hold!" The world fell silent as the seawater swamped their ears. Claire's chest heaved as she took the fluid into her lungs, now drowning before his eyes. He would have to get the door open, pull her to the surface and revive her. She wouldn't have long.

He lifted the handle and pressed his shoulder against the rear door. It didn't move. He wedged his foot against the dome light like a sprinter at the starting blocks and hurled himself against the door. Nothing.

It hadn't worked. He tried to slow his racing mind, focus on a plan, but his mind spun in haphazard directions. Pressure equalization. Wasn't that physics? Didn't physics always work? Maybe some air pocket had prevented it. He pounded on the glass with his fists.

Think, Mike!

He opened his eyes in the murky water, the headlights' reflection now filling his vision with green. He could spot Zach clearly, eyes open, holding his breath, waiting for his hero to save the day. The boy's pounding heart would use up his limited oxygen in about half the time as normal. Then he would start to drown. First Claire, then Zach, finally…*no!*

His lungs pleaded for air as his brain exploded with activity, spitting out random thoughts and ideas as if the organ had chosen to activate all its neurons at once in its last moments.

Stahl's eyes widened as if hit over the head with a hammer, and he nearly inhaled a lungful of frigid seawater. His gun. Firing it underwater would eject the bullet, but the slow pressure behind it would create drag and bring it to a stop in just a few feet. He would have to hold it against the glass to shatter it and create an opening.

Stahl snaked between the seats and banged on the glove box, reaching inside for the backup thirty-eight caliber revolver RG had used in the Sarnie interview. He rummaged through the space, pulling out driving manuals, insurance cards, and registration before wrapping his hand around the cold iron. *Please God let it be loaded.*

He peered at Zach's face, his eyes wide as the remaining oxygen in his lungs dissolved into his bloodstream. He only had seconds before the boy would reflexively inhale ocean water.

Goddammit!

He pulled the boy close and placed his mouth over the boy's, and with his last remaining breath transferred a few more seconds of precious oxygen into the boy's lungs.

Black spots migrated from the edges of Stahl's vision.

Zach's eyes widened as Stahl raised the gun. He held Zach at arm's length as he pressed the muzzle against the window glass and pulled the trigger three times, the deafening explosion shattering the Crown Vic's side window.

He kicked out the glass shards embedded in the frame and hurled Zach through the opening and into the darkness. His vision shimmered, black dots swimming in a flurry before his eyes. Teetering on the brink of unconsciousness, he followed the boy through the tight space, reaching back to hook his arms under Claire Simpson's shoulders and drag her drowned body through the window.

CHAPTER SEVENTEEN

Wednesday, March 30

Kacey

"RG, where the hell are you?" Kacey whipped her head back and forth inside the back bedroom of the Barnard Street house. She closed her eyes, attempting to locate and enter the portal that had swallowed RG, but she could only sense its obstinance. Kacey could access numerous portals to different times and places, otherworldly connectors operating like major highways crisscrossing the country, open to everyone and accommodating all travelers. But some portals were selective, constructed by darker forces. These portals made it difficult for just any traveler to access and could be deadly if entered. Kacey sensed this portal's construction had been for a purpose only Sarnie and RG could fulfill, and she wasn't on the guest list.

A connection between Sarnie and RG had developed, allowing RG to witness the dead man's brutality not once, but twice. Kacey shuddered, thinking about whether the connection allowed Sarnie to witness RG's life, and whether her and Robert Jr.'s lives were on display, too. But either way, RG would face Sarnie, and maybe Luther Greer, alone. Unless she could find her own way in.

Kacey paced the bedroom's perimeter, her mind racing, turning over the possibilities to find a solution. Stomping toward the far end of the room, she pivoted and threw a backward heel at the wall, like a horse kicking its stall, putting a dent, then a sneaker size hole in it. Nothing but drywall and two-by-fours, no stairway leading into Luther's underworld.

Brilliant.

She kicked herself for the irrational outburst, but somehow the crumbling hole in the death house's wall made her feel better.

A creaking hallway floorboard froze her in her tracks. She pressed herself against the wall, fearing Chatham PD had returned to work after devouring their donuts. She muffled an exasperated sigh as she imagined her arrest photos at an active crime scene gracing the *Cape Cod Times*. Not an easy one to explain to the Chatham Schoolboard. The floorboard creaked again under weight. A light pitter-patter thumped across the squeaky floor, like the barefoot steps of a child. She tilted her head to alter the acoustics.

"Hello?" Her voice faltered. "Is someone out there?"

Kacey eased into the hallway with cautious steps. The sound of running water gurgled from the hallway bathroom and puffs of steam misted from the door's narrow opening like a London fog. Kacey stepped through the hallway's mounting humidity and pressed her hand against the door, sending it rattling against the wall. But the bathroom had changed, flushed with a sepia haze, as if she had stumbled through a bend in time. Postwar acrylic floor tile and a sturdy claw-foot tub now replaced the cheap Linoleum flooring and Re-Bath shower. Kacey sensed the struggling child in the churning water before she could view her long curls wrapped around the drain, trussing her beneath the surface. The chapter in Raymond Knoll's eBook had come to life before her eyes.

"Oh my God!" Kacey threw herself arms deep into the tub. She gripped the little girl's hair next to the scalp, and, with her free hand, pulled the flowing ends engulfed by the drain. They wouldn't budge. The little girl's mouth pulled the bathwater into her lungs as she gasped for air, her body convulsing as it fought for life. Kacey continued to pull with both hands now, the little girl's long curls hopelessly caught deep in the trap.

Get a knife! Cut it off!

Kacey jumped from the tub but slipped on the slick flooring, driving her shoulder into the unyielding tile. She cradled a bruised limb as she rose, the air knocked from her lungs. Limping to the kitchen, she threw open drawers and cabinets until she found a carving knife.

When she glanced up, the house shuddered. Bracing herself against the counter, the dwelling transformed itself. Kacey sensed the pull in the pit of her stomach as she, and everything around her, fast-forwarded to a time when bright flowered prints adorned the kitchen walls and gaudy orange and yellow fabrics wrapped the living room furniture. The room had mutated into something from a sixties sit-com.

She pressed her hands against her crisp shirt, no longer saturated from her unplanned bath.

She sprinted back to the bathroom, but the girl with the long curls had disappeared, having drowned in a different tub, years ago, in another time.

Kacey readied herself for another vision, like Ebenezer Scrooge to a latter-day ghost of Barnard-Street-past. As she waited, a faint whistle resonated from the backyard. She raced to the kitchen to peer through the window above the sink at the woman pinning wet laundry to the rotary clothesline. The breeze blew back the curtains, the faint pollen scent filling her nostrils.

"Oh, shit." The next chapter in Knoll's book.

A boy in blue jean overalls shuffled around the corner with an overflowing laundry basket, humming an indeterminate melody, disappearing into the cramped laundry room beside the kitchen.

Kacey dashed into the room after him, the gleaming new Whirlpool washing machine open, resembling a hungry mouth with its top pushed open. If she could change the outcome, alter it somehow, maybe the house would lose its aura and the evil would stop. Maybe her actions might prevent future tragedies from occurring…or past tragedies. She wasn't sure.

The boy fed the washing machine handfuls of soiled clothes.

"Raymond?" she asked.

"Yes, ma'am." The boy scrunched his face, as if trying to place her.

"I don't want you to put any more clothes in the machine." Kacey used her teacher's voice. "Your mother said to leave them."

The boy snorted a laugh. "She did not."

"She did. She wants you to go outside and help her pin the wet laundry."

His eyes lowered. "I don't think so." He reached into the basket and continued stuffing clothes into the Whirlpool.

"You don't want her to be mad at you, do you?"

The boy turned a sad eye to Kacey. "It's too late, you know."

"Too late for what?"

His lips pressed together in a defeated grin. "Too late to save me."

"It doesn't have to end like this." Kacey reached for his hand, pressing it against the soft laundry. "You don't have to keep filling the machine. Just wait until your mom comes in. Just wait. I'll go get her."

Raymond stopped, resting his hand in the basket. "Okay. You go get her. I'll wait here."

Kacey backed out of the laundry room, glancing toward the back door. "Don't move. I'll be right back."

Kacey sprinted through the kitchen, pulling on the back-door handle, but it wouldn't budge. She dashed to the window and leaned over the sink, shouting through the screen at the woman, but she continued spinning the line and securing more damp clothes. The woman's pursed lips sent a tuneless warble cascading across the light air.

"Mrs. Knoll! Come in, please! I think if you come in, Raymond won't be hurt! We can change everything!"

The woman ignored her, or maybe she couldn't hear her, and continued with her work.

A mechanical thunk tore through the morning calm followed by an ear-splitting scream as the washer's heavy top slammed down on the boy's arm.

"No!" Kacey dashed from the kitchen back to the laundry room only to witness the young boy in the jaws of something indescribable…inhuman. The Whirlpool had vanished, replaced by a great winged bird with jaws of a hellish beast, a dog or the otherworld's twisted version of one. It shook the boy in its drooling maw, tearing at the limb now hanging by the remnants of muscle cords and tendons. With a powerful shake the beast ripped Raymond's arm from its socket, throwing back its head and scarfing the appendage down its massive gullet. Blood rocketed from the tear in the boy's body, staining the colorful wallpaper a more contemporary crimson hue.

She grabbed a handful of towels and raced to the boy's side as he lay on the floor, an ever-expanding pool bathing his quivering body.

"I told you," he said.

Kacey pressed on the open wound, attempting to stanch the blood jetting from his body. She leaned forward with all her weight balanced over her arms. "Why didn't you listen to me?"

"It had to happen this way. I'm sorry."

"It's not your fault, Raymond. I only wanted to protect you."

"Please," he pleaded, "listen to me for a minute." But his voice had changed. "Go to the portal."

"What?"

"*Your* portal. Just go!" A familiar voice rang in her head as instructions spilled from the boy's mouth in a young woman's tongue. "But before you leave here, take something with you… and leave something behind."

Ellie? In her confusion, Kacey leaned backward, relinquishing the pressure on the wound as the boy's blood resumed its pulsing cadence, spurting against the near wall. "Jesus!" She grabbed a towel from the floor to press on the throbbing wound and whispered to the boy. "I don't understand?"

The boy sat up, oblivious to the blood jetting from his wound. "You need something from the house to take with you." He rummaged his good hand through his overall pockets and pulled out a bright yellow butterfly yo-yo. "Here, use this.

It'll get you through the portal. But you have to leave something behind to help you get back."

"Back from where?"

"Through Luther's portal. If you leave something behind, it's like putting a stopper in the door."

The boy's blood pooled around Kacey, saturating her jeans and warming her legs. Raymond's shrill cries resumed from the boy's mouth. "Ellie, are you still there?"

The boy writhed on the floor. His eyes turned glassy and distant as if he remembered he had been bleeding to death, picking up where he had left off before Ellie had turned him into a ventriloquist dummy.

"Mom!" he launched an earsplitting scream.

"Go now." Ellie's voice spoke deep inside Kacey's head.

She stepped away from Raymond, backing out of the kitchen and into the living room as his mother burst through the back door. The frantic woman didn't appear to register Kacey's presence as she raced into the laundry room, her guttural wails filling the tiny house.

Kacey gripped the yellow yo-yo in her palm as she patted her pockets for something to relinquish, but she had nothing on her person beside her wedding ring. And she wasn't about to leave that anywhere. Her car keys dangled from the ignition and everything else resided in her purse, resting on the car's front seat. She brushed a hand against her ears, hoping she might have left a loop or stud resting in her lobes. Nothing. Her fingers went to her neck, fingering Wilder's locket hanging around her neck. She turned it over in her hand as she glanced at her wedding ring. With a defeated sigh, she unsnapped the locket's clasp and rested the trinket on a shelf beside the television console, hoping its modest sacrifice would ensure her safe passage home.

She could hear Ellie's voice. *Like putting a stopper in the door.*

Closing her eyes, Kacey struggled to find the fissure between worlds. The screams and wails from the boy and his mother shattered her concentration like daggers hurling through her mind. She pressed her hands over her ears to dull the cacophony. *Block it out! It isn't real!*

As the wails subsided, she slipped into a comforting calm, the silence descending like blanketing snow. A yawning chasm opened beneath her feet, suspending her in midair before dropping her into the soundless abyss. She rode along a swirling current through a turbulent tranquility, a route she had taken in her dreams countless times since childhood, as familiar as the run up Route 3 to Boston. Through the mist, the hazy outline of the Pancake Man materialized before her.

Entering the diner from the rear door, she paused to take in its comfort. She exhaled and hurried through the throng of regulars sampling their blue-plate specials and chatting over coffee. They shouted out greetings and wore welcoming smiles, but Kacey could only give a haggard wave as she dashed toward the front door.

At the front entrance, she glanced toward the server's window behind the counter and spotted Ellie and Sal in the kitchen doorway.

Kacey raised the yo-yo in her hand and forced a weak smile.

Ellie nodded and mouthed the word, 'Go.'

Gripping the toy in her fist, she faced the door, envisioning Luther's afterworld. She shivered as she recalled the elder Raymond Knoll's description of the dark stone underworld, the lost souls, and the slaughtered bodies suspended on wooden posts. Mumbling to herself, she directed the Pancake Man to take her there, to open the portal to hell.

She reached for the handle and threw the door open. But instead of the familiar brilliance of the next world flooding the entrance, darkness clawed at her, wrapping her in its grip and pulling her into the unknown.

* * *

Mike

Mike Stahl slumped in the stiff orange chair beside the adjustable bed, laptop open. His tapping fingers provided a percussive complement to the thrums and hisses of the machines keeping Claire Simpson alive. Zach snored softly as he slept beside his mother, arm draped across her shoulder. She lay on her back with thick bandages wrapped around her head and a tube down her throat to help her breathe. Her brain had been subject to considerable trauma. She had been unconscious without oxygen for god knows how long until Stahl had resuscitated her, and she had suffered a grade-three concussion. The ER docs at Cape Cod Hospital had placed her in a medically induced coma, cooling her body to near ten degrees below normal to reduce the damage. The first twenty-four hours would be critical, but the medical team couldn't estimate at this point the extent of the damage. Stahl gleaned from their stoic manner they weren't optimistic.

He glanced at the clock.

9:41 pm.

Visiting hours at the hospital had been over since eight, but he and Zach wouldn't be leaving Claire's side tonight. His weary gaze locked onto Zach in a dead stare. Despite being on the verge of drowning, the boy had waited with Stahl as he pulled Claire from the car, grabbing his mother's arm to guide her to the surface.

Zach's eyes opened for a moment. Stahl flashed a reassuring smile before they fluttered shut.

He had failed him, struggling too long inside the car and

putting the two people he loved most in his life at risk. How could he ever look at Zach again if the boy lost his mother? His gaze drifted to his wife, bandaged and struggling for life beside him. Where did her dreams take her in the dark place she slept? Did she sense the cold? She had gone from the frigid seawater that nearly killed her to the cool IV fluids flooding her veins and keeping her alive, but she had to be shivering in that in-between place she dwelled.

God, if you just bring her out of this, I promise to keep her warm.

Why had he been so stupid? Why had he squandered the months they had spent apart, all because he couldn't move on, he couldn't forget the past. *Just wake up, Claire. I'll make it up to you.*

His jaw clenched as he turned his attention to the computer, picking up where he had left off before his detour into self-defeat. He had been scouring the Internet, trawling for clues about what could have happened to the Crown Vic. But his search had yielded no hint as to why a vehicle with a sound mechanical history had driven itself into the bay as if it had a mind of its own.

Until he came across the article.

His weary eyes went from half slits to wide circles as he scoured the entry. Stahl's breathing picked up as he scrolled back to the top and read the piece again, finishing with his laptop balanced on his forearm as he stood on springs in the room's center.

It all fit. And it pointed to one person.

He dropped the computer and paced the narrow room. The rumbling engine's echo reverberated in his head like a familiar song. Late sixties, muscle car, its four-barrel carburetor's sound unmistakable.

Stahl paused at the window, parting the venetian blinds and staring out into the night. Whoever killed Alex Sarnie had tried to eliminate the one person who suspected him. Stahl had witnessed it before. Murder becomes more palatable once you've killed someone, and it proved easier to justify the more you did it.

He dropped into the chair beside the bed and grasped Claire's hand, his breath catching in his throat. Zach pulled his mother toward him in his sleep.

They won't get away with it, Claire. I promise you.

Fuck the Sarnie case and immortal forces. He had retribution of his own he would exact on the person who had done this. His free hand squeezed the chair's cheap vinyl armrests, his fingernails leaving deep pits in the fabric.

Time for a late-night interrogation.

* * *

RG

Alex Sarnie resembled a wax figure at Madame Tussauds, his corpse-like skin and pale complexion standing in sharp contrast to the living spirits surrounding him. But he exuded a power that belied his failing body. The others gawked at him with a reverence reserved for a savior, several averting their eyes as if gazing at the sun. Only Luther appeared to view him with contempt, his twisted scowl reflecting Sarnie's rebuke, as if it festered like an abscess inside the jumper's gut.

"So, you're the one." Sarnie stepped toward RG, circling him. "I've sensed you since the moment I died. Or the moment I was reborn, actually. The visions are strong. And you've been keeping tabs on me."

"Hardly." RG examined Sarnie with a measured glance. "You have an overdeveloped sense of self-importance. My mind shows me things whether I want it to or not. It just so happens they're snippets of you and your destruction. If I could clear your shit out of my head, trust me, I would."

Sarnie pivoted to face Luther. "Why are our minds linked like they are?"

Luther ran a finger across his moustache. "I've seen into both of your heads, and I know a little secret. You have something in common." He leaned and whispered in Sarnie's ear.

A wry grin spread across Sarnie's face. "Well, I'll be damned."

"I'm guessing you already are," RG said, scanning the dark cave. "Something in common, huh?" He sniffed the air and wrinkled his nose. "Certainly not our choice of deodorant."

"He won't be so brash for long." Luther pressed a calming hand to Sarnie's shoulder. "Not when he witnesses the fate awaiting him here. You see, Granville's part of a team preparing to kill you."

Sarnie turned to Luther but kept his eyes glued to RG. "So, we finish him here?"

Luther eyed the bodies behind him, affixed to wooden posts. "I'm envisioning a nice, slow death. He'd look pretty good with his insides torn out." He glanced about the cavern at the advancing horde. "Have the others hang him up. Let them do your dirty work. Then you finish him off…your way."

RG placed his hands together, the ring's warmth comforting him. "Isn't that shtick getting a bit stale? How about something a bit more original?"

Sarnie eyed RG with caution as he circled him. "Oh, I have some very original ideas for you, and I plan to take my time. And when I'm through with you, you'll be begging me to gut you."

"Careful of his ring," Luther directed. "It houses his power."

Sarnie chuckled. "Hand-me-down magic tricks from an

aging caretaker, nothing more. He needed an old man to protect him when he found himself on the run a few years ago. The 'Fugitive Professor' I think they called you, no?"

Even in the afterlife I can't escape it. RG shrugged. "What can I say? Has a bit of a ring to it, I have to admit."

"Now he's a celebrated otherworldly hero." Sarnie nudged Luther. "A cold-blooded spirit slayer. Protector of the weak. But deep down, he's a killer…just like me."

RG grimaced. "I'm nothing like you."

"Oh, but you are." Sarnie spoke into his ear. "And you're starting to get a taste for it, aren't you? That's why you keep doing it, telling yourself it's only a mission." He rolled his eyes. "Please…"

"I've killed to protect others in my world. You do it for fun. Not even in the same category."

"You sense the exhilaration, the same sensations you get when you send one of us into the abyss. You're more like me than you think." Sarnie ran his sticky nails through RG's thick mane and nudged Luther. "He even has my hair."

RG winced at his touch.

"And I know you better than you think. I've witnessed so much of your life, it's as if I've lived it right beside you, the visions playing out before me. A flaming spirit hovering beside you, pushing you toward your fall from grace. A dying woman tethered to a hospital bed with cords and wires, passing from this world to the next." He turned to Luther, "…Helen, if I recall her name. And, of course, the auburn-haired beauty sharing your home…and your bed. So many images and memories of her…it's as if I know her myself—"

"Be careful." RG turned on Sarnie, pointing a finger at his face. "You're not immortal yet."

"Oh, but I will be." Sarnie grabbed a fistful of RG's curls

and pulled. "You, on the other hand…" Sarnie snapped his fingers…"are about to find out just how mortal you are."

At the sound of his beckoning, a cluster of jumpers broke free from the pack and fell upon RG, grasping his arms from either side and taking him to the ground before he could manipulate the ring. Heavy hands yanked the gold band from his finger. Luther stepped forward and snatched it, rolling it between his index finger and thumb before threading a long nail and settling it on his hand.

"Well, that saves me a trip to Jared's." A glow filled his frame as his eyes fluttered closed.

Sarnie stepped toward a prone RG, held immobile against the cold cave floor. "So, are you ready for something…original?"

* * *

Mike

"You're up late." Stahl stood in Chris Daniels' workshop for close to a minute before announcing himself, The Rolling Stones' pounding backbeat on Cool 102 masking his presence.

"What are you doing here, Mike?" Daniels glanced across the barn from beneath the Challenger's hood, his elbow resting on the front quarter panel. "And where are my donuts? Your job to feed me, right?"

Stahl reached for the remote, tilting his head. "You know, I've already heard the Stones today." He clicked off the volume. "It's triggering some bad memories."

Daniels dimmed the light hanging beneath the hood and straightened up. "What the hell are you talking about?" He wiped the oil smudges from his hands with a rag in his back pocket.

"You want to know why I'm here?" He jammed his hands

against his hips. *Can't believe I'm saying this.* "I'm deciding whether or not I'm gonna arrest you."

"Arrest me? For what?"

"Crown Vic went off the road and into Jackknife Cove a few hours ago with me in it, along with Zach and Claire." He fell into a blank stare. "Claire's still in a coma. Funny thing, it happened in the same spot as Alex Sarnie's car a few weeks ago. I'm guessing his car had the same problems mine did before it hit the water."

"Oh my God. Claire…" His eyes bore a hole in the floor. "Is Zach okay?"

Stahl looked at Daniels with steel eyes. "Don't ask me about my family right now."

Daniels raised his hands in front of him. "Listen, I'm sorry, are you accusing me of something?"

"Someone hijacked the Crown Vic remotely," Stahl interrupted.

"Hijacked? What does that mean?"

"I've become something of an expert on the CAN bus system over the past few hours. You know, the device you're installing in your muscle cars. Turns out you can remotely disable just about any system in a car with an Internet connection and a computer. I stumbled across an article about a pair of computer security geeks who discovered a glitch in a feature found in most cars, including the Crown Vic. Turns out, if you have a vehicle's IP address, you can disable engines and brakes, accelerators and steering, any system controlled by a vehicle's CAN bus system. With Internet access, a cellphone to establish a WiFi spot, a laptop, and a vehicle's GPS coordinates, you can establish its location…remotely from just about anywhere. Including six inches from the back bumper."

"What does that have to do with me?"

"You tell me." Stahl folded his arms.

"Are you fucking nuts?" Daniels adopted a wider stance. "You saying you think I had something to do with this?"

Stahl worked his jaw.

"You think I killed Sarnie's family, too? With a computer? You gotta have high-end hacking skills to be able to do that. Christ, the IT guy, Malcolm, spends half his morning at my desk just about every day."

Stahl's hand drifted to his shoulder holder, unsnapping the retention strap. "Only one way to find out, really." Stahl took a deep breath before releasing. "You see, before I went through the fence and ended up in the drink, this car had been following me. Right up close, just about kissing my rear bumper. Had only one headlight."

"How are you possibly going to find the car? You have any idea how many cars driving around the Cape have only one—?"

"I remember that damn car. I'd recognize the sound of the engine anywhere." Stahl pointed to the vehicle in the second bay behind Daniels. "One thing I've learned from you. You can't mistake the sound of a muscle car, especially a Challenger. Now you're gonna turn on the lights for me."

"What?"

"I'm gonna stand here, and you're gonna pull the dashboard switch."

"And if the lights go on, am I off the hook? Or are you gonna read me my rights anyway, say I repaired them? I mean, what the hell am I doing in my own workshop close to midnight fixing a Challenger that drove you off the road, right?"

"You didn't repair them."

"Why not?"

"Because you figured I was dead."

"You're fucking crazy." Daniels pointed a shaking finger at his friend. "You've lost it, Mike!"

Daniels turned and rummaged through the drawers of the cabinet beside the Challenger.

Stahl unholstered his HK45. "Keep your hands where I can see them."

Daniels froze. "Relax. Just getting the keys. Need to fire this thing up to juice the battery. Haven't driven it in a while."

"You sure about that?"

Daniels dropped into the driver's side and pumped the gas to prime the engine. The engine sprung to life, firing on the first key twist.

"All warmed up, eh?"

Daniels exited the car and slammed the door. "Fuck off, Mike."

Stahl pointed to the headlamps. "The suspense is killing me."

"After all we've been through." Daniels shook his head. "I pull this switch and everything changes. Headlights go on, we're finished. One headlight doesn't and—"

"You're finished."

"Won't be enough to arrest me. You know it, and I know it."

"I have phone records." Stahl stepped to Daniels' workstation and held the cigar box above his head. "I have letters."

Daniels swallowed.

"I have enough circumstantial evidence to raise doubt. But we'll examine the computer systems in Sarnie's car and the Crown Vic, figure out who has been playing around in there. That will be the smoking gun. But right now, I just need to know if the lights go on."

"You're forgetting about Jimmy McKinnon? You talked to him like I said?"

"Funny thing about Big Mac." Stahl paced the workshop floor. "Someone gave him a call during our meeting. Told him things I didn't want him to know. Like my reason for going there. Ended up with two guns against my head. You wouldn't know anything about that, would you?"

"You think I know Big Mac?" Daniels threw his arms from his sides. "Just dial him up whenever?"

"You've been full of surprises, lately. I had no idea you even knew Jessie Sarnie until last week."

Daniels stepped to the Challenger's window. "I'm sorry it's come to this. You're running out of friends."

"What are you waiting for?"

He reached in the side window. He glanced up, fixing Stahl with a stony gaze as he pulled the knob.

CHAPTER EIGHTEEN

Wednesday, March 30

Kacey

Kacey crept along the cave floor on all fours, hiding behind the rocky outcroppings as she advanced toward the jumpers, huddled en masse at the front of the cave. She couldn't spot RG but, moments earlier, had seen a gang of dead souls take him down. With RG's ring glowing on Luther's finger and nothing but a butterfly yo-yo clutched in Kacey's fist, she conceded they had their work cut out for them. They had faced off with individual jumpers in the past, but now they faced a garrison of hundreds.

They were outgunned.

She reached to her neck for Ian's locket, pressing her eyes shut as she recalled the choice she had made in the Barnard Street house living room. *Sonofabitch!* She could have used a little time stoppage right now. She glanced at the ring sparkling on her hand. Had she chosen love over common sense? She already knew the answer. That's how she had spent her entire life and wouldn't regret it, but tonight it might mean dying for her decision. At least she would be beside RG if it happened.

As she inched forward, the yo-yo throbbed in her hand, its shape undulating and surging like a child's pull on its mother's hand. She glanced at the object, catching a hint of its eight-year-old owner amidst the swirling colors beneath the toy's stenciled butterfly wings. Kacey squinted and leaned forward, the yo-yo transforming before her eyes, images and distant memories pulsing within it. She pressed the butterfly image to her eye and peeked inside, spotting Ray Knoll strolling along Main Street in Hyannis with his mother on a late summer afternoon. Weighed down by shopping bags filled with new clothes and school supplies, he collapsed on a sidewalk bench and folded his arms across his chest.

"Can we go home now?" he had asked.

"Now you sit tight, Ray. We're almost done." His mother tenderly combed hair out of his eyes as a smile creased her lips. "I'll be right back." She crossed the street, dashing into Benny's variety store, emerging with her hands held behind her back. With a quick step, she dodged the oncoming traffic and joined him beside the bench.

"What have you got, Mom?" He grabbed at her closest arm.

She opened an empty hand. "What? You think I bought something for you?"

"Come on." He clutched the other arm, easing it from behind her back. "I saw you at the counter. What did you bring me?"

She waved another empty palm. "Whatever do you mean?" She giggled.

Raymond raced around his mother's back to discover what she had been transferring back and forth between hands.

"Whoa," he cried, turning the brightly colored toy in his hands. "A butterfly!"

"You like it?"

The boy tore the yo-yo from its package. "Like it? I love it!"

"I'm glad," she said, her son's joy mirrored in her eyes.

Raymond hesitated. "But why did you buy it for me?" He glanced at the shopping bags beside him. "I've been complaining all day. I don't really deserve it."

Kacey could sense the love percolating from within Raymond's mother, an unseen force filling her soul and bursting its seams. "Deserve has nothing to do with it."

"So, you bought it for me…just because?"

"Just because." She dropped onto the bench and put an arm around his shoulder, pulling him close and kissing the top of his head. They rested in silence, heat waves shimmering off the baking sidewalk. She closed her eyes and turned her face to the sky, love radiating like sunshine from her core, completely content on a street corner bench in Hyannis with a young boy nuzzled against her.

Kacey pulled her eye from the yo-yo as the images faded like an interrupted dream. The toy continued to flip and jump in Kacey's hand as she advanced along the cave's wall, hidden from sight. She scanned the restless throng of jumpers before her, their vengeance and enmity spewing a pall of hate, registering as a burning odor in her nostrils. The yo-yo nearly leaped from her hand again as Kacey crept forward. She sensed movement and retreated into the cave's shadowed darkness.

"Care to join your husband?" Luther Greer's lilting voice whispered from behind as razor-sharp talons caressed Kacey's shoulders. The jumper had assumed his other form, his dripping, wolf-like canines tickling Kacey's ear. "He'll appreciate the company."

The Luther-thing wrapped his claws around her, beat his wings, and took flight, pulling her from her hiding place high into the air. He hovered above the crowded cave like a mutant hawk with a trembling rodent hooked in his claws before descending toward the undulating jumpers circling their prized captive. Luther sheathed his talons and dropped Kacey to the hard cave floor mere feet from where a team of jumpers readied a set of his and hers gibbets. The yo-yo pounded in her grip like a heartbeat.

Kacey crawled across the cave floor until she reached RG, wrapping him in a desperate embrace.

"That was quite an entrance," he said, "but I wish you had stayed where you were."

"Can't be worse than the Barnard Street house." Kacey scanned the army of jumpers surrounding them. "Can it?"

"Not sure it can get much worse."

After a moment she grabbed his hand and steered it to her ribcage.

His face twisted. "What are you doing?"

Her heart thumped against her chest. "Can you feel that?"

"Your heart's pounding like a trip hammer." He brushed the tumbled strands from her eyes.

She surveyed the man in front of her, marveling at his restless hair framing his face's matching angles, the way his lips formed an almost perfect landing zone for hers, like a bullseye for her special arrow. A hundred women might stroll past him every day, never registering his presence or witnessing the miracles she encountered with each glace. "I love you more than I ever have, RG. Right now. That's why my heart's beating so hard. And I'll love you more five minutes from now."

"I'm not sure we're gonna be here in five minutes." RG glanced at the crude wooden beams looming before them, their shadows darkening their faces. "Why are you telling me this now?"

"I'm getting the strangest sensation. You better take hold of my hand."

"Something happening?" He grasped her palm, rubbing his thumb across her wedding ring. He glanced at his shriveled ring finger, scarred and naked without its gold band.

"I think so." She blew out a breath. "It's like an untapped energy source surging through me."

"Where's it coming from?"

"I think…us." She showed him the yo-yo thumping in her hand. "And this."

Alex Sarnie chuckled as he stepped toward them, eyeing the yo-yo. "You gonna show us how to 'walk the dog?'"

"Speaking of dogs," RG said, gazing into Luther's canine snout. "Looks like you'll be at the end of Sarnie's leash pretty soon. Hope you're comfortable with your place in the pecking order. Can only be one alpha, I guess."

Luther clicked his talons against the stone floor.

"I'm leaving you in the hands, or should I say, claws, of the very capable Mr. Greer…" Sarnie spread his hands across the wave of jumpers, "…and my new friends. They're ready to make things very unpleasant for you. I have business to take care of, and then I'm off to see my mother. She and I have a bit of…catching up to do. When I return, I promise something…original…" his eyes darted back and forth between Kacey and RG, "…for the two of you."

Sarnie clapped Luther on the back as he mounted the staircase to the Barnard Street portal.

"They'll be well taken care of, Mr. Sarnie." His grin disappeared as he turned his attention to his team positioning the gibbets. "It's time."

On Luther's command, the dark horde advanced toward the pair. Luther inspected the tips of his talons as if debating whether to take care of their disposition without Sarnie.

With their fingers entwined, Kacey placed her other hand on top of RG's. She sensed her husband's focus drifting as he struggled to devise a strategy against the approaching threat. She had to get him to concentrate, find a way to steer his energy back onto her again. Nothing else would save them now. "Do you love me?"

"Huh?" His eyes darted back and forth at the coming horde. "Strange time to ask, don't you think?"

"You need to show me. You only have a few seconds." Kacey's eyes fixed on RG's, ignoring the menacing forms rumbling toward them.

"What?"

"You know what this is?" Kacey opened her hand and revealed the odd-shaped plastic toy resting in it. "It represents love in all its simplicity. A mother's love. Raymond Knoll's mother gave this to him in a moment of complete adoration for her child."

"So what?"

"Look around you. Hatred surrounds us. It's coming for us, yet I feel nothing but love insulating us. It's bursting from inside this plastic toy…It's within you and pouring out of me in waves, like a haze enveloping us." She raised her head, her eyes flitting back and forth. "Our love will protect us."

RG threw his hands up. "It's the ring we need right now, but it's sitting on someone else's finger."

"Doesn't matter. Love remains the most powerful force in the universe. Your father said so. We have everything we need right here." She gripped Raymond Knoll's toy in her fist. "But you need to help me channel its energy…and ours."

"What should I do?"

"What you do best."

RG titled his head. "You mean, complain?"

Kacey shook her head and grabbed his face. "This, stupid." She pressed her lips against his as a sea of hands reached for them. Her heart swelled with emotion, building energy like a tidal wave hurtling towards the shoreline. She could sense the pressure intensifying in RG's core like tectonic plates about to shift and trigger an emotional earthquake.

She opened her palm, exposing the throbbing yo-yo.

A silent explosion burst from her outstretched hand and rocked the cavern. The energy wave sent jumpers spiraling in different directions, their bodies crushed and blown apart as they catapulted into cave walls and skipped across the unyielding ground. Kacey and RG remained ensconced in a protective cocoon, resting in the eye of the storm as the swirling winds decimated Luther's lair. Kacey's lips stayed locked onto RG's as she held her palm steady, Raymond Knoll's yo-yo unleashing its fury.

As his brethren's bodies flew past him and exploded against the stone walls, Luther braced himself against the tempestuous gale, clutching the base of a wooden gibbet in a death grip. But Kacey had channeled the universe's ultimate power, the true immortal force that gave life its meaning and opened the door to all possibility. Luther's skin blackened and bubbled as love's infinite energy washed over him like acid raining from the sky. His quivering muscles couldn't hold on any longer, and he spun through the air. As he exploded against the cave wall, his shattered core released his final winged beast. Spittle flew from its snapping jaws as it fought the oncoming turbulence and locked onto Kacey and RG.

Dive bombing the pair again and again, the beast raked its razor-sharp talons against their protective bubble and ripped through their defense. Kacey sensed the breach, disengaging from RG's embrace.

"Don't let go, Kacey, that's what it wants!"

As the two knelt beside each other on the floor, Luther's inner demon prepared for a final approach, unsheathing its talons for a high-speed double evisceration. Kacey rolled the yo-yo in her hand, coaxing its wavering energy to protect them a moment longer, but it lay silent in her palm. Placing it on the ground, Kacey stood to face the threat swooping toward them.

"Kacey, look!" RG rose to his feet, his eyes glued to the yo-yo.

A pair of brightly colored wings grew from the toy, black and orange with edges stippled with white, flapping rapidly to escape its yo-yo chrysalis. A cylindrical black body followed, multiplying in size before Kacey's eyes as if its DNA had mutated at warp speed. The Monarch's wings beat in a furious cadence, creating a wind gust that blew Kacey and RG's hair back as if they stood at the sea's edge.

The monster insect gaped at them, its flawlessly proportioned body the size of a hang glider. "God, I hope this isn't payback for all the butterflies I pinned to cork boards in sixth grade science class."

Kacey glanced at the elegant monstrosity, tilting her head at its face, registering the passing resemblance to Raymond Knoll's mother. The monarch lurched forward and fluttered into the air, directly in the path of the winged creature bearing down on them.

The Luther-thing beat its powerful wings as it descended, grasping the monarch in mid-flight. It dropped to the ground and pinned the butterfly beneath it as the beast's jaws ripped into its body and gutted it. Its talons sheared off chunks of flesh and devoured them like a lion pride surrounding a downed gazelle. The monarch's wings quivered against the cave floor as the beast's dog-like maw tore through them.

RG and Kacey huddled together as the Luther-thing feasted on the gift meal. It threw back its head and swallowed the final chunk of the butterfly, a massive bolus tumbling down the dog-thing's massive gullet.

RG's eyes darted to the remnants of the butterfly and back to Kacey. Raising a hand to the side of his mouth, he whispered. "I had hoped for a stronger showing from the butterfly."

Kacey swallowed. "Me, too."

Luther's hell-dog beat its wings and bounced along the stone floor until it loomed above RG and Kacey, preparing for its attack. It let out an ear-splitting shriek that shook the cavern, bringing rocks and debris raining from the walls.

The beast lashed out with a claw as RG stepped in front of Kacey. He pulled her to the ground as its arcing talons sliced the air above their prone forms, missing the pair by inches. Another shriek pierced the silence as the monster's head twitched, snapping violently from side to side. Foam erupted from his throat. It threw a wing toward the floor to maintain its balance before listing sideways.

"RG, what's happening?"

He threw an arm around her and lifted her from the floor. "Move!"

The Luther-thing stumbled forward, its talons raking the ground where RG and Kacey had rested seconds ago. A giant shudder erupted through the beast, and an ear-splitting shriek shattered the air. Its eyes rolled back in its head as it fell backward, convulsing and twitching before falling silent.

The great bird disappeared, replaced by Luther's still form. His dead eyes remained open and motionless, his mouth parted. Luther's hands clutched his throat as if he had been garroted a second time.

A tiny butterfly flew from his mouth. It had a monarch's shape, but its orange scales had gone black, as if scorched, and its tattered wings hung in ribbons from its body. It flitted about the cave before falling to the ground motionless.

"What the hell just happened?" RG gasped. He scrambled to his feet and approached Luther's dead body, inspecting the foam dripping down his cheeks. "It's like he was poisoned or something."

A light dawned in Kacey's eyes. "I suspect he was."

"How?"

"I think I get it. Butterflies store toxins inside themselves. When predators eat them, they transfer the toxins to their killer. They sacrifice themselves for the good of the colony."

RG shook his head. "How the hell do you know that?"

"A decade of teaching third grade, Mr. University professor. Insect units, trips to butterfly houses." Kacey blew on her nails and wiped them on her shirt. "It wasn't all just babysitting, you know."

"Butterflies, serial killers…" He snatched the ring from Luther's dead hand and inserted it on his mangled ring finger. "I'm learning so much about you this week."

Kacey inspected the monarch's remnants strewn across the ground. "This butterfly was born of love and engulfed by evil. No wonder Luther couldn't survive the toxic meal."

"The most powerful force in the universe…" RG grabbed Kacey's hand and planted a kiss on her waiting lips.

"Oh, my." Kacey fanned herself as she knelt and retrieved the butterfly yo-yo from the ground. "Let's get the hell out of here. It's time to find Sarnie's mother before he does."

CHAPTER NINETEEN

Wednesday, March 30

Mike

Stahl's shoulders dropped as he gazed at the Challenger's grill. Daniels stared back as he pulled his hand back through the window. Neither man spoke for a time. Wasn't much to say, really.

"So, what do we do now, partner?" Daniels folded his arms. "Or should I say…ex-partner?"

Stahl gazed at the pair of light halos piercing the workshop, boring electric holes in the opposite wall. "Chris…I…"

"And fuck you, by the way!" Daniels swept a pile of invoices and receipts off his workstation. They hung in the air before fluttering to the floor.

Stahl stood with arms against his sides, palms out.

Daniels shook his head. "I should have told you about

Jessie, but to think I would kill her and her family. To think I would try to kill you."

"All the evidence…it appeared to fit." Stahl stumbled to the counter and collapsed onto a chair. "Claire's condition… got me seeing red."

Daniels waved his hand. "Whatever."

"Listen. I—"

"Just, don't." Daniels turned, his hands pressed against his hips. "Doesn't matter right now. We have a more pressing problem."

"What's that?"

"Someone tried to kill you." He pivoted to face his partner. "And we gotta find a Challenger with one headlight."

"You're on suspension. I can't let you—"

"You owe me. And besides, what are they gonna do?"

Stahl scratched his head. "Um…fire you."

"Well, someone's got you in their sights, and despite the fact I wanna kill you, I'm not gonna sit here in the shop and let someone else do it." Daniels threw open his workstation laptop and powered it up. He pulled his cell from his back pocket, placing it on the desk as he dropped onto the hard-back stool. "Let's search the DMV database for…what do you think… early '70s Challenger? Can you pin down the year?"

Stahl stepped over to Daniels' workstation, pressing his hands on the table as he leaned forward to view the screen. "I may have learned a bit from your rambling bullshit on muscle cars, but not enough to ID the exact year."

"Can't be too many on the Cape." Daniels pecked away at his keyboard.

Glancing at Daniels' cell, Stahl straightened as if in slow motion. Daniels jabbered away, but his voice dimmed, the silence providing clarity to Stahl's scattered thoughts. When the tumblers fell into place, he dropped onto the stool beside Daniels. "You can stop typing..."

The tapping fell to silence as Daniels turned his head from the glowing screen. "Mike?"

Now it made sense. The cellphone. The call list. Daniels' name on the list had been a wild card, getting him so sidetracked he had forgotten the other calls.

"Mike?"

Stahl paced the barn floor. The evidence had been right in front of him the whole time.

When he had first viewed Doyle's phone log a couple days ago, he hadn't known the burner belonged to Jessie Sarnie. Once he discovered Jessie's relationship with Daniels and his partner's name popping up all over the phone log, Stahl had put blinders on, focusing on the wrong person with the wrong motive. But another number had come up on the list. Over and over. This love triangle had one more corner to it no one had measured.

"Come with me, partner. I know who tried to kill me."

A light burned in the upstairs office, and a single car rested in the lot's first parking space beside the building. Daniels eased the Cougar through the chain-link barrier surrounding the property and past the empty guard booth. Nestling his vehicle beside the Challenger, Daniels gave the muscle car a quick once over.

"Piece of shit restoration."

Here we go. "We're not here to debate workmanship. I need you to check the lights. If one doesn't glow, I go in and arrest the bastard." Stahl recalled the photo above the desk. How had he missed it? The gamer. The computer expert who thwarted hackers at the company. The car buff.

"And if it's got an alarm?"

"Why do you think I brought you here?" Stahl grinned as he reached for the door handle and stepped from the Cougar. He scanned the parking lot at Sarnie Trucking as Daniels circled the Challenger, cupping his hands against the windows.

"Don't see a security system. It's clean." He pulled on the locked doors. "Just give me a minute." Reaching through the Cougar's open window, Daniels extracted a small black bag from the backseat. He rummaged through it and pulled out a folded coat hanger.

Stahl shrugged. "Figured you might be a bit more high-tech."

"Still the best way to get into an old car." Daniels hooked the wire between the door and window and pulled. The swift, upward motion produced an audible click, unlatching the lock on the first try.

"Jesus. I'm getting a clearer picture of how you spent your teen years."

He smirked as he swung the driver's side door open, gripping the light switch between his fingers. "You ready?"

As Stahl nodded, Daniels pulled the lever. Light pierced the darkness and settled onto the wall in front of the Challenger, a single glowing light circle beaming from the driver's side.

Stahl shook his head as he examined the burned-out passenger's side headlamp. "It's gotta be the car. I don't believe in coincidences."

"Maybe you should." Wilson Sarnie held the thirty-eight-caliber handgun at Stahl as he stepped from behind the building. "You see, I have a refrigerated truck heading up to the Canadian border today and a couple of dead cops that are going to need a ride. If that isn't a coincidence, I don't know what is. Don't imagine they'll find your bodies until midsummer at least, after the snow melts."

Sarnie tilted his gun at the Cougar. "What is this hunk of shit?"

The cables stood out on Daniels' neck. "If you can't recognize an Xr7, you don't deserve the piece of shit you drive."

"Oh, one of those Mustang knockoffs Mercury tried to replicate?" Sarnie shook his head in a deliberate cadence. "Car couldn't decide what it wanted to be. Sports car? Touring car? Such indecision." He tilted his head toward the Challenger. "This one had a bit more self-confidence."

"Cougar could hold its own with any Mustang, including your Challenger."

"The Eliminator maybe, but not this one. What's it got, the 264? Factory engine for the father of four?"

"Want to find out?" Daniels jiggled his keys.

Stahl fixed Daniels with a stare, an overgrown teenager attempting to solve this dispute with a drag race. Wilson Sarnie would put them down quicker than he would a rabid dog. Stahl had to buy them time. "So, how did you do it?"

"You mean, put you in the drink last night? Just gotta know the right computer code for a piece of shit Crown Vic and take control of the operating systems through the CAN bus. Piece of cake. Should have gotten your speed up a bit more before I put you through the fence, though."

"My wife may not wake up again 'cause of you."

"I'm sorry about that. I hate collateral damage. Necessary, though. Only a matter of time before the trail led back to me. But with you two missing, and the 'House of Horrors' case going on, I'm sure they won't be spending so much time on the Sarnie case anymore."

"You killed Jessie, didn't you, you sonofabitch!" Daniels' face flushed red and a vein pulsed in his temple.

"Ah, the cop fucking her. Did you take a number like the rest of us?"

Daniels quivered like a bulldog chained to a front yard stake, ready to spring.

"Aww, you fell in love, didn't you? She tell you she loved you? She would leave my brother for you? Maybe wrote you a few love letters?"

Daniels' nostrils flared; his hands clenched in fists by his side.

"Yeah, she had a way with words, didn't she? When I found out about you and her, she had to pay. Now you're gonna pay, too." He raised the gun to Daniels' head.

"So, the target was Jessie?" Stahl intervened. "And Alex and Marlie just happened to be in the wrong place at the wrong time? What kind of man goes after his own blood?"

Sarnie turned the gun on Stahl. "For a detective you sure don't know shit. Alex and Marlie weren't my blood."

"Your brother and niece? What are you talking about?"

Sarnie chuckled. "Ever detect a resemblance between Alex and me?"

The question threw him. "Not really," Stahl replied.

"Because there isn't one. Or did that little observation just sail over your head? We don't share any DNA, my friend." Sarnie snorted a laugh. "Alex never caught on, either, the stupid fuck. Too dumb to put two and two together, kind of like you."

Stahl stood with his mouth open, the reality of this revelation impacting more than his survival right now. "You mean, your parents never told him?"

"They could never figure a way to tell him. At some point

it just became too late. My mother made me promise never to say anything." He waved the gun. "Doesn't matter much."

But it did matter. In ways Sarnie or Daniels couldn't imagine.

Alex and Wilson Sarnie, different mothers.

"How can you justify killing a little girl?" Daniels dabbed at the corner of his eye.

"Marlie came with the package. I had hoped I'd get Alex, too, but it didn't happen. Son of a bitch got lucky, really. His whole life, he had been nothing but a bully. Could never pass up a chance to put me down, humiliate me. Like sticking me in a basement office or paying me a pittance while he raked in the cash. He's still got it coming."

"What do you mean, still?" Daniels squinted.

Sarnie's gun dropped to his side. "He survived, goddammit! What the hell kind of cop are you?"

"Impossible," Daniels said. "I've seen the accident photos."

"Bullshit! The feds handed you a cover story to protect him. He's still off looking for his killers, the dumb sonofabitch. He has no fucking clue."

"Show him your case file," Stahl whispered to Daniels. "In the backseat."

"There's something you need to know, Sarnie. Your brother's dead. I have the photos in the car, I can show you." Daniels raised a thumb toward the Cougar. "Let me just reach through the back window."

Sarnie crossed his arms. "You're gonna show me pictures of my dead brother?"

"He's got them right here," Stahl added.

"Go ahead, but I'm not stupid, you know. It's obvious what you're trying to do. Typical cop bullshit, trying to mess with my head." He glared at Daniels. "There better not be anything else in the backseat or the first bullet goes into your brain."

"Easy." Daniels held his hands in front of him as Sarnie stepped to the opposite side of the Cougar, arm rigid, fingering the thirty-eight caliber's trigger. Daniels kept one hand in the air as he pulled a manila folder from a stack of files in the backseat. Opening the folder, he pulled the pictures of a drowned, bloated Alex Sarnie. He fanned them out in his hand like a deck of cards. "How do you explain these?"

"He can't." Alex Sarnie's voice dripped with contempt as he emerged from the shadows. "But then again, he has his own explaining to do."

* * *

Ellie

Ellie Daniels had served the last of the Pancake Man's evening regulars and finished clearing and wiping the tables. She collapsed at the counter, using her legs to pivot her body on the rotating counter stool. She accepted a cup of coffee and slice of peach cobbler from Sal, who gave her a fatherly smile.

"We're all so happy you've been working here, Ellie." He leaned forward on his elbows and stabbed a square of Ellie's pie with the fork from the silverware bin. "We don't get a lot of new help around here, and none as sweet as you."

"I love it here, Sal. You've all been so great to me. I couldn't be happier."

"The pie alone is worth spending eternity here. You'll never go hungry, and you'll forever be surrounded by friends."

He returned her warm grin.

"Sal?" Ellie gazed toward the front door. "Where do you go at the end of your shift?"

"What do you mean? I go home."

"But where? When you open the door to leave, I see nothing but white."

Sal glanced toward the entrance. "When you're ready to step through the door, you'll witness something different, something beautiful."

"Sometimes when I peek at it, I think it lets me view a world right through it." She rubbed a stain on the counter with her finger. "Or maybe I'm imagining things."

"Oh, I don't think so." Sal pulled out his rag, grinning as he lifted her hand and wiped the counter beneath it. "What do you see?"

"Little weathered houses along a bluff, and gift shops and ice cream stores dotting the main road in front of the store. And across the street, the harbor on the other side of the jetty. It's like home."

"We all go to the place that means the most to us. You will, too. Sometime soon, eh?" He aimed his fork at the cobbler and raised an eyebrow. Ellie nodded. Cutting the edge of the flaky crust with the edge of his fork, he raised it to his mouth. But Ellie's fork intercepted it, knocking it back onto the plate.

She smiled and scooped the dripping pie chunk into her mouth. "So, you didn't answer me. Where do you go when you leave?"

Sal wiped the corner of his mouth with a napkin and tossed it at her. "As a boy, I lived in New York City. In the summers, my mother would send me to my grandfather's vineyard in a country on the other side of the world. Papi would wake me before dawn to work the fields, teach me how to harvest the grapes and turn them into wine. It seemed like a million miles away. Farmland, vineyards, and dirt roads as far as the eye could see."

Sal leaned forward and took another bite of pie. "When I leave here at night, I go to my Papi's vineyard." He patted

Ellie's hand and straightened. "Don't forget to punch out, honey…finalize things before you go." He slipped back into the kitchen.

She attacked the peach cobbler and finished it off with a glass of milk. She waved to Sal through the kitchen window as she slipped off the stool. Glancing toward the entrance, Ellie circled the diner searching for one more task. She had already filled the salt and pepper shakers and cleaned off the menus in the tabletop wire racks. She had wiped the laminate table tops and arranged the napkins and silverware beneath the counter for the morning rush. Her gaze drifted to the front door. One by one the overhead lights flipped off, leaving her in near darkness. The only illumination settled over the waiting area. Her footsteps clicked on the Linoleum flooring as she approached and placed a hand against the door. She imagined the ocean on the other side of the street, the boats' horns sounding over the harbor. She imagined the size of the swells on the bluff's opposite side, where the rip currents folded beneath the surface layer. She pictured the new friends she would meet there.

Stepping toward the door, she glanced over her shoulder and caught Sal and the other restaurant staff observing from behind the service window. They quickly looked away, disappearing into the shadows.

She seated herself along the cushioned bench beside the front door. She sensed the vague connection to her body lying in Mass General. So far away now, as if it wasn't still part of her anymore. She turned to the door. The pull had gotten stronger.

Her vision clouded as the overhead light dimmed. She couldn't tell if the darkness had come from within or from an ebb in the fluorescent light above. Her vision now focused inward, her rods and cones scattering the light in reverse and showing her things only she could view. She could make out the figure's familiar outline clear as day. What she witnessed wasn't a vision or memory, but images of the man in real time, the *now* presented to her from within. She sensed the turbulence, like someone had roiled her internal waters. The symptoms Kacey described had bloomed as if she had tapped into some universal power, the physical distress signaling her of impending danger, that her brother Chris needed her. Her body let loose an internal convulsion, and she imagined the sensation must have resembled the moment before giving birth.

Ellie dropped her head and pressed her eyelids shut. *Help me, Kacey.*

She rested for a few moments in the dark, truly alone for the first time in her life, the front door looming before her. "Sal?" She glanced toward the kitchen.

No answer.

The blood drained from Ellie's face. *I'm not ready.*

Kacey's voice spoke in her head. *"Your brother needs you."*

Ellie stood and took deliberate steps toward the door. She turned to glimpse Sal emerge from the darkened kitchen, a bittersweet grin plastered on his face as he stood behind the counter.

Ellie pushed the door open to find her new home an exact rendering of how she had imagined it, the gray shingled homes littering the bluff and the dazzling sunshine glinting off the harbor's surface like a million sparkling diamonds. She fell into a soothing brilliance, as if she had dropped into a silk hammock. Her laughter echoed in her ears, so loud they must have been able to hear it back inside the kitchen.

In Mass General, the hulking gray machines sputtered and flatlined, the staccato blips turning into a high-pitched blare as Ellie stepped from the diner.

* * *

Mike

Daniels' eyes darted back and forth between Alex and Wilson Sarnie as the photos dropped to the ground and scattered across the parking lot. "What the——?"

"So, what do you say, Brother?" Alex Sarnie emphasized the last word as he circled Wilson. "Feels like we need to have a quick discussion, clear the air a bit, don't you think?"

Wilson swallowed, raising his piece toward his brother and taking aim.

"You really expect that hunk of iron will to do anything, Wilson? The way I am now? You saw the photos, didn't you?"

Daniels turned to face Stahl, his nose wrinkling as a wave of decomposition wafted across the parking lot. "What's happened, Mike? I thought he was..." His eyes searched Stahl's for reassurance, as if a word or nod from his mentor could normalize something as unbelievable as resurrection.

Stahl shrugged, accepting he would have to explain things to Daniels, bring him into a new reality. "It'll all make sense soon, Chris. I'll explain."

"Ah, Detective Stahl," Alex Sarnie began. "I figured if I stayed close you would lead me to my killer. And you must be Daniels." Sarnie sighed, resting his hands against his hips. "The detective fucking my wife."

Daniels held his ground but remained silent.

"Not going to bother denying it?"

"I loved Jessie."

Sarnie snorted. "Didn't everybody. Luckily for you, I have moved on from the earthly emotions like jealousy."

"So, he gets away with it?" Wilson Sarnie's voice rose as he turned the gun to Daniels.

Alex faced his brother. "As did you. I may no longer be

jealous, but I still have serious anger issues I'm dealing with." He took a step closer. "Ones you'll have to contend with. Do you know why I'm back?"

"Back from…where?" Wilson asked, as if he needed to hear the obvious, confirm what his squirming brain attempted to process.

A slow grin spread across Sarnie's face. "Back from the dead."

The stopper shook in Wilson's trembling hand, as if it suddenly weighed an extra ten pounds. "That's impossible."

"Is it? I'll let you decide." Sarnie pulled up his shirt to reveal the gauze encircling his torso. He unraveled the wrap, as if removing a garland from a Christmas tree. Maggots tumbled from the wide holes in his skin, the ones clinging to the medical tape fluttering to the pavement like a writhing snow. His skin had the consistency of wax, glistening with an exudate carrying the pungent odor of decay, like spoiled food left out too long. The skin holes revealed his inner organs sitting like a meat stew in his belly.

"I came back for you!" Alex Sarnie pointed to his brother. "I came back for the person who killed my family. I came back to make them pay for what they did. I figured I would maybe hang them from a hook and rip a hole in their body or maybe tear their heads off." Sarnie gave his brother a warm smile. "But seeing you has given me a change of heart."

Wilson Sarnie released a deep breath as he dropped to his knees. "Thank you, Alex. I know I did the wrong thing. Jessie…got me all mixed up. You know how she was. You gotta forgive me!"

A twitch pulled at the corner of Alex Sarnie's eye.

"There, there, Wilson." He reached out a hand and gently stroked his brother's hair. "You seek forgiveness?"

"I beg you."

Sarnie grabbed his brother by the neck and lifted him to his feet. "All those years, and you never bothered to tell me. You lived, pretending to be my brother," he said, sweeping his arm across the grounds, "reaping the rewards of my success. You deprived me of knowing my real mother. But no matter, I have a friend…more like a mentor, who helped me find her. I'll be visiting her soon, but the reunion will be short."

Stahl shuddered. Sarnie had no relationship with his mother. He would kill her without hesitation. Nothing would stop him from achieving immortality.

Sarnie patted his brother on the cheek. "So, I think instead of forgiving you, I'm going to take you to a place I know. A house I've been staying. Others await you there."

Alex Sarnie leaned forward and locked gazes with his brother. A tremor swept across Wilson's face, leaving his jaw trembling, a line of saliva sliding down his chin. His eyes bulged, as if his brother showed things to him, inserting pictures into his mind, things awaiting him in the haunted dwelling. Wilson's mouth widened to an impossible size, his eyes darting back and forth in their sockets, as if witnessing a terror he couldn't comprehend. Alex Sarnie broke the connection, driving Wilson onto the pavement. He tried to speak, his mouth moving and attempting to form words, but nothing came out. Only a high-pitched moan, an ancient emission of fear from his reptilian brain in response to what he had witnessed.

"Let's go, Brother." Alex Sarnie extended his hand. "You have new friends to meet."

In a fleeting moment of clarity, Wilson Sarnie raised his gun and pulled the trigger, waving it back and forth in an attempt to mow down everything in his path. Bullets caromed off the Cougar and building wall as they whizzed across the grounds, grazing Stahl's shoulder and riddling Alex Sarnie with divots. Before he could hit the ground and seek shelter, a pair of bullets pierced Chris Daniels' chest. He dropped to the pavement as if the bones in his legs had crumbled to dust. The empty chamber clicked as Wilson Sarnie continued to pump the trigger and swing the firearm back and forth.

Alex Sarnie leaned forward to inspect his chest. "More people putting holes in me." He pressed his lips together and shook his head before glancing at Stahl.

"Sorry about your friend, but it's time to drop off this trash and meet my new mother."

He grabbed his brother by the hair and pulled him along the pavement, kicking like a child dragged into the dentist office. Stahl shuddered as he imagined what he would soon face.

"I'm hit, Mike!" Daniels cried.

Stahl dashed to his friend, laying on his back in an expanding blood puddle. He dropped to his knees, unsure how to handle such massive trauma. He ripped off his shirt and pressed it to the hole in his partner's chest, but he couldn't seem to dam the leakage. Rolling Daniels onto his side, Stahl inspected the ragged exit wound. He wouldn't have enough fabric to plug that one even if he had stripped to his skivvies and brought a change of clothes. He snatched his cell, his finger poised to call 9-1-1. No point. Only one person had the power to save him. He tapped a bloody finger on the screen.

RG picked up on the first ring "Where the hell have you been, Mike? We waited at Barnard Street—"

"No time for that now, I need your help!" he screamed into the phone. "Sarnie Trucking…Daniels…he's shot! It's bad."

"I don't understand. Dial 9-1-1. There's nothing I can do for a—"

"The ring!" Stahl interrupted. "It fixes things."

RG hesitated. "I don't think it fixes that."

"You gotta try. Please!"

Mumbled conversation rattled in the speaker before Kacey's voice came over the line. "Mike, we're on our way to intercept Sarnie at his mother's house. If we leave—"

"It's not his mother!" Stahl interrupted. He could read in the silence her attempt to process this new information. "Just get over here, I'll explain everything."

"Okay, we're five minutes away." She disconnected.

He doesn't have five minutes.

Daniels' glassy eyes flitted between Stahl and the Cougar. "How's the car?"

"Fixable, buddy." Mike squeezed his friend's hand. "You won't have any problem patching the holes."

He stared at Daniels and the holes no one could patch, the dime-sized gap in the center of Daniels' chest, and the ragged exit wound on the opposite side. Judging from the blood loss, if the bullet hadn't been a direct hit on his heart, it had severed the major arteries around it.

"Hey, Mike," Daniels whispered, smacking his tongue against the insides of his mouth. "I'm thirsty."

"Hang on, brother." Stahl scrambled to the Cougar and pulled open the driver's side door, wrenching the bottled water from the center console's cup holder. He knelt beside Daniels and raised his head, pouring the water onto his friend's tongue.

"God, that's good." Daniels closed his eyes and swallowed, as if understanding the cold fluid might be the final thing his tongue would ever taste. His face glowed as he savored each drop.

Daniels' chest rose and fell in sync with his labored breathing. Stahl couldn't think of anything to say as he perched beside him, the parking lot falling deathly silent. After another minute, motor sounds swelled in his ears, RG and Kacey pulling through the gate.

"Mike…come here. Lean closer." Daniels struggled to keep his eyes open.

Stahl grabbed his hand once again and squeezed. "I'm here."

"I…forgive you," he whispered.

"What?" Stahl leaned closer.

Daniels struggled to breathe. "For thinking I would try to kill you. I know you feel like shit about it."

Stahl squeezed his eyes shut. "I—"

"It's okay," he interrupted. "I…forgive…"

Daniels eyes fluttered shut.

CHAPTER TWENTY

Saturday, April 3

Ellie

Ellie arrived moments too late to prevent her brother's fatal wounds. But had she gotten there on time, she still wouldn't have been able to bend physical laws and alter the bullets' velocities and trajectories like more experienced caretakers.

The slugs would have hit their mark either way. Fate had determined it.

Kacey and her husband knelt on the pavement beside her brother's body along with another man she didn't know. She could sense his love and friendship for her brother, the way he held Chris's hand and spoke to him. A thick emotional signature wrapped the man's body, like a thermal image on an infrared camera, the same aura surrounding Kacey and her husband. She grinned, comforted that the three would share their unique gift with the people in their world. So many lost souls she encountered during her time between life and death had been devoid of emotion and feeling, chugging like a mechanical engine without the oil to help them function. They had either forgotten how to release their heart's vulnerability or had let their experiences bury everything beneath layers of pain and disappointment.

She could sense the life ebbing from her brother's body. He lay there on fire. The stress chemicals coursed through him and triggered millions of pain receptors in his body, flipping them to overdrive. He looked dead, but he still had time left.

If she couldn't save him, she would comfort him in his final moments, the way he had comforted her throughout her life—after their father's death, or when she suffered her first heartbreak. Finally, as she had reclined in a hospital bed alone and unable to move. She would take him where he needed to go. Kacey had trained her well, and the time had come.

Ellie eased herself into her big brother's body, its contours as comfortable as if she had thrown on an old sweatshirt. Stretching her limbs, she filled all the inner nooks and crannies until she shared his body and mind completely. Pictures and remembrances sped through her brother's dying brain as he relived his life's moments. She relaxed and savored the images with him, smiling at the life he had lived, relishing his joys and successes. She also sensed his awareness of the unknown creeping toward him…and a growing fear. She sent a cooling breeze through his heated body and soothed his discomfort, stabilizing his breathing.

Daniels stirred. *"Is that you, Ellie?"* The words formed in his mind. He didn't speak them, but pushed them out in silence, setting them adrift into the void. He couldn't picture her in the traditional way either, but he sensed her.

"Who else would it be?"

"What are you doing here?" He cleared his throat. *"Are you…dead?"*

She nodded.

"Today?"

"Turned out to be my time, Chris."

She could sense his body deflate, not being with her when she passed. He had planned to visit her tomorrow. *"I'm sorry I couldn't be there."*

"But you were there. You've been there the whole time."

He reached for her hand and caressed her palm, lowering his head. *"Am I dying?"*

Ellie searched her mind for an answer, a way out, anything to prevent the inevitable. She had come to take him onward, but she now rejected that mission.

"Not if I can help it."

As she focused, a surge welled within her. A swirling power grew and multiplied, honing her energy into a tangible force, like a weapon in her grip. She corralled the flowing energy swirling through her body, controlling it with her hands, as if she'd taken a raging inferno and stored it inside her fingertips. She sensed the ability to set it free or reign it in with a mere thought. She recalled Kacey's words, how all caretakers have a unique power that will emerge over time. Ellie hadn't sensed the depth of her gift until now.

RG, Kacey, and the other man remained by her brother's side. She gazed at his chest. His labored breathing pulled his face into a pained grimace.

Another surge jolted Ellie's frame. She inspected the damage to her brother's body, the ragged hole piercing his core, his shattered ribcage, and his tattered heart struggling to push blood to his body through the severed arteries. She grinned as she pictured a brother and sister on a beach blanket, the boy patting the wet sand into the shape of a heart and handing it to the little girl.

He had fixed her broken heart once. Now she would return the favor.

Ellie closed her eyes as the power rose in her body, glowing in her core and surging through her arms and hands and into her fingertips. She sensed a moment when the surge could have engulfed her, a moment of uncertainty, but she reined it in, controlling the energy inside until it yielded to her demands. She wrapped her hands around her brother's heart, reaching for the shattered pieces and gathering them together beneath her palms. She patted the edges until they fit together and pressed her hands over the top, forming it into its proper shape. She massaged the pierced aorta, patching the tears. She let go and felt the strength inside, the blood pumping through his veins once again. His breathing resumed its normal depth and strength.

Ellie took her hands from his chest. *"You should be okay now."*

"You're not taking me with you?"

Ellie grinned. *"I changed my mind."*

He reached for her hand.

"I'll be back one day…when it's time."

She sensed Kacey and the weight of her smile. *"We'll take care of him from here,"* Kacey said.

"Do I go home now?" she asked.

"Everyone's waiting for you."

Ellie's spirit pulled from her brother's body, toward the place she belonged. She reached out for Kacey one more time, but a distance had spread between them. *"Maybe we can meet up again sometime."*

Kacey's voice replied, muted and distant as if filtered through an old-fashioned telephone receiver.

"I know a great little diner."

* * *

RG

RG and Kacey had dashed from their vehicle and fallen to the pavement beside Stahl and Daniels. Stahl sat in a trance beside his friend, blood stretching from the man's body and soaking the detective's pants.

"Take off the ring, RG. Put it on his finger!"

Daniels' blanched skin and still chest revealed no sign of life. "Mike, he's gone. The ring can't bring someone back to life."

"Can you at least try?" Stahl blinked like a frightened child. For a man who had witnessed so much, his partner's deteriorating condition appeared to have pushed him to his emotional limits.

"Ellie's inside him, RG. She's doing what she can from within." Kacey grasped her husband's hand. "The ring has done wonders for your severed finger. If it can help patch Daniels' holes, we may be able to slow things down until we can get him to the hospital."

"He's lost a ton of blood already."

"Just do it!" Stahl shouted. "Please."

RG slipped the ring from his finger, the twisted wounds and scars rising to his skin's surface as the digit shriveled before his eyes. He sensed a distant echo of pain along the knuckle where the jagged blade had ripped through it last summer. He positioned the ring on Chris Daniels' finger.

"Help me turn him over, RG." Stahl positioned his arms underneath Daniels' head and shoulders. "I need to check something."

After easing Daniels onto his side, Stahl probed Daniels' tattered, blood-soaked shirt. "I think the bleeding has stopped."

Slipping a hand inside the fabric's ragged hole, Stahl grinned. "His skin…it's mostly intact, more like a skinned knee than an exit wound."

"He's still unconscious," RG said. "But maybe now he won't bleed out. We'll leave the ring on until he gets to the hospital, then we gotta take it off."

"What? But his wounds will reappear. He'll bleed out again."

"The doctors can't fix something that isn't there, Mike," Kacey said. "At some point we have to take the ring back. Best place to do it will be the hospital. It will give him the best chance."

They loaded Daniels into the back of RG's Subaru. Less than an hour later, Daniels underwent surgery at Cape Cod Hospital to repair a massive hole in his back from a thirty-eight-caliber handgun. Afterward, Stahl, RG, and Kacey huddled outside the intensive care unit where Daniels would remain overnight. Sedated and pumped full of pain-killing drugs, Daniels would be unable to receive visitors until morning at the earliest. A cadre of Cape Cod police officers patrolled the hallway unable to visit their friend and unaccustomed to such restrictions. They grumbled to each other about hospital rules, their salty language not subject to similar constraints.

Chief Defranco sidled up beside Stahl and placed a hand on his shoulder. "So, what the fuck happened out there?"

"Wilson Sarnie surprised us."

"I see you have another souvenir." Defranco pointed to Stahl's bandaged shoulder. "You've got enough lead in you to start a munitions factory."

Stahl smirked. "Just a graze."

"So, Alex Sarnie's brother, huh? Kills his own family and tries to silence the cops on his trail."

"We gotta get an APB out on him. With Daniels going down, I didn't make the call." Stahl shuffled his feet on the buffed, white floors. "Sorry, Chief, I screwed up."

RG's eyes tracked to Stahl, both men understanding all the APBs in the world weren't going to locate the man. He had been taken to Barnard Street, a place no one would ever find him.

"Don't worry about it, Mike. We'll find the bastard. I'm not gonna ask why a suspended detective joined you on a call." Defranco raised his eyebrow. "I'm sure your report will provide an explanation in painstaking detail…in three-part harmony."

"You got it, Boss."

"By the way, Berrelli's in custody." Defranco folded his arms. "The sonofabitch did try to tip off Big Mac from outside the Kells, like you thought. GPS and phone records got him dead to rights. Oh, did you hear?"

"What?"

"Big Mac ended up separated from his head up in Saugus."

Stahl flinched. "Couldn't have happened to a nicer guy."

"Rest of his crew ended up about the same. I'm aware he made threats to Claire and Zach, but you don't have to worry about that now." A grin played at Defranco's lips "Why don't you head upstairs and sit with Claire awhile. Daniels will be fine. He's one tough kid."

"Good advice. Thanks, Chief."

As Defranco pushed against the double doors and stepped from the hallway, Daniels' surgeon entered the ICU from the opposite hallway, a stethoscope dangling across his shoulders. RG recognized Dr. Howser immediately, the guy who couldn't possibly have been old enough to reattach his finger last summer.

Howser tilted his head when he recognized RG. "Hey, I remember you. How's the finger?"

RG positioned his hands behind his back and tugged at the ring he had removed from Daniels' finger as they wheeled him in to surgery. He hesitated a moment for the transition to occur before he lifted his hand.

"Not bad." Howser pressed his fingers against the digit, the raised scars crisscrossing his shriveled skin like a roadmap. "Still having numbness?"

"A little."

"You may never have full sensation in it again. We're lucky we could reattach it. Speaking of lucky," Howser said, turning to Stahl, "your friend couldn't be any luckier and be alive."

"Daniels has always had the luck of the Irish with him," Stahl added.

"Well, there's gotta be something more than luck going on here." The doctor removed his glasses and rubbed his eyes. "Never seen anything like it. If you drew a line from the entrance wound in his chest to the exit wound in his back, you go directly through the heart. But somehow the bullet went *around* the whole mess without leaving a nick. There's no other explanation. Didn't so much as break a rib."

RG glanced at Kacey.

"He's gonna be fine," Howser said with a smile. He pointed back at RG as he traipsed down the hall. "And you take care of that finger. I don't want to have to see you in here again."

After Dr. Howser exited the double doors, Stahl turned to RG. "Sarnie's on his way to visit his new mother. That's the last thing he told me. We gotta find out where he's going."

"How?" Kacey asked. "Can we access adoption records?"

"Aren't those records usually sealed?" RG chimed in.

"Let me go upstairs and get Zach. We'll all head back to the station. I have an idea."

* * *

The desk lamp's cone of light illuminated the Chatham police station's foyer as RG, Kacey and Zach paced the polished tile floors. Stahl leaned against a desk and glanced at the wall clock. "He said he'd be here as soon as he could."

"You suppose he's having second thoughts?" RG asked.

Stahl gave a dismissive wave. "About what?"

"Oh, I don't know. It's Saturday morning before dawn, and a lead detective needs his IT guy." RG rolled his eyes. "Nothing suspicious there."

Four heads spun toward the entrance as a knock rattled the glass doors. Stahl hopped off the edge of the desk and raced to the foyer.

A lump of a man stumbled through the double glass doors, bed head pushing his cropped, black hair in unnatural directions. A thin line of sweat bathed his upper lip. He fumbled with his tortoise shell glasses as Stahl greeted him. "Jesus Christ, Mike. What the hell's going on here? Who are all these people?"

Stahl introduced Malcolm Meyer to the team. "Malcolm, we have a serious problem, and I need your help. But I gotta ask you a question first."

Meyer's eyes darted back and forth. "Shoot."

"You're a computer guy, right?"

Meyer shrugged. "What's this about?"

"You could work cyber security for any large corporation or head the IT team at one of the top universities in this state." Stahl folded his arms across his chest as he circled Meyer. "But you're sharing a seat with your ass in a windowless cubicle in Chatham upgrading our computers to Windows 10. Why?"

Where the hell is Stahl going with this?

Meyer hesitated, rubbing his chin. "Well, if I work in Chatham I can still live with my mother, and—"

"No, I don't think that's it," Stahl waved his hands. "You see, I suspect you have an adventurous spirit. You want to be part of the action here."

"Action? Well, I did play on the softball team last year."

Stahl blew out an exasperated sigh. "I mean police work, Malcolm! You ever considered being a cop?"

Meyer slumped. "I wouldn't come close to passing the physical. Especially after I wrenched my ankle last October sliding into home plate—"

"And that was my fault," Stahl interrupted, raising his hand. "I never should have waved you around third. But bum wheel or not, you'd be a great cop. Take me, for example. I hobble around and I'm still a cop. You'd be a natural."

"You think so?" He straightened.

Stahl threw a glance at Kacey, already rolling her eyes.

Wrapping an arm around Meyer's shoulder, he steered him into the man's cramped workstation. Computer parts and tangled wires lay scattered across every table and desktop. "You have all the tools. Good attitude, an analytical mind. You can't be a computer programmer without being able to think logically. The way you run those bases, I can also tell you have no fear. That's something else you need."

"No fear," Meyer repeated.

"But the most important thing about being a cop is to follow your hunches. Take chances. You see, I'm trying to solve a case, prevent a murder, and I need someone with no fear. Someone who's willing to go out on a limb with me to make this happen. What do you think, Malcolm? You ready to partner with me on this?"

"Partner, huh?" Meyer unzipped his windbreaker and dressed his chair back. "What do I need to do?"

Stahl pressed Meyer's shoulder, forcing him into the seat. He glanced at Zach. The boy winked and gave him a thumbs up.

"You need to help us stop a murder. Tonight. The only way we can do it will be to find the killer's birth mother. She's in danger. The Registry of Vital Records lists all Massachusetts adoptions, but I can't access it. I could get a court order, but—"

"It would take too long."

Stahl placed a hand on Meyer's shoulder and squeezed. "Look at you, thinking like a cop." He gazed at Meyer like a proud father.

"Well, I watch a lot of *Law & Order* on Netflix."

"With a life on the line, you gotta take chances. We can't wait for the courts because we're out of time."

"So, you want me to hack into the Registry, find the killer's birth mother. Basically, break the law?"

Stahl held his breath. "Your actions might save a life tonight."

"Jesus, Mike, that all? I figured maybe you needed me to delete porn or steal files from the Chief's computer." Meyer repositioned his glasses and straightened the keyboard "Child's play."

Meyer logged onto the Registry, his fingers tapping the keyboard as he attempted to breach the Registry's stubborn firewall. RG, Kacey, and Stahl huddled over Meyer's shoulder in anticipation as his fingers flew across the keyboard. But as the time dragged, the team dispersed, pacing the small cubicle as Meyer muttered to himself while hitting dead end after dead end. Soon, Meyer's mumbles turned to expletives.

"Let's give Malcolm some breathing room." Stahl directed the group from Meyer's workstation.

Outside the cubicle, RG checked his watch. "What are the chances Buddy Holly breaks the code and gets us in?" He pulled at his face. "We're running out of time."

Stahl shrugged. "He's the best I got on a Saturday morning."

Freshly brewed coffee aromas imbued the department's open floor as the time dragged, with no progress coming from Meyer. As the team rested on desktop edges or paced the cramped department, faces grew long. RG stared through the blinds into the night. The morning hadn't yet shed the night's shadows, but a hint of dawn swelled within a mixture of pink and orange just below the horizon. Time passed, and Stahl's ace hadn't been able to break into the system.

"Hey, guys," Stahl spoke in somber tones outside Meyer's cubicle. "I'm guessing he's not gonna be able to access the registry. Why don't you head back home and get some rest? I'll get working on the court order. It won't be more than twenty-four hours, at the latest."

"We give Sarnie a twenty-four-hour head start, and we're sunk." RG clasped his fingers behind his head and pulled his elbows together. "Christ, right now he's on his way to see her!"

"We can only hope he hasn't found her yet." Kacey rubbed his back.

"The best you got, huh?" RG gestured toward Meyer's desk.

Stahl glanced inside the cubicle. His son, Zach, huddled beside Meyer, observing the man's keystrokes.

"Hang on a minute." Stahl's perked up as his eyes targeted Zach. "The best I got? Jeez, why didn't I think of it before?"

"Think of what?" RG rubbed his eyes.

"Zach. The kid can fix every blue screen, virus, and software glitch we've ever had at home."

"Of course." Kacey raised her eyebrows. "I see him more the computer lab at school than anywhere else. The kids say he's a prodigy."

"Maybe the best I got isn't the one I thought. Still, I don't really know what the kid is capable of."

RG grinned. "Only one way to find out."

Stahl ducked his head into Meyer's cubicle and waved Zach over. "Whatcha doing, bud?"

"Just watching Mr. Meyer do his work."

He escorted Zach into the neighboring cubicle and lowered his voice. "How's he doing?"

Zach scrunched his face. "He could use a little help."

"How come you're so quiet then? Could you have helped him?"

"Well, I didn't want to say anything. I didn't want to hurt his feelings."

"I have to ask you a question, Zach, and I need you to tell me the truth." Stahl folded his arms. "You know anything about hacking into computer systems?"

"Well…um." Zach lowered his eyes. RG could sense the boy's hesitancy. Classic no-win situation with either answer, both with the potential for disappointing his father.

"I won't be mad, and you won't get in trouble. I promise. Have any of your friends at school shown you anything?"

"Maybe a few little things."

Maybe they had found their ringer after all.

Stahl grinned. "How about you give Malcolm a hand in there."

Zach placed a palm to his father's ear and whispered. "He

actually needs a lot of help, Dad. But I think I can figure it out."

Stahl dragged a hand through the boy's locks. "Well, can you make a few suggestions, you know, tell him what to do without hurting his feelings?"

"I'll try." Zach returned to the seat beside Malcolm and glanced at the screen. He shrugged as RG, Kacey, and Stahl assembled at the cubicle's opening. "Are you still doing your port scanning?"

"Uh…yeah," Meyer huffed, gesturing toward the screen.

"Using Nmap?"

"Obviously."

"Did it give you an IP address yet?" Zach leaned forward on his elbows.

"I haven't seen any yet."

Zach pointed to a line of green numbers buried in a mountain of code. "How about those?"

"Hmmm." Meyer pulled off his glasses and rubbed his eyes. "Where did those come from?"

Zach grinned at his father. "Maybe you should drop the incoming data packets on port 22. It looks open. What do you think, Mr. Meyer?"

Meyer gaped at the boy beside him. "Why don't you sit up here closer?" He pushed the keyboard in front of Zach and leaned back in his chair. "Now what?"

Zach grinned as he adjusted his seat, his fingers dancing across the keyboard. Window after window opened, taking them deeper into the Registry's labyrinthine security levels.

RG poked an elbow into Stahl's ribs. "You know, the kid might have a future in cybercrime if he chooses to go that way."

Stahl shifted his weight from one leg to the other. "Well, he may speed things up a little, but we still have a long time before—"

"Hey guys, take a look at this!" Meyer shouted.

"Whatta you got, Malcolm?"

"The kid got us in." He threw an arm around Zach's shoulders.

Stahl met Zach's eyes in a silent communication that left them both grinning. He pressed his hands against Meyer's desk and leaned forward. "Okay, now the real work starts. We're looking for the birth mother of Alex Sarnie. S-A-R-N-I-E…type it in. I figure an agency in the Springfield area, maybe northern Connecticut. We're guessing sometime in the late seventies."

Meyer commandeered the keyboard, giving Zach a high-five before returning his gaze to the computer screen. "Let's see…Springfield adoption agency, late seventies." Meyer's fingers clicked and tapped as his tongue poked through his lips. Looking up from the screen, he said, "I got a Sarah and Tom Sarnie."

"Is the birth mother listed?" Mike asked.

"Got it. Looks like Abigail Carver."

RG stepped into the cubicle. "What did you say?"

Meyer squinted toward the screen. "Carver…Abigail Carver, unmarried high school senior."

"Where's she from?" RG leaned over the computer monitor, trying to read the screen from the desk's opposite side.

"Looks like…Connecticut."

"What town?"

"Huh?"

RG knelt beside Meyer's chair, spinning the computer monitor toward him. "What town in Connecticut?"

"Says here, Enfield."

"Abigail Carver," RG mumbled. *Oh Christ.* He rose to his

feet and wandered toward the door, steadying himself against the wall as his knees gave way. Kacey rushed to his side, waving Stahl over to help. They shouldered his dead weight and eased him into a chair.

"Kacey, what just happened?" Stahl asked.

She shrugged, smoothing the hair from RG's forehead. "Not sure, Mike."

Stahl filled a paper cone from the Culligan and handed it to RG. "Who is Abigail Carver, RG?"

He emptied the cup and dropped it to the floor. "The Carvers are family…on my mother's side. Abigail went by her middle name." RG held his head in his hands as he leaned forward, a groan escaping his lips. *This can't be right.*

"There should be a middle name on the document, Malcolm." Stahl pointed at the screen.

"Yeah, I found it. It's Helen. Abigail Helen Carver."

"Helen Carver…Oh my god." Kacey leaned against the wall and slid toward the floor until her legs splayed out in front of her.

Stahl stood frozen, as if waiting for an explanation.

RG sat up. "It all makes sense now. The connection between Sarnie and me. The visions."

"Wait a minute," Stahl's focus remained aimed toward the floor as if his brain attempted to press the final pieces together. "Are you saying—?"

"My mother was Helen Carver," RG interrupted, "before she met my father and became Helen Granville."

"So, Alex Sarnie is—"

"My half-brother," RG interrupted, lifting his gaze. "And he's on his way to kill her."

CHAPTER TWENTY-ONE

Thursday, March 31

Alex

Alex Sarnie rested on the bench on the boardwalk facing the
inn. The brilliant sun warmed his waxy skin as he closed his
eyes and leaned his head back. He took the moment to relish
the culmination of his journey, the anticipation of what lay
before him. He had found his killer, or at least the detective
had, and he had fulfilled his obligation to Jessie and Marlie.
When he returned to Barnard Street, he had discovered the
work the Granvilles had done there. His brother and sister-in-
law's power had surprised him, taking out nearly the entire
cave, including his mentor. Sarnie chuckled. Others would
come to replace the dead, and he had learned what he needed
from Luther. The man had harbored grand aspirations, but

only one Immortal Force could lead a legion of jumpers who couldn't die, and now it would just be him.

He would make sure to thank the couple for their help.

The destruction of Luther's home, the dead strewn about and smashed against the cave's floor and walls, and the unearthly silence, had added a touch of horror to Wilson's final moments. Although he had brought him to Barnard Street to share his bounty with Luther and his throng, Sarnie had enjoyed exacting Wilson's punishment alone, whispering his final intentions for his ex-brother as he lay inverted and nailed to a rickety post. After gutting him, Alex Sarnie had grinned as the light bled from the man's eyes, his innards trailing down his chest like butchered squid until they covered his writhing features. The moment had been intoxicating, and once he achieved immortality, he would continue to exert his power within his new kingdom. He would be the most powerful man who had ever lived, and he would live forever. Caretakers would beg for a mere ounce of his immortal blood. He could demand whatever he wanted from them until he decided, if ever, to bestow upon them his gift. But he wouldn't. Ever. Humans would line up to kiss his feet and serve him as the second coming of their savior. They would build cathedrals for him and write his story in their religious tomes. He would let the others have their fun with them, and from time to time, he would, too. The living remained plentiful, enough to go around for everyone.

He gazed across the road at the older woman hustling between customers with steaming plates balanced on her shoulder, disappearing back and forth from the inn.

Mother.

Had she ever held him in her arms? Even briefly? Or had he been whisked away at birth to ease her suffering, quell any attachment she might have had. Sarnie would make sure to hold her hand as he drained her blood, caressed her brow, and filled her head with beautiful thoughts of her world. Or maybe he would hang her upside down and gut her. He couldn't decide. Either way, she would leave here believing she had done the right thing, giving of herself as a mother should for her son.

As the lunch hour passed and her customers drifted from the porch and along the boardwalk, Sarnie rose from the bench and crossed the street. Helen had bussed and cleaned the tables and relaxed on a patio chair with a cold drink. She held the sweating glass against her cheek as he mounted the creaking stairs.

"Are you still serving?" Sarnie asked.

Helen smiled as she met his gaze, but Sarnie sensed a hidden revulsion at his waxy skin and putrid stench. "Of course." She looked away as she cleared her throat. "Let me get you a menu?"

"Actually, that won't be necessary." Sarnie's eyes darted to the vein pulsing in her neck. "I know exactly what I'm hungry for."

* * *

RG

The sun had dropped below the horizon as RG and Kacey raced along the boardwalk toward the inn. Morrow kept pace beside them, one hand clamped to his fedora to protect it from the sturdy headwind. The evening chill had chased away most of the realm's denizens, creating an unnatural calm to the typically bustling seaside avenue. Despite the conditions, sweat leached from RG's pores. He moved as if every second counted. Before transitioning across planes, Helen had spoken to him again, the words infiltrating his brain dropping him to his knees.

"He's here."

From a distance, the inn appeared deserted. No light bled from its darkened windows or revealed a living soul's shape behind its glass. Either everyone had checked out or a power outage had struck the boardwalk's far end. The lights blazing in the surrounding structures torpedoed RG's latter theory and sent his mind careening in troubling directions. He cast a glance toward Morrow, his father's grim features revealing he, too, entertained similar suspicions.

"Has she reached out again? Like before?" Morrow asked.

"Nothing since. I've tried to find her in here," he pointed to his head, "but it's like there's a brick wall between us. It's as if she doesn't exist—" RG pressed his lips together, regretting his words.

"We don't know anything yet," Kacey assured him. "Let's get in there and find out what's going on."

When they reached the end of the boardwalk, they crossed the empty street and disappeared into the darkness, swallowed beneath the inn's shadow. On the porch's confined space, the swirling winds buffeted their hair from side to side and front to back. Kacey cupped her hands and peered through the window glass.

"I can't see a damn thing inside."

RG rattled the door handle, but it wouldn't budge. Jamming the back of his elbow into the door's rectangular glass pane, he shattered the window and reached through the jagged cleft. He unlocked the door and threw it open.

As they stepped through the entryway, a gagging stench belched from the room's interior, its odor unmistakable in its origin, unrecognizable across every existential plane.

Death, and a lot of it.

"Oh, God," Kacey bent over at the waist, covering her nose and mouth.

Reaching toward the wall, RG triggered the light switch, unprepared for the scene before him. Bodies lay crumpled throughout the foyer, ragged gashes running from neck to waistline. Blood collected in pools on the hardwood floors beneath the corpses and dripped from the walls and ceiling. Guests lay clustered beside kitchen crew and inn staff in an indiscriminate slaughter.

RG blinked, hoping he could erase the scene before him. But when he pressed his eyes shut, the image remained burned into his retinas as if he'd stared at a bright light in a darkened room. He took a deep breath.

"Come on."

They proceeded to the upper floors, checking rooms and common areas, the results the same. Splayed bodies in suffering agony strewn about before them.

Everyone. Dead.

RG steadied himself against the wall as Kacey approached, resting her hand on his shoulder.

She turned to Morrow. "Do you think she's—?"

"Dead?" Morrow shook his head. "Can't say for certain." He perused the carnage surrounding them. "He wanted privacy, for sure. He didn't want to be disturbed in his quest." He removed his hat and combed his fingers through his hair.

RG advanced along the corridor. "I can feel her. She's close."

In an instant, RG sprinted down the stairs to the lobby like a bloodhound clued in to an irresistible scent. He navigated the dead body maze, throwing open the double doors leading into the kitchen. Morrow and Kacey followed on his heels, the path ending at the inn's back door.

"Dead end," she whispered.

"Dammit! He must have taken her somewhere else." RG pressed his face against the backdoor glass and stared out into the blackness. They had to be long gone by now.

As he turned from the door, a gurgling sound caught his attention. A kitchen employee, no more than a teenager, lay prone beside a stainless-steel oven. A plastic bin lay overturned beside him, and broken plates framed his body. The teen's pierced sternum oozed a runny liquid, and his innards dripped from the fissure running vertically to his pelvis. His outstretched arm extended through a reddish stream trickling from beneath his white uniform.

"This one's still alive!" RG cried, dropping to his knees beside him.

The boy closed his eyes and coughed a spattering of blood onto RG's shirt.

"We'll get you help." RG whispered. "You're gonna be fine."

The young man's mouth stretched into a slight grin, as if considering the absurdity of the statement. He turned his head, his attention turned to the boy's rigid, outstretched index finger pointing toward the walk-in pantry.

RG placed a hand against the boy's face. "What is it?"

The boy's eyes blinked slowly, as if each repetition required extraordinary effort. "He's…there."

RG glanced into the storage room, finding nothing but boxes of dried food and cans scattered across the floor.

"He took her…down." The boy pressed his eyes shut as he tapped the floor with his extended finger.

RG peered at the floor. "I don't understand."

The teen raised his finger, pointing toward the storage room.

Kacey stepped across the blood-stained floor and peeked inside. "There's another doorway in there."

"He must have taken her through it," Morrow said. "Wherever it goes."

RG rose from his knee. "What should we do with the kid? He needs…" He glanced down. The boy stared blankly toward the ceiling, his eyes half-lidded and glassed over.

RG lowered his head. "Oh, Christ."

"Come on, there's nothing we could have done to save him." Grabbing his arm, Morrow led him through the pantry. "But maybe there's time to save Helen."

Kacey pulled on the cellar door, but the handle wouldn't budge.

RG whipped his head back and forth, searching for something he could use as a battering ram on the ancient wooden door. Retracing his steps, he dashed into the kitchen and grabbed the first implement he could find, a meat cleaver resting beside a cutting board. He bounced it up and down in his hand, assessing the weight, satisfied the heavy handle might do the job.

"Stand back."

He raised the hatchet and slammed the butt against the cellar door until his hands ached and wood chips peppered his hair, but he couldn't breach the barrier. Raising the miniature machete above his head, he brought the gleaming knife-edge down on the door handle. The blade exploded into pieces as it sliced the handle from its moorings, sending it pinging across the floor.

The door creaked open.

"Now what?" Kacey eyed the dark opening.

RG tossed the handle stump to the floor. "We find out who's mortal and who isn't."

* * *

Water trickled along the damp stone wall as they descended the warped staircase, a mildew odor swelling in RG's nostrils. Approaching the bottom step, he scanned the cramped space. The room appeared to be a storage depot for the inn, its positioning below ground lowering the already chilly temperature another twenty degrees. Old furniture and assorted junk sat piled on either side of a cement corridor leading toward a short stairway and bulkhead on the opposite side.

As RG's eyes adjusted to the gloom, his breath pulled from his lungs. The room turned on its axis as his knees jackknifed, spinning him to the floor. "Oh, God. No!"

Helen Granville hung suspended from the ceiling, her feet tethered to a thick, wooden joist running from stairway to bulkhead. A bucket perched beneath her slowly revolving body.

Kacey and Morrow raced across the floor and grabbed Helen to support her hanging weight. Morrow's foot contacted the bucket and sent it rattling across the floor.

"It's empty," Kacey shouted. "Sarnie hasn't gotten to her yet."

"Thank, God!" RG scrambled to his feet, stumbling forward. Helen's eyes blinked open and her mouth attempted to form words as recognition dawned in her eyes. RG sensed her confusion as she attempted to place the nice couple she had met on the boardwalk within the hellish context of death and slaughter where she now found herself. He pulled an old chair from a rickety furniture pile and climbed to the wooden joist, unraveling the rope lashing her to the ceiling. Helen dropped into Kacey and Morrow's arms, the pair bracing themselves against her weight's sudden momentum.

"Please help me!" Helen's voice wavered, her body trembling as Morrow pulled the tattered ropes from around her ankles. "There's a...mon...a monst—" Helen's eyes widened as she peered over RG's shoulder toward the stairs, her gaze fixed and unmoving.

A rank, decaying odor filled the confined space. RG pivoted to find Alex Sarnie blocking the stairs.

"A monster?" Sarnie shook his head. "Oh, Mother. That's no way to talk about your own flesh and blood."

* * *

Sarnie's state of decay had accelerated. Fluid leaked through jagged fissures crisscrossing his skin, and globs of maggots dropped through his ragged clothing. His body appeared close to complete putrefaction, and he didn't have much time left. But the carnage on the upper floors revealed the spirit's undying power.

"I hoped I wouldn't have to resort to such measures, but she fought me the entire way," Sarnie addressed the three caretakers. "Still, hanging remains the best method to get blood flowing before slitting the throat."

Morrow curled his fingers into tight fists.

Sarnie surveyed his opposition, a grin curling on his lips. "Not sure what you expect to accomplish here. You must have viewed my handiwork upstairs." Glaring at RG, he added, "You're no threat to me, Brother. No matter what you wear on your finger."

"Your friend Luther made a similar miscalculation," RG said. "He learned firsthand what we can do."

Sarnie grinned. "And now you're gonna learn what I can do."

The jumper raised his arms, his fingertips glowing blood red as he extended his hands like a preacher's at a southern revival meeting. His body shuddered as an energy surged through his palms, ripping through the confined space and sending RG, Kacey, and Morrow cartwheeling through the air. Furniture and stacked boxes flew like bowling pins as their tumbling bodies came to rest against rigid stone walls.

An unparalleled stillness enveloped RG as he pulled himself to a sitting position. He glanced toward Kacey crouching on all fours and shaking out the cobwebs. Morrow had made it onto his knees, his black jacket and hat covered in dust. A deathly silence fell, as if someone had hit the mute button on his brain's speaker. He banged a palm against his temple in an attempt to dislodge whatever blocked his ear canals.

"*I knew you'd come.*" His mother's sweet voice filled the void.

RG turned to face Helen still sitting against the wall, unscathed by the recent destruction. Somehow Sarnie's energy blast had bypassed his meal ticket to immortality. Her eyes remained glued to the monster by the stairs, oblivious to RG's identity.

"*He's my brother, isn't he?*"

"*I'm sorry I never told you.*" She sighed. "*We keep the biggest secrets from the people we love most…and sometimes they come back to haunt us.*" Helen didn't speak for several moments. "*Is this… revenge for what I did?*"

"*He needs your blood. It's the life force he needs to preserve his body and make himself immortal.*"

"*How do we stop him?*"

RG glanced at Helen. "*Haven't figured that one out yet.*"

Morrow's voice burst from the silence of his brain's center. "*I can hear you, RG. I can hear both of you.*"

RG glanced at Kacey, sensing from her expression she hadn't been invited to the group chat. The link between father, mother, and son had tapped into some other power Kacey still didn't have access to. He took a quick peek at Sarnie, advancing from the stairwell. They didn't have much time before he launched another offensive.

Morrow crawled toward Helen and grasped her hand. She gazed at him, but no recognition dawned in her eyes.

"Benton, you need to break the spell. Wake me up. I can help you stop him."

RG inspected his mother, knees tucked under her chin and her body shaking with fear. He turned to Morrow. *"What could she possibly do?"*

"I'm not sure, Son, but right now she has powerful blood flowing through her body. She's they key to this whole thing. Has been all along. We have to find a way to link this to Helen," he squeezed her hand, *"with the one on the inside."*

"Wake me up, Benton." Helen pleaded.

After a moment, RG spoke. *"Tell her the words, Dad."*

A wry grin played at the edge of Morrow's lips as he nodded his head. *"The words."*

RG had come across the words before. He had listened to his mother reveal them with her dying breath in a hospital bed a lifetime ago and had read them in his father's letters to her. They represented the link between past and present, the bridge between this world and the previous one. The tangible string between their hearts. If anything in the universe could shatter the barrier between these distinct worlds and awaken the parts of her earlier life she didn't know existed, Morrow's words might be the wrecking ball.

Kneeling beside Helen, Morrow rubbed her hand. "There was a man once…a man you loved."

"What…?" She locked onto Morrow with a blank expression RG could only interpret as confusion at his words strange timing.

Morrow's voice wavered. "He would say, 'Goodnight, goodnight. Parting is such sweet sorrow…'" He placed his opposite hand on top of hers. A brief glow surged from the shadows beneath his fingers.

RG searched Helen for a spark of recognition, something behind her eyes, but her gaze returned nothing but a wary distance.

"'That I shall say goodnight…'"

But before Morrow could continue, Helen straightened. "'That I shall say goodnight,'" she repeated, raising her head and scrutinizing the man before her. Her body softened and her face flushed, as if someone had slipped into her mind and had opened a curtain. RG sensed the string between their hearts tighten as she awoke to a world once removed, remembrances flooding her like a wave's undertow pulling her back into the sea.

"'…till it be morrow,'" she mumbled, unable to catch her breath. Fat tears tumbled down her cheeks as she threw her arms around Morrow in an embrace that cut across decades and multiple worlds.

"Benton? How can you be here?" Helen's eyes darted about, resting on RG. "You've all come back to me—"

"Well, isn't this touching," Sarnie interrupted, stepping forward and closing the distance. "Mom, dad, and little brother all together again. One happy family."

Helen broke off her embrace and struggled to her feet. She took a step toward her son. "The hardest thing I ever did was give you up. You have no idea."

Sarnie stopped.

She took another step forward. "They told me a family in Springfield adopted you. I would drive to Forest Park and sit on a bench all day looking for you. A hundred times a day I would convince myself I'd found you."

"And a hundred times a day you'd forget about me, too, I'm sure."

"Not ever. You're wrong."

"It doesn't matter now." Sarnie raised his palm. "You can make things right by giving me life again."

"I already gave you life. I didn't have to, but I did. I could have snuffed you out like a flame when you grew in my womb. A mother can give life or take it away. You should be grateful for what you had."

Sarnie dug his nails into his palms. "And now I want more. You owe me." He glanced down at his rotting shape. "Look at my body, dying before your eyes."

Helen closed the distance and pressed a palm against her son's cheek. "It's your soul you should be worried about."

"My soul can't be salvaged. The body is all I have left, and you're going to save it." Sarnie reached a sticky hand to Helen's neck. With one arm extended, he lifted her off the floor as her feet struggled for purchase. Gasping for breath, she pounded her fists against his arms and shoulders.

Morrow and Kacey raced to her side, clutching Sarnie's outstretched arm to free her. But the connection between mother and son—Helen's immortal blood just millimeters from Sarnie's own pleading blood vessels—created another energy surge that blew the caretakers across the room the instant they touched his electrified skin.

His wife and father's groans rumbled from the room's corners. RG stood unmoving, the reality dawning on him that the team's combined caretaker powers proved no match for the overwhelming strength inside Alex Sarnie's shriveled form. He had been toying with them, and soon he would dispatch them and have Helen to himself.

He glanced at the ring, hoping to call on its salvation power. *Tell me what to do.* But it rested cold on his finger, no heated glow emanating from its smooth edges. Dead, its strength overwhelmed by the immortality power play raging between mother and son, everlasting life resting on the strength of the thin skin layer separating them. Her heated blood wafted from her arms in waves like a fog, shimmering in the air, as she struggled against her tormentor. The hazy miasma grew, swirling around Sarnie's arms, his chest, and legs as if seeking a hidden access point, a single cut or abrasion it could use to infiltrate and salvage his dying body.

Helen's eyes rolled back in her head as she weakened, her arms dangling from their sockets. RG reached for the ring as Morrow's voice bellowed from across the room.

"Don't wait for the ring to tell you what to do! Tell it what you need it to do!"

RG glanced down at his finger. The time had come to take control. A heated energy built inside his chest, pressing against his walls and surging into his extremities. His father hadn't simply passed along his power to an inanimate gold band as he had believed. He had passed his power to his son, and RG sensed it coursing through him like never before. The ring warmed on his finger, glowing like a heated ember. He spoke to it.

Kill the body.

Kacey's words from the Pancake Man repeated in his head like a mantra. He had dismissed them as folly weeks ago, but at the moment they made perfect sense.

Kill the body.

RG closed his eyes, visualizing what he would need to separate Sarnie from his body. He reached for the ring, but found the meat cleaver's blunt handle clutched in his hand, caressing the ring's edge.

What the…?

He could have sworn he had dropped the stumpy handgrip in the storage room when he hacked open the cellar door. Hadn't he?

Lot of good this will do.

As he was about to toss away the useless timber, a hint of steel appeared, molten fire spitting from the weapon's broken end. Under the ceiling bulb's dim light circle, a blade formed and grew in length, narrowing out and curving upward. He tested the steel's weight in his hand. Perfectly balanced, as if the ring had forged it for his hand only.

"Kill the body!" Kacey shouted from her knees.

With his mother struggling for breath, RG stepped forward and delivered a thunderous blow to Sarnie's raised elbow, slicing through the shriveled tendons like scissors through paper. Sarnie's sheared forearm spilled a flurry of maggots as it dropped to the cement floor. Helen Granville tumbled to the floor beside it.

"You sonofabitch!" Sarnie dropped to his knees to retrieve the appendage. "You have any idea how hard it'll be to fix this," he said, hissing. He raised his head and glared at his brother with fury. As Sarnie inspected his amputated arm, RG took his cue, drawing the cleaver back and swinging it in a mighty arc. The blow to the front of his throat caught Sarnie by surprise, separating his head from his body.

"Try fixing that, you bastard."

Sarnie's head bounced across the dusty floor, his body twitching and squirming in a final death dance. His mouth opened and emitted a wail that shook the inn as he appeared to grasp that RG's severing blow had cost him his shot at immortality, and he couldn't fix this one. RG pressed his hands against his ears to quell the roar as Sarnie's spirit burst from his useless body. He exploded through Kacey, Morrow, and RG, in quick succession, like a silver ball pinging across a pinball machine's bumpers, scattering them across the room before rocketing inside Helen and driving her to the floor.

RG struggled to his knees, his head spinning. Kacey lay

writhing against the stone wall as he crawled over to tend to her. Morrow followed, blood trickling from a gash across his forehead. RG fought the urge to grab them both and get the hell out of there, but he couldn't leave his mother with that otherworldly parasite infecting her.

RG kissed the top of Kacey's head. "You rest. I got this."

Her eyes fluttered as she rubbed her temples.

"Take care of her, Dad. I'm going after Sarnie."

Morrow nodded as he cradled Kacey's head in his lap. "You go."

As RG prepared to penetrate his mother's body and square off against his brother, she opened her mouth. Sarnie had hijacked her vocal cords, his voice bellowing from her throat as violent spasms tore at her body. "You took my body, but I think I've found another one I like."

RG blew out a breath and took two running steps, throwing himself at his mother and piercing her frame. For a moment, he found himself in complete darkness, Sarnie's proximity laying a dark shadow within her. But Helen's soul lit a path for him to follow, like a sliver of sunlight peeking out from a black cloud. Her image appeared, but devoid of time and dimension. More of an amalgam than a rendering of her at any one particular point, her form and shape blurred into a single undefinable moment. Her presence aroused his senses and unearthed childhood's obscure familiarity and comfort. He had returned to the womb, indescribable sensations of security and unconditional love filling his soul.

Invading the inexpressible peace, Sarnie cast a darkening aura that overwhelmed his mother's essence and filled RG with dread. He had battled deadly jumpers and defended the human form in the past, but the stench of Sarnie's soul remained infinite, tickling his nostrils with an emitted odor worse than the formaldehyde and sodden corpse. As RG opened himself to his mother's spirit radiating through him, he sensed the offerings deflect off Sarnie's impenetrable soul and crumble around him.

"Just you and me now, little brother."

RG couldn't see Sarnie. None of the earthly physical senses manifested when souls intermingled. But Sarnie's voice, his manifestation, and his darkness grew like instant weeds in a once-flawless garden and surrounded him, blocking out his mother's light.

"It's time to let this go, Alex."

His chuckle rumbled in the darkness. *"You took away my shot at immortality. You're gonna pay…and she will, too."*

"You can end this now. We can end it, together. Look where you are right now. Don't you sense the light shining from her? She's your mother. You could be part of this. You can live in the light if you choose."

For a moment, RG sensed his brother's indecision, a wavering as he considered his choices. But Sarnie's spirit form mobbed him in a brutal mugging, enveloping him and skewering his core with a high voltage invasion, dropping him to his knees.

"That's for Luther, little brother. But this next one's from me." Sarnie placed his hands on RG's chest and expelled his brother from Helen's body with an explosive shove that sent him rocketing into the ceiling joist above the cellar stairs. RG tumbled downward on his back, crashing through the stair railing before coming to rest with his head dangling off the third step. His momentum pulled him down the stairwell in a series of thumps, his sweaty cheek coming to rest against the cold cement.

"Your turn, Mother," Sarnie hissed.

RG raised his head, still tuned into the conversation, the connection between them as clear as FM radio on a cold night. *"Don't hurt her. Please."*

Sarnie's deep laugh bounced in his skull, rising in volume until his ears rang. *"I'm going to kill her, little brother. Then everybody else in this godforsaken place."*

RG drew himself to his knees and glanced at his mother, a change taking place before his eyes. Light simmered from every inch of her translucent form, radiating from her skin and permeating the cellar with a brilliant light that chased the shadows from every cobwebbed corner. The room glowed as if the sun had pried open the bulkhead door and seated itself on the bottom step.

Helen grinned, and her voice spoke in his head. *"You rest. I got this."*

* * *

Alex

Sarnie had considered RG's proposal to shed the cloak of darkness and live in the light, but his rational mind couldn't sway whatever universal forces had guided him to his destiny. At some point, a person's fate gathered a momentum no one could overcome. As a jumper, he remained destined to live in the dark places between worlds. He could have been more had it not been for his brother, whose quick decision with a transformed meat cleaver had bested him. Defeat snatched from the jaws of victory. He had been too close to immortality to let his rage off the hook.

They would all have to burn.

But he sensed a change in the engine powering his soul, an impotence following the expulsion of his brother from Helen's core. He attempted to control his mother's hands, guide them to her own throat, and choke the life from her. But the sizzling electric power he had wielded now turned against him, controlled by another and directed to his center. The burning tore through his chest, erupting into a fire Sarnie couldn't extinguish. It spread to his arms and legs until his nerves screamed to match the pained sounds spilling from his open mouth. He couldn't breathe, the air heavy with heat and fire, but no oxygen to feed his starving lungs.

"Mother, please!" Sarnie fell to his knees, unable to withstand her assault.

"It's too late. I hoped to save your soul, but you gave me no choice."

The shove came from behind.

Stumbling forward, Sarnie lost his balance. He tumbled downward, his body weightless. His stomach clenched, as if Helen had swallowed him and sent him through her gut. He fell into flaming water, his weight pulling him under as he inhaled the simmering fluid scalding his lungs. He flailed his arms to keep his head above the surface. Sarnie sensed the walls closing in on him, and he found himself back in the Lexus submerged at the bottom of the bay, burning seawater swamping him and filling the vehicle. He threw himself against the car door, but it wouldn't budge. The pitch blackness swarmed him as the scorching water filled the vehicle. He clawed for the door handle as the water rose above his neck and filled his nose and mouth, but the door vanished. He wasn't in the Lexus anymore. He found himself drowning again, this time alone in his mother's womb. He pounded on the walls of Helen's insides as they closed in around him.

She had left him no way out.

* * *

RG

RG sensed a change in the room's energy, a shifting momentum inside his mother. The electric touch zapping RG into the ceiling beams now fizzled in Sarnie's soul like a packet of wet matches but burst from Helen and blanketed the room with light. She had pummeled her unruly son's spirit to nothing, his presence no more than a gnat buzzing beside her ear. Sarnie's gasps and cries filled RG's head as he pleaded with his mother, but she would not relent.

Helen stood and surveyed the radiant cellar, her eyes darting from Morrow to RG, and to Kacey. She wrapped her arms around her midsection as her son struggled inside her. *"This is for hurting my family."*

Sarnie cried out again. A squeezing sensation pressed against RG's chest and he struggled to breathe, as if a vice had gripped his entire body and held it underwater. RG couldn't imagine what punishment Helen imposed on Sarnie, but their brotherly connection had afforded him a glimpse of his agony. Helen crushed Sarnie tighter and tighter in her core, as if preparing to abort the parasite inside her.

RG crawled across the floor to Kacey and Morrow. He placed the back of his hand against Kacey's cheek. She returned a pained smile.

"He's weakening, isn't he?" Kacey asked.

"Something's happening inside her…I can feel it."

Kacey tilted her head. "But how? She doesn't have any special power."

"Today, she does," Morrow interjected. "All mothers can give life or end the life inside their bodies. They can give birth, or they can…abort. The universe grants them such power. How she uses it remains her choice. Sarnie made the mistake of going back inside her, but he didn't realize that a mother always has ultimate power over her child."

"I can hear him." RG pressed his hands over his ears. "He's screaming."

Morrow shrugged. "Years ago, Helen made the decision to choose life. Today, she's making another."

Helen gave a final shudder as Sarnie's flew from her body and landed on the dusty floor with a splat. He resembled nothing of the jumper that entered her, his translucent spirit scorched and encased in a gooey film, reduced to the size of a fetus. His naked form had blackened as if singed by his mother's touch. Sarnie's toothless mouth opened and closed as a high-pitched cry rumbled from his quivering throat and wound down to silence.

"What is that?" Kacey strained to kneel, her eyes glued to the gelatinous mass oozing onto the cement like a jellyfish out of water. As the three rested their eyes on the shape, a flame erupted from within, burning it to a crisp.

"Jesus, Helen." Morrow shuffled toward his wife, grasping her hands. "Remind me not to piss you off in the future."

She reached to his face and pressed her fingers against his skin, taking in with her hands what her eyes couldn't capture. "Can there be…a future?"

"How about an eternity from here on out?"

As Morrow and Helen embraced, RG grasped Kacey's hand and led her to the stairs. Grinning, he dropped onto the second step and helped Kacey beside him, marveling at the scene before him, his parents in each other's arms after nearly forty years.

"Jeez, get a room you two." RG grinned.

"Take a picture," Morrow quipped, looking over his shoulder. "It lasts longer."

But RG's eye remained wide and unblinking. *I don't think so.* Nothing would last longer than this.

CHAPTER TWENTY-TWO

Tuesday, April 5

Mike

Mike Stahl's eyes closed as he lay in the hospital bed beside Claire, fingers intertwined, her bandaged head resting on his shoulder. Zach lay fast asleep on her opposite side. After coming out of a four-day medically induced coma, Claire had spent the previous day slowly waking and gaining strength until she uttered her first words at just past midnight. Since then, she hadn't stopped talking, as if trying to make up for the previous days of silence. Stahl had almost forgotten the sound of her voice, but its sweet sound filled his heart and head like a fine wine until he was drunk just listening to it. Her voice opened the dam inside him, releasing the angst and stress and flooding him with a welcomed, whole body exhaustion. The walls faded and the floor fell away as he dropped into a brief slumber, imagining the world expanding before him. He drifted across miles of unexplored earth, remote snow-capped mountain peaks, tropical rain forests, dazzling sugar-sand beaches, places he would never visit in his lifetime. Not on a detective's salary. He had only dozed for a second or two before jerking awake and rubbing his eyes. He shook away the images in his head, aware the things had seen held nothing for him. None of it mattered. Everything he had ever wanted or needed, his whole world, rested on a twin-sized bed beside him, in a tiny room in a small corner of old New England.

And that was good enough for him.

Claire squeezed his hand. "I can remember the icy dark, not being able to breathe. I have a good idea what you must have gone through in Plymouth, when you swam through the pipes in the pitch black cold."

"You got me through that mess, Claire. If it wasn't for you—"

"It wasn't me," she interrupted, propping herself on her elbow. "You got yourself out of there. And you rescued me from the darkness of a watery tomb."

Stahl drew her close. "I don't want you to move to Boston. I want you to come back home."

"We've been over this, Mike."

"I nearly lost you. I'm not letting you go this time. All those things…the things I couldn't move past. I've let them go."

"They'll keep coming back. It's the thing we can't overcome."

Stahl leaned his head against the pillow and pictured Daniels laying in the parking lot at Sarnie Trucking. Days ago, the man had mumbled, with what could have been his final words, an absolution for a man who had been convinced his friend and partner had tried to kill him. And yet Stahl had not been able to pardon his wife for the things she had contemplated and voiced in a moment of terror and confusion nine months ago. But tonight, as he gazed at her damaged body, the flecks of blood still caked on her skin, all the things he couldn't forgive or forget disappeared like a forgotten memory.

"I learned something from a friend, Claire. Let me spend the rest of my life showing you what he taught me. Come back to the house. Give me one more chance. I promise you won't regret it."

Claire lifted her head and grabbed the sides of his face, pulling him close. She gazed into his eyes as if searching for something, maybe a spark, whatever had been missing back there. Maybe the light she had waited for. Her eyes grew wide and a grin spread across her face as she sunk into the pillow. Her fingers remained against his cheek. He turned his head to kiss her palm, folding her hand in his.

"Well, look who's back…" she mumbled as she drifted off to sleep.

CHAPTER TWENTY-THREE

Friday, April 8

RG

Kacey guided the Outback along Nauset Light Road as the wipers squelched the driving rain from the windshield with a rhythmic thump. Since their return from the inn and their defeat of Alex Sarnie, it had rained on more days than not, the Cape initiating squalls and torrential rain to power-clean Sarnie's stain from its sandy pores.

Kacey squinted through the rain-stippled glass to pinpoint the house, pulling up along the weathered fence separating the road from Knoll's beach grass front lawn. As they hoofed from the vehicle to the front door, the wet sand shifted beneath their feet like quicksand, slowing their progress and creating near stationary targets for the drenching rain's dead aim.

Kacey banged on the door and waited as her hair flattened to her scalp. After a long minute, she shouted, "Mr. Knoll!"

"He's gotta be here." RG cupped his hands to the side of his face and peeked through the window. "His car's right out front."

"Well, he's not here now. What do you want to do?"

RG stepped from the porch and stared upward into the falling rain, his arms held out from his sides. "No point in trying to stay dry now. Let's head to the back of the house, maybe try another door."

"Hey, look!" Kacey pointed toward the horizon.

RG followed Kacey's gaze across the beach. The sky and sea had merged into one indistinguishable shade of gray, but a lone shape rested upon the rock jetty extending into the Atlantic, a silhouette against the horizon's grim backdrop. The roiling sea cascading against the rocks, combined with the blanketing rain, converged to shower the figure from all sides, but he didn't move from his perch.

"What's he doing out there?" Kacey wiped hair strands pasted to her forehead.

RG shook his head as the pair trudged along the sand. Within minutes, they had arrived at the rock pathway extending from the shore into the sea.

"Mr. Knoll," RG shouted, but the man gave no indication he had heard him.

"This is crazy," Kacey muttered as they took their first tentative steps from boulder to boulder, careful not to lose their balance. In minutes, they reached Raymond Knoll sitting cross-legged as the incoming waves greeted the stone barrier broadside. His clothing hung off his body like wet laundry on a clothesline, accentuating his gaunt build and adding an extra decade to his battered appearance.

"If I were a gambling man, I would have bet against you

coming back from Barnard Street." Knoll's voice rang above the storm's din, his gaze locked on the horizon. "I guess you're a better fighter than liar." The surf collided with the rock's base, sending a salty spray cascading over them.

Kacey reached for RG to keep her balance. "What are you doing out here, Mr. Knoll."

"I love the rain." Knoll lifted his gaze and grinned. "As a kid, I used to sit in the backyard of the Barnard Street house when the skies opened. Seemed like the only time things were…normal there. Safe. I could just be a kid. This spot," he gestured with his one hand, "makes me feel like a kid. Makes me feel…I don't know. Safe again."

You, maybe. RG ran his foot along the rock's sleek surface. One rogue wave or a stiff breeze would be more enough to dislodge the three of them from their roost.

Knoll bounced to his feet. "Did you find what you were looking for at Barnard Street?"

"We did," RG said, "and you never have to worry about Luther again."

"Worry?" He gave a dismissive wave. "Luther got what he wanted from me long ago, what did I have to worry about?"

RG pictured the acres of eviscerated bodies hanging upside down on wooden poles in Luther's dwelling. *You got off easy.* "Well, he got what was coming to him."

Knoll narrowed his eyes. "Why did you come back here?"

RG checked Kacey with his eyes. "We need to tell you our secrets."

"Secrets?"

"Let's just say there are things you need to know. How about we head back to the house and talk awhile." RG leaned over and peered into the churning surf. "Before we end up as shark bait."

"The last time you came here, you didn't have much to say about anything. Why the change of heart?"

"Because we owe you." Kacey reached into her pocket and pulled out the yellow butterfly yo-yo, pressing it into Knoll's palm.

He turned the toy over in his hand, rubbing the butterfly emblem emblazoned on the side. "How did you get this? I haven't seen this since I was——"

"Eight years old? You gave it to me after your accident. It opened the portal to Luther's world." Kacey knelt beside him. "When we got there, it saved our lives."

His face flushed as a mist formed in his eyes.

"*She* saved our lives."

The rain rolling down Knoll's face mixed with the tears building in his eyes. "I haven't thought about her in a long time." He turned his head and covered his eyes with his hand, his body shaking in spasms as the emotions washed over like the seawater breaking against the jetty. Kacey stepped beside him and rested a hand on his shoulder.

"Come on, Mr. Knoll, let's get back to the house."

As the three treaded back to shore, another wave sent a saltwater mist sweeping across the rocks. RG and Kacey baby stepped their way forward, but Knoll navigated the nooks and valleys with a practiced cadence, never taking his eyes off the yo-yo. His face had assumed a childlike wonder, as if the simple act of holding the toy had resurrected the eight-year-old boy he had once been. Reaching the shoreline, they trudged across the beach, the shifting sand doubling their steps and filling their sneakers.

Standing on the back deck, RG removed his gritty sneakers as Knoll and Kacey disappeared through the slider. Banging the soles together, he cursed the thick paste embedded in the grooves that would soon relinquish its granules in his car's floor mat and home's wall-to-wall carpeting. Knoll knelt before the hearth, arranging the kindling and igniting the timber until the flames' rumbling exhale filled the room with heat.

Disappearing into his bedroom, Knoll returned with a pair of towels. "Here." He tossed them to RG and Kacey, huddled before the fireplace.

Knoll dropped into his chair, his face aglow with the dancing fire. "I had a dream, you know. Luther lay on the ground in his cave. A butterfly fluttered from his mouth."

RG and Kacey locked gazes.

"A butterfly did leave his mouth," Kacey said. "But it only flew a couple feet before it dropped to the ground."

Knoll clutched the yo-yo with a tight fist. "The ancient Greeks must have been right."

"Ancient Greeks? Right about what?" RG asked.

"About butterflies."

RG tilted his head.

"You know, the soul…" Knoll paused, searching RG's face as if waiting for a spark of comprehension. "And you're a college professor?"

"Didn't they believe the butterfly represented the soul leaving the body?" Kacey asked.

"Very good." Knoll's eyes lit up. "You know your literature."

RG jaw dropped as he swung his gaze toward his wife.

"Third-grade teacher, remember?" she communicated.

"He's gone, Mr. Knoll," RG said, swiping the towel through his damp mane. "No matter what the ancient Greeks thought."

Knoll pushed against his arm rest and hoisted himself to his feet. "I have something for you, Mrs. Granville."

He shuffled to his roll top desk and reached into the bottom drawer. Returning to the fireplace, he knelt beside

Kacey, opened his palm, and relinquished the object clutched in his fist. Kacey caught it in her outstretched hand.

"I think this belongs to you," he said.

"Oh my God." Kacey's mouth dropped open as she rolled the locket in her palm.

"Where did you get it?" RG's eyes darted to Kacey's.

"I've had it forever, since childhood. I figured someday I would find its rightful owner."

"But we used it a few days ago—"

"I left it in his house," she interrupted. "A long time ago."

RG dragged a palm across his jaw. "What are you talking about?"

Kacey recounted her adventures in the Barnard Street house after Luther's portal had sucked him from the back bedroom into the earth, how she had left the locket in Knoll's house as her return ticket home. Knoll opened his laptop and pecked away at the keys, trying to keep up with Kacey's recollection. "The locket kept the portal open for us, allowed us to get back. But when we returned to Barnard Street, the house had changed. Mr. Knoll's boyhood home had been replaced by Sarnie's 'House of Horrors.' The locket was long gone."

Knoll glanced up from his keyboard. "I used to carry the locket with me all the time, every time I left the house."

"What for?" RG asked.

"When I had it with me, the hours would stretch somehow. I can't explain it. Gave me more time before I had to go back to Barnard Street. Any extra time I had before I had to return to that hell proved a blessing. I know what I said doesn't make any sense, but it worked somehow."

"Makes all the sense in the world." Kacey turned the locket over in her hand.

"I tried to pry it open once, but I got the distinct impression I shouldn't, that it harbored a power inside that wasn't meant for me."

"It gave you what you needed."

"But what does it do?" Knoll asked.

Kacey stood. "Let me show you." She held the locket in her outstretched fist and closed her eyes. As she turned her hand, the world ground to a screeching halt, followed by a deathly silence. Time stood still before them, the rain halted mid-flight against the windows and the sea waves froze like silent towers poised to crash onto the waiting sand. Knoll struggled through the thick air to press his face against the living window, like a child peeking into the world for the first time. Kacey opened her eyes and released her fist to halt the interruption as time resumed its natural progression.

Knoll pressed a hand to his forehead as he stepped from the window, nearly stumbling as he made his way back to his chair. "I need to write all this down." He pecked at the keyboard.

"We have a lot to tell you. Enough to fill a book, if that's what you want." RG stood and gazed out the window toward the ocean. "It's the reason we came back, Mr. Knoll. No more secrets. It's time for people to know."

"I just have a small readership through Cape and Islands Press. I'm not sure this one-man operation can tell the world what they need to know."

"You're the only other person outside our circle who has seen the world the way we've seen it. You're the only one we trust to tell our story. It may take a while, but the truth will get out." He reached for Kacey's hand. "The world can decide what it wants to do with it from there."

"Then let's get started." Knoll fished around in the roll top desk, pulling out an old tape recorder and cassette tape. He positioned it on the coffee table as RG joined Kacey on the sofa. Pressing the record and play buttons together, Knoll sank back in his chair with fingers poised above his laptop.

As Knoll leaned back, a ray of sunlight split the clouds, flooding the room like a glittering spotlight. He leaned forward and peered out the window. "The clouds are breaking up. Just like that, the sea will quiet and the sky will turn blue. By tomorrow, it will be like the storm never happened."

"But it did happen. Like everything I'm about to tell you. People should know there could still be a storm coming."

Knoll settled into his chair. "Why don't you start at the beginning?"

RG rubbed his hands together, his foot tapping underneath the coffee table. "It doesn't seem that long ago, but it was. A lifetime ago, really." A peace descended across his features as the weight of the world slowly lifted from his shoulders. "I came home from work one night to find a stranger in my living room..."

THE END

ACKNOWLEDGMENTS

I want to thank Chris, Kaylee, and Dylan for their love and support in my pursuit of this strange passion. I couldn't have done it without you. I also want to thank my former agent, and current editor, Linda Kasten at Fix-It-Write.com, who has been a champion of the Caretakers series from the moment I pitched it to her. She has immersed herself into my world to help shape my ideas into novels to be proud of. Thank you for joining me on this ride and applying a steady hand to the wheel.

ABOUT THE AUTHOR

Stephen Paul Sayers is a college professor and internationally best-selling author of supernatural thriller and horror fiction. His debut novel, *A Taker of Morrows*, was published by Hydra Publications in June 2018, followed by *The Soul Dweller* in November 2018. His short fiction has appeared in *Unfading Daydream* and *Well-Versed*.

As a research scientist, Stephen yields to the left-brain world of data analysis and statistics by day, but releases the demons in his slightly twisted right-brain by night. It gets strange around dusk when neither side is fully in control. He makes his home in Columbia, MO and Plymouth, MA—not far from the Cape Cod locations he writes about in the Caretakers novels.

For more about the author, visit https://www.stephenpaulsayers.com

ALSO BY STEPHEN PAUL SAYERS

A Taker of Marrows

The Soul Dweller

www.ingramcontent.com/pod-product-compliance
Lightning Source LLC
Chambersburg PA
CBHW070421170726
48291CB00002B/302